I'm No Angel
I'm No Saint
I'm Just A Man

I'm No Angel
I'm No Saint
I'm Just A Man

S. L. SHARP

I'M NO ANGEL - I'M NO SAINT, I'M JUST A MAN

This is a work of fiction. All of the characters, names, incidents, organizations, and dialogue in this novel are either the products of the author's imagination or are used fictitiously.

iUniverse books may be ordered through booksellers or by contacting:

iUniverse
1663 Liberty Drive
Bloomington, IN 47403
www.iuniverse.com
1-800-Authors (1-800-288-4677)

Because of the dynamic nature of the Internet, any web addresses or links contained in this book may have changed since publication and may no longer be valid. The views expressed in this work are solely those of the author and do not necessarily reflect the views of the publisher, and the publisher hereby disclaims any responsibility for them.

Any people depicted in stock imagery provided by Thinkstock are models, and such images are being used for illustrative purposes only. Certain stock imagery © Thinkstock.

ISBN: 978-1-4917-5623-2 (sc)
ISBN: 978-1-4917-5624-9 (e)

Printed in the United States of America.

iUniverse rev. date: 12/26/2014

COVER PHOTOGRAPHY
The author provides special thanks to Linda for the magnificent cover photograph entitled "Christopher".

DEDICATED TO THE PEOPLE OF
ATLANTIC CITY, THE BOARDWALK OF
DREAMS AND MY BROTHER, ROD.

ACKNOWLEDGEMENTS
THE AUTHOR IS GRATEFUL TO THE
FOLLOWING INDVIDUALS DURING THE
BOOK DEVELOPMENT JOURNEY
JULIE, LINDA & ROD
AND SPECIAL THANKS TO
JULIE, BRUCE, EMILY, ANDREW, JEFF,
DOUG, JACK, JANICE AND NGOC.

Contents

Introduction

The book explores the expansive caverns under the four-mile Atlantic City Boardwalk which provide housing for hundreds of the poor and downtrodden people including Christopher, a grey bearded, long haired, unkempt middle aged man. He possesses godly connections and remarkable powers to assist fellow unfortunate acquaintances, friends from the boardwalk, casino visitors and residents of the Atlantic City.

Enjoy the roller coaster ride with Christopher in the pages ahead while he unselfishly serves as the city's unofficial guardian. The action filled book reveals Christopher's amazing relationship with a seagull named Sanabrio who is his confidant, regarding issues with the battered women, criminals, HIV challenged, desperate gamblers, the mentally challenged, and impoverished children. Christopher is a believer that all godly creatures are placed on earth for a special purpose and devotes his life to the development of their unfulfilled potential using his special powers.

Christopher's life of scorn by casino security personnel and devotion to servicing challenged humans takes an unexpected turn with the meeting of Lady Noreen, an attractive, affluent middle aged woman suffering from depression. Christopher cleans up his act in the grooming department and moves to Lady Noreen's magnificent Oceanside home in Ventnor. Their relationship quickly blossoms into a remarkable love story and brings purpose to their lives. They form an unlikely partnership committed to the enrichment of Atlantic City. And under their stewardship, the Atlantic City Boardwalk evolves into a year round 7/24 entertainment center featuring dancers, singers, and musicians at charity events, competitions, celebrity events, fashion shows, fireworks, and marathons. The charity coffers quickly overflow with financial resources for healthcare, education and enrichment programs for battered women, children, teenagers, and the elderly. The reader will meet a cross section of the Atlantic City populace including desperate gamblers under the mentorship of Christopher and Lady Noreen. One will treasure the stories sparked by these two remarkable humans.

The reader will meet a cast of memorable characters including Alex, Angela, Arthur, Baba, Big Luke, Bredele, Brook, Bruce, Mrs. Chang, Cora, Crazy Kay, Daisy, Delilah, Deuce, Devlin, Eleanor, Elijiah, Elliot, Emiliann, Emily, Linda Gagliano, Father Garrison, Grandpa, Feymale, Fernando, Gary, Hannah, Harvey, Heffe, Hilten, Jeff, Jasper, Jeremiah, Jessica, Joshua, Josey, Julie Marie, Kashmir, Lady Noreen Kagey, Kyleen, Lamar, Leon, Lisiah, Marcus Lowery, Laurel Mitchell, Mama Cane, Mack, Marcena Zinicola, Mr. Marcuso, Mr. & Mrs. McBriden, Mariah, Marie, Morton, Captain Matthew, Sergeant Leon Mussack, Ngoc, Odessa, Ogbonna, Old Bessie, Orlando, Patrick, P.J., Prentis, Raul, Joy Rhapsody, Rico, Dr. Rior, Russ, Christopher Saint, Sarge, Spencer, Starlett, Teresa Y., Tisha, Jumbo Tiny Tut Tut, Dr. Vay, Whitney, Winkie Wiskey, and Nicholas Zyvosky.

Hopefully, the book, I'm No Angel - I'm No Saint, I'm Just A Man, will serve as an inspiration to the reader about the self-satisfaction, that one enjoys from mentoring contemporaries and the next generation. These outcomes have important potential for catalyzing social change.

THE BLACK ROSE
BY S. L. SHARP

SHE'S A GROWIN' WILD
IN BLOOM TO A NEW DAY
SHE'S A SWAYIN' TO THE
COLD WINDS IN HIS OWN WAY
THE LOVLIEST BEAUTY
OF HER TIME
CREEPIN' OVER THE GROUND AND SOIL
LEAVIN' THIS EARTH BEHIND

SHE'S OPEN TO THE
SUNLIGHT OF A NEW DAY
SHE'S BLOWIN' IN
GOD'S DIRECTION ALWAYS
OVER THE BANKS AND
UP HIS HILLS
PROTECTING HIS HYBRID'S PETALS
THE WEEDS HE KILLS

SHE'S A LIVIN' BEARING
SEEDLINGS UP TILL THIS DAY
SHE A DRYIN' OUT
AT THE ROOTS TODAY
THE WAR OF THE SEASONS

TOOK HER ON
BUT GOD SAW HIM THROUGH IT
AND HER EARTHLY LIFE IS GONE

KEEP ON GROWIN' TO THE
HEAVENS BLACK ROSE
DON'T LOOK BACK ON YOUR
DEEP TROUBLES AND WOES
JUST KEEP GROWIN' TO THE
HEAVEN'S RAMBLING ROSE

BECAUSE GOD WILL TURN
YOUR HARDSHIPS INTO SMILES, AND
YOU'LL GO UPWARD
TO HIS HEAVENLY HOME
CAUSE IN GOD'S WORLD
NO ONE DIES

BUT WATCH THE THORNY
STEMS ON YOUR WAY
AND LISTEN TO
THE WORDS, I SAY
YOU WILL BLOSSOM
AGAIN IN YOUR NEXT LIFE
WHERE THERE WILL BE NO
TURMOIL OR EARTHLY STRIFE
KEEP ON GROWIN' BLACK ROSE
KEEP ON GROWIN'

DEDICATED TO CELESTINE

Chapter 1

His Plan For You

Christopher, a bearded middle-aged man, slouched down in his chair in a hospital waiting room with his eyes half closed.

Joshua, a young blonde haired, 6'3" hunk of a man, comes over to him and nudges him on his shoulder.

Joshua blurts out, "Christopher, she's going into labor. I'll come back and see you when the baby is born."

Christopher remarks, "I can hardly wait! We've waited for this moment, it seems like forever! Come back for me as soon as our babies are delivered."

Joshua looking puzzled replies, "Christopher, the doctor said Marcena was just having one baby."

"Well, Joshua, the doctors aren't God. They don't know everything without an ultra sound and Marcena never had one. Therefore, only God knows everything," responds Christopher to him.

Joshua smiling, "You're right Christopher! But most of the time the doctors are right."

Christopher winks at Joshua and laughingly says, "You're probably right, Joshua, but let's wait and see."

Joshua leaves Christopher in the waiting room.

Christopher slowly gets comfortable in his chair once again. His eyes begin to slowly close as he goes back into a deep, sound sleep which takes him back into time.

Suddenly in a flashback, you see Christopher, sleeping on a sandy beach on a hot sunny day. He slowly is awakening. He opens one eye

1

and sees a seagull staring right in his face. Gradually, he sits up and sees the frothy waves rolling onto the beach from the ocean. As he looks around the beach, he sees footprints all around him.

A truck slowly moves across the sand and goes under the C. T. Royal Ocean Mall and disappears behind the sand.

People in the early morning are starting to walk on the beach. A heavyset woman walks toward him dressed in golden yellow shorts carrying her purse. She runs to the ocean, wets her feet, and looks around the area with a giant smile on her face. Next, she runs to a trash can and rummages through it to find something to eat.

As Christopher observes what she is doing, he sees that this woman finally ends her search finding some food and walks back to the Boardwalk.

Christopher starts laughing to himself as he sees one seagull on top of another seagull. The one on top, like an acrobat, finally gets off of the other one. Then, the two seagulls start to peck each other's beaks as he observes their courtship into the mating bird season.

One of the seagulls lands on Christopher's arm. Christopher calls this one, Sanabrio.

It almost seems like this one is his pet.

A cool gentle breeze hits Christopher's unshaven face. He rubs his stubby, whitish gray beard.

Next, he sees a young boy and girl walking down to the shoreline hand in hand. Happy and in love, they stop upon their adventure on the beach to pick up treasured seashells. The young man then throws them like flying saucers back into the water where they sink swiftly into the ocean.

Christopher suddenly spots an empty bench on which no one is sitting in as of yet.

Next, he sees a middle-age couple strolling arm and arm closely next to one another. The woman gives the man a big hug and a tender kiss.

As Christopher looks up into the air, he sees the clear blue wondrous sky. A plane moves slowly across the white puffy clouded sky.

The sounds of the ocean and of the boats speeding in the water echo in his ears.

With his feet bare he uses his toes to move the sand so he can bury both of his feet underneath it.

Christopher speaks out, "Good morning, God! I'm ready for another day. It is almost time for me to go to work. I chose someone to win the casino jackpot. I spotted her last night. Her name is Lisiah. She's leaving with her husband for home today. I'll catch her before she leaves Atlantic City. So many people are in need of money these days, God. They are losing their houses, jobs, cars, land, jewelry, furniture, money, and everything that they own. Well, God, I best get up and go and see all of your children this morning. Everyone has been pretty happy lately. It's getting harder to find who I am looking for these days to win."

Christopher slowly gets up and begins to walk toward the Boardwalk. He strolls toward the sand dunes and walks up the steps leading to the Boardwalk. He puts his sunglasses on and happily walks down the Boardwalk. He soon approaches his favorite casino and walks into it. Then, he makes a right and enters the men's restroom. After he is done going to the bathroom, he washes his hands and face.

A bathroom attendant by the name of Lamar in the casino bathroom gives Christopher some paper towels to dry off his face.

Christopher calls back to him saying, "God bless you!"

"Thanks, Christopher. It looks like you got some sun yesterday," Lamar adds.

"I sure did. It was beautiful on the beach yesterday with a high of 90 degrees. The water was warm and a cool breeze blew across the beach. The birds were talking with each other through their mating calls and kissing one another. The human beings were hand and hand strolling on the beach last night, too."

"Christopher, I'll have to take a quick peek at the ocean, when I get off work today," Lamar states aloud to him.

"I hope you do, Lamar. Some people are so busy working these days that they stop living and looking at all of the beauty in their surroundings. Sad to say, workaholics never learned how to play when they were children. Their parents only gave them praise for their work accomplishments, not their enjoyments or contributions to our world. So, please, take the time to enjoy your life, Lamar. Remember, God never promised any of us a tomorrow. Don't get so involved in man's world that you miss out on the enjoyment of God's world. I'll see you later. Bye for now!"

Christopher walks out of the bathroom and onto the casino floor. Everyone is gambling all around him. Bells, noises, and lights are going off everywhere. All the people around the casino can visually see the lights and rainbow colors of the computer slots. The excitement of winning at the slots and the laughter of playing at the machines can be heard throughout the casino.

Christopher is seen by the casino employees as a middle-aged, sloppily dressed, homeless man. He is, slowly approaching a section of the casino where he is getting ready to sit down next to a sophisticated middle-aged woman, who is playing at a five-dollar slot machine.

Christopher dressed in his old clothes calls out to her, "How are the machines hitting today?"

The red headed woman snaps back at him by saying, "Get lost you dirty old bum. I can't concentrate on my game. Leave my sight before I call the casino security on you! You're probably on drugs!"

"Old bum, dirty old bum, that's not my name. My name is Christopher to you, madam! And I go to the Laundromat every week and wash my old clothes. You should not judge people by what they wear, but by what is in their heart and soul. I have a heart that was created in heaven by God. I'm not about material things; I'm about living things. On top of all of this, I'm not on drugs and I do work. I clean the beach every day. I'm an environmentalist."

The woman yells back at him, "You are plumb crazy, old man! I'm going to get someone right now to throw you out of this casino, so I can concentrate on my slot game and win!"

"Just sit still lady. I'm leaving your sight right now. I certainly wasn't put on this earth to bother you. This is not Judgment Day today, is it? If so, well, bye for now!"

Christopher walks down the casino aisles, and as he gets ready to leave the casino and go out of the front door, he sees a picture of a child on the face side of a slot machine.

He walks over to the picture and asks the woman, "What is the name of your child?"

The woman whispers back to him, "Her name is Angela."

"What is wrong with her?" asks Christopher.

"She needs an operation on her leg. She was born with one leg longer than the other one."

Christopher places his hand on the woman's shoulder and prays out loud, "May you be blessed with a blessing from the Lord." With that Christopher walks away from the woman. But before he leaves the casino; he glances back at the woman. When he does, he sees the light above her machine going off and the sound of exploding firecracker sounds being heard all around her.

Immediately the lady starts jumping up and down repeating, "I've won! I've won! I've won $31,500.00. The three lost bottles of fortune, finally lined up on the dollar machine. I've won the progressive jackpot! Oh, my heavens! I've won money for my daughter's operation!"

The woman's husband finally hears her yelling and runs to her saying, "Oh, Lisiah, I can't believe you've won the jackpot. This is truly a miracle in itself. Oh, do I love you. Now, we can get a check for the money you have won and leave the casino for home."

Christopher watches Lisiah from the entrance of the casino doorway. The woman and her husband are so happy! Their dream of winning at the casino really did come true today.

Finally, Christopher sees a tall young man in his late twenties come over to her from the corner of his eye. Then Christopher looks at all of the pictures of the jackpot winners on the sidewall of the casino with a smile on his face, and walks back out to the Boardwalk.

Once outside on the Boardwalk, an elderly man with one arm comes up and hugs Christopher saying, "Christopher where have you been lately? The baseball game is on right now. Come down with me under the Boardwalk steps so we can listen to the game together. I borrowed Samson's radio today."

"Okay, Sarge, let's go listen to our game right now!" happily replies Christopher.

The two of them go straight to the steps leading back to the beach and walk right underneath the wooden Boardwalk. They then sit down on the sand and get ready to listen to the baseball game.

Then Sarge and Christopher listen to the baseball game in its final inning. When the game is finally over with, Sarge looks over at Christopher and says to him, "I guess you are wondering how I got here aren't you? Well, I lost my left arm in the Vietnam War. When I came home from the war, it felt to me as though my own people had turned their backs on any soldier who returned from the war. I felt like an outcast from what we call the human race. Therefore, I purchased a one way ticket to Atlantic City and I never went back home to Ohio ever again. I guess you can say the person that I once was actually did die in the war. The stranger who came home from the Vietnam War was only an American hero to the people underneath the Boardwalk. Sad to say, the American people turned against their own soldiers in that war. I guess you can say, the responsibility for the failure of the war lied with our Congress not with the men who fought in the war. This being the case, this is the reason why the American soldiers came back home as unsung heroes after our country's withdrawal from Vietnam."

"So true," agrees Christopher with Sarge.

"Come back here underneath the boards, Christopher, I have some pictures that I want to show to you." Sarge pulls out three pictures in a battered up old plastic briefcase. "This picture is of my wife and two kids. This one is of my buddies in Vietnam with me. It breaks my heart to tell you this Christopher, but all of my buddies died there in the war. This final picture is of my mother. She was killed in a car accident before I came back from serving my time in Vietnam."

Christopher pauses a minute and looks straight at Sarge and philosophically says to him, "Life isn't fair, Sarge, but each one of us must get through life in our own way, and always remember that the people, who judge us will be judged by God in the same way that they judged us. Don't feel bad for yourself, Sarge; just feel sad for the people, who judge you. You do have a purpose here on this earth, Sarge, up until your very last breath."

Sarge blurts out, "Christopher, what am I supposed to do with my life?"

"My friend, I really don't know exactly what you are to do with your life. Each man, woman and child must find their own purpose on this earth during their own lifetime. Your purpose could be as simple as listening to the baseball game with me today, or it might be something so spectacular that you have to work at it to make it happen. There is no crystal ball on this earth to tell you why you were put in Atlantic City, Sarge. You must live out God's plan for you, my friend."

Chapter 2

Life Is An Irony

Bredele shouts out, "Look, Joshua, here comes that bum from the Boardwalk again. He is always around here. He leads a double life. When he is here, he is part of us. When he is outside of the casino, he's part of the underground subculture crowd underneath the Boardwalk. Who does he think he is anyway? He's just a low life, bearded, homeless bum."

Joshua voices out to Bredele, "Don't be so hard on the man. He doesn't hurt anyone. Just leave him alone. He always looks clean."

Bredele with a vicious grin on his face grumbles, "I'm going to kick him out of the casino today. I can hardly wait to do it! He's always joking and laughing with our casino crowd patrons. If he doesn't gamble in the casino today, I'm going to make sure that he goes face first out of the casino doors."

Bredele slowly starts to walk over to where Christopher is sitting. Christopher is talking to a lady, who always talks to him at the dollar machines located in the "Pirate's Ship Dollar Island" section of the casino.

Christopher hollers out, "Noreen, how's your day today?"

Noreen laughingly complains, "Christopher, I'm just putting in time on this earth ever since the deaths of my husband and son. Now I just gamble to break the monotony of my life. I will never win again in this life. I've lost everyone who I really cared about. Now I'm just serving a life sentence every day of my living existence."

"Noreen, you still have exciting years ahead of you. You know, you're not dead yet, baby!" Christopher snickers.

"What do I have to look forward to, Christopher?" sadly replies Noreen.

"You must start living more, Noreen. You are not the one that died. You still are beautiful! You should go to the casino shows and use your comps to get the delicious free meals and dinners. Use your comps! Stay overnight in those beautiful hotel rooms facing the ocean and go to the chance drawings. You will have so much fun doing all of those activities. Since you have oodles of money you should spend it like water, and enjoy the life that you can buy from your gambling!"

"But Christopher, I have no one to escort me to any of those activities or events. I don't have a male companion. I don't want to go to these functions all by myself. I hate being all alone. It is the worse curse that could ever have been put upon me in my life."

"Well, lady, as nice as you always dress, I need to win some money on the slot machines today so I can accompany you to your events and activities. Do you mind lending me $20.00, so I can invest the money in your new life after today?"

Bredele comes up on the two of them in deep conversation. "Pardon me, is this bum bothering you, Mrs. Kagey? If so, I will gladly escort him immediately out of the casino for you! It will be my pleasure to do it for you!"

"Excuse me, sir. Would you mind your own business! Christopher is helping me gamble. He brings me good luck, just by sitting next to me. Would you leave us alone and mind your own business unless I call on you, or else I will see the casino floor manager about you harassing my friend," responds Noreen to Bredele in an overbearing tone of voice.

"Good luck, madam! I'm so sorry - I thought this man was bothering you."

Bredele storms away from them with a devilish grin on his face whispering under his breath, "Mrs. Kagey is truly crazy! Who would want to be seen sitting next to that no good, worthless bum?"

"Christopher, now that Bredele is gone, what machine would you like to play?"

"Let's go over there and play on the one-dollar, "Pot Luck Seven Slot Machines," in the last row.

"How much money do you need again, Christopher?"

"Noreen, just lend me $20.00, and after I win, I'll give you your money back with some human interest."

Christopher and Noreen walk to the back of the casino and sit down with a group of women yelling and cheering for one of their friends on the machines that Christopher wants to play on.

Christopher sits down next to their friend and has Noreen stand behind him. He tells Noreen, "Rub my hands for good luck."

Then Christopher puts his borrowed $20.00 bill into the slot machine. The twenty-dollars registers on the computerized slot machine so now Christopher can play it.

"Christopher, are you sure that you don't want more money from me to gamble with?" Noreen asks him.

"No, Noreen! This is enough money for me to win on today."

The board game pops up on the computerized slot machine. Christopher hits the three-dollar play button on the board. Noreen sees the sevens spin and stop.

The woman next to him hollers, "Go! Go! Go!"

Christopher looks at the number of credits that he has earned on his spin. The machine registers $2,500 dollars. He has just won on the machine by getting the three purple sevens on the line.

Everyone screams with excitement seeing that Christopher has won on his slot machine.

Noreen is in shock at his winnings.

Well, Noreen, "Thanks to you, we've won $2,500.00. That can buy me some new clothes so I can get ready to escort you to your parties at the casino. But first things first! I'm going to give you your $20.00 back. I never have taken anything in life from anyone that I didn't give what I borrowed back to them. Then I want to treat you to lunch at the Lunch Box Restaurant on the Boardwalk today."

Christopher sits with Noreen and the other gamblers around him as he waits for a slot machine attendant to pay her in cash since he doesn't have a driver's license.

The slot attendant comes over to Christopher in a happy way saying, "Congratulations, sir! You've just won $2,500.00. I'll go and get you your money, right now."

"Thanks, but it is Noreen's money. She will give you her license. Would you please bring her one- hundred-dollars in tens and the rest of the money in hundred-dollar bills?"

The woman next to Christopher gets the spin on her casino slot machine. Christopher shouts out in a very loud voice, "Go girlfriend, get those lucky sevens."

Noreen and the rest of the girls join in with Christopher to cheer her on. It sounds like a cheerleading squad cheering the home team on at the casino.

One by one the credits start to mount up. Everyone is shouting in full force voices, "Go - Go – Go, Diana!"

The woman accumulates over $400.00 worth of money in credits.

Christopher questions Diana, "Girlfriend what are you going to do with all of that money?"

"I'm from New York. I'm going back home on the bus tonight and I'm going to buy my mother a nice birthday gift. She deserves one. She has unselfishly looked after my father and her four children all of these years. My brother was diagnosed with schizophrenia at the age of twenty. Because of my mother's love for him, she was able to find an outstanding psychiatrist, and at the present time my brother has a normal life.

When my brother was committed into the state institution, our family was scared to death that he would never recover. However, through my mother's prayers, my brother's psychiatrist and the medication he was put on, my brother is now home once again. He is now actively involved in his life. Our family is so happy about his recovery! It is so hard on a family when a member of it has a severe disease or mental disorder. So many people in society want to turn their backs on the mentally ill these days. They fear these people like my brother are living time bombs just ready to explode at any second. Too often, the American people don't hear the success stories about people like my brother. My brother today is a functioning citizen in his community, thanks to my mother's love, his psychologist, his psychiatrist, his medication, and his family."

"Diana, you are so right! Family is so important in life. It sounds like you are going to make your mother's birthday a very special day to remember this year."

"Yep, my two sisters and I, plus my five friends, came down here last night on the bus to spend the day in Atlantic City. This Saturday has gone by too fast for all of us. It is so much fun being here with everyone. You don't have to think or worry about time or anything. It's just like being on a mental vacation from your real life."

"Well, congratulations on your win, Diana! This is Noreen, my friend. As soon as we get our money, we're going to go outside and take a walk on the Boardwalk. Then I'm taking Noreen to lunch. That is the human interest reward that I told her I was going to give her after we won at the slots today."

"That sounds like lots of fun," in laughter replies Diana to Christopher.

The cocktail waitress passes by all of them calling out, "Coffee, drinks, sodas, beverages…"

Christopher stops the cocktail waitress and addresses her by saying, "Drinks are on the house for all of these New Yorkers."

The waitress happily responds to Christopher by saying, "What does everyone want to drink?"

The friends yell out in unison, "3 waters and 5 diet sodas!"

Christopher asks, Noreen, "What do you want to drink?"

Noreen responds, "I want an iced tea."

Christopher winks at the waitress named Wendi and says, "I'll take an iced tea and water on the rocks."

Wendi laughs at Christopher and says, "I think I can handle that order," and then she goes merrily on her way to get everyone their drinks.

In the next few minutes, Joshua comes back to Noreen and Christopher with her money. He counts it out in his hand, and happily tells them once again, "Congratulations!"

"Thanks, my name is Christopher. What's your name?"

"Joshua," Joshua hesitates to answer him.

"I bet you love your job, Joshua."

"Yes, I do!" he answers.

"What is more important to you – love or money?" Christopher asks Joshua.

"Love of course, Christopher!"

"Are you in love with someone special at this moment, Joshua?" Christopher asks him.

"No, Christopher, I've never found the right woman to fall in love with, but I haven't given up yet, and I am still looking for my other half."

Wendi brings everyone their drinks.

"Let's salute Joshua, and let's hope that he finds the woman of his dreams. The one, who he is supposed to meet and fall in love with," toasts Christopher.

Everyone salutes Joshua and toasts to him and his happiness. Then Christopher hands Joshua a hundred-dollar tip.

"Well, Joshua, Diana and friends, Noreen and I have a date so we best get going right now," says Christopher to all of them.

Diana, with all of her friends, yell good-bye to Christopher. Then, they all congratulate him once more on winning at his slot machine.

Joshua, I hope that Noreen and I will get to see you again real soon," Christopher blurts out.

Noreen in her stylish pants suit and sandals walks away with Christopher for a luncheon date with him on the Boardwalk.

Once out in the breezy, warm air, Christopher gives Noreen her $20.00 back.

"Christopher, I don't need this money back. I have lots of money. Money doesn't mean anything to me. (She starts to cry.) You see, I've been cursed. My husband, Allan, died from colon cancer. Then not thinking that my son, Aaron, would get it, I never tested him for it. However, in college, during his junior year, he started having severe stomach cramps and rectal bleedings. By the time he told me about it, it was too late. He ended up having six months to live before he died from colon cancer, too. Why didn't I have him tested for cancer earlier? Why was I so stupid? Why did both of the people that I loved so much in my life have to die?"

"Noreen, I can't answer you why. You just have to find peace of mind somehow in your life. If not, the rest of your life will be full of endless pain which will drive you mentally crazy. You'll never forget what happened to your loved ones, but you must try to face your life and start living once again my friend. So please, just have it in your heart to take your money back. Let me feel like a man. Please don't take my manhood away from me! I'm not part of your past! I've never hurt you! Please let our relationship be a new page in your life," Christopher pleads to Noreen.

Then he takes Noreen out on the Boardwalk and he asks her to sit on the bench where an old woman is sleeping. Noreen and Christopher sit down next to the old lady. Together they watch all of the people walking up and down the Boardwalk. Some people are by themselves, some are with their loved ones, friends, and families. Everyone is dressed very light for the 90-degree weather.

"One thing for sure, Noreen, no matter whether the people are rich or poor, they all still get to share the Boardwalk and the ocean together on this glorious day," states Christopher to her.

Next, Christopher has Noreen sit on a bench where a woman has her head dropped down and is in a very deep summer sleep.

Christopher then says to Noreen, "This old woman next to you is Old Bessie. She carries everything she owns in her backpack. She lives underneath the Boardwalk with all of us. She is sort of like the mother of our family. She keeps all of the young ones in line."

Then Noreen and Christopher listen to all of the sounds of the people soliciting business without a license on the Boardwalk. One man is playing the trumpet, one is preaching the Gospel, another man is doing magic tricks, and a group of teenagers are just street dancing at the side of the casino.

People from the casinos and people from the beach pass by all of these performers. They hear and see what they are doing with their talents. The people who pass by these gifted people, put dimes, nickels, and dollars into their cups or guitar cases after seeing them perform their talents on the Boardwalk.

"See, Noreen, this is the way mankind survives. Everyone gives a little money to everyone else. It is a trickle down system. No one ever gets it all, and sometimes when they do get it all, it is a curse to the person that wins it, inherits it, or steals it."

Finally, Christopher puts out his arm for Noreen to take it, and he escorts her down to the Lunch Box Restaurant. As they walk to the restaurant five doors down from the casino, they take in all the sounds and sights of the Atlantic City Boardwalk. Once inside the restaurant, Christopher asks Noreen what she wants to eat for lunch.

Noreen shrieks, "Surprise me, Christopher! I haven't been this overjoyed in my life for so many years."

With that Christopher goes up to the counter and orders two cheesesteaks topped with fried onions, two large fries, and two iced teas.

The counterman, who they call Baba Buddham on the streets, responds to Christopher by questioning him, "Christopher, who is that pretty middle-aged dame with you? What are you doing with the likes of her?"

"Baba, she is just a classy lady, who I am having lunch with today. That is all that is happening between us!"

"I'm sure of that, Christopher. No woman like that would want to be in your company for too long. I thought maybe she was one of those women from the church trying to get you back in touch with your spiritual religious values."

"Baba, you never know, who will change whose life in time. Life is an irony. Sometimes it is a stranger that changes your life in a mysterious way; not the person that society stereotypes to be the one."

"Christopher, I like you, but you certainly talk in circles. Well, here's your food so go enjoy your lunch with that magazine pin up woman. This will be a once in a lifetime luncheon for you Christopher. Thanks for bringing Noreen to the best restaurant on the Boardwalk. You really made my day!"

Christopher takes his tray with all of the food on it and goes over to the counter to get straws, napkins, salt and ketchup. Then he pays the cashier for the food. He digs into his pockets and pulls out some money from his winnings. The cashier, Tisha, winks at Christopher, and he winks back at her.

Tisha jokingly bursts out saying, "Enjoy your lunch Christopher with your red hot date. When are you going to take me out on a date with you and buy me lunch?"

Christopher laughing comments back to her, "Tisha, you are too young for me. I'm an old fossil, baby. I'm much too old for you!"

Tisha kiddingly pesters Christopher in return, "Shucks, Christopher, I've wanted to go out with you for years!"

Christopher chuckles back at her by saying, "Tisha, you are too young for me. I am old enough to be your father. I have to go now. My date is waiting for me. Bye for now!"

Once back at the table, Christopher distributes all of the food on the tabletop to both of them. When he is done, Noreen looks at him and sighs, "What are you talking to everybody about?"

"Everyone wants to know, who you are, and why you are with me, Noreen?"

"Let me put it this way, I have nothing to live for, Christopher. If you kill me it is fine. I really don't want to live. I am sick of my life and everything in it. Even though you seem crazy, you are very nice to me. Therefore, what do I have to lose? If I end up being wrong about you and you are a psycho killer, well, at least I will have had a little fun in my life. I haven't been truly happy with myself for such a long time," sadly shares Noreen with Christopher.

"Thanks a lot! I'm not a psycho! Noreen, I am going to change your life and your name. You are now going to be called Lady Noreen and you are going to laugh again. You are going to see the stars in the sky, the birds in the air, and smell the ocean in the breeze. This I can promise you!" pledges Christopher to her.

After they eat their lunch together at the Lunch Box Restaurant Noreen looks at Christopher and quietly whispers, "Well, I best be going now."

With that Christopher gets up from the table and walks his Lady Noreen to the Boardwalk and asks her, "Do you want me to walk you back to the casino, so you can call your chauffeur to take you home?"

"That is not necessary. I only live in Ventnor. I think I'll walk home today. I haven't done that for years. You're right, Christopher, I haven't been alive for such a long time. I'll just follow the Boardwalk

from here to Ventnor. Thanks for a great lunch. You are strange, Christopher, and different. Yet, you make more sense to me in my mind than all the shrinks and doctors have made to me during these past few years of my life. I thank you for that Christopher. Maybe if you're not too busy next month, you might want to escort me to the show and dinner event at the casino."

"I'd love, too, Lady Noreen. Christopher watches Lady Noreen walk slowly on a new path back to recovery. Then he goes back to the Boardwalk and sits back down on a bench next to Old Bessie. She is still sound asleep dreaming about her past life.

Seeing this, Christopher slowly moves from the bench and walks down the steps and takes off his sandals. Then, he walks down to the beach barefoot on the wet sand near the ocean.

Chapter 3

Life Is Precious

Christopher wakes up the next day and after cleaning up the trash on the sand. He slowly walks down to the beach to see his best friend, Big Luke. The summer days seem to be flying by one by one so fast.

Big Luke sees Christopher from the Boardwalk and he comes over to greet him. Together, they see hundreds of people in crowds on the Boardwalk enjoying the sights of Atlantic City.

Big Luke utters passionately, "Christopher, why are there so many handicapped people on the Boardwalk, the casinos, the restaurants, and in the massage parlors?"

Christopher explains, "It's just God's way of showing us not to give up because sometimes the willpower and love of life of these handicapped people can become a factor in helping us turn our lives around."

Big Luke states to Christopher, "I wish I hadn't dropped out of high school. Now, all I can do is hustle on the Boardwalk. I have no education or skills to get a real job."

Christopher adds, "We are all like the seagulls, Big Luke. Have you ever watched them?"

Big Luke responds, "Christopher, I've slept underneath the Boardwalk for so many years, yet I've really never watched the seagulls. In fact, I've never cared to watch them. I just notice them from time to time, when the people on the Boardwalk feed them, or when they steal food from the kids or people eating on the Boardwalk, or on the beach. One pooped on me while it was in midair one day, and I wanted to kill it."

"Well, Big Luke, watch the seagulls right now. Here I have some pretzels in my hand. Let me break them up and throw them onto the sand."

Christopher throws the crumbs onto the beach. The seagulls start to squawk and land all around the crumbs. He sees his favorite seagull, Sanabrio, who lands on the beach to fight for his share of the pretzel crumbs. The other birds and the pigeons pick up the crumbs with their beaks and begin eating the crumbs. A lot more squawking is taking place on the beach.

The pigeons move in to eat the crumbs and the seagulls start squawking more at them and fighting with them to defend their territory. The pigeons try to get a crumb or two from them else they leave the area to get food elsewhere.

"Like the seagulls, you can either go get your GED, Big Luke, or leave this territory and begin a new life somewhere else with no education. But you can't keep running from what scares you. It is never too late to start your life over again. You have to decide if you want to stop learning or if you want to go back to school and have another learning experience in your life. If you become brain dead Big Luke, you'll just spend most of your time gossiping about other people because you'll have nothing new to talk about."

"I guess you are right, Christopher. But life is made up of everyday habits, and I don't know if I am ready to break any of my everyday habits just to go back to school. At the moment, I feel so angry with myself over what my life has become. Yet, I am comfortable with my routine for right now."

"Big Luke, when you are ready to go back to school and move on with your life, you'll know! But always remember it is never too late to learn again and you have the rest of your life to work on your education. You could even graduate from college one day. That is, if you want to do so. Your life is your life. You can do anything with it that you want, but it is never too late to begin a new adventure.

Well, Big Luke, I have to go! I have to go! I am going to go buy some new clothes. I have a date in three weeks with my girl, Lady

Noreen. Lady Noreen and I are going to a show and out to dinner at the casino.

Just remember if you ever want me to help you get into a GED program just ask me, and I'll be glad to help you. In fact, I'd be privileged to help you," Christopher promises Big Luke.

"Thanks, Christopher, I never thought about going back to school before. I guess you've given me something to think about. Are you sure I am capable of learning once again?"

Christopher exclaims, "If a young bird can jump from the nest then nothing can stop you. You just need to take the first step. Only you, Big Luke, can make a difference and learn how to fly. You can walk into a classroom and get your GED certificate, but you must do it all by yourself."

Then Christopher suddenly says, "Good-bye for now," to Big Luke, and walks down the Boardwalk towards Mississippi Avenue so he can cut over through the side streets to the downtown area of Atlantic City. Once there, he spots a Marcuso's Men's Clothing Store. He goes into the men's apparel store and tries on several suits before choosing the right one to buy.

At first, the store manager and owner is hesitant in helping Christopher. But when Christopher gets so overexcited about trying on the different suits, Mr. Marcuso just starts bringing him everything in the store to try on. Then, the two of them begin to interact and have so much fun together.

After trying on so many suits, Christopher tries on casual pants and summer knit shirts. Mr. Marcuso has the time of his life dressing Christopher up and having him model the different styles of men's clothing for him.

Finally, Christopher starts having his own fashion show in the heart of the store. The people gather while Christopher is his own master of ceremony of his own show. While modeling he sings, dances, raps, and tell jokes.

As the audience starts swarming around Christopher, people begin purchasing clothing items and asking for Christopher's autograph. Everyone in the store is in shock at what this comedian/model is capable of doing as a model.

At the end of Christopher's floor production, he has the two suits that he is going to buy pinned for alterations. Then, he chooses two pairs of casual pants, a pair of jeans, two shirts, a jacket, some underwear, socks and a pair of shoes. With all the summer sales taking place on men's clothing at this store, he gets some great bargains. As he gets ready to go, Christopher tells Mr. Marcuso that he will pick up his new suits in two weeks and he will take everything else with him.

Then Christopher starts to get ready to leave the store wearing one of his new outfits. He tells Mr. Marcuso, that he is getting ready for a special date that he has planned with a beautiful woman.

With that Mr. Marcuso wraps everything up and puts his merchandise neatly into bags for him.

"Christopher, if you ever need a job. Feel free to call me. I'd love to have you as a model for my new fall line. You can sell!" insists Mr. Marcuso.

"Perhaps, I'll see. Would I get a steady income from working with you, Mr. Marcuso?" wonders Christopher.

"Of course, I'm sure we can negotiate an appropriate salary for your employment with our company. Please think about it, Christopher. It would be a great kick-off for introducing our new fall fashions."

With thanks, Christopher shakes hands with Mr. Marcuso, and everyone in the store. He then takes his bags and departs for the Boardwalk. In a happy-go-lucky mood, Christopher heads for Mama Cane's house to get his haircut and his beard shaved off. Mama Cane is an elderly grandma.

Once at Mama Cane's house, he is welcomed by her foster children. Christopher has helped Mama Cane for the last few years by doing odd jobs including maintenance jobs on her house. He recently painted the house for her during the month of May. Mama Cane, in return, would do anything for Christopher.

Christopher very mannerly asks, "Mama Cane, I notice that you cut people's hair all of the time. Would you have the time today to cut my hair, and when you are done doing it, could I please shave my beard off in your bathroom? Would you happen to have a razor for me to use?"

Mama Cane loudly laughs out loud and answers him, "Christopher, what has happened to you? Who are you getting all of this done for? Are you doing this for a lady friend? Tell Mama everything!"

"Mama Cane, I've met a lovely lady and she needs someone like me in her life. Therefore, I have to clean myself up a little so she won't be embarrassed being seen with me," shares Christopher with Mama Cane.

Mama Cane screams at him, "No one would ever be embarrassed with the likes of you, Christopher. You are the kindest man that God ever let out of heaven. You'll grow on her in time just like you have on my five foster children and me. All of my kids love you. You give them quality time. You help them with their homework, you teach them how to do repairs on the house and you spoil each one of them. What more could a woman want?"

"Well, right now, Mama Cane, please cut my hair and make me look like a human being once again."

"Okay, Christopher, go take your new sports shirt off and sit down in that chair right over there. Then, I'll have Whitney put a towel around your neck."

Christopher does what he is told to do. Whitney, Mama Cane's next to the youngest teenage foster child, helps Christopher prepare to get ready for his haircut.

Next, Mama Cane comes over to him and starts cutting his hair. Long lockets of whitish gray hair starts to fall below on to the floor. Christopher closes his eyes and asks Mama Cane to awaken him when she is done with her human hair sacrifice.

Slowly, the children come in to spy on Christopher and laugh at him. He is very comical as he closes his eyes and makes noises while being transformed into a different Christopher.

Finally, Mama Cane tells Christopher to open his eyes and to look into the mirror. His haircut is done.

Then Mama Cane has Christopher go into the bathroom and shave his beard off.

After about fifteen minutes, Christopher reappears outside of the bathroom into the kitchen looking like a brand new man.

By this time, Mama Cane has everyone in the house lined up to see him.

When Christopher walks out of the bathroom everyone claps and cheers for him. Mervin, Mama Cane's youngest foster son who is nine years old, starts yelling at Christopher, "You've got a girlfriend. You've got a girlfriend."

Mariah, age fifteen, Jepson, age eighteen, and Gregory, age nineteen, join in with teasing Christopher on his new image.

Christopher looks like a new man. He looks at himself in the mirror in shock saying, "I wonder if Lady Noreen will even know me. I hope I don't scare her to death looking this way," wonders Christopher to himself.

Mariah gives Christopher a hug. Then, says to him in a high-pitched voice,

"Oh! Christopher, your lady friend will think you look bad!"

"Bad, Mariah, I don't want to look bad!" remarks Christopher.

"Christopher, bad means good. You'd rather be bad good instead of just good. You are the bomb and I love you Christopher!" laughs Mariah.

With that Christopher gives Mariah and all of the children a big hug. As he goes to leave Mama Cane's house he reaches into his pocket to give her some money. "Mama Cane this money is for you and the kids. I know you'll need this extra money for the kids this summer."

"You are a blessing to me, Christopher! What would I do without you! You have helped me so many times with the kids. Thanks for the money for them. With school starting in the fall they will need some new clothes and their school supplies. I only wish that I were giving you some money instead of you giving me this money. You do so much for all of us. I will never be able to repay you, Christopher."

"You have paid me back enough, Mama Cane, by just being you and loving all five of your kids!" confirms Christopher to her.

With that, Christopher picks up his bags and off to the casino he goes to see if Lady Noreen is at the casino yet, so he can get a firsthand answer on whether he looks like a psycho or not.

He hurries as fast as he can back over to the casino. Once there no one knows him. He looks around, but does not see Lady Noreen so Christopher gets ready to leave the casino. As he walks out of the casino, he passes right by Bredele. Bredele doesn't even know who Christopher is as he passes right in front him.

As Christopher walks down the steps to go out of the casino, he sees a young man in his early twenties sitting on one of the steps holding his head.

Christopher approaches him and begins by saying to him, "What is wrong, son?"

"You really don't want to know and you shouldn't really even care about my problems."

"Well, I do so, please, talk to me. I sense you need someone to confide in right now."

"I just blew $500.00 on that dollar machine right over there. I have none of that money left. I need that money if I am to pay my college tuition on Monday. Otherwise, mister, I have to drop out of college."

"Don't look so sad. I have a few twenty-dollar bills left in my pocket. Let me give them to you so you can play a different machine to get your money back. Okay?"

"I don't know! I don't know you! What do you want in return from me?" nervously asks the young man.

"I want nothing! I just want you to leave the casino when you are done winning your money back. I also want you to pay your college tuition on Monday. That's all I want from you! By the way what is your first name?"

"My name is Mack that is short for Mackenzie."

"What are you going to major in at college?" asks Christopher.

"I want to become some type of engineer. I'm not quite sure right now what type of engineer yet." responds Mack.

"That's great, Mack!"

"I should never have gambled all of my money away today," admits Mack to Christopher.

"Well, you did! That is why you must promise me that you will leave the casino immediately after you win; so you don't gamble your winnings back into the machine?" explains Christopher to Mack.

"Yes, I promise! But how can you predict that I will win on a machine?" questions Mack.

"I can't! Only the chip or the dealer can determine the turn of a machine or the deal of a hand, and sometimes it's a blessing from the Almighty. But let's give it a try. You have already lost all of your money! Anything you win will be for your college education, plus you'll owe $20.00 in human interest," states Christopher to Mack.

"Human interest, what's that?" inquisitively asks Mack.

"I'll explain it to you if you win!"

"By the way, what's your name? Mack asks.

"Mack, my name is Christopher."

"What do you do?" questions Mack.

"I'm an environmentalist," replies Christopher to him.

Christopher then points to Mack to follow him way in the back of the casino where the dollar machines are located in an aisle. Next, he tells Mack to wait a second while he runs over to the coat attendants in the far back of the casino to deposit his bags until they are done gambling.

He then hurries back to Mack and directs him to play the third machine from the end of the row.

"Mack, put these two $20.00 bills into the machine. It will give you 20 credits in dollars on the machine. Good luck!"

Mack begins to hit the button on his machine. He can play from one to three dollars on each bet on the machine game. He needs to get 3 popped bottles on a three dollar bet to get a game board of bottles. Then, he has to touch the board to open the bottles to win money. However, when all of the bottles have been opened on the screen the game is over with.

Mack gets a few matching figures on the first ten hits and brings his credits up to 200-dollars. Then his money amount starts dropping to 150-dollars.

"Christopher, I'm afraid, I'm going to lose all of your money. This is the way I lost all of my money before. The machine just went dead on me and it ate all of my money up."

"Stop being a pessimist, Mack. Make a bet of three dollars on the next spin this time. Boy, don't you have any faith in miracles?"

"I don't know if I do! Three dollars, Christopher, you must be crazy!"

"It seems that way, Mack, but in truth, I'm not! You have to have faith in yourself, not in me, if you want to try and win at this game."

"Okay, Christopher, here I go!"

He closes his eyes and pushes the button for a three dollar bet on the machine. With that the board game starts to spin. Next, more bottles appear upon the screen of the dollar machine.

"Oh, my look, it worked!"

"That was the easy part. Now let the game pick the winning bottles for you."

"But what if the board loses on the first pick? Then, I still will not have my $500.00."

"Mack, just have patience, son," insists Christopher.

With that the game board starts to open the bottles. The first bottle is $200.00, the next bottle is a triple bonus bottle for $246.00, the next bottle is for $1,250.00, and the bells go off. The game is over with for Mack.

"Christopher, let's play this game again!"

"Mack, you gave me your word that you would leave here when the game was over with so just cash out your machine. Aren't you happy with the money that you just won, Mack? Don't be so greedy that you not only lose all of your money right now, but your soul because of your greed. Son, no one ever really wins in this life. Life is not a win-win situation. People just survive and get by for the most part, so just try it my way."

"You're right, Christopher! You're right. I've won. How did you know that I'd win?"

"I just had faith, Mack!"

Mack then waits to be hand paid.

Joshua and Bredele walk over to Mack to give him his money.

Joshua says to him, "Congratulations! You've just won $1,696.00 dollars and you have $147.00 left in the machine to play."

"Thanks!" replies Mack.

Bredele runs to the cage to get Mack's money. When he returns he pays, Mack, his money and has Mack sign the casino W-2G form.

Mack gives each of the attendants a $10.00 tip.

Joshua thanks him, but Bredele hardly says anything to Mack. He is insulted that Mack only gave him a $10.00 tip.

Christopher has his back to both of the casino attendants and neither one of them recognize him. To them, he is just another gambler on the floor gambling away at the machines.

"Mack, let's leave so cash out your machine. I want you to meet one of my friends. Then I will walk you to your destination. Where might that be?"

"I'm parked in the casino deck on the fifth floor, Christopher."

"Well, Mack why don't you go with me to get my bags right now? When we return, I want to walk you out to the Boardwalk to meet by friend, Deuce. He lost all of his family in a house fire. After that he had a nervous breakdown and he was never the same ever again. Then, one day I found him passed out, and I dragged him underneath the Boardwalk. After I fed him, I took him to a halfway house in the area to recover. Since then, he has worked and lived at that house, and every night he plays his heart out on his saxophone on the Boardwalk. It's the only way he can express all of his pain to others."

"Why did God do that to him, Christopher?"

"God didn't do that to him, Mack! The electric wiring in his house did it to him! It seems like people always want to blame God for the bad things that happen to them in their lives. They never thank God for the good things in their lives. God doesn't hurt or destroy us!

Then Mack goes with Christopher to get his bags. Christopher tips the girl, who works in the coat claim, they walk back to the front of the casino to exit. After that, Christopher takes his new friend, Mack, out to the Boardwalk to meet Deuce. As they approach him they take in the sounds of one of his jazz songs. A crowd is surrounding Deuce at the present. Some people are dancing to his music and others are putting money donations into his bucket. After Deuce is done playing several selections of music for his audience, Christopher walks over to Deuce to introduce Mack to him.

"Deuce, this is Mack."

Deuce asks Mack, "Hi! Did you like my music?"

"You are great on that saxophone. You really have a gift. I enjoyed listening to you play your saxophone."

"Thanks, kid! My music is my sanity. Without it, I would have no purpose. I had to lose everything in my life to find that out. When I was married and so happy with my wife and my children, I stopped playing my saxophone. I was too caught up in living and my job. Then, when I lost everything, I found myself again only through my music. Now, I give it free to everyone because it is all I have left to give to anyone."

"Deuce, I have to walk Mack to the casino parking deck. When I am done doing that I will come back with my harmonica and join you, buddy," replies Christopher to him.

"Great! We'll have a great time, as usual, together," Deuce impulsively blurts out.

Then Christopher and Mack walk back toward the casino so Christopher can walk Mack to his car and see him leave the casino. On the way to the casino parking deck, they pass a handicap woman in a wheelchair. Christopher looks at Mack and says, "Do you remember me saying that you owed a human interest reward for winning tonight?"

"Yes, what did you mean by that?"

"I meant that you should give back to one of God's people for winning tonight, so why don't you give that handicap woman something. They call her Daisy on the Boardwalk. She deserves it! She has to survive. It is like giving a church offering to God."

Together they walk over to the woman. Mack takes twenty dollars out of his wallet and puts the twenty into the woman's hand.

The handicap woman yells back to him, "God will bless you, young man! Thanks!"

As the two of them walk back through the casino and to the elevator Mack says to Christopher, "Can I give you your $40.00 back."

"No, son, I don't want anything back from you. You have already given of yourself to Deuce, Daisy, Joshua and Bredele. Now you deserve the rest of the money that you won today."

They get off at the elevator on the fifth floor. Christopher walks Mack to his car. Mack asks him if he can give him a ride somewhere since he is carrying so much stuff in his hands.

Christopher agrees to get into his car and go with him.

When they get to the street level Mack gives Christopher a hug and sincerely says to him, "I'll never forget you or this night. Thanks so much!"

"More importantly, Mack, never stop believing in God and miracles. Bye for now, son," Christopher quickly says to him in a loud voice.

Christopher walks back to the Boardwalk to meet up with Deuce. As he walks by the side of the casino, he sees three teenage boys getting ready to hurt a dog near a historical monument sight for the veterans.

One of the angry boys cries out to the other boy, "Hold that ugly dog, I want to kill it."

The other boy follows his order.

Then, the evil boy starts to pour lighting fluid on the little dog's fur. When Christopher sees this his eyes become enlarged and he runs over to the tiny mongrel.

"Stop what you are doing to that dog right now. I will not let you hurt it," yells Christopher at both of boys.

"Shut up!" The second boy shouts to Christopher. Then, that boy pulls out his lighter and lights it up, and starts moving toward the terrified dog.

The third boy runs away scared from all of them.

Christopher quickly runs over to the second boy and squeezes the boy's hand in which he is holding the lit lighter. The boy's hand gets burnt and the flame goes out. Then Christopher runs over to the dog and grabs it from the other boy.

Just then a policeman on the Boardwalk sees the third boy running from the monument and fears trouble in the making for the boy running away looks very familiar to him. In fact, he looks like one of the boys in one of the local gangs which are always getting into trouble throughout the city with the police.

The policeman runs over to the monument area thinking there might be trouble going on somewhere around it.

As Christopher turns around with the dog in his arms, the boy with the burnt hand pulls a switchblade on Christopher and threatens him by saying to him, "Give me the dog back right now old man or else!"

"I am not afraid of you! I will not give you this dog back for his life is precious, son. You are not going to kill this dog just because you hate yourself and your own life. Just because everyone else fears you, I don't."

With that the boy runs over to Christopher and stabs him twice. As Christopher falls to the ground with the dog in his hands the second boy runs over to the first boy, and they both flee the area just in time as a policeman appears.

Seeing this happening the policeman runs over to Christopher and says to him, "What has happened to you? Can you talk?"

"Some teenage boy just stabbed me. He wanted to set this little dog on fire. I wouldn't allow him to do it," weakly replies Christopher to the officer.

"I have to get an ambulance for you and get someone to apprehend those boys right now. I just need to know how many boys there were altogether, sir?"

"Three! I need a favor from you. Would you please keep this dog for me until I get out of the hospital?"

"Keep the dog? I hate dogs! Ask one of your other friends to take care of the dog for you, but please don't ask me."

"Please keep the dog for me. I don't have anyone else to help me with the dog. I'll be glad to pay you. It will just be for a few days. And look at it this way, dog spells "god" backwards, so you will be helping Him, too." Out of breath, Christopher begs the policeman to do this favor for him.

Just then the ambulance arrives and a crowd surfaces around Christopher. One of the men in the crowd hears Christopher talking to the policeman and walks over to Christopher as they start to put him onto the ambulance.

"Christopher is that you?" in shock asks Joshua.

"Oh, Joshua, I'm so glad you're here. I need you to help me. Please tell Lady Noreen when you see her at the casino that I've been detained, but I do plan to take her to the casino show and dinner in a couple of weeks. Also, I need a favor from you. Would you please hold on to my bags until I leave the hospital? I really don't have any place to put them."

Joshua questions Christopher by asking him, "How long do you think that will be?"

"I don't know, Joshua, I'm not a doctor, I'm just going to be a patient."

A paramedic finally yells out, "Sir, please clear the area. We're putting this man in the ambulance. Are you going with him to the hospital or not?"

Joshua slowly sighs, "Ugh! I don't know!"

The paramedic frustrated with his answer inquires once again, "Are you going with him or not?"

Joshua just stares at Christopher as the paramedics start to take the dog from him, and hears Christopher yell, "Where is the policeman? Where is he?"

The policeman hearing him responds, "Here I am."

Christopher sighs in relief and mutters to him, "By the way, what's your name?"

"My name is Sergeant Leon Mussack."

Christopher then in a breathless tone says to him, "Leon, please take my dog and care for it until I recover. Please!"

Sergeant Mussack screams at Christopher, "Okay, I'll take your dog. But I'll be checking on you every day until you get out of the hospital so you can take your dog back home with you. You know I hate dogs!"

Christopher whispers to him, "Thank you so much. Here is the dog. You two will have a great time together while I'm on a vacation at the hospital."

"By the way, what is the dog's name?"

"The dog doesn't have a name. You name it!"

With that the policeman walks away with the little dog tucked under his arm.

They place Christopher inside of the ambulance. The paramedic looks back at Joshua and shouts out at him, "Sir, are you coming with him or not for the very last time?'

In hesitation, Joshua, with all of Christopher's bags in his hands, replies to the paramedic, "Yes".

They help Joshua into the ambulance and off they take Christopher to the hospital.

Once at the hospital, the paramedics immediately take Christopher into an emergency room. The doctors are shocked that Christopher hasn't bled more and that he is still awake and talking. It looks like Christopher has two stab wounds. One to his left lung, another one in his right arm, and his right hand is very, very bruised. The doctors immediately send Christopher to the x-ray department and request a room for him.

As the hospital staff gets ready to take Christopher to his room, Christopher calls out for a nurse to come to him. With that a nurse by the name of Marcena Zinicola goes over to him.

"Would you please help me? If there is a good-looking young man waiting for me in the waiting room, would you please go tell him the hospital is admitting me and that he can go home," in a faint voice Christopher tells the nurse.

"How will I know him?" asks the young nurse.

"You'll know him, his name is Joshua," Christopher responds to her in a quiet tone.

"Okay, I'll go find him for you," replies the nurse to Christopher.

"Hurry!" begs Christopher.

Marcena goes out to the waiting room and spots a good-looking hunk of a man. She walks over to him and asks him, "Is your name Joshua?"

"Yes!" Joshua quickly answers her.

"Your friend sent me out here to tell you that he has been admitted into the hospital and you can go home now," Marcena tells Joshua.

Then, Joshua reacts to her by saying, "Oh, thanks, that was very nice of you to come out to the waiting room to find me. How long will Christopher be in the hospital and how badly hurt is he?"

"That I can't answer until all his x-ray results and tests are completed and given to his doctor. However, it is unbelievable that your friend is still awake and coherent. He is really a strong-willed human being," laughs Marcena.

"Yes, he is! He is quite a character. Okay, well thanks. I guess I'll be leaving then. By the way, what is your name?" with interest Joshua inquires.

"It's Marcena."

"Is it okay if I call you at the hospital to see how he is doing?"

"That will be okay. Here is a card with the hospital number and my extension number on it. Just ask for Marcena Zinicola on the third floor."

With that Joshua walks out of the emergency doors headed for home.

Chapter 4

Miracles Aren't Impossible

The next day, you see Joshua on the casino floor with Bredele. At his break he spots Lady Noreen and goes over to her.

"Lady Noreen, I have a message from Christopher for you. He was stabbed last night near the casino, when he tried to save a dog from being killed. He was trying to find you to tell you that he was going with you to the upcoming casino show and dinner," Joshua sadly tells Lady Noreen.

Lady Noreen gasps out sobbing, "Is he going to live?"

Joshua calmly responds, "It seems like he is. He was awake during the whole ordeal."

"Bless his heart. He almost got himself killed over a dog. That man is something else and here I thought he was psycho," sadly Lady Noreen responds to Joshua.

"Also, I have to prepare you. Christopher is a changed man. Yesterday he went and bought new clothes, had his haircut, and shaved his beard. You won't know him when you see him," anxiously Joshua tells Lady Noreen.

Lady Noreen madly yells out, "Why did he go and do all of that? I liked him for just being Christopher. Here I'm the one who wants to die and he almost got killed on me. I do indeed call that reversed fate!"

Joshua talking in a hurry continues to say, "Well, I have to go back to my shift. Is there anything else that you want me to tell Christopher for you, Lady Noreen?"

Lady Noreen in shock whispers softly to him, "Yeah, tell him not to die yet! I have just started living once again!"

With that Lady Noreen collects the money out of her machine and leaves the casino.

Joshua walks back to Bredele at the cage. They go back to work handing out money to people who are winning on the machines.

As the evening slows down Bredele questions Joshua, "What were you doing with that middle-aged woman today? Do you have the hots for her or something?"

"I was telling her that her friend, Christopher, was almost stabbed to death last night," in defiance Joshua answers Bredele.

Bredele in his evil voice raves on, "Shucks, you mean that waste of human flesh didn't die! How sad, Joshua!"

Joshua responds to him by saying, "Bredele what an awful thing you just said. Don't you have a heart?"

"Listen, Christopher is a loser. He's scum! That woman would be better off without him. Unless she is buying drugs from him, she should get as far away from him as possible. He is bad news! He's a homeless beach bum. You better listen to me, Joshua," Bredele yells in a loud voice at him.

Joshua sarcastically exclaims, "Bredele, you don't like anyone, do you?"

Bredele full of sarcasm snaps back at Joshua saying, "No, I don't. See all of those people out there on the floor gambling, I hate each one of them. They just sit there and gamble their lives away. How sick all those gambling addicts are as they gamble throughout the days, weekend, months, and years in our casino!"

"Bredele, those people out there pay our salaries. They're just out there on the casino floor having fun. They're not hurting anyone. Why don't you take your anger and inferior complex out on yourself, Bredele? With that mouth of yours, you just gossip and say evil things about almost everyone you know. I feel so sorry for you," expresses Joshua in anger to Bredele.

Bredele in a belittling rage cries out in anger, "Don't feel sorry for me, Joshua. Feel sorry for your scum bum friend. He's the sicko – not me!"

"Well, my day is done with for now. I have to go," Joshua answers him in quickly.

"Where are you going?" Bredele smirks.

"I'm going to the hospital to see Christopher," Joshua eagerly answers him.

"He's a con man. He has you as his caretaker now, too. I have to go! I can't take any more of this do-gooder stuff today," Bredele bitterly replies to Joshua.

Joshua leaves the casino and starts walking to the hospital. Once he gets to the hospital, he goes to the information desk and asks for Christopher. No one can help him because he doesn't have a last name for him.

Next, he goes to the third floor to find Marcena Zinicola. He looks in the nurse's station and he spots her.

"Hi! Do you remember me from yesterday?" Joshua shyly remarks.

"Of course, I do! I don't have amnesia!" jokingly states Marcena.

"Do you know what floor my friend is on?" Joshua asks her.

"Of course, I do, Joshua. He is on the seventh floor in room 735."

"By the way, what is Christopher's full name, Marcena?"

"His name, you're going to laugh, Joshua, is Christopher Saint."

"You're kidding! That's really his name, Marcena?"

"That's what the hospital office pulled up under his social security number and that's the name he gave to the hospital, too," Marcena answers Joshua.

"Well, I guess it isn't a fictitious name then. Again thanks for your help, Marcena. I hope I see you around the hospital again sometime."

"You never know!" Marcena chuckles inwardly back to him.

Joshua smiles at Marcena. Then he runs to the elevator and goes up to see Christopher. He finally finds his room and enters it. Christopher is resting peacefully. As Joshua slowly walks into his room, Christopher's eyes pop wide open.

Then Christopher a little out of breath quietly whispers to Joshua, "Hi, there!"

Joshua in shock impulsively responds, "How are you doing, Christopher?"

"The doctors tell me I'm going to live. You have to tell Lady Noreen the good news. I have a punctured lung, stitches in my right arm where I was stabbed, and a bruised right hand. But the good news is I'm alive! I told the doctors, I was going to heal up real fast because I have a date with Lady Noreen in four weeks to see the impersonator show at the casino and I can't let her down. Lady Noreen has almost given up on living these days. She doesn't have any desire to live anymore. Without it, miracles aren't possible," replies Christopher to Joshua.

"Well, Christopher, you must get well then. It sounds like you are ready for your big date with her," jokingly Joshua tells Christopher.

"Tell Lady Noreen that I'll see her at the casino as soon as I get out of here. If she can wait that long and that her psycho escort is still very much alive. Also, tell Marcena that I'm okay, too, Joshua. I don't want my beautiful nurse to worry about me. When I woke up in the emergency room after surgery, I woke up to the face of an angel. I thought I was dead! But I wasn't, it was Marcena's face. Marcena does have the face of an angel doesn't she?" Christopher states to Joshua.

"Yep, Christopher, she is really beautiful."

"Joshua, she isn't married, but she does have a boyfriend. I have to check him out!"

"Christopher, leave well enough alone. You just take care of yourself and get well."

"Huh, my friend, Joshua, I thought you wanted to find true love?"

"I do, Christopher, but in my own time. By the way Christopher, before I leave you, is your real name Christopher Saint?"

"Of course it is! Don't you believe me, Joshua?"

"I do." Joshua walks out of Christopher's room with a big smile on his face.

Later that day, Christopher has another surprise visitor. This time it is Lady Noreen.

"What are you doing in this hospital, Christopher?" Lady Noreen full of emotion yells at him.

"I tried to protect a dog last night, Lady Noreen, and I ended up here."

"You are the craziest man that I have ever met in my entire life. In fact, I wouldn't even know you today. You don't look like my, Christopher. Why did you have to shave your beard off and cut your hair?"

"I wanted to look presentable for you, Lady Noreen!"

"Are you crazy – you looked fine the other way you looked, Christopher. On top of that, Christopher, I'm the one with a death wish and you're the one who almost got killed for a dog. I don't believe it! I need a shrink to understand you!"

"Listen, you should be happy. I lived, Lady Noreen!"

"I guess I should be, Christopher! You're the first saint that I've ever known. Is that really your name or is that one of your aliases? Are you a murderer or an undercover agent, Christopher?"

"No, Lady Noreen, I'm just an ordinary man."

"Nothing about you seems very ordinary to me, Christopher Saint."

"I am! Are you all right, Lady Noreen? I bet I gave you quite a scare? I'm not going to die. I have too much to live for in my life."

"The doctor told me that you would be okay. He said that your lung, arm and hand seem to be mending really fast. I was happy to hear that, Christopher, but where are you going to go when you get out of the hospital?"

"Now, you know where I live, I live underneath the Boardwalk in Atlantic City, Lady Noreen."

"Christopher, when you get out of the hospital why don't you stay in a room at my place. You can do some repairs on my house for your room and board. I have a real big house in Ventnor and no one lives in it with me because everyone is dead. Why don't you join me?"

"Lady Noreen, what will your neighbors say?"

"Who cares what the neighbors think! I am over 60 years old. I can do whatever I want to in my life."

"But you don't even know me, Lady Noreen. I'm just a stranger to you."

"That's true! But, Christopher, I have fun with you. You are the first person in my life after all of my pain to make me think about my life. I guess you could say you have given me a wake-up call for the very first time. For that I'm thankful."

"Well, then I guess I'll move into your house as soon as I am released from the hospital, Lady Noreen."

"Great! I better go now and start getting your room ready for you, Christopher. No one has stayed in my house for years. Maybe, I'll even redecorate the room for you."

"That sounds great! Write down your address and telephone number on this piece of paper so I know your address when I get ready to leave the hospital, Lady Noreen."

"Okay, I will, Mr. Saint."

"Thanks for visiting me, Lady Noreen. It meant a lot to me."

"I'll never do this again, Christopher! You never even gave me your last name. I had to go to all of the hospital floors to find you. I'm exhausted and out of breath. I'm too old for this. I'm part of the menopause generation!"

"What are you talking about, Lady Noreen? You look great for your age. You're no spring chicken but I'm nothing to crow about either."

"There you go with your sick humor! I have to go home and start getting your bedroom ready for you right now, Christopher."

"Is your chauffeur here to take you home, Lady Noreen?"

"No, I walked here. I couldn't believe that you almost got yourself killed over a dog, a little dog on top of that, Christopher!"

"Did you enjoy your walk, Lady Noreen?"

"No, Christopher, I was hoping someone would hit me, mug me, or kill me, but nothing happened to me. I mean nothing! That's how boring my life is. You're the one with all the excitement in your life. Well, I'm leaving you now!"

"Bye for now – I'll miss you, Lady Noreen!" happily Christopher replies to her.

"No, you won't! I won't miss you either! So long, Christopher!" snaps Lady Noreen at him.

In an irritable mood, Lady Noreen walks to the elevator for her long walk home. She is seen by the motorists that pass her talking to herself.

S. L. Sharp

The next morning, after Christopher finishes his breakfast, Marcena enters his room.

"Well, how is our patient today? You look much better," Marcena states in a pleasant tone of voice.

"Oh, Marcena, I feel like going to the ocean. The ocean is my sanctuary and my sanity," happily Christopher tells her.

Marcena responds to him by asking, "Christopher, did you file charges against those boys?"

"No, I'll handle the situation in my own time. Jail never solves the problem. It only turns juveniles into criminals. Therefore, I won't file any charges against those three boys, Marcena."

"Please don't take the law into your own hands, Christopher. I don't want to see you getting hurt again."

"I won't! I promise! I am not here to judge or solve the problems of the world. I am just here to live, Marcena."

"My precious nurse, would you mind straightening my pillow before you leave my room?"

"I'd be more than glad to do that for you, Mr. Christopher Saint."

As Marcena goes to fluff his pillow for him, Christopher observes several bruises on her arms.

"Marcena, why is your arm so black and blue? Did someone hurt you?"

"Christopher, your imagination is going wild. You are watching too many soap operas. I helped a young man named Rico, who lives next door to my apartment. He has Spina bifida. I think I bruised my arms when I lifted him out of his wheelchair the other day."

"That sounds like a very good reason for your bruised arms, but if anyone ever physically abuses you, I want to know about it. I am your protector, Marcena."

"Okay, Christopher, I promise you if that ever happens that I will tell you!"

"You have my word on that Marcena."

Marcena leaves Christopher's hospital room and he takes a nap.

Near midevening, a distinguished looking man is wheeled into Christopher's room. The man has white hair and a moustache. When the nurse leaves the room, Christopher hollers over to the man, "Are you alive over there?"

"I'm just barely alive! I feel like a guinea pig! They keep doing all of these tests on me to keep me alive. On top of that, I have been on so many different types of machines and medicines that I feel like I'm almost half dead."

"What is wrong with you?" Christopher asks him.

"The doctors say I have cancer and that it has spread all over me. They tell me I only have 6 months to live. So you see, I really don't have anything to be happy about."

"You have a lot to be happy about. You are still alive and you can still bring a lot of happiness into other people's lives in 6 months. Oh, by the way, my name is Christopher."

"I don't get your point! I know that I have a lot of money, but I don't even have any heirs. I'll probably give the state all of my money; I haven't even made out a will yet. I'm just so mad about dying!" yells the man at the top of his voice in front of Christopher.

"Wait a minute! What is your name?"

"Nicholas Zyvosky!"

"Well, Nicholas, why don't you stay at the shore when you get out of the hospital and you can work at the beach with me. You'll meet a lot of wonderful people and maybe you'll have a little bit of fun. Who knows what is in your future!"

"Give me your address, Christopher. Maybe when I get out of this hospital, I'll look you up."

Chapter 5

The Secret To Life

Finally the next week, Christopher is discharged from the hospital. All the staff members on his floor give him cards before he leaves the hospital.

Marcena comes to see him that day bringing him a special cupcake with a lit candle on it. She asks Christopher to blow out the candle and make a big wish.

"I've made my big wish. I sure hope it comes true. If so, Marcena, there will be double trouble for you."

"What do you mean by that Christopher?"

"Just wait and see, Marcena."

"Christopher, sometimes you make no sense at all to me."

"Marcena, does anything in this life really make any sense to you?"

"You're right, Christopher."

"Maybe one of these days, I can take Rico and you out to eat, Marcena?"

"Rico loves pizza, Christopher."

"Put your address and telephone number on this piece of paper with Lady Noreen's address on it. That's where I am going to stay for the next few days until I get back on my feet, Marcena."

"Here's my address and telephone number, Christopher. I hope to hear from you one of these days."

Christopher gets his things from the hospital closet in his room and gets ready to leave. He gives Marcena a big hug and then goes to see Mr. Zyvosky, his room partner.

"The offer still goes, Nicholas. I hope you will come and visit me. We'll go fishing and you'll have a great time at the beach with me. In fact, Nicholas, you might have so much fun that you'll never want to leave the beach or the ocean ever again."

"Thanks for your offer, Christopher. I have really enjoyed your company. Let's see how everything ends up here. If, and when, I get out of here, I'll try to remember to look you up for the day."

"Okay, that's a deal. Bye for now, Nicholas."

Christopher walks from the hospital to his favorite spot – the ocean. Once there, he takes off his shoes and shirt and walks up the beach to Ventnor to find Lady Noreen's house. As his feet feel the warmth of the sand, he feels so alive once again.

Thirty minutes later, he makes it to her street. Her house has a front side view of the ocean. He can't believe how giant her house is. He walks to the front door of her house and rings the doorbell. Finally, Lady Noreen answers it.

"Hi, there, stranger, I've been calling the hospital every day to find out when you would be released and ready to come home. Today the woman at the front desk on the telephone told me that this was the day that Christopher Saint would be released from the hospital."

"Lady Noreen, your house is simply beautiful. I never expected it to look like this."

"Did you think that I lived in a dump, Christopher? In fact, I've given you the master bedroom in this house which faces the ocean since you like the water so much."

"Let me see my room, Lady Noreen. I'm so excited about seeing a view of the ocean from it."

Lady Noreen takes Christopher on a tour of her house and up to his bedroom. It is a giant plush room that has been redone and redecorated from the ceiling to the floor.

"Lady Noreen, I love it. It has the most beautiful view of the ocean. I just love it!"

"I never really noticed the view until right now, Christopher. It is beautiful, isn't it?"

S. L. Sharp

"It truly is! Is it okay if I go to the police station to find Sergeant Leon Mussack, so I can get the dog back that he has been keeping for me?"

"That is fine with me, but can we go together to the casino tonight for the big drawing?" wonders Lady Noreen.

"That sounds great," Christopher answers her with a smile on his face.

"Christopher, why don't you ask my chauffeur to drive you to the police station, so you don't overdo it too much today?"

"You sure you don't mind, Lady Noreen?"

"I don't mind! I pay Brook a lot of money for doing nothing. He would love to drive you to the police station. Believe me! He has nothing better to do today."

Christopher waits for the chauffeur to come for him as he puts his few things into the closet and drawers in his room. When Brook, the chauffeur arrives, Lady Noreen calls Christopher to come downstairs.

"Thanks for all of your help, Lady Noreen. I'll be back in a little bit. Do you want anything?"

"A serial killer would be a nice gift for me today, Christopher!"

"Please stop it right now, Lady Noreen! You're not going to die yet, so try to enjoy your life just a little if you possibly can!"

"Thanks for the sermon, Christopher Saint. Are you a preacher or a saint now?"

"I do have a calling and it is to help you, Lady Noreen! Let's see if I succeed in my mission."

"Funny! I'll see you later, Christopher."

Christopher gets into the limousine and Brook is overjoyed to see him.

"Good day! My name is Brook. Where can I take you?"

"I'd like you to take me to the police station, Brook."

In jest, Brook replies, "Is it for a visit or a stay?"

"It is just for a visit, Brook. One of the policemen there has been watching a dog for me."

"Then off we go, Christopher!"

Brook finally arrives in front of the station and drops Christopher off.

"Where do you want to meet you when you are done, Christopher?"

"In front of the florist shop four blocks down from here, Brook."

"I'll see you there, Christopher!"

Christopher enters the police station and asks for Sergeant Leon Mussack. The receptionist at the desk says, "The Sergeant is with someone at the moment. However, when he is done I will call your name. Wait in the lobby please."

Christopher sits down and reads the newspaper. Finally, Sergeant Mussack comes out to the receptionist area to get him.

"It is really good to see you again, Christopher. It looks like you are back on your feet once again!"

"I came to take the dog off of your hands. I know you hate dogs, Sergeant Mussack."

"Christopher, I don't know how to explain this to you, but that dog has gotten to me."

You didn't get rid of the dog did you? You said that you were going to check on me every day at the hospital and you never did. I thought maybe the dog got sick or something bad happened to it."

"No, Christopher, nothing like that happened to the dog that I now call Delilah. In fact, she is in perfect health. I took her to the veterinarian the next day after your mishap. The vet checked her over and she was fine. Then, I went and got some dog shampoo and toys for her since my wife and two kids were visiting with my mother-in-law that week. After that, I took her home and bathed her. She was a doll. That night, we watched TV together and I played ball with her. I haven't had that much fun for years. I really don't want to give her back to you, Christopher. I wish I could keep her. Can I buy her from you?"

"Sergeant, I thought you hated dogs."

"I do, Christopher, but Delilah is more like a person than a dog to me. She just makes me so very happy. It's like she totally adores me. Delilah is like my best buddy. I knew that when you got out of the hospital, you'd want her back. That is why I never called on you at the hospital or came to see you. It was for my own selfish reasons, Christopher."

"Well, Leon, since you put it that way, she belongs with you. I just saved her life. On the night that I saved her, she was just an abandoned dog waiting to be found or killed. It is apparent that you've won her heart over, so now she is your dog. But, if Delilah ever has puppies can I have one?"

"Of course you can, Christopher! If she does, I'd I feel like a proud father. Here take one of my cigars before you leave. You have made me the luckiest man today. Oh, thank you, thank you, and thank you once again, Christopher, for giving me Delilah."

"I must be going, Leon, I'm taking my girl, Lady Noreen, to a drawing at the casino tonight. Keep me informed about our girl, Delilah. Let me give you my new address in case you need to get in touch with me."

"Thanks, Christopher! I can never thank you enough. You have made my day the best one yet!"

Christopher leaves the police station genuinely happy. In an upbeat mood he struts down four blocks to the florist shop. Once there, he sees Brook drinking a cup of coffee inside the limousine. Christopher goes and taps on the window of the limo and tells Brook that he has to buy something at the florist shop and he'll be right out."

Once Christopher is inside the shop the florist asks, "Can I help you, sir?"

"Yes, sir, I'm looking for an exotic bouquet of flowers for an exotic woman. What can you make up for me and how much will it cost me?"

"I can make you a somewhat exotic bouquet for $ 50.00 or a wild exotic bouquet for $100.00," the florist quickly answers him.

"Give me the wild exotic bouquet that fits this woman to a tee. Will you make the bouquet up for her yourself?" questions Christopher.

"I certainly will!" replies the florist.

"Then make it the way you described it to me. It's the exotic bouquet that I want to buy for my Lady Noreen, and by the way, what is your name?" Christopher asks the florist.

My name is Patrick. I'll go to the backroom of the florist shop to prepare the bouquet for you.

Christopher moseys around looking at all of the plants and flowers. Within 15 minutes, Patrick comes out with the most beautiful arrangement of exotic wild flowers that Christopher has ever seen.

"Patrick, you outdid yourself! That is a gorgeous bouquet of flowers! If I ever need flowers ever again, I'm coming directly to you!"

"I am so glad that you like the arrangement. So often, I make arrangements for people and they don't stop to look at my talent, or the art, that I put into the arrangement. People wait too long to give flowers to people while they are alive. Instead, they wait until they are dead."

With a giant flower bouquet in front of him, Christopher approaches the limousine.

Brook gets out of the limo and offers to help Christopher get into the limo.

Once inside of the car, Christopher asks Brook to put the sky window down so he can stand up and look out of it.

Soon they are back at Lady Noreen's house. Christopher asks Brook to go and get Lady Noreen for him.

Brook immediately runs to the door and Lady Noreen opens the door.

"What do you want, Brook, your money? Or did Christopher leave me already after 30 minutes of putting up with me?"

"For neither reason, madam, Christopher wants me to escort you to the car. He has a surprise for you."

"A surprise for me, Brook, I'm too old for surprises!" yells Lady Noreen at Brook.

"Madam, no one is ever too old for surprises. Please come with me. Christopher is waiting for you. For heaven's sake, don't spoil his surprise!"

Brook gives Lady Noreen his arm and he escorts her to the car.

As Lady Noreen bends down to sit down next to Christopher in the limousine, he hands her the bouquet.

"I'm not dead yet, Christopher. Who are these flowers for?" baffled Lady Noreen asks him.

"You are a diamond in the rough. These flowers can only bring out the beauty that I feel when I am around you."

"Thanks, Christopher, but are you sure that you are talking about me? I think you are talking about the other me that died a long time ago. She went away and never came back home."

"Is your name Noreen Kagey?"

"Yes, that is my name, Christopher, but are you sure you don't need my shrink, or my prescription drugs? Maybe you hurt more than just your lung, arm and hand when you were attacked on the Boardwalk."

"You are the one that I'm talking about and I'm mentally sane, Lady Noreen."

"Well, thank you, Christopher, the flowers are truly gorgeous. I've never had a bouquet of flowers ever like these in my whole life."

Christopher then gets out of the limousine and goes to the other side and offers Lady Noreen his arm to walk her into the house.

Brook just watches the two in amazement and scratches his head, he can't believe that Christopher is with her. He is puzzled about the whole relationship and feels a great sense of pity for Christopher.

Once inside of the house, Lady Noreen runs to the kitchen and puts her flowers into a vase and sets the vase on the dining room table.

"They are very beautiful, Christopher. It was very nice of you to buy them for me."

"You deserve them. You have been very kind to me, Lady Noreen. You have taken me, a stranger, into your house. That is truly a great human act."

"Christopher, do you want to leave early for the casino, so we can eat there before the drawing? If you're not up to it, I'll understand.

"Lady Noreen, let's walk to the casino and grab a bite to eat on the Boardwalk. The walk will do us good.

"By the way Christopher, where is the dog?"

"The dog now has a new owner, Lady Noreen."

"Who is the new owner, Christopher?"

"Sergeant Mussack."

"Oh! I thought it was going to be your dog?"

"No, Lady Noreen, the dog fell in love with Sergeant Mussack."

"Oh! Now I understand."

"Lady Noreen, you must see the ocean at night and meet some more of my friends."

"I never go out on the Boardwalk at night, Christopher, and I never really look at the ocean anymore. I haven't eaten on the Boardwalk for years."

"Lady Noreen, you're going to have a great time tonight. Just wait and see."

With that, the two holding hands begin their walk to the Boardwalk. First, Christopher has Lady Noreen stop on the Boardwalk at the Mango Tango Bar & Grill. There they have two super mango tango burgers with onion rings and iced teas. Lady Noreen insists on paying the bill. Then, they walk further down the Boardwalk and see some teenage kids rapping on the Boardwalk and putting on a spectacular dance show for everyone to see. Finally, Christopher has Lady Noreen take off her sandals and walk with him down the beach the rest of the way to the steps leading up to the Boardwalk entrance to the casino. But, before they walk up the steps, Christopher excuses himself to go and get something underneath the Boardwalk. After he picks up his harmonica, he runs back to Lady Noreen and they walk up the steps to the casino and enter it.

Inside the casino the lights are going off on the machines and the music is playing really loud. The beverage waiters and waitresses are delivering drinks and the slot managers are giving money to the slot winners. It is another exciting evening at the casino in Atlantic City.

Christopher and Lady Noreen walk to the elevator and take it upstairs for the drawing. Once inside the casino's main ballroom, Lady Noreen, deposits her card entry inside of the large drum with all of the other invited people who have entries for this big drawing at the casino tonight.

Lady Noreen and Christopher then take a seat in the ballroom to wait and see if she has won any of the prize cash amounts. The drawing then begins.

Christopher notices Joshua and Bredele over near the drum. They are over there tonight to draw the entries from the cage.

The master of ceremonies informs all of the guests about the rules and regulations used for the drawings. When he is done with his announcements the drawing begins. Hundreds of names are drawn from the drum.

"Christopher, let's leave. They've drawn all the names. Only one name is left for the big prize of $15,000.00. If we don't hear my name, let's leave," impatiently Lady Noreen keeps telling Christopher.

"The final 1st prize winner is Jenna Peyton. Jenna, are you here in the audience? You've just won $15,000.00. Jenna, where are you? You are a very, very lucky winner tonight!"

"Christopher, let's go. I didn't win. I never win at these drawings."

"Lady Noreen, let's just wait a second to make sure the prize is claimed. No one has gone up on the stage yet."

"Christopher, I'm leaving, I'll meet you downstairs."

"Are you in such a hurry, Lady Noreen, that you have no time to enjoy your life?"

"Christopher, that's not it. I know when I've lost!"

"But, you haven't lost yet, Lady Noreen."

"Hello! Hello! Is Jenna Peyton in the audience? Your time is almost over with Jenna," the casino vice-president announces.

"5-4-3-2-1 - It's time to draw another name. Portia reach in there and draw another name out."

"And the winner is Noreen Kagey."

"Oh, my God, Christopher, it can't be! I never win anything at these drawings. It can't be me! And I wanted to leave. You were right like always, Christopher."

"Go claim your cash prize and I'll meet you downstairs near the Rainbow Seven Machines. Go get your money, you lucky winner."

Lady Noreen goes in back of the curtain to claim her big winnings. She asks for a check for $14,500.00 dollars and $500.00 in cash. She has to wait there for a while to get her winnings and sign the casino form.

Meanwhile, Christopher is sitting near the Rainbow Seven Machines waiting for her. As he sits there, a beverage hostess comes around taking drink orders. Christopher orders a diet soda.

Next, Joshua comes over to him.

"Christopher, it is so good to see you once again. How do you feel?"

"I feel a lot better than I did when you saw me at the hospital, Joshua."

"By the way, Christopher, I still have your bags of clothes. When do you want me to give them back to you?"

"Let me see, today is Sunday. How about getting together with me on Wednesday, Joshua?"

"That day would be great! That day is my day off, Christopher. What time?'

"Joshua, let's meet around noon."

"Great, Christopher! I'll be looking for you outside on the Boardwalk in front of the casino at that time."

"Bye for now, Joshua."

"See ya, Christopher!"

The beverage waitress soon comes back to Christopher with a diet soda.

"Here you go, sir. Wait a minute aren't you the man that Mama Cane always brags about to me? Yeah, you are him. She just can't say enough good things about you. She believes you can make dreams come true for people."

"I wouldn't go that far... but I will listen to what your dream is and maybe I can help you with it in some small way."

"My name is Hilten Lytle. My dream is to try-out for the big talent show in late October on the Boardwalk at the President's Boardwalk Plaza, but I don't have a band or dancers, or costumes, or anything to do it. I just have a dream. I think I can win it! If I have the best original song and I win the talent show, they'll record the song and put it on the radio. But first, I have to have a hit song, and I don't have one!"

"Well, dreams do come true! You do have a few months to plan for it, Hilten."

"But, Christopher, I don't have any money or anything else to compete in the show."

"Well, let me think about it. Maybe your dream can come true, I don't know about it right at this exact moment."

"Christopher, I have to get back to my job, but thanks for listening to me."

Just as Hilten walks away from Christopher, Lady Noreen comes down from the elevator and walks over to Christopher.

"Are you mad at me, Christopher?"

"I'm not mad at you! You did nothing wrong for me to be mad at, Lady Noreen. However, please don't be so impatient about your life. Don't hurry it up so fast, because it's over before you know it."

"I guess your way of thinking makes sense and my way of thinking is just my way. I am sorry, Christopher, how can I make it up to you?"

"Let's leave here right now and let me introduce you to my friend, Deuce."

"Okay, I'm ready, Christopher."

Finally, Christopher hears Deuce's saxophone playing in the breeze of the night. With Lady Noreen, he hurries over to him. Deuce already has a big crowd surrounding him. As Christopher and Lady Noreen move closer into the crowd, Christopher grabs something out of his pocket.

"Christopher, where have you been? You were supposed to join up me several days back, but I heard some kid stabbed you. So you had a good reason for not joining me that night. Will you accompany me tonight on your harmonica?"

"I certainly will; however, not long since I am still healing from injuries. I have "Harmony," my harmonica, with me tonight, and this is my friend, Lady Noreen."

"Lady Noreen, it is a pleasure to meet you! Christopher and I go way back quite some years together."

With that Christopher goes up front with Deuce and they start playing music together. Christopher plays on his harmonica and Deuce on his saxophone. Lady Noreen stands in the audience and starts dancing to the music. She then goes up to Deuce's instrumental case and puts a $100.00 bill in it. Christopher looks at her and smiles.

As the night warms up a drummer and a violinist join Deuce and Christopher in their musical group. Finally, the hour gets late and Christopher puts his harmonica back into his pocket and gently touches Lady Noreen's hand to go home.

"Christopher, where did you learn how to play the harmonica like that?"

"Lady Noreen, a girl by the name of Angel taught me how to play it a long time ago."

"She must have been a great teacher for you are a professional musician on the harmonica. You could be in a band as talented as you are, Christopher."

"I never thought of that, Lady Noreen. I think you've given me a vision of a future dream. You're really something! I saw you put a hundred-dollar bill in Deuce's saxophone case. You are really changing, Lady Noreen. You are starting to understand what the human interest in life is all about. I am really proud of you. You will make something good happen with your money now. You now understand the secret to life - that without people and love in your life, money has no value."

Christopher has Lady Noreen walk with him down to the beach and they walk hand in hand back to her house. Once inside the house, Christopher says good night to Lady Noreen and goes to his bedroom.

Lady Noreen has a cup of hot tea. Then, she gets all her eight bottles of pills lined up and takes her medication for her manic depressive disorder. Finally, she looks at all of her bottles and says, "Tomorrow I'm going to see my shrink and I'm going to start cutting back on all of you, my pretty pill friends. I don't need all of you to live anymore. I've finally come to the point that I can live on my own just fine!"

With that Lady Noreen gulps all of her pills down like she is taking a shot of liquor, and goes up the stairs to go to her bedroom.

Chapter 6

Oh, God, Help Me!

During the next few days things begin to change around the Kagey house. Christopher spends a lot of time of painting and working in the lawn. Lady Noreen is now constantly redecorating the house and planting flowers, plus going to her doctor's appointments so she can cut back on all of her medication dosages. She is determined to get on with her life without relying on prescription drugs.

On Wednesday, Christopher reminds Lady Noreen that he is to meet with Joshua to pick up his stored bags of new clothing and suits from Marcuso's Men's Clothing Store downtown. Afterwards, he tells her that he is going to call on one of the nurses from the hospital and meet her friend named Rico, who has Spina bifida. Christopher asks her to accompany him. However, Lady Noreen decides to go grocery shopping and pick up some more flowers for the flowerbed in the backyard, but she thanks him for inviting her.

Christopher walks down the Boardwalk to the beach steps with some bread in his hand. Then as he walks down the shoreline he calls out for Sanabrio, one of the seagulls. Eventually the seagull hears his name and flies directly to him.

"Oh, Sanabrio, I've been so tied up with life that I haven't been able to get to the ocean to see you. Real soon, I will put a bird pond near the house, so you can visit me. I truly miss you! Here is some food for you to eat right now.

Then Sanabrio lifts his strong wings into the air and flies out over the ocean with the bread hanging from his beak. The seagull looks like he is buried into the deep blue clouded sky.

As Christopher walks down the beach he screens the area seeing surfers, lovers, homeless people and lost souls walking and laying on the beach. Once he reaches his final destination, he sees three young children building sand castles and designing sand sculptures into the sand. They are happy as they play master engineers within the sandbox of the beach. He can feel their free energy and joy of life in his soul.

Christopher finally walks up to the Boardwalk and sees his friend, Joshua, who is standing in front of the casino waiting for him.

"Joshua, have you been waiting here long for me, my friend?"

"No, Christopher, I just got here. Here are all your belongings that you gave me to hold for you."

"Thanks a lot for helping me, Joshua. Do you have time for me to buy you a soda or take you out for lunch?"

"I have made other plans for today, Christopher, but maybe we can make plans to get together for a bite to eat on another day."

"That is a great idea! Again thanks for everything, Joshua. Lady Noreen and I will see you real soon. Bye for now."

Christopher walks back towards Atlantic City and takes a few side streets to reach Marcena's apartment building on Iowa Street. Once there, he steps inside of Mario's Pizza to use the payphone telephone booth to phone Marcena to see if she is home so he can take her and her friend, Rico, out for lunch.

"Hi! Can I please speak to Marcena?"

"She is speaking."

"Marcena, this is Christopher, I'm in your vicinity and if you and Rico are available, I'd like to take both of you out for lunch."

"That sounds like a great idea, Christopher. Come on over and I'll buzz you into the apartment complex. While you take the elevator to my floor, I'll go knock on Rico's door and see if he can go with us today."

Christopher departs from Mario's Pizza and walks over to Marcena's apartment building. He pushes her buzzer and she opens the front door to let him into the building. He then goes to the elevator and goes up to her floor. When he gets off the elevator there stands Marcena and Rico in his wheelchair waiting for him.

"Christopher, it is so good to see you. This is Rico, my good friend and neighbor."

"It is a pleasure to meet you, Rico. I hope you like pizza."

"Pizza! That is my favorite kind of food, Christopher. I bet Marcena already told you that's what I love to eat."

"Yes, Marcena did tell me that, and we are going to eat as much pizza as you want to eat at the restaurant, Rico."

"Yeah, that sounds great!" remarks Rico.

"Marcena, is it okay with you if I leave my bags and packages here in your apartment so I don't have to carry them to lunch with us?"

"I'll open my apartment door and you can leave your things anywhere you want to leave them in my apartment. Your things will be very safe here, Christopher."

Then the three of them leave Marcena's apartment. Christopher and Marcena walk together as Rico wheels his wheelchair to the Miletti's Italian Restaurant across the street from the apartment building. Once inside of the restaurant, the smells of spaghetti, ravioli and pizza are all around the place.

The waitress comes to take their order and Christopher has Rico order an extra-large pizza for all of them to eat.

"Well, have you been busy at work, Marcena?" asks Christopher.

"There have been a lot of car accidents this month, Christopher. I must admit we've been pretty busy throughout the entire hospital."

"Well, Rico, tell me all about yourself."

"I have been very busy with my wheelchair racing this summer. I love to compete against others, Christopher. It is so exciting!"

"That sounds like lots of fun, Rico! No wonder Marcena is so proud of you."

"Marcena is like the sister I never had in life, Christopher. Ever since my parents died a year ago, and I became 21 years old, Marcena has looked after me. She always tells her boyfriend, Spencer, that she won't marry him unless he includes me in the marriage package.

Since Marcena's parents aren't living either, we've become like family to one another."

"I know Marcena loves you a lot; she always talks about you at the hospital. She is very proud of you, Rico. Now I see why both of you are a family to one another."

The pizza is brought to the table and everyone eats up. When everyone is done eating, Christopher accompanies Rico and Marcena back to their apartments. Then, he takes them both up the elevator with him. He helps Rico into his apartment, and when he walks Marcena into hers, her boyfriend, Spencer, is there sitting on the couch.

"Christopher this is my boyfriend, Spencer."

"It is a pleasure to meet you. In fact, I've been waiting to meet you. I knew you must be a very special guy to have a great girl like Marcena in your life."

"Christopher, you have it all wrong! Marcena is lucky to have a great guy like me in her life. She can actually say that she has the best of everything in her life now."

"Huh, I guess, I do! Thanks for straightening me out, I had it all wrong didn't I?" mumbles Marcena.

"You certainly did, and now I think it is time for you to leave, Christopher, so Marcena can get ready for work," impolitely states Spencer in front of both of them.

"Like usual you're right, Spencer," Christopher answers in a reluctant voice.

"Thanks again for a wonderful day, Christopher. Rico and I loved the pizza. Maybe Lady Noreen and you can go with me to one of Rico's wheelchair races? Rico would love having lots of fans to cheer him on to victory. Did you know he is a champion racer?"

"I didn't know that, Marcena! Well, I best get going now. Bye for now," remarks Christopher to both of them.

Marcena walks Christopher to the door and says to him, "Bye, Christopher, thanks for the wonderful day!"

The door closes and a major drama scene breaks out in the living room of Marcena's apartment. Spencer is in a rage over the fact that Marcena went out with Christopher and Rico for the day without him.

"I don't believe you went out with them over me. What were you thinking? Do you like that old man, Marcena?"

"It's not like that Spencer. He's just a friend that I made at the hospital a few weeks ago. He's like the father I never had to protect me from evil."

"Huh, he's your friend, father figure, and your protector, Marcena. He's more like your lover to me."

"Get off of the subject right now. I don't want to fight with you, Spencer."

"You don't want to fight with me, you cheap bitch! Well, I want to fight. It looks like I have to teach you another lesson on how not to look at other men or go out with them when I'm not there with you. You see you're mine and don't you forget it, Marcena. Come here right now!" orders Spencer in a malicious voice.

"Spencer, just leave me alone. You can get out of my apartment right now.

You're not going to hit me again. If you do our relationship will be all over with for good! I will not allow you to hit me anymore. People at work have noticed my black and blue arms and legs. They haven't seen the rest! You are an abuser! I have put off reporting you to the police because I thought that you would change, but it has ended up that I'm the one who has changed in this relationship. I am now a victim. I now live in fear of you each and every day of my life. I fear you! I grew up with an abusive father, and now I have an abusive boyfriend. My life has never really changed has it?"

"Come here right now. I won't hurt you. I'm sorry for everything I did and said to you, Marcena."

Christopher takes the elevator down to the first floor and gets ready to leave the apartment building when he realizes he has forgotten his packages and bags in Marcena's apartment. Realizing this, he walks back to the elevator and goes back up to Marcena's floor to get his things. As he gets off the elevator, he hears loud voices arguing back in forth at each other. As he walks further down the hall, he sees Marcena's door opening as if someone is trying to leave her apartment.

"I won't ask you again, leave right now!" in anger yells Marcena.

Spencer walks over towards her and the door. He pauses right when he gets in front of her. Then he slaps her across the face and slams the door.

Marcena flies across the room and lands on the floor. She struggles with all of her energy to get back up.

Seeing this, Spencer then slaps her across the face again. He then pulls her back up and starts shaking her in a furious rage.

Marcena screams out, "Help, me. Help! Oh, God, help me!"

Spencer covers her mouth and starts punching her in the chest. "Shut up, bitch! Shut up, right now!"

"Stop it! Stop it!" Blood is coming from her lip and nose. "Get out! Get out of here right now, Spencer, or I'll call the police."

"Oh, no you won't!" With that Spencer uses his fist and hits her directly in her face.

Marcena lets out a final scream of horror before he lands his final punch on her.

Christopher hears Marcena's cries for help and with all of his strength he pushes her apartment door wide open.

Spencer looks in shock to see Christopher standing right in front of him.

Christopher immediately runs over to Marcena to help her. He sees that she is badly beaten up and in an unconscious state. He fears she is near death if he doesn't get her immediately out of the apartment and away from Spencer.

"Get out of my way Spencer I am not going to let Marcena die. Get out of my way!"

"Old man, you are crazy. This is between Marcena and me. You caused all of this to happen to her, Christopher."

"I didn't! You did! You are mentally evil, not sick, but evil. So many parents lose their daughters to evil lovers like you. You murder a person's soul. This time you won't get her back so you can't violently kill her. I have big hopes and dreams for Marcena, Spencer. You're not going to take her life or dreams away from her."

With that Spencer gets up and runs over to him and starts hitting Christopher. However, each time he hits Christopher, he hurts his fist. The harder he hits Christopher, the more damage he does to his own fists.

Christopher within a moment picks Marcena up in his arms. He touches her neck to get her pulse.

Spencer has blood coming from his hands, he shrieks at the top of his voice at Christopher, "Who are you? Look what you have done to my hands! You must be wearing a metal chest plate! I get it; you're a secret serviceman gone undercover. You're a policeman!"

"I am Christopher Saint, and if you ever hit or hurt another person in your life, you will die. If you ever come into contact with Marcena again or try to see her, you will die. You've abused people all of your life. Now, I've put all of your abuse from all of those years back into your own body. Spencer, do you now feel all of the pain and torture that you have caused everyone throughout your whole life?"

"I'm in pain! Help me, Christopher!" yells Spencer back at him.

"The only way you can help yourself, Spencer, is by you finding yourself through God. If you don't do that the abuse that you have given to all the others in your life will destroy you. I beg you to seek the Lord," Christopher urges Spencer.

Spencer lies on the floor and starts to cry.

Christopher walks into the hall holding Marcena in his arms.

Rico opens his door and comes into the hall in his wheelchair and sees Christopher holding Marcena.

"Oh, no, Christopher, he's done it again to her. Oh, no! She is all I have! She is my mother and my sister all in one. Christopher please, please don't let Marcena die. Please save her life!" frantically screams Rico.

"I'll try, Rico! Hang in there. Marcena will make it through this! Here is my girlfriend's telephone number. Call her right now. Have her and her chauffeur come and get you. I will meet up with all of you at the hospital."

Marcena's neighbors gather in the hall. One of them calls the police on Spencer.

Christopher runs holding Marcena tightly in his arms to the elevator.

It is the next day. You see Marcena in the hospital on life support machines. She hasn't regained consciousness as of yet. In the waiting room sits Lady Noreen and Brook. Rico is asleep in his wheelchair with his head bowed down. Christopher is in the hospital chapel praying for God to spare Marcena's life.

"Please God, let her live. She has so much good to do for you down here. I've seen her life in my dreams. She will serve you and love you for the rest of her days upon this earth. Please heavenly Father, bless her with a miracle to live." Christopher then stands up and walks to the elevator to go to the waiting room on the third floor of the hospital where Marcena is struggling for her life in the intensive care unit.

On the way up to the third floor on the elevator, Christopher hears a ringing sound in his ears. He tries to shake his head to stop it, but the ringing sound won't stop. The elevator finally stops and he gets off of the elevator. As he walks to the waiting room the ringing gets louder in his ears. The pain of the sound hurts him so much that he closes his eyes and in that moment he sees a giant rainbow in his mind. He immediately opens his eyes and Marcena's doctor comes out into the waiting room.

"Who is Christopher?"

"I am!" nervously answers Christopher.

"Hi! I am Dr. Rior. Marcena is finally conscious and she is asking for you. She has suffered a few broken ribs, a broken nose, and a broken leg. I am afraid if you had not gotten her to the hospital as fast as you did, her boyfriend would have killed her. Thank God, you were there to save her, Christopher."

"Oh, doctor, thank you so very much! Through you knowledge, God saved Marcena. Thank you for being an instrument of God's glory, Dr. Rior. Today you have won a battle over evil!" Christopher assures the doctor.

"Christopher, I never thought of it that way. It is my job to save people lives. I do it every day," the doctor sincerely replies to him.

"I know you do, Dr. Rior. Yet it is God's job to save lives every second of the day, too! Therefore, you are both miracle workers," Christopher states with a strong conviction.

"Well, thank you. I never thought of it that way, but maybe I am. Let me take you to Marcena's room right now," Dr. Rior responds.

Christopher walks behind Dr. Rior to Marcena's room. Once in it, he sees four other patients in the emergency room beds hooked up to tubes. Christopher realizes how blessed Marcena is that God saved her life.

"Marcena, you can only talk for a few minutes to Christopher. I will see you later today," reassures Dr. Rior.

Christopher goes over to Marcena and holds her hand. Slowly with all her strength she opens her eyes and focuses on him.

"Oh, Christopher, thank you so much for saving my life," Marcena struggles to say to him. "I really must be out of it or else the doctor has me on too many pain killers. I had a dream that you were a giant angel who took me up to the top of my apartment building and flew with me in your giant arms to the hospital. You were such a handsome angel, Christopher. Isn't that a funny dream?" softly whispers Marcena to Christopher.

"That was quite a dream, Marcena, for I'm no angel, I'm no saint, I'm just a man! But listen now, you have to get well real fast. I have some big plans for you. You are going to love them, too. I have to go because I want you to get well as fast as you can."

"I hope so, Christopher. Ever since my father beat my mother to death and my father was sentenced to death by lethal injection, I stopped dreaming. I was in my late teens when all that happened to me and I never faced my fear of being abused. Therefore, I fell in love with an abuser in my early twenties. I wonder if everyone is just like me and continues the circle of constant pain for their entire life."

"Sad to say, many do, because they never tell their darkest nightmares to a professional therapist. Then one day, the pain explodes again within them, but this time they are no longer the child but the victim again in a different situation. That is why I want you to get some professional help. It will help you mend, Marcena, for the scares on the inside mend so much slower than the scares on the outside of your body. Well, listen I must go. Is there anything else I can do for you, Marcena?" inquires Christopher.

"Would you please have Rico come in my room to see me? He must be frightened to death about my condition. He wanted me to report Spencer to the police and to get help, but I thought I could change Spencer. Rico was right! I was wrong! I will never ever try to change someone else from being who they are Christopher," declares Marcena.

Christopher gives Marcena a kiss on her cheek and she closes her eyes.

Christopher goes back to the waiting room and tells Rico to go and see Marcena.

Rico is so relieved to know that his best friend and mother figure is alive. He, like an Olympian wheelchair champion, wheels as fast as he can to her room.

Then Sergeant Leon Mussack sees Christopher and walks over to him.

"Christopher, I'm so sorry about the girl. Are you up to giving me a statement on what happened in her apartment last night?"

"Yes, I am Sergeant! I forgot my packages and bags in Marcena's apartment so I took the elevator back up to her apartment to get my things. When I got on her floor, I heard Marcena scream for help. I walked down to her apartment door; it was not locked, it was slightly ajar so I walked right into her apartment. Then all I remember is seeing her boyfriend, Spencer, hitting and slapping her around. I went towards Spencer and Marcena so I could grab Marcena away from him. Then Spencer and I exchanged some physical fist blows to each other's bodies. Spencer, finally, went down on the floor and I ran with all my energy with Marcena to the elevator so I could get her to the hospital."

"Christopher, some of the tenants in the apartment said they saw you run with Marcena to the elevator and they saw Spencer walk out of the apartment with a dazed look on his face holding his hands and crying.

In fact, one of the apartment tenants overheard him saying, "Oh, my God, what have I done? Please, heal me, I hurt so bad inside. I am so sorry for what I have done. I'll never hurt her or see her ever again. Please don't kill me, Christopher."

"How strange, Sergeant Mussack!" Christopher answers him with a puzzled look on his face.

"Christopher, the guy must have had a nervous breakdown or something, for he just seemed to have kept rambling to himself all the way down the hall," states Sergeant Mussack.

"Sergeant Mussack, Spencer has to find peace within his own soul. All those years that he refused to get professional help for his mental condition have caught up with him. Hopefully, he will turn himself in and beg the judge to get him some professional help. It will be the only way that Spencer will ever find any peace of mind ever again. If he doesn't do this, he will bear the pain that he has put Marcena and so many others through for the rest of his life."

"You're right like usual, Christopher. Oh, I meant to tell you that I have taught Delilah some new tricks. My wife and kids love her. Next, I am going to teach her and my kids on how to catch a Frisbee. Just between you and me, I was having some marital problems with the wife - that's why she took our kids to her parents. Now, since I talked her into coming back to me, we've had such a great time together. With the dog, we are a real family now. We go to the park, on picnics, hiking, and to the beach a lot. Delilah has really saved my marriage. She has made all of us so happy and here I hated dogs!"

"When hate turns into love – miracles like what you are telling me about right now can happen. Aren't you glad that your heart of stone turned back into a loving heart? Now you have the love to give your wife, two kids, and Delilah. Sometimes our jobs turn us into human machines. When that happens we need a reason to laugh once again. You found your reason to laugh again through Delilah. Now that simple reason has spread to your whole family. Leon, you are truly a blessed man. Bye for now, but I'll look forward to seeing you with your family and Delilah on the beach one of these days playing Frisbee," chuckles Christopher to himself.

Sergeant Leon Mussack leaves Christopher and walks to the hospital floor elevator.

Lady Noreen stands up and hugs Christopher inquiring, "Is she okay?

"Lady Noreen, she is going to be better than she was before. Once you get a second chance at life you live it better than the first time around. She is a fighter. She'll pull through!"

"Did they ever find her boyfriend, Christopher?" angrily asks Lady Noreen.

"Rumor has it that he packed and left Atlantic City. Hopefully, the police will find him on the run somewhere. I feel bad for him, but only he can save his own life from all of his own pain and destruction. God does give second chances to all of us. However, so often the person when he or she gets the second chance; they just repeat the same behavioral pattern over and over again. That's why most people destroy themselves and their lives," remarks Christopher to Lady Noreen.

"Christopher let's wake Brook up, get Rico, and go home. You've had quite a night!" slowly whispers Lady Noreen to him.

Lady Noreen goes over and wakes Brook up.

Brook smiles at Christopher and says to him, "Do you want me to open the sunroof of the car going home so you can show Lady Noreen how you like to ride in the limousine?"

"That sounds like a great idea, Brook!" laughs Christopher.

"Wait a minute, Brook, here comes, Rico. I will get him."

The three of them walk to the limousine that is parked in the hospital parking deck. As Christopher pushes Rico in the wheelchair to the limo, Brook opens the door to let Lady Noreen into the car. Then Christopher hops in the back seat to be with Lady Noreen.

Then, Brook assists Rico into the front seat of the limo, and puts his wheelchair in the trunk.

Finally, Brook opens the sunroof and Christopher takes Lady Noreen's hand and he helps her stand up in the back of the car.

With Lady Noreen and Christopher standing up in the sunroof, they drive off to Rico's apartment building on Iowa Street. Everyone is listening to the beautiful music on the radio in celebration of Marcena's miraculous recovery tonight.

Chapter 7

This Is A Sign From Heaven

You see, Christopher is enjoying himself out on the beach feeding his favorite seagull, Sanabria.

Lady Noreen is weeding her flowerbed and having the time of her life doing it.

Her cell phone rings outside. She answers it saying, "Hello!"

"Hello! Is this Lady Noreen Kagey?"

"Yes, it is!"

"This is Nicholas Zyvosky, I was wondering if I could please talk to Christopher. I was his roommate a few weeks ago, when he was in the hospital."

"Hold on a minute. I'll walk the phone over to him. If I lose you, call back."

"Thanks!"

Lady Noreen walks out of her yard to the Boardwalk and finds Christopher playing and talking to a seagull, while he feeds him. Lots and lots of birds are all around Christopher. Lady Noreen immediately runs to him and hands him her cell phone.

"Hello, this is Christopher."

"Hi there, Christopher, you might not remember me, but I was your roommate a couple of weeks back. This is Nicholas Zyvosky."

"Hello, Nicholas! How are you doing?"

"So-so!"

"Listen I was wondering if I could come down and visit you. I have a timeshare condo down in Ventnor for this month. I thought I would take you up on your invitation to go fishing. I haven't done anything exciting since I was diagnosed with my death verdict. Do you really want to go fishing with me?"

"I would love to go fishing with you, Nicholas. We can rent a boat for the day and go deep ocean fishing with a few other people, if you would like to do so?"

"Boy, would that be lots of fun."

"By the way, what are you doing tonight, Nicholas?"

"I'm just going to be with my favorite friend these days, my television."

"If that is all you are going to do, why don't you join my girl and me for a casino date. You'll have a great time. I'm sure Lady Noreen can get comps for you to come with us to the casino tonight. Nicholas you might even end up being the life of the party there!"

"Ha! Christopher, you think so…?"

"Nicholas, I know so…!"

"Then, I'll join you and your girlfriend. Where should I meet both of you?"

"Let's meet on the Boardwalk near the mall, around 6 o'clock. We can grab a bite to eat together before the casino show."

"It sounds like lots of fun!" happily responds Nicholas.

Christopher finally finishes feeding Sanabrio, and all the other birds. Then he runs the cell phone back into the house to Lady Noreen.

"Lady Noreen, are you hiding from me? Where are you?" teasingly Christopher asks her.

"Christopher, are you blind? I'm right in front of your eyes!" replies Lady Noreen to him in an agitated tone of voice.

"Is that you, that beautiful hunk of a woman over there?" quickly states Christopher to her.

"Stop the flattery, Christopher, it will get you nowhere!" insists Lady Noreen.

"Lady Noreen do you think you could get an extra comp to the casino for one of my friends tonight?"

"I'll have no problem doing that Christopher for you! I've put so much money into the casino slots and tables that I own the whole main ballroom!" laughs Lady Noreen.

"Thanks, Lady Noreen. You're incredible! By the way, I have to go pick up my suits at Marcuso's Clothing Store, and I'll call Rico to see if he will let me into Marcena's apartment so I can get my bags and packages. I want to look nice for you tonight."

"Christopher, I liked you with your beard!" Lady Noreen shrieks these words out loud.

"Then, I'll grow my beard back just for you. By the way, what is different about you, Lady Noreen? You seem so much happier and content with your life these days."

"I don't know maybe it is because I've cut back on my medication last week under the directions of my psychiatrist. You see, I used to take more medication than I had to take. I thought it would deaden my pain and put me out of my misery. I used to lie to my psychiatrist about my drug addiction problem. Isn't that funny, Christopher, I actually started to have a drug addiction problem? Most people think of drug addicts as having these types of problems, not nuts like me," giggles Lady Noreen.

"That's great Lady Noreen that you've done that with your life. Now, if you start exercising on the Boardwalk, you'll even feel healthier. The body and the mind are integrated. Each one of them must be exercised each day through mental exercise and physical exercise if they are to stay strong and healthy," Christopher tells her.

"Oh, Christopher, I don't know if I'm up to that yet. I just started walking a little and working around the house a couple of weeks ago. I don't think I'm ready for an exercise training program right now. But I must admit, I do feel somewhat better."

"I'm so glad to hear that Lady Noreen. Well, I'm going to call Rico, so I can start getting ready for tonight. Can I borrow your cell phone, Lady Noreen?"

"Of course, Christopher!" replies Lady Noreen.

Christopher calls Rico, and Rico is very excited that Christopher is coming over to see him. Rico has alternated shifts with some of Marcena's friends so everyone who loves Marcena can visit her at the hospital. Today is Rico's day to visit Marcena.

"Rico, I'll be at your place in about 30 minutes. Why don't you meet me outside with my bags? Then, I can walk with you on your way to the hospital. You see, I have to stop by Marcuso's Clothing Store to get my suits."

"That would be perfect, Christopher! I have a lot to tell you," excitedly answers Rico.

Christopher runs out of the house in Ventnor to the beach, and walks from there to the Boardwalk. Once on it, he walks to the steps and starts walking towards the side street to Iowa. As he walks straight ahead of him, he hears someone calling to him from a bench.

"Christopher, come here! It's me!"

"Hello there, Old Bessie! How is the mother of all of the children on the Boardwalk today?"

"Not too good! I miss you, Christopher! Ever since you moved away from all of us on the Boardwalk things have gotten crazy. There is a runaway kid that I took in that scares me to death. His name is Dev. The kids on the Boardwalk nicknamed him Devil, but his real name is Devlin. I probably shouldn't have taken him in – he's evil, Christopher," explains Old Bessie to him. "The only good news, Christopher, is that Big Luke has been watching after all of your possessions underneath the Boardwalk. He misses you, too!"

"Old Bessie, where is this boy, you call Dev? I've never heard you talk about any kid like this before. Should we call the police on him?" Christopher asks her in a concerned tone of voice.

"Christopher, that won't do any good. They'll just put him back on the streets, and then he'll hurt one of the other kids or kill me," Old Bessie answers him all frightened.

"Is the boy around here right now so I can meet him, Old Bessie?" Christopher asks her in a strong tone of voice.

"No, I hear he is shacked-up with some girl. Rumor is that he was the kid that beat the elderly, old man, from the nursing home to death last year with a baseball bat. No one ever found the murder weapon or the murderer of poor, Mr. Irwin Baumgarten. It makes me so sad to know that man was a victim of such a brutal crime. I don't know why there are so many hate crimes in America today. What worries me even more than that is thinking that Dev might be the boy who stabbed you, Christopher! I can't believe it was over that little mongrel dog. I've asked the other kids if it was Dev, and no one says anything.

I think they are all so scared to death of this boy that no one will talk. Why, oh why, Christopher, do these hate crimes continue against people and animals in America?" cries out Old Bessie as tears start to come to her eyes.

"It seems that people are so unhappy and bored in their lives these days that they have to abuse and victimize others to feel happiness and pleasure. That is because people do not feel any love. Love is free, but money and material things mean more to people today than love. After a while when you don't get any love, one becomes numb to everything in his or her life. Eventually that child or adult has a mentality of kill or be killed. That's the way it is, Old Bessie."

"That's not only sad, it's heartbreaking, Christopher!" blurts out Old Bessie.

"Do you have a piece of paper and a pen, Old Bessie?" Christopher asks her.

"Let me go through my purse. I see it. Here is a piece of paper and I think I feel a pen somewhere in the bottom of my purse," insists Old Bessie.

"Give the paper and pen to me. I'll write my new address and telephone number out for you. Call me, Old Bessie, if you see Dev again. I will talk to him. I don't want anything bad to happen to you!" Christopher assures her.

"Thank you, Christopher. You always make me feel so much safer here on the Boardwalk by myself," Old Bessie confesses to Christopher.

From the Boardwalk, Christopher walks over and cuts down Iowa, and finds Rico outside in front of his apartment building. Rico is looking all around trying to spot Christopher. Finally, he sees Christopher coming near him.

"Howdy there Christopher, here are your bags and packages."

"Thanks, Rico, I finally have my new clothes. Now I can dress up tonight."

"You're so welcome! It is so good to see you. I have great news for you. Marcena is coming home in about two more weeks from the hospital, but she has no one to take care of her, Christopher. What should I do?"

"Oh, don't worry about that, Rico. I'll help you take care of her when she comes home. Maybe you can help Lady Noreen plan a home coming party for her. Would you like to do that for Marcena?"

"Oh, that would be so much fun to do, Christopher. I've never done anything like that before for anyone in my entire life."

"Well, I have to be going so you can get to the hospital so you can be with Marcena, but don't tell her about the surprise party, Rico."

"I won't, I never tell my sins or secrets to anyone, Christopher."

"I'll call you sometime this week, and Lady Noreen will help you to arrange all of the details for Marcena's party with you."

"That sounds great, Christopher. Oh, by the way, would you like to come to my wheelchair race in November? I have been exercising and building up my arms for the big race for the last six months. I'd love to have you watch me try and win my race."

"I'll try to make it there for you, Rico."

"Is that a promise, Christopher?"

"Cross my heart, Rico!"

"Christopher do you have any messages to give me for Marcena, before I see her?"

"Just tell her, Rico, to have happy dreams and that dreams really do come true!"

"I hope so, Christopher!"

Christopher then carries his bags and packages to Mr. Marcuso's Clothing Store. As soon as he arrives there, Mr. Marcuso looks up and is so happy to see him.

"Where have you been, Christopher? I was afraid that something awful had happened to my number one model for this fall," jokingly responds Mr. Marcuso to him.

"I was stabbed a few weeks back over a boy trying to kill a little dog, Mr. Marcuso."

"Are you okay now, Christopher?"

"I'm fine," Christopher assures him.

"What about the dog?" asks Mr. Marcuso.

"She, Delilah, is now the most loved dog in this world, Mr. Marcuso."

"I'm so glad about that, after all, you almost died for her, Christopher."

"Are my suits ready, Mr. Marcuso?"

"They certainly are ready! Christopher, would you like to try them on?"

"Would you mind if I do?" asks Christopher.

"Be my guest, Christopher."

Christopher then tries his new suits on and models them all around the store. He sings and dances as he models for the sales employees. Everyone is having so much fun watching him model his clothes, especially Mr. Marcuso.

"Christopher, are you going to model for me in the fall?" Mr. Marcuso asks him.

"I don't know yet, but I'll try to work it into my busy schedule. By the way, which suit should I wear tonight?" Christopher asks Mr. Marcuso in an uncertain tone of voice.

"Wear the black one, Christopher, and here is a tie to wear with it. It is a gift to you from me. Your girlfriend will be shocked at how good-looking you look in that suit."

"She will be, Mr. Marcuso! That's great! She needs a little shock treatment every now and then just to keep her on her toes," laughs Christopher.

"Is she sick?"

"No, she just thinks she is all of the time."

"Is she going through the change of life like my wife is, Christopher?"

"Yeah, Mr. Marcuso, but she never changes. I guess that is why they call it menopause. I guess you pause in your life, and sometimes you never return to it."

"God help you, Christopher! One moment my wife is cold, the next moment she is hot. Then, she wants the air conditioner on because she can't breathe. Then, she gets too cold. In fact, she gets a lot of headaches now even though she doesn't have her period anymore. Although I think she has a constant period now, but it is invisible because the Red Sea in her is all dried up."

"Mr. Marcuso, that's what it is like, but I love Lady Noreen that way all of the time!" states Christopher.

"Thank heavens you do, Christopher!"

"Let me get changed back into my old clothes, Mr. Marcuso, and get going. Lady Noreen and I have to meet one of my friends that I made at the hospital. He is going to the show with us tonight and sometime this next month, we are all going fishing."

"Do you think I could come with both of you fishing? It is my last sane month before the Marcuso fall fashions come out. I could use a vacation. All I ever do is work. My wife and daughter tell me that all of the time!"

"Maybe they are right, Mr. Marcuso."

"Please call me Marc, Christopher. Mr. Marcuso seems like such a formal name."

"Okay, Marc, we will all go fishing in the next couple of weeks before the fall season gets here."

Christopher goes into the dressing room and changes his clothes. The sales clerk gets both of his suits and puts them into a wardrobe bag for him. When she is done doing that Christopher grabs the wardrobe bag and his other bags. After he organizes everything, he starts his long walk back to Ventnor. On his way, he meets a cashier manager from one of the fast food restaurants on the Boardwalk, who is walking home to Ventnor, too. They strike up a conversation.

"It looks like you're going somewhere special tonight with that fancy wardrobe bag and all those other bags that you are carrying," responds the young woman to him.

"You are right! I'm taking my girl to a big show at the casino this evening," replies Christopher to the woman.

"Which show?" the woman asks him.

"The impersonator one!" replies Christopher.

"It is great! I am a singer and I know a lot of the other singers in that show," claims the young woman.

"Oh, do you know Hilten Lytle?" responds Christopher.

"No, should I?" the woman questions him.

"I thought you might know her since she is a singer, too," remarks Christopher.

"Where does she sing?" blurts out the unknown woman.

"Nowhere yet, Hilten is trying to form a group to compete in the Boardwalk Talent Show in late October to see if she can win the song contest, so she can become an upcoming singing recording artist," Christopher remarks.

"Well, if she needs some back-up singers, my friends and I might be interested in joining up with her. We are trying to get as much exposure as possible to get into the recording industry. This might be a big break for us, too, if the girl can really sing."

"Hilten might just need you as a back-up singer in her group. Who are you?"

"Here is my card. My name is Joy Rhapsody. Have Hilten call me if she is serious about performing in that show. If she is talented, who knows, my group might join her."

"I will try to see her tonight at the casino to tell her about you, Joy. Who knows, maybe together all of you will win the A. C. Boardwalk Talent Show."

"Wouldn't that be fantastic? By the way what is your name?"

"My name is Christopher Saint."

"You must be kidding me!" laughs Joy.

"No, Joy, I'm serious. That is my God given birth name."

"Really, you're not pulling my leg, Christopher Saint?"

"Honest! That is my real name."

"Ha! Ha! I've walked all this way with a saint and I never knew it. Well, this has been some day for me. Don't forget to tell Hilten about me, Mr. Saint."

"I won't, Joy."

Finally, Christopher makes it to Ventnor. As he approaches his street, he sees Lady Noreen running from the Boardwalk to her house. He can't believe that she has started to run. He is so happy about this. He runs to the door to greet, Lady Noreen saying, "Lady Noreen, you are something else! Just look at you! Did I see you running just now?"

"Were you spying on me?" groans Lady Noreen.

"Hardly!" teases Christopher.

"I wasn't running, I just thought I heard the phone ringing and I was walking quickly to answer it, Christopher."

"But how did you hear the phone inside the house, Lady Noreen?"

"I don't know how, Christopher, but I did, and that's that!"

"Okay, whatever you say is right!"

"Thank you, Christopher."

Lady Noreen and Christopher walk into the house and go to their individual bedrooms to get dressed for the casino show. Once dressed, Lady Noreen goes downstairs and waits for Christopher.

Finally, Christopher is done dressing and he walks down the stairs.

Lady Noreen sees him, and walks over to him. She can't believe it is him. She almost faints from the excitement of his new look.

"What's wrong, Lady Noreen?"

"I just got lightheaded. It is one of those menopausal things. You know, Christopher, one of those change of life things."

"Are you sure you are okay, Lady Noreen, you are so hot!"

"Christopher, during menopause when you are hot, you are real, real hot. When you are not-you're real, real cold. Your temperature is never right again during the change. Do you get it?"

"I guess so, Lady Noreen!"

"You look like a fashion model tonight, Lady Noreen."

"Thanks! I'm a fashion model from the 1900's."

"Hardly, let's get going so we can meet Nicholas Zyvosky. He will have a great time with us at the casino."

"Let's get going! Brook is outside with the limousine ready to take us to the side street where the C. T. Royal Ocean Mall is located at near the Boardwalk. Would it be okay if we eat at the Private Players' Lounge in the casino before we go to the Impersonator Show, Christopher?"

"That would be just perfect, Lady Noreen. It makes sense to eat in the casino lounge before we go to the show."

They walk out to the limousine and Brook can't believe his eyes. He opens the door and both of them get into the limousine. He drives them directly to the Boardwalk location near the C. T. Royal Ocean Mall. Once there, he lets them out to meet their guest and goes back to the car and waits for them.

When Lady Noreen and Christopher approach the Boardwalk all eyes are on Christopher. Lady Noreen gives the women, who are eyeing Christopher a nasty look.

Finally, Christopher sights Nicholas and he walks over to greet him with Lady Noreen.

"Hi! Nicholas! It is so good to see you. I am so glad that you called me today. Nicholas Zyvosky this is Lady Noreen Kagey."

"It is a pleasure to meet you," responds Nicholas.

"Follow us to our limousine," requests Lady Noreen.

Nicholas follows them to the limousine. Brook gets out and opens the doors for everyone.

"Nicholas, this is my other friend, Brook. By the way, Brook, what is your full name?"

"My full name is Brook Paul Wilkins," answers Brook.

"Nicolas Zyvosky this is Brook Paul Wilkins."

"It is great to meet you!" utters Nicholas.

"Brook is the best chauffeur in the whole wide world. Without him, I wouldn't get anywhere with Lady Noreen," proudly brags Christopher.

"It's good to have a man like that these days! Most people don't like their jobs. They'd rather take a false medical leave than work," protests Nicholas.

"Maybe their jobs make them sick because they are abused by their bosses. There are too many bosses today that boss people around. Not enough leaders to lead people to success not only on the job, but off of the job," points out Christopher.

"What do you mean by that?" Nicholas breaks in.

"Well, if people were appreciated and awarded on their jobs, they would feel fulfilled and they wouldn't miss so much work. Often when people are sick all of the time they are taking mental health days because of the stress at their workplace," claims Christopher.

"I never thought of it that way before, Christopher. Maybe that is why my employees missed so much work during their work year. Maybe they were all sick of me. I finally lost so much money at work because of all of them that I started to get sick of all of them, too. Now

I am dying from cancer. The thought of all of this makes me truly sick!" asserts Nicholas.

Brook pulls up in the black stretch limousine and drops everyone off at the casino door. Nicholas, Lady Noreen and Christopher get out of the limousine. As they get ready to walk into the casino, Christopher turns around to ask Brook if he would like to join all of them for the evening.

Brook in shock replies, "No, not tonight but maybe some other time. Thanks though for asking me. No one has ever included me in any of their activities or events in my thirty-year career at driving a limousine. Thanks, Christopher, for treating me like I have some purpose or human worth."

"Brook, you have true worth in this world. Without you no one could function in this hectic world. Do you like to fish, Brook?" mentions Christopher.

"I don't know I've always been so busy working that I've never had the time to go fishing, Christopher!"

"Well, Nicholas, and I will be planning a fishing trip sometime in the near future, Brook. When we get all the details ironed out, I want you to come with us."

"Christopher that would be impossible, you see, I live with my father. He is in a wheelchair. I can't leave him for a long period of time," with great sorrow Brook divulges this to Christopher.

"Don't worry about that Brook. We plan on taking your father with us on the fishing trip, too."

"Oh, Christopher, you are the best! My dad will be so excited about being invited to your fishing trip. Thanks for making me feel so special."

"You are special, Brook, and don't ever let anyone treat you otherwise."

"Well, you better join Lady Noreen and your friend, Nicholas, they are waiting for you, Christopher," responds Brook.

"I will, Brook, and we'll meet you at this door around midnight." Christopher informs Brook.

"Okay, Christopher, I hope all of you have a great time and win lots of money."

"Thanks for your good wishes, Brook!"

Christopher goes and joins everyone. They all take the escalator to the second floor to the exclusive Private Players' Lounge. Once inside of it, Lady Noreen presents her card at the lounge. Her casino hostess has already reserved her table. The three of them then proceed to the table, and then to the gourmet buffet to get their food and then to the side table to get their beverages. Nicholas is very impressed with the private club. He goes to the bar at the side of the dining area to get a drink. Everyone enjoys their food and conversation before the casino show. After everyone is done with their dinner, they proceed to choose their desserts at the dessert table and get their flavored coffee at the beverage table. Everyone on the staff at the private club and Lady Noreen's assigned casino hostess, Kyleen, treats them to everything and makes their time in the club exceptionally pleasurable for them. Kyleen gives everyone in the casino room the best service possible.

Once everyone is done eating, they proceed down the escalator to use their three complimentary tickets to see, "The Ageless Impersonations of all Times," live. The talented summer show is truly a spectacular one. Lady Noreen, Christopher and Nicholas can't get over the talent of the impersonators as they imitate individual singers and groups of the past. Each performer does an all-star performance. The crowd claps and cheers the highly talented singers and musicians throughout the night.

When the show is over, Lady Noreen, Christopher, and Nicholas head to the slots. Once at the slots Lady Noreen heads for her dollar machines. Christopher and Nicholas stand behind her and converse as she plays her favorite lucky slot machine. Christopher, while he stands watching Lady Noreen play her slot machine, sees Hilten Lytle. She is taking beverage orders from the casino players at the machines.

"Hi! Christopher. Long time no see! What can I get for you?" asks Hilten.

"Hilten please bring Lady Noreen a diet soda and an iced tea for me. By the way, Hilten, I'd like to introduce you to my good friend, Nicholas Zyvosky. He is our guest tonight."

"Nicholas, it is a pleasure to meet you. What can I get for you to drink?" asks Hilten.

"Please, bring me a Black Russian."

"I'll be back with your drinks in a few minutes," Hilten advises them.

Hilten takes off to get all of their drinks. Noreen keeps winning and losing on her favorite machine and having the time of her life. Christopher finally sits down with Nicholas next to Lady Noreen and seriously talks to Nicholas about a business opportunity for him tonight.

"Nicholas, do you remember that you talked to me in the hospital about leaving all of your money to the state when you die?"

"Yes, I do, Christopher, and I still plan to do that! Why do you want my money?"

"No, Nicholas, I only want to be your friend. I don't want your money!"

"Well, Christopher, I don't know how to be someone's friend. Sad to say, I've been so busy accumulating lots of money for so long that I haven't had time to have friends or have any fun.

Now, that I have been given a death sentence, I feel like I don't have any time left to make friends or have any fun at all."

"Nicholas, that is not true. It is not important how much time you have left. It's how you live each day to its fullest, Nicholas."

"Well, how do I do that Christopher?"

"The girl I just introduced you to needs help. Hilten wants to win the A. C. Boardwalk Talent Show in late October. She needs you to back her, if she is going to be able to win with a hit song. You see, Nicholas, Miss Lytle has no back-up singers, band, costumes or anything else to make it happen. She only has a dream and you, Nicholas, don't have a dream or even a purpose for living anymore. The girl has great potential but no manager or agent. You, Nicholas know how to transform a project like this into a full business success. Would you monetarily back her as her manager/agent and take her the full route to success?"

"Christopher, you must be crazy? I don't even know this girl. She might not even be able to sing. I've never been anyone's manger or agent before. Your proposal is an impossible scheme. I must say no to this stupid idea of yours. I can't be a part of this creative adventure of yours!"

"What would it take for you to change your mind and give me your word of honor to do it for Hilten?"

"See that small circle of $5.00, $25.00, and $100.00 slot machines over there? Well, Christopher, I would have to win $10,000.00 on that machine right there for me to become a believer in your scheme," sarcastically replies Nicholas to Christopher.

"But, Nicholas you don't need any money, you are filthy rich to begin with."

"I know I am Christopher, but it would take a miracle for me to believe in your scheme. I mean a miracle!"

"Well, if that happened would you give me your word to do it?"

"Christopher, you must be crazy. It's not going to happen. First of all, I'm not going to win on that machine, and second, you are going to feel like a fool when I lose on that machine. Then you are going to realize that you are a fool and that you are really, really crazy, and we will probably never see one another ever again in this lifetime."

"Nicholas, that might be the case, you might be right, everything you are saying to me sounds true. However, you might win. If that happens, you can be a different you. You might actually pull it off for her, and help Hilten win the talent show."

Christopher stands up and excuses himself from sitting next to Lady Noreen for a moment. He then gestures for Nicholas to follow him to the $5.00 slot machine that Nicholas has pointed out to him that he wants to play. Side by side the two walk to the circular pattern of the high player slot machines. Nicholas has a disgruntled look on his face and Christopher has a smile on his face.

Finally, the two reach the machine. Nicholas sits down at it and looks to Christopher to give him $100.00.

Christopher responds back to him, "Listen, Nicholas, you have more money than I'll ever have on this earth. Just put one of your hundred-dollar bills into the $5.00 slot machines and play $15.00 each time for six times and then push the button twice for your last $10.00."

"Christopher, this is a rip off. You have insulted my intelligence. First off, your brainstorming ideas are all crazy to me. Secondly, you've insulted my intelligence by making me play my own $100.00. This whole idea of yours is crazy, but I'll do it to prove that you are wrong. I'm not usually a betting man, but since your girlfriend has taken me to dinner tonight and to the show, I'll put my own money into this machine just to give back to her the cost of the evening. However, after I lose on this machine I never want to see you again. You promise never to call me, and we won't go fishing together either. Do you understand what I'm saying to you, Christopher?"

"Yes, I do, Nicholas, but you must promise me that you will be Hilten's backer if you win, and you'll go fishing with me and all of my friends."

"That will be a dark day in hell, but I promise you, Christopher, I will!"

Nicholas sits down at his machine and does what Christopher has told him to do. He plays $15.00 on the machine 6 times and he wins nothing. Then, he looks at Christopher and gets ready to cash out his last $10.00 from the machine.

Seeing what he is ready to do, Christopher yells at him, "Stop!" But it is too late a printed ticket for $10.00 comes out of that machine. With that Christopher picks up the $10.00 ticket out of the machine and hands it back to Nicholas and emotionally says to him, "Play this $10.00 ticket in the machine. You promised me that you would do that for me. Aren't you going to keep your word?"

With that Nicholas nastily takes the $10.00 ticket and puts it back into the slot machine and hits the play button. Immediately the light goes off and the music at his machine goes on. Nicholas has won $10,000.00 by getting two triple bars with one double bar on $10.00.

Nicholas is in shock. He can't believe that he has won. He looks at Christopher embarrassed and sadly whispers to him, "How did you know that I would win. Did you fix the machine or something?"

"Nicholas, I didn't do anything. This is a sign from heaven that you must help, Hilten. Now you have your $10,000.00, so I expect you to keep your word to me that you will help Hilten out."

"Okay, Christopher, I will, I will! I have nothing to lose. I'm going to die anyway, so I will do it for her, and I'll even go ocean fishing with you and all of your friends, too."

Hilten seeing the excitement over at the winner's circle takes their drinks over to them after giving Lady Noreen her diet soda. Once she goes over to the winner's circle she gives Christopher and Nicholas their drinks. Then in a sincere way, she says to Nicholas, "Congratulations on your win! Good luck!"

"Nicholas shyly looks at Hilten and nervously says to her, "Thanks!"

Christopher in front of Nicholas excitedly shouts out, "Nicholas and I would like to see you tomorrow about your singing career and the A. C. Boardwalk Talent Show. What would be a good time to see you?"

"Would 10:00 a.m. tomorrow morning be okay for both of you, Christopher?"

"Nicholas is that time okay for you?" asks Christopher.

"Yeah, I can meet with both of you at that time. I haven't made any big plans for my day," Nicholas responds in an arrogant tone of voice.

"Then we'll both meet you at Prentis's Breakfast & Lunch Grill which is right next to the casino tomorrow morning. It's a date," happily Christopher replies.

"Oh, Christopher, thank you so much! I can hardly wait until tomorrow morning to meet with both of you about my singing career. This is the most exciting news that I have ever had in my entire life. Thank you both so much!" in a happy state of mind Hilten answers Christopher.

Hilten walks away from both of them like she has just won a lottery jackpot. All she keeps doing is taking beverages orders and looking back at the two of them with a million-dollar smile on her face.

Joshua and Bredele seeing the machine go off go over to the machine to Nicholas for his driver's license in order to disperse his request for a check to be drawn up. Nicholas gives Joshua his driver's license so Joshua can go and get his jackpot/cash transaction paperwork report. Joshua congratulates Nicholas on his big winnings.

Nicholas in disbelief is humble and thanks him for his words of praise to him.

Christopher is delighted to see Joshua. The two say hello to one another. Joshua then goes with Bredele to get all of the paperwork for Nicholas's winning slot machine.

As Joshua walks away, Bredele remarks to Joshua, "There is that sickening friend of yours! He should be put out of this casino. He is a mess. What is he doing with that other distinguished looking man and why is he wearing a suit? Is he a con man?"

"Stop it right now, Bredele. Christopher hasn't ever done anything wrong to you. Just close your mouth. He is just friends with Lady Noreen and he is here with one of his friends just like anyone else having a good time. Just get off of his back and leave him alone."

Hearing Joshua's words, Bredele looks back at him in total anger. He then looks at Christopher totally disgusted and says to Joshua, "Just wait, one of these days, you'll see I am right. One of these days Christopher will leave Atlantic City and the Boardwalk. Just wait and see, that guy is a con artist. I know a farce when I see one."

"Oh, be quiet, Bredele. You talk too much! One of these days that will get you into a lot of trouble."

With that they both go and get Nicholas's paperwork and bring it back to him. Nicholas signs the paperwork and gives it back to Joshua. Then, Christopher walks over to Joshua and whispers to him, "By the way, Marcena will be getting out of the hospital soon. Would you like to attend her coming home party that Rico and Lady Noreen are going to throw for her at Lady Noreen's house next week?"

"You'll have to tell me when it is and I'll have to look at my schedule to see if I can come to it."

"What day are you usually off work, Joshua?"

"Christopher, I am off on Fridays."

"Well then, Joshua, it will probably be next Friday. Do you think you can make it?"

"Yep, Christopher, if it's then, I can make it!"

"I'll see you before then, Joshua, and I'll give you all the details about the surprise party."

"Okay, Christopher, I have to go now, someone in that group over there just won a jackpot. All seven of those girls are down here celebrating a bachelorette party for that girl with the crown on her head. She is becoming a bride next week. They are all having a great time tonight."

"Did you meet anyone special in the group who isn't married for yourself, Joshua?"

"Christopher it isn't that easy. I just am getting over a two-year relationship. My girl left me for my best friend. I really just want to date right now until I am over the loss of my former girlfriend."

"Always remember, Joshua, anyone who is that easy to lose is not worth fighting for ever again. She will only break your heart for a second time. Some people are just plain love hunters. They keep hunting for love their whole life and never find it, for they don't have any idea what they are hunting for. Therefore, they break a lot of their lovers' and children's hearts and in the end they die from a broken heart for they hurt so many other people that they break their own hearts in the end. Just wait Joshua, God has a big plan and a happy marriage planned for you in the very near future."

"I hope so, Christopher. I have to go now."

Joshua goes to the bachelorette party group. Nicholas follows Christopher over to Lady Noreen's spot at the slot machines. Lady Noreen cashes out about three hundred dollars in a slot ticket from her machine. Christopher takes her ticket to the casino cash dispenser and gets Lady Noreen's money out in three one-hundred bills. Then, Christopher, Lady Noreen, and Nicholas walk out to meet Brook. Brook, like usual, is punctual and outside drinking a cup of coffee as he waits for them. Finally, the three of them get into the limousine and head off to Ventnor.

Once to Lady Noreen's house Brook drops them off. Lady Noreen runs to the house for she has to go to the bathroom real bad. She yells back to Nicholas, "Thanks for coming with us, you lucky winner! You'll have to join us again some other time."

Then, Christopher asks Nicholas if he will come in for a drink with him before Brook takes him home.

"Christopher, I best get going if we are to meet Hilten in the morning. I have to do my homework tonight so I have a game plan ready for tomorrow's meeting."

"You're right like usual, Nicholas!"

"Christopher, are we going to take the limousine to the Prentis's Breakfast & Grill tomorrow?"

"Oh, no, Nicholas, we are going to walk there. I'll meet you at your condo and we'll walk together on the Boardwalk to the restaurant to meet Hilten."

"But Christopher, I don't know if I am up to walking there with you. I haven't exercised in years."

"Well, let's try it, Nicholas, and if it is too much, we'll take the jitney or a cab to the grill. Don't worry about it! I'll pay for it."

"Oh, that won't be necessary, I have lots of money, and now I even have a lot more money! Funny thing, Christopher, but money is all that I do have in my life."

"That's not true, Nicholas, you now have me as your friend. I won't let anything bad happen to you. Your friendship means a lot to me!"

"Even after the way I treated you tonight, Christopher?"

"Yes, even after how you treated me tonight! You have a good heart Nicholas; you just have to learn how to be someone's friend."

"Well, thanks Christopher for giving me another chance. I will try to be nicer to you, and not to verbally abuse you in the future. I guess I never had any friends in my life because I always abused everyone so I could get ahead in my life."

"You know, Nicholas, it is never too late to change."

"I just realized that tonight, Christopher! I'll see you tomorrow."

Nicholas jumps back into the limousine with Brook to go to his condo a few blocks over in the Ventnor area. He knocks on the dividing window in the limousine and asks Brook to open it. Brook does as Nicholas requests him to do. Then, Nicholas asks Brook to stop somewhere so he can get a cup of coffee and something to eat.

Brook drives a few blocks back to Atlantic City and stops at a donut place.

Nicholas asks Brook to run in with him and he buys Brook a dozen donuts to take home with him and a cup of coffee for both of them. Nicholas also buys two lemon donuts for himself to eat on his ride home to his condo.

Brook is now in Seventh Heaven for he loves his coffee.

Then, the two of them return to the limousine and Nicholas asks Brook if he can ride up front with him and listen to a music radio station on his way home to Ventnor.

Brook finally reaches Nicholas's condo and he gets out of the limo to let Nicholas out of the passenger's side of the limo. But Nicholas beats him to opening the door for him.

Nicholas then walks over to Brook and puts a paper and a folded bill into his hand.

The paper says, "Thanks for the ride home. I really enjoyed it. The donuts I ate were great! I haven't eaten a donut for years. In fact, I haven't had any fun in my life at all!"

Then, Nicholas walks to his condo and opens the door to it, never looking back to see the dazed look on Brook's face when he opens the bill and sees that it is a $100.00.

Brook then gets back into his limousine with his eyes as big as flying saucers and drives to his apartment in Atlantic City with the radio in the limousine blaring, while he dances to the music in his seat singing along with the songs on the radio. Brook is overjoyed as he thinks quietly to himself that he finally has an identity to some people in his life now. Usually, Lady Noreen just treated Brook like a robot not as a human being with any human worth. As of tonight, Brook is a man with pride and self-respect, who would have an extra hundred dollars to help his elderly father.

Chapter 8

I Have All The Faith Possible
In You, My Friend

The next morning Christopher wakes up at 7 a.m., and he runs to his window to take his first peak at a new day. After he finishes dressing, he hurries to Lady Noreen's door and knocks on it saying, "Lady Noreen, I miss you! Are you awake?"

"Christopher, I haven't gone anywhere since last night! I'm talking to you right now. So darn it, I guess, I am alive again today!"

"Lady Noreen, please don't talk that way. That is such a depressing way to look at your life. I just wanted to ask you, before I meet up with Nicholas this morning to discuss a business matter with him, if Marcena Zinicola could come here next week? She doesn't have anyone to look after her, and you are the best at everything you do. You know how to do everything just right. You could make a temporary bedroom in the den for her. You have a couch that converts into a bed there, and that room is so big. It would be the perfect room for her."

"Just wait a minute, Christopher, what are you trying to talk me into doing for you? I don't want to be a human/animal caretaker like you are to everyone! I don't want to take care of her or anyone. I'm too old to take care of other people. I can't even take care of myself. I am an adult misfit, who doesn't care about anything or anyone in this world. So there!"

"You're not too old to help someone out, and Marcena needs you desperately Lady Noreen. Both of her parents are dead, and she doesn't have a mother to look after her during this awful period in her life.

87

Please, Lady Noreen, if you have just a little pity for this young woman in your heart please do this for her."

"Oh, Christopher, I don't want to do it! I want a life filled with no responsibility. I don't want to take care of someone else's child."

"Lady Noreen, I'm shocked at you saying something like that to me. What if God said something like that about taking care of your husband and son in heaven? How would that make you feel?"

"I wouldn't feel anything! I'm so numb at this point in my life from the Lord taking the two most important people from me in my life, that I'll never feel anything for anyone ever again."

"Okay, Lady Noreen, never mind what I asked you, I'll ask someone else to help Marcena. Evidently, you died too, when your loved ones died, and you're never going to come back to life in this lifetime to help another soul. You really fooled me, though. I thought you would really want to help this young woman recover and come back to life. You know, she was almost beaten to death by her boyfriend. I guess, I was wrong about the whole idea! You don't have any room in your heart to feel for anyone else, but yourself. I'm sorry that I asked you to do me a favor. I'll never ask you to help me ever again, Lady Noreen."

With that Christopher storms up the steps to his bedroom to get his backpack. Then he runs all the way back down the steps to leave the house to go and meet Nicholas in Ventnor. On his way out of the door, he hears his name being called. He walks back inside the house and sees Lady Noreen walking over to the screen door to meet him.

"Christopher, I've thought about what you said to me. Marcena, can stay here with us until she recovers from her traumatic experience, and heals once again back to good health."

"I thought about her coming here, too, Lady Noreen! It is best that she doesn't come to your house. I don't want you to be her maid. On top of that, I should have never asked you to help her. If she comes here, I need to bring her young friend, Rico; he is only twenty-one years old. He is in a wheelchair because he has Spina bifida, and you wouldn't have any place for him to stay either, unless he stayed in the bedroom downstairs. However, I know that was your son's bedroom, and you would never let anyone stay in that bedroom."

"Christopher, I can never win with you. First, I say, "yes," to your first request, and then you come back to me with another favor for me to do for you. You never stop asking me to do favors for you!"

"But Lady Noreen, my favors aren't that wrong for me to ask you to do. You should be serving the Lord with all of your heart, instead of just thinking about yourself all of the time. You are being so very, very selfish!"

"That's a low blow, Christopher, I don't think of myself all of the time. That is an insult to me! Just forget me ever thinking of having Marcena stay with us for a while. I don't want to talk to you about this subject ever again!"

Christopher then walks back out the door and begins walking towards Ventnor to meet his friend, Nicholas. On his journey down the Boardwalk there, he throws pieces of bread to the birds and greets his favorite seagull, Sanabrio. Finally, from the Boardwalk, Christopher can see Nicholas sitting on a bench on the Boardwalk reading his newspaper.

Christopher shouts out to him, "Good morning, my friend. Well, are you ready for our big meeting with Hilten this morning?"

"Yes, I am, Christopher! I read a lot of newspapers this morning to update me a little with what is happening in the world these days. I never had any involvement with the music industry. I made all of my money in investments on Wall Street. This is a new, unexplored industry to me. Therefore, I will call later today to buy a computer so I can research the music industry on the Internet."

"That sounds like a great idea! I know, Nicholas, that you can make Hilten's dream a reality. You can make her career spin off and her songs go all the way up to the number one spot on the charts. I have faith in you, my friend."

Christopher and Nicholas walk down the Boardwalk to the Prentis's Breakfast & Lunch Grill on the Boardwalk near the casino. There waiting patiently inside the restaurant for them is Hilten.

"Good morning, Christopher and Nicholas. I have been up all morning waiting excitedly for this day to happen! So what is happening concerning the A. C. Boardwalk Talent Show, Christopher, and how do I fit into your plan?"

"Well, Hilten, Nicholas is here with us today to help you put a plan together so you can perform in the A. C. Boardwalk Talent Show in late October. It will take a lot of work on everyone's part, but we are all going to make this event happen for you!"

"Do you really think we can do it, Christopher?"

"Hilten, we can do anything that we put our mind to doing, and with Mr. Nicholas Zyvosky as your manager/agent, you can't help but win this big event in Atlantic City in the fall."

"Is that true, Nicholas, you're going to be my manager and agent?" Hilten asks him.

"It was a difficult decision, because I wasn't sure if I could commit to do this or not. I guess I was scared of failing at representing you, Hilten, but Christopher has convinced me to represent you. Plus, I have given him my word to do it for you. So yes, it is true, Hilten!"

"When do we begin Christopher? I need a band and backup vocalists plus dancers. Where can I find all of those people to be part of my group?" excitedly inquires Hilten.

"Let's do it this way, Nicholas. You help her get her songs and music together, and I'll find her, her band, dancers, singers, and costumes for the performance.

By the way Hilten do you know a girl by the name of Joy Rhapsody?" Christopher asks.

"No, Christopher, I don't!"

"Well, Hilten, her group may be interested in backing you up for the talent show."

"Christopher, are they good singers?"

"I don't know if they are good singers, or not, but my instinct tells me that they are.

"Okay, Christopher. Will you need any money to begin this project?" inquires Nicholas.

"Not right now, Nicholas! I just need you to invest in getting the music and lyrics written for Hilten to perform for the talent show. I also need contracts drawn up for everyone to sign in case the song that they record is a big hit. This way, you, and everyone else will get paid. Last but least, however, you might want to determine whether or not it is cheaper to buy or rent music equipment and a sound system for the show. That should be about it! The main thing is, Nicholas, you must protect this group, so they can go all of the way up to the top of the charts."

"Christopher that gives me goose bumps!" hollers out Hilten.

Well, if your song and group wins this contest, you are on your way to the charts, Hilten!" exclaims Christopher.

Arthur, the owner and manager of the restaurant comes over and serves Hilten, Nicholas, and Christopher their breakfast. However, everyone is so busy talking and so excited about getting everything done for the big day in late October that they hardly eat anything.

Finally, Nicholas pays the bill and takes Hilten to the recording studio in Atlantic City with him to start learning about the music industry before she has to go on her evening shift at the casino.

Christopher starts putting this plan into action on how to make Hilten's dream come true by walking up and down the Boardwalk recruiting his friends from the Boardwalk to be musicians in Hilten's band. First, he finds Deuce eating breakfast at the Lunch Box Restaurant and Christopher recruits him to play the saxophone in Hilten's group.

Then, he runs underneath the Boardwalk to find his best friend, Big Luke, who he hasn't seen since he was hospitalized a few weeks back. He finds Big Luke reading a book as he sits on the Atlantic City beach. He runs over to him and finds out that he wants to register to take a community college program. However, he first must take his GED test. That is why he is reading the book. It is in preparation for his test in ten weeks. Christopher remembers that Big Luke once was a very talented electric guitar player in his youth so he asks him if he'll be in Hilten's band.

Big Luke answers him, "Yes," as long as you will provide me with a top quality electric guitar, Christopher."

Christopher then gives his friend, a big hug and tells him, "I am really proud of you for having the courage to take your GED Test."

Next Christopher races down the Mississippi Avenue to find his friend, Ogbonna. Ogbonna is a young twenty-five year old originally from West Africa. He plays the drums like wild fire on the Boardwalk.

Christopher talks to him about an opportunity for him to play as a professional drummer in Hilten's band.

Ogbonna, is filled with so much joy about this opportunity. He responds to Christopher with his acknowledgement of an absolute yes. Ogbonna is extremely excited about joining up with her band.

Now Christopher has a saxophone player, a drummer, and an electric guitar player for the band. He then decides that he will play the harmonica in her group. However, he still needs an electric keyboard player and a tambourine player.

As he thinks to himself, he remembers that Sarge is also very musical, so maybe he can play the tambourine for the group. If so, then maybe if he can find Winkie Whisky Scullin, he can be the band's electric keyboard player. Winkie is the man who does the sand sculptures on the beach when he isn't drunk.

Next, Christopher walks down the Boardwalk to the fast food restaurant where Joy Rhapsody works. He sees her inside the restaurant taking orders. He goes to her aisle and tells her that he will call her tonight about becoming part of Hilten's singing group. Then Christopher asks Joy if she will to call the other members of her group to see if they are in agreement of joining Hilten's group, too.

Once he leaves the restaurant, Christopher slowly jogs to Mr. Marcuso's Men's Store to see Marc. He asks Marc if his band members can wear some of his new fall fashions if he announces at the Boardwalk Talent Show that these fashions were supplied by Marcuso's Men's Store.

Mr. Marcuso is very excited about this opportunity for his clothing store. He agrees to do it for Christopher, if Christopher will provide him with money to design and create new fashions for this big musical event.

Christopher agrees to it, and Marc shakes hands on the deal with Christopher. They are both very excited about Marcuso's Men's Store new fashion line of men's sports and casual clothes for this fall.

From downtown Atlantic City, Christopher walks up from Iowa Street to Patrick's Floral Shop. There he talks to Patrick about having him donate some flowers to wear in the girls' hair. Then he asks Patrick if he knows of a fashion designer that can design some upbeat fashions for the singers and dancers to wear for the Boardwalk Talent Show. Patrick shares with Christopher that he used to be a fashion designer before he became a florist, and that he would love to do it for him. However, he would need the money up front for the cost of the materials, and a $1,500.00 salary to pay some of his other bills for the next month. Christopher totally agrees to all of his conditions and then leaves his floral shop waving good-bye to him.

Then, Christopher walks as fast as he can to the C. T. Royal Ocean Mall. Once there he looks for Orlando and his street-dancing hip-hop group. He finally finds Orlando, and he asks him if the two boys and the two girls in his Boardwalk Dance Group would be willing to join up to be part of Hilten's group.

Orlando is overwhelmed by the offer and he agrees that Christopher can count on him and his whole group, if he'll pay each member $50.00 for the night.

Christopher enthusiastically agrees to the deal, and together they walk out to the Boardwalk so that Orlando can talk it over with his group and demonstrate some of his new dance ideas for the event.

By the time Orlando's group is done doing some razzle-dazzle street dances for Christopher, it is 7 p.m. in the evening. Christopher slowly moves his way down to Ventnor. Once he arrives home, Lady Noreen is busy working in her garden. As he approaches her house she calls him over to her.

"Christopher, where have you been all day?" in a sad way, Lady Noreen snaps at him.

"Lady Noreen, I told you that I had a business meeting with Nicholas Zyvosky and Hilten Lytle."

"Oh, that is right! I forgot, Christopher."

"Well, while you were gone, Marcena Zinicola called to thank you for everything that you have done for her. I told her that you would bring her home here to my house next Wednesday and for her to call her best friend, Rico, and tell him that my chauffeur, Brook, would pick him up next Monday. This way, he will be all moved into his room downstairs before Marcena comes home from the hospital and I can help him organize his room. I will have a ramp built onto the house at the front of the steps next week, so Rico can wheel in and out of my house."

"Oh, that is a great idea! It was really nice of you, Lady Noreen, to invite both of them to your house. You are doing a wonderful thing for both of these young people. The Lord will truly bless you, Lady Noreen."

"Quit all of that rambling, Christopher. I just did what I thought I should do for these two young people since they are both like orphans to me. Someone had to help them, and I guess that someone was me because all the other people in their lives are dead."

"Let me take you on a walk to the beach with a bottle of wine to celebrate your change of heart and your most generous deed so far. The night is young and so are we."

"I don't see why we should celebrate anything, I just did what anyone would have done and you had nothing to do with my decision at all, Christopher."

"I know I didn't. That's why we should celebrate what you did – you did it all by yourself, Lady Noreen."

"Well, you can do something for me now, Christopher."

"What?'

"Would you please grow your beard back for me? I really liked you with a beard. I told you that before but you never really listen to me, Christopher."

With that Christopher runs to the refrigerator and grabs a bottle of wine and some cheese. Next, he reaches for two glasses from the kitchen cupboard. Lady Noreen, seeing what Christopher is doing, runs to the couch and pulls a quilted blanket off of it, and folds it up for them to take with them to the beach. Then, Christopher puts his arm around Lady Noreen, and they run together to the beach to enjoy the music of the waves.

The next day, Lady Noreen and Christopher end up waking up from sleeping on the beach underneath the Boardwalk. Lady Noreen can't believe she fell asleep in Christopher's arms during the night. She hurriedly sits up, for she is embarrassed for being all tangled up with his body. This is the first time she has ever been romantically involved with a man since the death of her husband. She doesn't know quite what to think of the whole situation.

"Good morning, Lady Noreen!"

"Good morning, Christopher!"

"How did you sleep last night under the Boardwalk, Lady Noreen?"

"I slept like a new born baby. Funny though when I was young, Christopher, I never would have slept on the beach. Now that I want to die, I just sleep on it. In fact, now I do everything I want to do in my life. I guess I was always afraid to do what I wanted to do in my life before. Now, I do everything I want, and I'm still alive! Nothing makes any sense to me anymore."

"Lady Noreen, you don't get it!"

"Get what?"

"One never dies in life! When you die in this life, you just go onto another life. Life is never ending! Just like the sky never comes to an end, well life doesn't come to an end either. That's why people should really have a celebration party for their deceased loved ones instead of a funeral. Children understand this theory better than grown-ups. That's why they often laugh at a funeral until an adult corrects them. Children want to think of the deceased member in their family with laughter not with lots of tears."

"Christopher, nothing that you say to me ever makes any sense! It's like you talk an alien language to me."

"Maybe I do, Lady Noreen, but in some small way it should make a little bit of sense to you! Oh, by the way, do you think you could plan a homecoming celebration with Rico for Marcena for next Friday? That is Joshua's only day off during the week, and I really want him to come to her party."

"There you go again, I just bring two orphans into my house, Christopher, and now you want be to have a party on top of it! Christopher, you are never appreciative of anything that I do for you. You always want me to do more and more for you. Well, I won't have a party for Marcena!"

"Suit yourself! But don't call them orphans. You are as much an orphan as they are. Aren't all your family members dead, too?"

"Yes, but that is different, Christopher. Adults aren't considered orphans, just kids!"

"Well, maybe someone should adopt you. You are all alone, too, without a family to care for you in your old age."

"Shush up, Christopher! Shush up! You are enough to drive me crazy, if I wasn't already crazy. I am too old to have to think! Just get out of my sight for the day and leave me alone. And for the last time, there will be no party in my house – just a wake when I am gone!"

Christopher calls up his friend, Nicholas, and tells him that he is getting ready to meet with him to discuss his business strategy for the song. He tells Nicholas that he will meet him in 30 minutes at the Prentis's Breakfast & Lunch Grill. Christopher, then slowly goes out the front door yelling back to Lady Noreen, "I love you! I wish you loved me! Bye for now."

Christopher happily walks down the Boardwalk feeding all his bird friends and talking in a serious conversation to Sanabrio, as though the bird could understand every word he was saying to him. Finally, Christopher comes to the end of his destination and he leaves his ocean flying friends to meet his human friend, Nicholas.

"Well, Nicholas, what is your plan on how to pull this big deal together?"

"As I see it, we should have the group meet every night until the Boardwalk Talent Show at a common place and have all of them rehearse there. But, I don't know where that common place should be."

"Nicholas, let me take care of that! Can you spare the $10,000.00 that you won to pay for salaries, costume costs, fees, flowers, and music equipment?"

"Of course, I can, Christopher! I'm so filthy rich that I can afford anything! Better yet, I can use all of these costs as write offs, if I don't croak first."

"Don't talk that way, Nicholas. You have too much work to do for Hilten and her group that you don't have time to croak."

"I need you, Christopher, to get us the lyrics for the song, and you need one of your band people to write the music."

"I'll take care of that for you, Nicholas."

"Well then, I guess I better get going. I told Hilten that I would meet her at the studio to start working with her on her style. You know, Christopher, that young girl is a great kid. I hope I live to see her go straight to the top of the charts. She is truly a multitalented Diva."

Nicholas walks out of the restaurant after paying the bill.

Next, Arthur, the restaurant owner and manager comes up to Christopher loudly saying, "Christopher, I hate to be nosy or anything like that, but I overheard you talking to Nicholas about how you needed a song for Hilten, for the talent show contest. Well, Christopher, I can write the music for you. Can I help you write the hit song for your group with you? It has always been my dream to write a hit song during my lifetime!"

"Of course, Arthur, you can write the hit song for Hilten's group with me. I'd love for you to be the one to help me with the song. I really don't want to pressure you or anything like that but we have to write the song by tomorrow."

"I don't know if I can compose a song with you that fast! What is the theme idea for the song, Christopher?"

"It hasn't hit me yet, Arthur. I'll call you later today with an idea for some of the lyrics for the song."

"That would be great, Christopher! Here is one of my business cards. I'll expect you to call me later today, Christopher."

"I have to get ready to plan the group's first rehearsal for tomorrow, Arthur, could I borrow twenty of your business cards so I can put the address and telephone number down of the place where we are going to rehearse on them?"

"Of course, Christopher, here are the cards."

Christopher writes down all of the names of the people involved in the group plus the address and telephone number of the place where they are all to meet to practice every day until the Boardwalk Talent Show. Then he stands up and shouts to Arthur, "I'll call you later today. Thanks for all of your help. You are a lifesaver! Bye for now."

Christopher then slowly begins to jog down the Boardwalk to meet up with everyone in Hilten's group. First, he stops to see if Joy Rhapsody is at work on the Boardwalk. It isn't time for her shift to begin yet; so Christopher leaves her a note and a card for her to call him later at home.

Next, he runs into Deuce playing his saxophone for people on the Boardwalk. Christopher doesn't interrupt him, he just drops the card into his saxophone case. Deuce sees what Christopher is doing and after glancing at the card, he shakes his head "yes".

Down the way, he sees Big Luke with Old Bessie and Sergeant Leon Mussack. Once he catches up to them, he sees Sergeant Mussack giving them a composite sketch of a teenage boy that killed a boy for his sneakers last night on New York Avenue in Atlantic City. When Christopher looks at the composite sketch, he sees the picture of the angry boy who tried to kill him. Old Bessie sees the face of Dev for the first time. She now realizes that her intuition was right about him.

Sergeant Mussack tells all of them, "Beware of this boy. He will kill again!"

Old Bessie and Christopher share with Sergeant Mussack that they know that he is telling the truth that this boy is a murderer.

Old Bessie tells Sergeant Mussack that the rumor is that this same boy who the people on the street call Dev, killed dear, old Mr. Irwin Baumgarten, with a baseball bat because he was Jewish.

Christopher tells his friend, Sergeant Mussack, "This is the same boy who tried to kill me and torch Delilah to her death."

Sergeant Mussack after hearing all of this replies to both of them saying, "We must find this angry boy before he kills more innocent people and animals. This boy loves to kill! His passion and hobby is killing for a living!"

"Sergeant, you are so right! The worse crime in life, however, is not to love a child. Too many parents get rid of their children these days. Children today are like throw away children. People create them by mistake, and then throw them away at birth. Shed tears for the teens!" Christopher sadly blurts out.

"What did you say, Christopher?" asks Sergeant Mussack.

I said, "Shed tears for the teens."

"Christopher, that statement is so true. Too many teenagers today die for the mistakes of their parents and because of child abuse. It's like parents are raising mentally challenged time bombs to go off. I guess it is because so many people don't have any love to give to their child or children. Yet these people still give birth and become baby manufacturers."

"I don't see it exactly like that! Every child born has a free will. They can decide in their own minds if they want to repeat their family's history in their own generation or go and get help and get an education to go beyond where they came from. I believe that this Dev took the easy path in life. He chose to follow the devil with his whole being and soul. Now he will pay the price for this by being in eternal hell in his next life, for he will not die after this life. He will live on and on until he learns how to find love in his life," Christopher adds.

"I never thought of it that way, I don't know if I believe, my friend what you are saying or not, but you do have a point! By the way, when are you going to come meet my family and visit with Delilah?" asks Sergeant Mussack.

"I hope to get together with you, your family, and Delilah, in a couple of weeks to go ocean fishing with all of you. I will call you about the date," responds Christopher.

"Sounds like lots of fun! I'll look forward to your call, Christopher! Meanwhile, all of your friends and you beware of this kid. Call me if you see him on the Boardwalk immediately! Remember, he is a professional killer, and he loves to kill! Don't forget that! Any of you could be his next victim," firmly states Sergeant Mussack.

Sergeant Mussack walks back to his police car and leaves the premises.

Christopher gives Old Bessie a big hug as he sees the fear of God in her face. He tells her not to worry that everything will be okay and that this boy, Dev, will be caught real soon.

Old Bessie just closes her eyes. Christopher's words have comforted her for now so she can sleep. She has not been sleeping during the night on her Boardwalk bench in fear that Dev might sneak up on her and kill her. She knows in her mind that Dev knows that she is scared of him.

"Old Bessie don't worry, I will always look after you. I will not let Dev hurt a hair on your head," Christopher promises her as he gives her a kiss on her cheek and walks further down the Boardwalk from her.

Christopher then sees Big Luke on the beach near them. He runs over to him and nudges him on his shoulder. Then says to him, "Here is a card with the address of where you are to come tomorrow for the first band rehearsal. Go pick up the bill for your electric guitar today, and bring me the bill tomorrow. I'll have the money for you to purchase your electric guitar. By the way, how is your program going?"

"Great! I am so happy that I am going back to get my education. I feel like my brain is alive, Christopher. I felt brain dead before I started the GED program."

"That's great, Big Luke! After I see you get your GED's, I'll see you next attend college and graduate from college with honors."

"How do you know all of that, Christopher?"

"I don't know how, I just do, Big Luke?"

"Will I see you at the rehearsal tomorrow?" asks Christopher.

"You sure will! I wouldn't miss it for anything!" firmly states Big Luke.

Next, Christopher spots Ogbonna playing the drums for Orlando's street dancing hip-hop group. They are performing for a huge crowd on the Boardwalk. Christopher goes over to Ogbonna and puts a card next to him while he is playing the drums.

Then he hands a card to Orlando while he is performing a hip-hop dance with great energy for his audience.

Just as Christopher is getting ready to turn to go back towards Ventnor, he sees Sarge walking down the Boardwalk with Samson's radio getting ready to listen to his baseball game.

"Hey, Sarge, stop a minute! I need you to do me a big favor!" urges Christopher.

"What is it, Christopher?"

"I would be so honored if you would play the tambourine in Hilten Lytle's music group. I really need you to do that for me. No one else can do it, but you," raves Christopher.

"Are you sure you really want me? I only have one arm, Christopher."

"Aren't you the best musician on the Boardwalk in Atlantic City, Sarge?" exclaims Christopher.

"Well, yes!" agrees Sarge.

"Then you've answered your own question about yourself. Here is a card with the address and time for the rehearsal tomorrow. Please show up!" replies Christopher to him.

"Thanks, Christopher! I really needed you to come into my life to give me a second chance. Thanks for doing that for me!" responds Sarge with a grin on his face to Christopher.

"Don't thank me, Sarge. Everyone deserves a chance to live life to its fullest.

No one is put upon this earth to judge everyone else. Too many people today have taken God's job away from him. They'll find that out on Judgment Day. Until then though, I'll give you as many chances in your life as you need, Sarge," pledges Christopher.

Finally, Christopher walks down the steps to the beach. There, he sees little children and people collecting seashells. Further down the beach, he sees a fraternity group playing volleyball in competition at the shore for the day. Then, from nowhere he sees his friend, Winkie Whiskey Scullen coming from underneath the Boardwalk stinking drunk with a whiskey bottle in his mouth. Slowly, Winkie staggers over to see his friend, Christopher.

"Winkie, come here for a minute!" requests Christopher.

"What you want?" babbles Winkie.

"I need you to play the electric keyboard in Hilten Lytle's band for me," confides Christopher to Winkie.

"Will I get paid for doing it?" Winkie asks stammering with his words.

"Of course you will, as long as you are sober! Why don't you go back to your support group for alcoholics until the project is over with Winkie? You loved it when you were sober! In fact, Winkie, when you were off your liquor a year and a half ago, you were the happiest man on the Boardwalk. Why don't you go back to that help group for just two months until the talent show is over with?" Christopher pleads with his friend to do it for him.

"Just for two months?" groans Winkie.

"Yes, and after that you can choose whether or not you want to drink or not drink alcohol again. It is your choice, Winkie! But right now I need you," begs Christopher.

"You do?" shrieks Winkie.

"I do, so here is a card with the address and the time for the rehearsal tomorrow. I hope to see you there on time, sober." Christopher explains to his friend.

"Why do you have so much faith in me, Christopher? No one else does. Everyone else thinks I'm a loser and a sloppy drunk!" grumbles Winkie.

"Well, Winkie, everyone else thinks I'm a loser, too! Do you really believe the people who judge you?" Christopher asks him.

"I don't know! I don't know! I don't know anything anymore!" rants Winkie.

"Well, I do, Winkie! You're not a loser. You are the best electric keyboard player in Atlantic City, and I need you tomorrow. If you don't show up, Hilten's band won't have a keyboard player in it. Bye for now, Winkie."

"But I don't have an electric keyboard to play, Christopher," screeches Winkie.

"Well, Winkie, when you sober up today or early tomorrow go over to the instrumental music shop on the Boardwalk and pick out an electric keyboard, and bring me the bill for it. At that time, I'll have the money to buy you one. Plus, get me what the cost is to rent or buy all of the sound equipment that you'll need for the entire group," responds Christopher to Winkie.

With that, Winkie Whisky Scullen stumbles back to where his blanket is underneath the Boardwalk. Then Winkie struggles to fall down on his blanket so he can get some sleep and sober up.

Christopher seeing that he has contacted everyone about the rehearsal tomorrow turns his course back to Ventnor. He longs to help Lady Noreen work in her garden and help her around the house to prepare for the arrival of Marcena and Rico at her house.

On his way home, Christopher finds a stray cat underneath the Boardwalk. He picks it up, and carries it in his arms.

Once home, he sees a man inside of the house cleaning the carpets and another man painting the walls in Lady Noreen's deceased son's room.

Christopher hurries out into the backyard so he can start working in it as he grabs a milk carton from the refrigerator and some sandwich meat from a shelf to eat. He also grabs a bowl from the cupboard for the cat. Once in the backyard, he starts working in it, and he feeds his new found cat.

Lady Noreen hearing Christopher's presence around the house runs from her son's room to find him. As she walks up on him she is in a fit of anger as she sees him with a cat on his lap.

"Whose cat is that?" yells Lady Noreen at Christopher.

"I guess mine," confesses Christopher to her.

"You guess? Why don't you know?" argues Lady Noreen with him.

"Lady Noreen, the older I get the less I know! I don't know anything for sure these days. All I want to do is feed this pathetic, starving animal, and bless it with restored energy and life. That's it!" declares Christopher.

"Well, when you are done doing that let it go back to wherever it came from!" Lady Noreen orders Christopher.

"What if it has no other place to go to, Lady Noreen?"

"Well, then it can die like everyone else, Christopher."

"Whatever you say, I'll do, Lady Noreen."

"By the way, Christopher, Rico called me this morning. He is all excited about coming to stay with me on Monday. Did you say something to him about a surprise party for Marcena, Christopher? He is all excited about planning a party for her with me. I didn't have the heart to tell him I wasn't going to do it with him. Therefore, I told him that we would plan the surprise party for her next week."

"That was so nice of you, Lady Noreen." exclaims Christopher.

"After my conversation with him, I thought it was best that I call the painter to have his room painted a new color. It has been so long since I've been in David's room, Christopher. After I went inside it today after my conversation with Rico, I realized it was the right time to bring life back into David's old room once again even though I miss my son so much!"

"How do you feel about painting his room, Lady Noreen?"

"Christopher, I almost feel at peace with myself. I guess I don't hurt as much now as I did because now I can talk about David and feel his presence with me. Before, I was in so much pain from his death. I chose to lock him away in his bedroom and never to remember his death ever again," gasped Lady Noreen with tears in her eyes.

"That is what life after death is all about. There is no such thing as death, Lady Noreen. Life goes on forever and ever. Every day you say the name of your deceased loved one, they are with you. I may make a believer out of you yet!" Christopher confides to her.

"Well, what are you going to do today, Christopher?"

"I am going to mow the grass and work in the yard all day. Lady Noreen, do you need me to help you in the house to prepare for the kids coming next week?"

"No, Christopher! That's what I am paying all of those men in my house to do for me today."

"Great, Lady Noreen!" remarks Christopher to her.

"By the way, Lady Noreen, is it alright if I have a few people come over here tomorrow to work on Hilten's hit song?"

"How many people are coming in all, Christopher?"

"Maybe 16 people or so, will be here tomorrow, Lady Noreen."

"What did you say? You have sixteen people coming here? On top of that, you have Marcena and Rico coming here next week! You must be crazy, Christopher!"

"Lady Noreen, they won't be in the house, just in the backyard for their rehearsal. Please help the upcoming singer, Hilten. We'll dedicate her song to you! Please help her. I can't make her project a success without you!" Christopher begs.

"I guess so, God, hasn't let me die yet, because he wanted to put you into my life to make me suffer. God please take me, please take me. This man is driving me plumb crazy! I bet he drives you crazy, too! That's why you stuck him here with me!"

"Oh, go ahead, Christopher, but don't ask me for another favor. Do you hear me Christopher?"

"Thanks, Lady Noreen!"

Lady Noreen goes into the house and works in it throughout the day. Now and then, she takes a glance at Christopher, who is constantly busy doing things in the yard while in conversation with his cat. Lady Noreen just looks out her window at him in question. She can't understand why he is talking to the cat. The more he does it, the more upset she gets with him as the day goes on. Finally, at the end of the day, Lady Noreen comes out to compliment him on how nice the yard looks, but on how crazy he looks talking to the stray cat.

"Christopher, the yard has never looked so great ever! However, what are you talking to that stupid cat about?"

"First, thanks for your compliment, and second the cat isn't stupid! Her name is Tigress, for she is blessed with beautiful tiger eyes. Please, don't make fun of her. She had to go through a lot to survive underneath the Boardwalk these past few months. She doesn't need your negativity or abuse! Sometimes animals are more human than the human animal, Lady Noreen."

"Christopher! So much for the sermon in the backyard! I hope you give a good church service for me, when I kick the bucket."

"That will never be! With all the good you are doing upon this earth now, you'll never die," Lady Noreen."

"Thanks, Christopher, that's just what I wanted to hear."

"Listen, Lady Noreen, I have to go see Arthur before he closes his restaurant today. I was going to call him on the phone, but I have too much to tell him about my great idea for the song. Do you want to go with me?" Christopher asks her.

"No, I don't want to go with you, Christopher. You have me doing too much work inside the house! I'm not finished with my own work yet," snaps Lady Noreen back at him.

"I see, then, I'll go see him by myself right now. However, I do have one problem."

"What is it?"

"Can I leave Tigress with you, Lady Noreen? I don't want her to go back to the Boardwalk until she gets her health back. I guess what I am telling you is that I don't want her to die yet. Since you don't like her, would you please get rid of her while I'm gone? I'd feel better about it, if you did it, instead of me. Then, I can live with myself."

"Go, Christopher, I'll get rid of her. If she dies, I don't care. Just go!"

"Thanks, Lady Noreen, I knew I could count on you."

"Just go, I'll be her murderer," Lady Noreen takes a deep breath and finishes her words.

Christopher slowly jogs over to the Breakfast & Lunch Grill just in time to see, Arthur, before he closes down his restaurant for the day.

"Christopher, I thought you were going to call me tonight?" Arthur shouts out to him.

"I was, Arthur! But I got this idea for a song while I was working with my cat, Tigress, in the garden today. All day, I went over these lyrics with Tigress, and I think you can shape these lyrics into a hit song for Hilten. Let me write them down on a piece of paper for you. Do you have a few pieces of paper for me?" Christopher asks him.

"Sure, Christopher, here are a couple of sheets of paper for you."

Arthur continues to close down his restaurant while, Christopher writes out the lyrics to the song. When Arthur is done closing the restaurant, he comes over to read Christopher's lyrics for Hilten's hit song.

"Let me see your lyrics now, Christopher, so I can get a feel for the song?" asks Arthur.

"Go right ahead, Arthur, you're in charge of this song from here on in until you finish the music for it," Christopher exclaims to Arthur as Arthur reads the lyrics to the song out loud.

SHED TEARS FOR THE TEENS

A boy cries out
At night so loud
Hoping to rid his fears,
But no one listens
In the night
To hear the bullet
End his life
Shed tears for all the teens that no one heard
Shed tears - shed tears - shed tears

A girl in love
With all her heart
Finds out it's all a game
The boy just laughs
And uses her,
Thinking she is dirt-
Pills will ease her hurt
Shed tears for all the teens, who lie in pain
Shed tears - shed tears - shed tears

A boy and girl
Running in fear
Can't tell anyone - she's with child
Together in shame
They'll play the game
Hurting inside all the while,
Cause living like this ain't their style
Shed tears - shed tears - shed tears
For all those teens
Who will never be seen
Again!

"The lyrics are great, Christopher, where did they come from?"

"Well, Arthur, I was with Old Bessie, Big Luke and Sergeant Leon Mussack on the Boardwalk earlier today talking about a kid. Suddenly, when I told Sergeant Mussack about throw away kids in America, I said to him the words, "shed tears for the teens.""

That's when Sergeant Mussack replied to me, that the words were so true.

That's when the bulb in my head lit up. At that very moment, I knew that "SHED TEARS FOR THE TEENS," was going to be a hit song for Hilten. I even thought of a few kids that I had known in my life. They died in their youth. Even though they are dead, their messages will be carried on for everyone in the world to hear. So now, Arthur, since you always save the day for me, I am counting on you to come up with the music to go with these lyrics for the song."

"How do you want the music to be for it, Christopher?" responds Arthur.

"Fast, with lots of drum and tambourine parts. I want to play my harmonica at the end of the song. Also, I want you to leave parents with a message to remember. Make the music loud and powerful. Plus, I want the dancers to be divided into three groups. One group will do street dancing and the other one will do hip-hop to the verses of the song. A third group will do a mime to the chorus portion of the song, and laser colors of red, orange, pink, and yellow will cast a shine all over the group. At the end of the song, flowers will be thrown into the audience in memory of all the dead children, who have died because they were cast away by society's rules. You see, the laws of the land didn't protect these children from being killed."

"What other instruments will you have in your band, Christopher?"

"There will be an electric guitar, a keyboard, a drum and a saxophone, Arthur."

"Everything sounds great, but why don't I add a violin to play with you for the final message of the song," requests Arthur.

"Arthur, I don't know anyone, who plays the violin. Do you know someone?" asks Christopher.

"Yeah, I know a talented young girl in the performing arts high school in Atlantic City. Her friends call her Teresa Y. Maybe, she would be interested in playing in your group, Christopher."

"Ask her, Arthur. The more the merrier! Give her this card and have her show up at practice tomorrow. Again, Arthur, this project all depends on you; please, have the music to the song done by tomorrow," pleads Christopher.

"Don't worry, Christopher. It will be done by tomorrow!"

"Thanks, Arthur, I can always depend on you. Bye for now."

With that Christopher walks through the downtown area back to Ventnor. He wants to buy Tigress a collar and some food at the pet store. He makes a beeline to the pet store. Once inside the store, Christopher has the time of his life picking out toys for Tigress, who is the new baby girl in his life.

After he is done at the pet store, he stops by a flower stand on the sidewalk that is selling flowers and picks up a bouquet of daisies and assorted flowers to take home to Lady Noreen. Then, he proceeds on his walk back home.

Once home, he sees his Lady Noreen and Tigress asleep in the wicker lawn chair on the patio in the backyard. With sweat on his brow, he bends over and kisses Lady Noreen, and lays the flowers on the glass table in front of her. Then, he goes and tenderly pats, Tigress, and leaves her food, collar, and toys on the table with Lady Noreen's flowers.

Exhausted by the heat, Christopher lies on the grassy ground next to both of them and dozes off to sleep. As he sleeps, he dreams of his plans for the rehearsal for the talent show at Lady Noreen's house tomorrow.

Chapter 9

Dreamers In Search Of A Dream

The next day is quite hectic, Arthur shows up at Lady Noreen's house at 6 a.m. in the morning. He is so excited to deliver the hit song to Christopher, for he stayed up all night composing the music for the song and completing the lyrics to it. However, in his excitement he scares Lady Noreen to death. She thinks a crazy man is at her door. She runs down to open the door hoping the man will kill her or beat her to death and nothing happens to her. Arthur just runs into her house yelling for Christopher.

Christopher hearing all the loud noise and commotion downstairs runs down there in his shorts as fast as he can. There he sees Arthur all hyper standing next to Lady Noreen, who is ready to kill him.

"I finished it! I finished it; here is your hit song! I hope you like it, Christopher!"

"Like it! I'll love it! I can hardly wait until the band shows up so they can start working on the song. Make sure you copyright the song today, Arthur."

"Oh, I will! Here are the forms. I want you to sign them with me for you wrote the lyrics to the song, Christopher."

"You don't have to include my name on the copyright form, Arthur. This is your song; I don't want anything out of it for myself."

"Christopher, I couldn't have written the song without your lyrics; please let's co-author this song together. Please!"

"Okay, hand me the papers to sign, and I'll sign them. Are you staying all day with us for the practice, Arthur?"

"No, I'm sorry I can't, Christopher, but please stop at my restaurant sometime today to tell me how everyone likes the song."

"I will do that for you, Arthur!"

Then Arthur leaves for work.

Next, Nicholas shows up with Hilten. They both come to the door, and Christopher lets them both into the house. He then introduces Hilten to Lady Noreen. After that he escorts both of them outside to the backyard where Christopher finds Big Luke, the Sarge and Winkie sleeping on the grass, waiting for him.

Lady Noreen is beyond her limit when she sees these strangers sleeping in her backyard. She storms off hitting everything in her way and goes back upstairs talking hysterically to herself underneath her breath.

Quietly, Christopher goes and wakes everyone up and introduces them to one another. He hands the sheets of music for the song over to Sarge for him to begin developing it with the band and Hilten. Then he runs back into the house to see if his Lady Noreen is all right. He runs into her bedroom and sees her playing on her bed with Tigress. She has one of the new toys that Christopher bought for Tigress in her hand.

"Lady Noreen, I am so sorry that Arthur scared you to death this morning and the guys outside look like they stayed up all night for a party for the dead. I hope you will forgive me. I will do anything for you."

"Well, your friend didn't do a good enough job trying to scare me to death, and the guys didn't time it right for my wake, but last and most important did you say you would do anything for me?"

"Yes, I did, Lady Noreen!"

"Then would you take me to the sweepstakes drawing at the casino tonight. It starts at 9 p.m. sharp!"

"I certainly will! Can the band continue to rehearse at your house while we're gone?"

"Of course they can, they can even rob the house, and I won't care."

"Then it's a date, but please, don't call my friend's robbers. They are just dreamers in search of a dream."

"Whatever you say, Reverend Saint, I will do. Amen!" Lady Noreen replies laughing out loud.

Throughout the day Nicholas works with Hilten on the lyrics. The Sarge works with his whole band on the song once Ogbonna and Deuce arrive to the rehearsal.

Later in the day, Orlando arrives with his group, Heffe, Jessica, Emiliann and Alex. Christopher goes over his idea with them of having the groups do street dance, hip-hop dance, and mime to the song. The group then goes over to Sarge to have the Sarge have the band play the music for them. Then he has Hilten sing the lyrics of the song to the music. Everyone plays the music for Hilten except Big Luke and Winkie since they don't have their equipment yet.

Orlando's group loves the beat of the song and they get a great surge of energy to do the steps to the dance for the song. Then the dancers move off to the patio area to start working on the dance steps for the song and the mime motions.

While this is all happening, Nicholas leaves in the limousine driven by Brook to go and buy the rest of the band equipment needed by Winkie and Big Luke. Nicholas rides up front with Brook as they drink their coffee together that Brook bought for Nicholas and himself earlier.

Around 2 p.m., Joy Rhapsody and the three other singers in her group show up.

They are Ngoc, P.J., and Faymale. All of them are very anxious to meet Hilten.

Christopher escorts them to her.

Once they are all together, they want to hear her sing so they can determine whether they want to be a part of the A. C. Talent Show Event or not.

Hilten sings for them, and they are all sold on the idea that with her voice they can make a hit song happen. All of them go off with Hilten and Sarge to work on their part of the song with Hilten.

Next, Christopher sees a catering crew coming out of the backdoor of the house to the patio with lots of trays of food, plus sodas, and coffee for them led by Lady Noreen carrying Tigress. Christopher can't believe his own eyes. Being so proud of his Lady Noreen, he winks his eye at her. Lady Noreen in return lifts Tigress's paw up in the air and waves it back at Christopher.

At 3:30 p.m., Nicholas returns with all of the band's instrumental equipment and Brook helps him carry everything to the patio area. When Winkie and Big Luke receive their musical instruments, they look like two small boys receiving their first gift for Christmas. Once Winkie plugs in his electric keyboard his eyes light up like sunbeams. When Big Luke starts strumming his electric guitar with his fingers, the energy thrust that goes into him playing his music not only transforms his inner being, but the power of it is felt by everyone around him.

Finally, while Lady Noreen is having the dessert trays brought around for everyone to select their goodies, the doorbell rings and there stands, Teresa Y. at the door.

Christopher takes her outside and introduces her to everyone. Christopher is so glad that she is there for Teresa Y. will play the final part of the song with him. Then the two of them go over to Winkie, Big Luke, Deuce, Ogbonna, and Sarge to rehearse the song together with the whole group as Lady Noreen sits in her white wicker chair with Tigress watching them as the group presents their song to her, tears come streaming down her cheeks like a waterfall.

Seeing the time on the clock, the members in the group who work depart for the day, while the Boardwalk homeless people, Big Luke, and Sarge, are invited by Lady Noreen to stay for the night in her garden shed. Everyone in the group knows that they are to practice the song at Lady Noreen's house until the day of the A. C. Boardwalk Talent Show.

Christopher in shock at Lady Noreen's invitation to his friends from the Boardwalk replies, "Are you sure you want them here, Lady Noreen? What will the neighbors think of what you are doing?"

"I don't care what anyone thinks anymore, Christopher! Maybe if they stay, a mentally ill drifter will come here and kill me for my money or jewelry."

"Oh, Lady Noreen, I give up on you! You never stop plotting your own death, do you?" yells Christopher at her.

With that Lady Noreen picks up dear Tigress and puts her paw to Tigress's mouth to throw Christopher a kiss. Then Lady Noreen runs to her room to get dressed for the sweepstakes drawing.

Finally, after Lady Noreen and Christopher are both dressed, they are ready for Lady Noreen's big night at the casino. On their way, Christopher has them stop to see Arthur at the Breakfast & Lunch Grill to tell him how everyone loves his song.

Arthur is so happy to hear the great news that he treats both Christopher and Lady Noreen to cheesesteaks, fries and iced tea. Arthur tells both of them that their breakfast and lunch will be on him for the rest of the year for them making him so happy. Then he hugs Christopher and Lady Noreen and tells them he'll be at tomorrow's rehearsal to hear the song.

Once Christopher and Lady Noreen are finished eating, they stroll down the Boardwalk to the casino. Then they take the elevator to the seventh floor to the ballroom for the sweepstakes drawing. Lady Noreen gets into line to throw her hundreds of small sweepstake cards for the drawing into the drum for the grand prize drawing. As they are standing in line, Christopher starts to talk to the woman in front of him. This woman tells him that she wants to win the million dollars for her mother, father, sister and nephew. She explains to him how her sister almost died giving birth to her nephew, and how her sister came home later from the hospital needing a heart transplant. This devastated her whole family since her sister's husband had been killed in combat six months before her operation in Iraq. No one in her family has the money to settle her medical bills. Now that her sister is well and has a new heart, if she could win the jackpot for her sister tonight, she would be so thrilled. She would then be able to send her parents on a cruise and give her sister some money to pay off some of her medical bills. Plus, she would have a big birthday party for her nephew, Gary, this year.

When, they get to the drum, the woman asks Christopher to throw her one sweepstake card in for her. He takes it from her and fires it straight to the middle left of the wire cage for her.

Then Lady Noreen puts her hundreds upon hundreds of sweepstake cards into the drum. One falls to the floor and Christopher bends over and spins it like a Frisbee into the drum. Then Lady Noreen and Christopher go and take their seats in the ballroom.

Pretty soon the sound of the drum begins. Thousands upon thousands of cards are spun around and around. Finally the drum stops and Joshua, Bredele and Fhina reach into pick the winning tickets. The $1,000.00 winner is called, the $2,000.00 winner is called, the $3,000.00 winner is called, the $4,000.00 winner is called, next Lady Noreen's name is called as the winner of the $5,000.00 prize, and finally Linda Gagliano's name is called as the one million dollar winner.

Lady Noreen can't believe that she has won again. She yells to Christopher, "People will think this is fixed with me winning again. The sad thing is, I keep winning all of this money and I hate every penny of it. But maybe someone will see that I won all of this money tonight and kill me for it."

"Oh, Lady Noreen, be thankful for your gift from God and do something nice with it for someone. Don't forget to give human interest on God's blessing to you."

As Lady Noreen goes behind the curtain to get her check and sign papers for it, Christopher goes over to talk to Joshua saying, "Joshua, can you come to Marcena's party next Friday at Lady Noreen's house?"

"I am pretty sure I can come, it is my day off. What time do you want me there by, Christopher?"

"Joshua plan oncoming around 6 p.m. so you can visit with Marcena's friends for a while. Marcena has been through a lot as you know. She will enjoy being with you. That I am sure of, Joshua."

"I can't say that she will, Christopher, but I look forward to coming to her party. She is a really wonderful girl."

"Well, then, I look forward to seeing you next Friday. Bye for now, Joshua."

As Lady Noreen finishes with all of her paperwork for her money, she walks back over to Christopher. She tells Christopher that they have to wait a moment that someone wants to see him. Then suddenly the woman that he had talked to him in line runs over to him and kisses him on his cheek.

"Mister, I don't even know your name. I am Linda Gagliano. You brought me good luck tonight! Can I give you some of this money or buy you and your wife dinner? Can I do anything for either one of you?"

"First of all, Linda, he isn't my husband. I only like men with beards. Secondly, let us treat you. I have club access to the private players' lounge. We would be honored to have you as our guest," Lady Noreen answers.

"Since Christopher brought me so much luck tonight, I'd love to join both of you for the evening. Do they have a phone there so I can call everyone in my family and share the good news with all of them? This way my parents can start planning their cruise. I will tell my sister the good news when I get home in person."

"Of course, Linda, they have phones that you can use in the lounge, or if you want to, you can use my cellular phone. I have it with me," responds Lady Noreen.

Christopher grabs both of their arms and escorts them to the casino's private club.

Linda gives Christopher another hug and says to him, "I can't believe it; I never thought I'd win the jackpot. I can't believe it, Christopher."

Christopher answers her by saying, "I knew you would win, Linda! You understand what human interest is all about."

"Christopher, no I don't know what it is all about."

"Basically, Linda, it is a concept that you must give back to others when you have an abundance of money or anything in your life. This way, your blessing from God can go full circle. It is like throwing a stone into the water and seeing the circle in the water get larger and larger. I call that circle in the water the ripple effect of life. Now you can give back to your mother, father, sister and nephew. You've not only been blessed with a beautiful family, but by your Heavenly Father, too."

As the three of them walk to the casino's private club to celebrate their winnings, Bredele spots Christopher. He points to Christopher saying to Joshua, "There goes your rags to riches friend. He is a

Casanova. He sponges off of that poor, rich lady. What a worthless hunk of cells were put into that man by the creator."

"Bredele, leave Christopher alone. Why are you so caught up in his life? He hasn't ever done anything wrong to you. Leave him alone," yells Joshua at him.

"I can't believe that you are defending that man. You'll see one of these days that I'm right. He is a gold digger and a loser. You'll see, Joshua! Only the gospel truth comes out of my mouth."

"One of these days, Bredele, your mouth is going to get you into a lot of trouble."

"Not as long as there is freedom of speech it won't, Joshua."

"But Bredele, you use your mouth as a weapon to harm others with your words. You just enjoy saying awful things about people. You don't really care who you hurt as long as you just hurt them. That is so sad! Let's get back to work."

Inside the club you see Linda, Lady Noreen and Christopher having the time of their life. Linda is calling everyone on Lady Noreen's cellular phone. Lady Noreen is eating all sorts of goodies. Christopher is watching the weather report for tomorrow to see if his music group can have another practice at Lady Noreen's house.

Once the news report is done on TV, Christopher goes to get Lady Noreen and Linda so they can get their food at the buffet. It looks like food heaven there!

After everyone has eaten, Christopher and Lady Noreen say their good-byes to Linda, and get ready to walk back to Ventnor. Lady Noreen wants to walk off all the pounds that she just gained after eating all the rich foods at the buffet. She wants to stay fit and healthy by getting the proper amount of exercise these days.

Chapter 10

Do Not Be Afraid, My Child

The next day, Christopher is so excited about the band's practice that he is up with the dawn of the new day. He hurries down to the beach in the early fog. There he feeds Sanabrio and the rest of the seagulls. As he throws them their food Christopher talks to them about his deep concerns and tries to make sense of his daily ministry. When he is done feeding all of the birds, he walks along the shore to the rhythm of the ocean's waves and listens to the answers to his questions from up above.

On Christopher's way back to Lady Noreen's house, he meets up with Deuce and Ogbonna, who are walking on their way to join him for the band's practice today.

Once at Lady Noreen's place, Christopher finds Lady Noreen up and about with Tigress at her heels cooking breakfast for Big Luke and Sarge. They stayed overnight in her garden house last night, and the rest of the group is outside now, too. Hilten and Nicholas are sitting in the chairs on the patio, while Brook is setting up the musical equipment for the group's rehearsal. Slowly, Orlando's dance group and the backup singers join up with everyone so they can begin their daily practice.

Arthur shows up with more food from his restaurant for the group and everyone eats prior to their big day of practice. After everyone finishes their breakfast they begin an intense day of work on their song, "Shed Tears for the Teens". Arthur finally gets to hear his song come to life with Christopher's lyrics. He is so touched by the group's presentation of his song that tears begin to swell up in his eyes.

As everyone is practicing, the doorbell rings, and there stands, Teresa Y. and Marc Marcuso together waiting to join the group. Once Lady Noreen lets them both inside, Teresa Y. goes outside to join the band, and Marc asks to see Christopher and Nicholas.

Then the two of them join Mr. Marcuso, they have a great time reviewing the different fall fashion styles and looking at some of Marc's sketches for his new fashion line. Both Nicholas and Christopher are very impressed with it. Christopher tells Marc to go and get all of the band and back-up singers' measurements, so he can begin designing their wardrobes for the A. C. Boardwalk Talent Show in October. Then, Nicholas writes Marc a big check for him to purchase the fabrics and accessories needed to design the autumn wardrobes.

Next, Nicholas pulls Marc over to talk business with him about investing in his new line of men's merchandise and having Mr. Marcuso design some new suits for him for this big event, too.

With a smile from ear to ear, Mr. Marcuso, goes throughout all the different groups and starts getting the men's measurements. He can't believe that his fall line is going to be part of the A. C. Boardwalk Talent Show. To say the least, he is overjoyed!

A few hours later, Patrick appears at the door. He wants to see Christopher and he is deeply upset. Christopher comes to the door and speaks to him.

Patrick shares with Christopher that his former partner, Tony, has recently died from complications caused by the AIDS virus. He is very emotional about the whole situation and he tells Christopher that maybe he should choose someone else to do the wardrobe designs.

Christopher calms Patrick down and says to him, "Patrick, you are the man for the job. Only you can design the most gorgeous upbeat fashions for my girls. I need you to put the final touches on this show for it to be a great success and for the group to win. Please do this for me! I need you!"

"Christopher, since you are so sincere and passionate about me being the designer, I'll do it for you, but do you promise to pray for me?"

"I promise to do that for you. I am so sorry that you had to go through the final stages of your loved one's life and face his painful death, Patrick. But I promise you that something good will come out of all of this for you. In fact, Patrick, I once wrote a poem about being afraid. I think I have it memorized somewhere in my head. It goes like this-

DO NOT BE AFRAID MY CHILD

LIFE IS A THUNDERSTORM BUT ONLY THE STRONG SURVIVE. THE WIND TEARS AT ONE'S SPIRIT AND THE STORM'S WATER FLOODS ONE'S EYES.

BUT DO NOT BE AFRAID OF IT MY CHILD, FOR I WILL GIVE BIRTH TO ANOTHER DAY, AND YOU WILL HARVEST A FIELD OF NEW DREAMS. FOR MY WILL, AND ONLY MY WILL, MY CHILD, WILL BE DONE UPON THIS EARTH. SO DO NOT TREMBLE, OR BE AFRAID MY CHILD, FOR YOUR LIFE OF CONFUSION AND LIGHTNING BOLTS WILL SLOWLY DISAPPEAR ONE DAY INTO A PEACEFUL AND GLORIOUS NEW DAWN.

AGAIN I SAY TO YOU, MY CHILD, "DO NOT BE AFRAID OF THE STORM, FOR I WILL ONCE AGAIN GENERATE MAGIC BACK INTO YOUR WORN-OUT SOUL ON THIS TREACHEROUS NIGHT, AND I WILL GIVE YOU AN ETERNAL EVERLASTING LIFE."

"Oh, Christopher, you have made me feel so much better about my life. Show me to the girls, and I'll begin designing the sketches for their wardrobes. I also need to develop ideas about the color schemes I'll use for their outfits. Once I know this, I can visualize the flowers that will go into their hair."

"That sounds great, Patrick! Do you have any other ideas for the show?"

"Well, just one other thing. Can someone throw some flowers into the audience during the song? I think this would give the song a more visual effect. By the way, Christopher, what is the name of the song?"

"Shed Tears for the Teens," so the flowers will go right with the theme idea. Great idea, Patrick, let's go with it!" answers Christopher.

"Great!" The only thing I need right now is some money so I can purchase the materials. Once I have everything, I can get started."

Christopher asks Patrick, "Do you see that man over there with the moustache?"

"Yes! I sure do Christopher."

"Well, Patrick, go over and tell him what you need. He will either cut you a check, or go with you to the bank to get you your cash."

"I wish I had someone in my life every day like him. My life would be so much easier to live," sadly responds Patrick to Christopher.

"That's what we all think, Patrick! But sometimes the greed of money only leads to misery and destruction in one's life. Sometimes, an abundance of money is like an overdose of drugs."

"I never thought of it that way, Christopher."

"Well, let's get going and meet all of the girls. Don't forget my girl, Lady Noreen! She'll need a dress for that night, too, and she has great ideas for fashion designs. You might want to work with her on your fashion designs. I know that she would love being your partner on this project. Why don't you ask her for her assistance, Patrick?"

"That sounds, great! With my partner dead, I will not be so alone. In fact, this way, I can discuss my ideas with her. That's a great idea, Christopher."

Patrick leaves Christopher and walks over to Nicholas and introduces himself to him. They discuss the costume design project.

While they are talking, Nicholas goes over and gets a legal pad of paper out of his briefcase to take notes on the cost of the entire project. Next, Nicholas has Patrick sign a legal document and receipt for the upfront money. Nicholas then tells Patrick that when he is done getting all of the girls' measurements, and making all of the sketches necessary for their outfits, to tell him. Once Patrick does that, he will go to his bank with him to withdraw the funds for his work.

Meanwhile, Christopher goes over to Lady Noreen, and grabs her by the hand, and escorts her over to Patrick.

"Patrick, this is my Lady Noreen. She loves clothes and fashion as much as you do. Tell her your ideas for the girls' outfits and she'll consult with you on the costume designs."

"Great, Christopher! It is a pleasure to meet you, Lady Noreen. I really need your input on my fashion design ideas. I want them to be stylish and send an upbeat message to the audience. I bet you have some great ideas for me, for the dress that you are wearing is divine."

Lady Noreen and Patrick sit near the patio table. They begin the outfit design creative process for the singers, dancers, and Teresa Y. When, they are done compiling their ideas on paper, Lady Noreen runs over and grabs Marc Marcuso to see if their costume designs compliment his men's clothing line designs. The three of them talk back and forth for about twenty minutes, and then Patrick goes and starts getting all of the girls' measurements and sizes. When he is done, he measures Lady Noreen for her outfit, too.

On the way out of the house with Nicholas, Patrick yells at Christopher, "Who do you want in the group to throw the flowers out into the audience?"

"I don't want anyone from the group to do that, Patrick. Do you want to do that Patrick?"

"No, Christopher! I see an older woman throwing the flowers to all of the fans in the audience."

"Well, Patrick, I think I know the perfect woman to do it. I'll ask Old Bessie, a homeless woman, on the Boardwalk, who loves everyone in the city. She is the mother of all of the throw away and runaway kids in Atlantic City. Old Bessie will be the perfect one to do it."

"Tell me, Christopher, where can I find her, so I can go and get measurements for her outfit?"

"Look for her on the beach near C.T. Royal Ocean Mall tomorrow. You'll be able to identify her; she has a birthmark on the left side of her face. She is out there sitting on the bench in that area almost every day of the year. She never goes down to the beach area for she is afraid of the water."

"I'll try and find her tomorrow on the Boardwalk, Christopher. I meant to tell you, your Lady Noreen is not only going to help me design the fashions for the show, but she is also going to do all of the groups hair styles and make-up for them. I really enjoy working with Lady Noreen; she has great ideas," Patrick shares with Christopher.

With that Patrick walks off quickly and he grabs Lady Noreen.

Lady Noreen yells at him, "Where are you taking me, Patrick?"

"I want you to go shopping with me to purchase the materials needed for the costumes and to the bank with Nicholas and me. I need you. You have great ideas! Please come with me. I don't want to do this project all by myself."

"Patrick, you don't need me. I'll just be in your way. Your own designs and ideas are positively fabulous!"

"Lady Noreen, it may seem to you that I'm all there, but I'm not. If you don't come with me right now I don't know if I will be able to do this project for Christopher. Please, Lady Noreen, please come and help me."

With that Lady Noreen runs over to Christopher and tells him she is leaving with Patrick and Nicholas, and she runs to get her precious cat, Tigress. Then they all run out of the house together with Brook and get into the limousine. Nicholas sits in the front seat with Brook and Lady Noreen sits in the back seat with Patrick and her pet cat. The limousine backs out of the driveway bound for the bank in Atlantic City and a fabric store in Margate.

Slowly the day withers away from everyone's sight. Christopher takes a look at all the action taking place in setting the stage with the lyricist and composer for the lead song. By him seeing that everyone is giving 100%, and is totally involved in the project, Christopher sneaks out for a moment to go and find Old Bessie, so he can ask her if she wants to be a part of the group for the Boardwalk Talent Show. As he gets closer to C. T. Royal Ocean Mall it starts to rain in Atlantic City. Through the drizzle of the rain, he can barely see an image of Old Bessie sitting on her bench with an umbrella mounted to her head as a hat.

"Old Bessie let me take you home with me right now! You'll catch pneumonia if you continue to sit out here in this storm," Christopher sincerely tells her.

"Christopher, this is my home. This is the healthiest place for me to be right now. If I get too wet, I'll go either into the mall or a bathroom. A couple of times during a really bad thunderstorm, some of my friends, who work inside one of the casino hotels, let me sleep in a casino corridor for the night. People always seem to be at the right place at the right time to take care of me. You see, a lot of these people knew me when I was a lawyer as a young woman down here. At that time, I started gambling and it got out of control. Eventually, I lost so much money gambling that I lost my job and my home. I guess you can say I gambled my life away. Even though I gambled my whole life away, I found myself a whole new life. I found God's world! Now, I wake up every day right in his world and I have everything I need. Funny, but I once had everything in my life, yet I was so unhappy and lonely, my only sanity was my gambling. Now, I have nothing but everything. I'm a woman, who aged on the Boardwalk and grew up there to become a mother and grandmother of all the castaway children on the Boardwalk. I guess you could say my gambling problem gave me a new sanity, which enabled me to survive in this world and have a purpose to live. Sometimes, one must lose everything to find themselves. However, probably most people don't think of it that way."

"Well, Old Bessie, when you put it that way, I see why you want to sit out here in the rain. You understand that the rain is another one of God's miraculous ways in which to not only cleanse the earth but beautify the world all around you through His love of nature."

"Maybe it is more than that Christopher. Maybe it is God crying because he feels all of the pain and the sorrow that all of His children feel upon His earth."

"Maybe one never knows God's reasons! Anyways, Old Bessie, can you be at the A. C. Boardwalk Talent Show with us in late October?"

"Christopher, you don't want me in the show with you. I'm just an old, homeless woman, who will embarrass your group if I'm in the show with all the entertainers."

"But, I do want you in the show with all of us, Old Bessie! I need you to throw the flowers into the audience during the chorus part of the song."

"What is the name of the song, Christopher?"

"Shed Tears for the Teens," and you are the one with Sergeant Mussack, who inspired me to write the lyrics to the song. Therefore, I think it is only appropriate that you join up with us, and be part of the first performance of this new song."

"I guess if it means that much to you, Christopher, I should say, "Yes, and do it!"

"Thanks Old Bessie, you'll bring all of us such good luck. I'm so glad that you're going to be in the show with us! A man by the name of Patrick will come here sometime tomorrow to get your measurements for your outfit."

"Ok, Christopher! I look forward to having Patrick design a beautiful new outfit for me. Can I keep it after the show?"

"I'm pretty sure you can, Old Bessie."

"When do you need me to rehearse with all of you for the big day?" Old Bessie asks Christopher.

"You can do that with the group during their morning practice in October, before the show."

"Do I get paid for doing this, Christopher?"

"I'll make sure that you do, Old Bessie! Plus, we'll have a big celebration after the performance on the Boardwalk for you and everyone else in the show."

"But even if we lose the contest, Christopher?"

"Yes, Old Bessie, even if we lose. For life is a celebration! You see, it isn't important whether or not one wins or loses in life. The most important lesson in life is that we continue to try our hardest. Success is measured by trial and error in one's life, not by keeping record of all the wins and losses in it. The secret to life is – just seize the moment and something good will come out of it for you."

With that Christopher hurries back to his house in a heavy downpour on the Boardwalk. When he gets to there, everyone in the house is bedded down for the night. Even Lady Noreen is tucked into bed and fast to sleep with the love of her life, Tigress.

Christopher, whose clothes are all soaked from the heavy rain outside goes into the bathroom and changes into his nightclothes and in a second goes straight to bed. Just as he is ready to doze off, Tigress squeezes her thin body through the crack of his door's room and jumps into bed with him. Then Tigress wraps her tiny little body around Christopher's neck, so she can go to sleep, too.

Chapter 11

God Intercedes For Us

The next day everyone prepares for Rico's move into Lady Noreen's house on the following Monday. Lady Noreen has Christopher reorganize the bed and other furniture in her deceased son's room, so the room will be more wheelchair accessible for Rico. The bedroom looks so alive and different with newly painted walls, new rugs, and a new bedspread on the bed. With the ocean air seeping into the room, one can feel the presence of life once more in the chamber that once housed only the memory of a dead child.

Christopher is very busy with Lady Noreen. All day he has been helping Lady Noreen clean the house. He does all of the yardwork and weeds around the flower beds outside after feeding all of his birds, especially his pet seagull, Sanabrio. At the end of his day, he invites Lady Noreen to join him up on the Boardwalk for a big, big surprise.

"Christopher, what is my surprise? I am too tired to move and you want to surprise me with something stupid. You must be crazy! Else you must want to kill me off and be done with me forever. Well, whatever it is, I can't die now. I have too many things to do, and too many people are counting on me to live. Patrick needs me to help him with the A. C. Boardwalk Talent Show and Rico needs me to help him plan Marcena's homecoming celebration. So don't kill me now. I don't have any time left to die!"

"Lady Noreen, you must be sick! This is the first day in all of the days that I have known you that I have heard you say, you don't want to die. Something must be wrong with you! You must be tired and totally exhausted from all of the work you have done in the house. Bless your heart! You need a little surprise rather than a big, big surprise to bring your soul back to life, so meet me on the Boardwalk in thirty minutes."

Thirty minutes later, Lady Noreen meets Christopher on the Boardwalk. Together they walk down the Boardwalk feeling a warm, gentle August breeze. Christopher watches the small children running from the beach with their bathing suits on holding their wet towels with their tiny little hands. The children are getting ready to depart from the Boardwalk to go home.

As Lady Noreen and Christopher continue to make mileage in their walk on the Boardwalk, they soon enter Atlantic City. There, they approach a young man by the name of Aizen, who has the physique of a body builder. Christopher asks Aizen for a rolling chair ride on the Boardwalk for Lady Noreen and himself.

Aizen replies, "Gladly, I'll give you a ride." First, Aizen assists putting Christopher and Lady Noreen into the chair. Then he puts his headphones on, and starts pushing them down the Boardwalk to an unknown destination.

As Lady Noreen and Christopher pass all of the people walking down the Boardwalk, they observe so many people from different countries and walks of life sharing the Boardwalk with them. It looks as if anyone can find some kind of peace of mind in a casino on the Boardwalk. Once in one, time ceases, since there are no clocks on the walls and no windows anywhere to be found within the casinos.

Lady Noreen notices the seagulls perched on the light posts, the paintings on a few buildings, and the advertisements of all of the merchants, who are trying to sell their summer merchandise.

As the rolling chair is rapidly in motion, Lady Noreen asks Christopher to have Aizen stop rolling the chair, when they get near the plaza where the Boardwalk Talent Show will be held in October. She tells Christopher that she wants to get an idea about the size of the area there.

Once to the President's Boardwalk Plaza, Christopher has Aizen stop the rolling chair. Then, Christopher helps Lady Noreen out of the chair and goes to pay Aizen for the invigorating ride.

Aizen seeing what Christopher is getting ready to do, takes off his headphones and says to him, "Christopher this one is on me, I owe you!" Then, Aizen smiles at him, and goes on his merry way, pushing the rolling chair back up the Boardwalk to a new destination.

Lady Noreen noticing what has just occurred whispers to Christopher, "Why does he owe you?"

"Well, once Lady Noreen, when he was sick from heat exhaustion, I pushed his rolling chair for him for two days, and gave him all of the money that I made to him."

"Why didn't Aizen share the money with you, Christopher?"

"Because Aizen needed all of the money for his entrance fee for a boxing tournament which he was going to enter at the casino. He was going to be in one of the fights there. He is a boxer. He wants to be the next middleweight champion of the world someday. He trains and workouts every day for his big matches. He has 35 KO's, so far and 40 wins and 3 losses. He is one of Atlantic City's most talented upcoming boxers."

"Now I understand why he doesn't want any money from you. That was really nice of you to help that kid. Now, I see why he is returning the favor to you. I sure hope he wins that title someday. Everyone deserves to go for their dream, Christopher!"

Christopher shows Lady Noreen the Boardwalk area where the A. C. Boardwalk Talent Show will take place in late October. Lady Noreen asks Christopher lots of questions as to where the band with Hilten and her singers will be positioned on the stage with the dancers. Also, she asks him if he knows what area Orlando's dancers will be positioned on the stage in respect to everyone else in the show.

Finally, Lady Noreen understands the order of where everyone will be positioned on the stage. She then takes Christopher by the hand and they begin their long walk back together to Ventnor.

On the way home, Christopher stops at Jacque's Snack Bar. There he buys two large soft pretzels with lots of mustard on them for Lady Noreen and him to eat on their stroll back home on the Boardwalk.

Once home they say good-night to one another. Christopher gives Lady Noreen a gentle kiss on her cheek. Then, to their separate rooms they go to get ready for bed. They are both looking forward to having Rico come to Lady Noreen's home tomorrow.

Finally, Lady Noreen gently picks Tigress up and gives her a quick kiss on her nose. Next, she puts her precious cat onto her bed and off to La-La Land they both go!

Christopher rises around 7:00 a.m. the next morning. Then, he calls Rico, to tell him that he will be picked up around 9:00 a.m., and to look for a streamline limousine in front of his apartment. Christopher then goes and gets Lady Noreen and has her call Brook to have him come and pick them up around 8:30 a.m. today.

Eventually, Brook arrives at Lady Noreen's place. He picks up Christopher and Lady Noreen and off they go to get Rico. Lady Noreen is a little uptight for even though she has talked on the phone to Rico several times, she fears that her late son's room in her house might not be right or handicap accessible for him.

Finally, Brook pulls the limousine up in front of Rico's apartment building on Iowa Street. Rico is in the front of the building waiting for all of them to pick him up and drive him to Lady Noreen's house. Christopher gets out of the car and gets Rico's apartment key from him so Brook and he can go upstairs and collect Rico's luggage for his move to Ventnor today.

Lady Noreen runs over to Rico and introduces herself to him. The two of them instantly strike up a conversation with one another.

Next, after Brook and Christopher put all of Rico's things into the limousine, Christopher lifts Rico up and puts him into the limo as Brook puts Rico's wheelchair into the trunk of the limousine. Then off they go to Ventnor.

Once to their destination, everyone moves Rico's things to his room on the first floor. Then Lady Noreen takes Rico on a guided tour through her house to make sure everything is handicap accessible for him. Seeing that Rico can't get in and out of her house, Lady Noreen immediately requests Christopher to see if he can build Rico a ramp in the front and the back of the house with railings at the sides of the ramps. She feels these safety measures must be done to protect him.

Christopher assures Lady Noreen that he can make it happen. He tells her that he will give her a list of materials and tools that he will need to do the job. He then asks Lady Noreen if she would have Brook go pick up the items for him once his list is done.

Lady Noreen goes into her deceased son's bedroom with Rico and puts all of Rico's clothes and shoes away. Then, as Lady Noreen goes to unpack another one of Rico's boxes, she notices all of Rico's awards from his wheelchair racing events. Lady Noreen places each one of his awards on top of the dresser in his room with such pride as she looks at him with such great respect.

The rest of the day, Christopher and Brook work on the ramp and the railing project as Lady Noreen goes out on the patio with Rico.

Later in the day, she has a special barbecue for Rico. Brook and Christopher have never seen Lady Noreen this happy. It is like her purpose in life has been fulfilled once again through the love of another child.

The next three days fly by so fast, as Brook and Christopher complete all the projects that Lady Noreen has lined up for them to do.

Meanwhile, Lady Noreen and Rico spend the next few days planning Marcena's homecoming celebration and calling all of her friends to attend it at 7 o'clock p.m. on Friday. They've named it Marcena's Mardi Gras Celebration.

In the evenings before bed, Rico shares with Lady Noreen, Christopher and Brook all of the details of his racing events and shows them loads of his scrapbook pictures. He even shares with them several newspaper articles written about him.

This pleases Lady Noreen so much to hear about Rico's races and victorious championship adventures.

Rico also shares with Christopher and Lady Noreen that he is worried about his next race, for he needs to continue to work out and race on the Boardwalk in the early mornings if he is going to compete in it.

Christopher says to him, "No problem! Rico, I'm up early every morning, I'll work out with you!"

Then, Lady Noreen interrupts Christopher by saying to Rico, "I need to work out more, too. I'll set the dining room up as a workout room with equipment in it for you. Then we can both work out every day together until your race."

"That's great, Lady Noreen! Then, you can be my coach!"

"I can't be your coach, Rico. You must be crazy! I'm too old be your coach!" jokes Lady Noreen with him.

"No, you're not! Some of the coaches are in their 70's and 80's. You are young, Lady Noreen, in comparison to the ages of some of the coaches. You know, Lady Noreen, I need a coach, or I won't be able to make it through my race."

"But Rico, I hate to exercise! I'll work myself to death if I exercise every day. Why can't Christopher be your coach?"

"He'll be my trainer, Lady Noreen, but I need you to be my coach. Then, I'll be like some of the other kids, who have their parents involved in their racing competitions with them. Lady Noreen, I'm twenty-one years old, and all I have ever wanted out of my life is for my parents to see me race. Christopher and you can make that happen for me."

"Okay, Rico, I'll do it for you, just this once though!"

The next morning, Christopher takes Rico to the Boardwalk at 6:00 a.m. to race on it. The two of them have a great time. On their way back from their training practice, they see a young Hispanic guy, singing on the Boardwalk in Spanish; as he cleans the Boardwalk with a broom. They see that he is so happy in front of the casino as he gets it prepared for a big Luau Party on the beach today.

"Christopher, what is a Luau Party?" asks Rico.

"Rico, it's a Hawaiian feast. Have you ever been to one?"

"No, I haven't! Well, maybe Lady Noreen will take you to this one today. She loves to party," replies Christopher.

"Christopher, do you think she would really do that for me?" inquires Rico.

"Let's go home and ask her, Rico," responds Christopher.

Once back home, Christopher finds Lady Noreen outside on the patio warming up pancakes and sausage on the grill for them to eat. She is so into her cooking that they startle her as they come out onto the patio.

"Lady Noreen, Rico, has something to ask you," blurts out Christopher.

"Lady Noreen, will you take me to the Casino Luau Day. I've never been to one. In fact, I've never been on the beach because not until now was the beach handicap accessible for me."

"Okay, Rico, I'll take you to the Luau this afternoon. Oh, by the way, dear, I read the books that you gave me to read last night on how to train for your race. You can begin your training today if you would like to do so. If you look in the dining room, you'll see that I had some workers setting up some of the equipment that you selected from the catalogue this morning. So now you can work out!"

"That's great, Lady Noreen. Let's begin working out together after we eat breakfast."

"Christopher, will you be going back to the Boardwalk today?" asks Lady Noreen.

"Yes, Lady Noreen, I have to go and remind Joshua about Marcena's party. I also want to see if he will meet us at the hospital tomorrow when we pick her up. I'll do all of this after I drop Rico and you off at the Luau Party this afternoon."

"Great! Then Rico and I will meet you around 3 o'clock this afternoon. That will give us enough time to exercise and go with Brook to pick up the decorations for the party. A catering service will provide the food and beverages for tomorrow's Mardi Gras Party. I'm too old to cook anymore, Christopher."

With that Rico, Christopher and Lady Noreen enjoy breakfast on the patio. Then Lady Noreen and Rico go into the dining room to begin working out for Rico's upcoming wheelchair race.

Christopher finishes reading the directions on the boxes on how to put up a few more exercise equipment pieces in place for Rico and then goes outside to work in the lawn.

Finally, midafternoon approaches and Lady Noreen with Tigress and Rico are ready to depart for the Casino Luau celebration.

Christopher, who has started to grow his beard back for Lady Noreen, comes back into the house, cleans up, and accompanies both of them to the Luau. Lady Noreen feels great from her workout with Rico today.

Once to the Casino Luau, Christopher pushes Rico's wheelchair down to the beach and puts him under one of the beach huts there.

Once Rico gets under the beach hut, he looks all around at all of the sights he has never seen on the beach before. He sees three birds, where one bird is constantly calling to the other ones, while they fly away. He also sees the white frothy waves from the ocean roll in to the shore erasing human imprints from the sand. He can't believe all of the sights he gets to see on the beach. It is like he has been awakened into a New World.

Christopher points out for him to look at the children surfing on their boogie boards in the ocean. He also has him look at the lifeguards as they blow their whistles at the swimmers to protect them from being off course in the unending ocean.

Lady Noreen goes over and gets Rico, Christopher, and herself, a plate of food with exotic non-alcoholic Hawaiian drinks. Then, as a family, they watch the Hawaiian Grass Skirt Dance take place in front of them on the beach. After the dance is completed, the singers begin to sing Hawaiian songs to their audience.

When all of them are done eating, Christopher pardons himself to go so he can see Joshua. He tells Rico and Lady Noreen to enjoy the rest of the Luau Party, and that he'll come back and get them right after he is done seeing Joshua at the casino about Marcena's big party celebration.

As Christopher departs from the beach, he sees a grandfather sitting on the sand with his granddaughter digging up the sand and putting it into a bucket to form shapes. They are creating a space station in the sand for mankind. Then, he looks back at Lady Noreen and Rico and sees them happily sitting next to each other enjoying the entertainment at the Luau.

On his way up the steps to the Boardwalk, Christopher hears his friend, Remick, selling his ice cream on the beach. As Remick walks down the beach he shouts, "Ice cream and cold drinks! Enjoy them now!"

Christopher walks several steps away from the beach onto the Boardwalk and then to the casino. Instantly, he starts to zoom with his eyes the casino floor to find Joshua, but he can't find him. Finally, he goes over to the Winning Circle Dollar Machine and spies a woman playing the "Give Me Five Machine Slot Machines". She is engrossed in playing the machine. As she puts the dollar coins into the slot machine one-dollar drops down on the casino floor. Christopher sees it behind her and picks it up for her.

"Here it is. Good luck!" calls out Christopher.

"I was just down to $30.00 and then I hit three triples and went up to $120.00.

I'm trying to win $3,000.00. You see my daughter and son-in-law's dog, Savannah, was hit by a utility truck at their home in Virginia two weeks ago. They were moving to New York on that day, since my daughter and son-in-law have been admitted into graduate school. One is going to Columbia University in New York, and the other is attending Rutgers University in New Brunswick. They had to postpone moving from Virginia to New York because the dog almost lost her leg from the tragic accident. But, thanks to great veterinarians in Virginia and Pennsylvania, they were able to save the dog's leg.

The dog now lives in New York with them in a studio apartment. I just would like to win enough money to pay the dog's medical bills off."

"Well, miracles do happen when you least expect them to happen lady. Life is the unexpected, the unknown chance! Being at the right place at the right time! Good luck!" After saying that to the woman Christopher sees Joshua and hurries over to him.

"Can you meet Lady Noreen, Rico, Brook and me at the hospital tomorrow morning, Joshua? We are going to take Marcena at that time to Lady Noreen's home?"

"I guess so, Christopher!"

"Great I will meet you at the hospital at 11 a.m. tomorrow. Lady Noreen is going to have her move in with us. I don't want anything else to happen to her. She is too nice to have any more abuse or sorrow come her way. I guess you can understand that after having your girl leave you for your best friend. But always remember, my son, what bad or harm one does to another person will come back to them in this life. You both still have time to find true love and happiness in both of your young lives. However, you must not be afraid of trying to love again, Joshua."

"Christopher, you're not matchmaking us up together are you?"

"Joshua, I wouldn't do anything like that! I just want you to help me get her to Lady Noreen's place tomorrow. I am an old man; I also want you to come to her party at 7 p.m. tomorrow night."

"Well, you can count on me! I'll be there for you tomorrow at the hospital and I'll also come to her party, Christopher."

"Joshua, thank you! You are always my lifesaver. I am so glad God created you! Bye for now."

As Christopher leaves Joshua and gets ready to walk out of the casino, he sees the lady, who dropped her one dollar coin, laughing and talking to the people all around her, "I can't believe it! I wanted to win $3,000.00 to pay my daughter and son-in-laws dog's veterinarian bills, and here I have won $10,000.00. I don't believe it! I don't believe that I've won $10,000. Thank you, God, so much!"

The casino manger and host come up to her and take her picture holding a giant check made out for $10,000.00 in front of her. Then, a crowd of people gather around her. Her best friend comes in from calling her mother on her cellular phone to find out that her girlfriend just won $10,000.00. Both of them are in shock. Neither one can believe that their day at the casino ended up like this.

As Christopher walks in her direction, the woman pauses from her conversation with her friend, and gives Christopher a big hug and happily says to him, "I've just won! I've just won! I can't believe it, I've just won! I was with my daughter last Saturday in New York. I helped her transport her dog, Savannah, from the veterinarian's office in Pennsylvania where the dog was boarded for two weeks to recover and heal from being hit by a truck to New York. Once we arrived to New York, I had to wait in the car while my daughter took the dog upstairs. Then, my daughter went to park their car and walked back to join me to take her dog for a walk. When we returned from the walk, there standing in the doorway of the apartment building was an older woman holding a picture of the blessed mother. I looked at the woman and in belief said, "That's the blessed Mary. I don't believe that you are holding a picture of the blessed Mary."

The woman didn't think I was crazy! Instead she gave me the picture of the blessed Mother. I took the picture home with me. I will cherish the picture of Mary Immaculate that the woman gave to me forever. I told my daughter that we would be blessed with a miracle, but I never thought it would be by winning a slot jackpot for $10,000."

"God intercedes for us when we least expect Him to! Congratulations! You have just been blessed with a miracle!" excitedly announces Christopher to her.

With that, Christopher gives the woman a hug and walks out of the casino door. As he does, he passes by Bredele.

As Christopher passes by Bredele, you can hear Bredele say under his breath, "Good riddance to you, you scum bum!"

Christopher hearing him pays no attention to him, and just passes by him as if he heard nothing. He then goes down the steps and out of the door to join Lady Noreen and Rico. Once back at the hut, he sits with both of them and they tell him all about all of the entertainment at the Luau.

As the evening goes on the moon begins to reflect upon the water and the waves begin to dance in the shadows of the darkness. Christopher then leans over and asks Rico if he is ready to go home and call it a night?

Rico sleepily says to Christopher, "Yes!"

Once Lady Noreen hears Rico's answer, she has Christopher wheel Rico in his wheelchair up the ramp. As Christopher does this, Lady Noreen notices the marked up condition of Rico's old wheelchair as it is pushed up the ramp and onto the Boardwalk.

Christopher then notices that Lady Noreen and Rico both have on grass skirts over their clothes from the Luau Party as he pushes Rico back to the Boardwalk to meet up with Brook to have him take them all home.

On the ride back to the house, both Lady Noreen and Rico fall asleep on each other's shoulders. Christopher realizes that they are both exhausted from exercising today and getting totally relaxed at the wonderful Luau Party on the beach. It truly was the time to call it a night!

Once back at the house, Christopher carries Lady Noreen into her bedroom and Brook carries Rico into his bedroom.

As Brook walks back out to the limousine, Christopher smiles and says to him, "Thanks for all of your help with the family tonight."

Brook looks back at Christopher, and shakes his head. "You know, Christopher, I have known Lady Noreen for many, many years. I have never seen her as full of life as she was tonight. Christopher, what have you done to her?"

"Brook, I haven't done anything to her. Rico has! He has changed her life. She has been transformed by the love of this young man. In this world, people die from the starvation of not having any love. Love is free, but most people are incapable of sharing their love with another human being."

"Christopher, you are so right. I think the only reason that my father stays alive is because he knows I love him so very, very much. I still need him in my life! Without him I would have no family."

"Brook, you are so right. Please enjoy the evening with your father. Bye for now."

Chapter 12

Life Without Laughter Is A
Slow Death Within

The sun reflects in brilliant colors on the water as everyone celebrates Marcena's miraculous recovery from her close to death experience. The entire household is up by 7:00 o'clock a.m. preparing for Marcena's big party. Brook arrives early with the limousine so he can help Lady Noreen, Rico, and Christopher clean the house, and decorate the backyard and patio area for the big party today. Party trucks with tables, linens, silverware, balloons, flowers and decorations pull up in front of the house all day to unload these things for the Mardi Gras Party.

By 10:00 a.m., everyone in the house starts getting ready, so they can leave with Brook by 10:30 a.m. to go and pick up Marcena at the hospital. At 10:30 a.m., Brook tells everyone that it is time to pick up Marcena at the hospital. Lady Noreen gets into the limousine. Christopher and Brook help Rico into the limo. Then, off to the hospital they all go.

Once there, Christopher, Lady Noreen, and Rico go to Marcena's room. Marcena is sitting in a wheelchair and is so glad to see all of them that she breaks down crying. She has lost a lot of weight. Her little body still has visible bruises on it. Marcena's eyes are still a little blood shot from her broken nose. She still has her cast on her broken leg and her chest area is still tender from her broken ribs. But she is glad to be alive and with people who will not hurt or abuse her ever again. She is also very happy to see Rico and Christopher. Marcena gives them both a hug and a kiss. Then, Christopher introduces her to Lady Noreen and to Brook. Marcena is so happy that they came along to make her day going home so special and she is so thankful to Lady Noreen for letting her stay with her until she is better and able to get back to work.

The hospital gives Marcena balloons and sings a silly little farewell song to her. All the nurses and doctors on the floor come out of their rooms to say good-bye to her, too.

Just when she gets ready to leave the floor for the elevator, Joshua appears in the hallway to help push her in the wheelchair to the elevator. Instantly, Christopher looks at Joshua looking at Marcena and feels the magic moment of attraction between the two of them. Then, Rico, Lady Noreen and Brook join all of them on the elevator to go to Lady Noreen's house.

Once down to the first floor, Joshua wheels Marcena to the limousine and helps to put her inside of it. Christopher and Brook help Rico into the limo. Then Joshua, Lady Noreen and Christopher pile in the limousine as Brook gets ready to take everyone to Ventnor.

Once home, everyone is unloaded from the limousine except Brook, Lady Noreen, and Marcena. Christopher and Joshua load up the trunk of the limousine with some extra boxes in case Marcena has more things than just what goes into her suitcases for them to pack up at her apartment.

Joshua then says good-bye to Marcena.

Rico informs Lady Noreen and Marcena that he has to go train with Christopher for his wheelchair race in November. He is so sorry that he can't help them clean up Marcena's apartment with them today.

Finally, Brook drives Lady Noreen and Marcena uptown to Marcena's apartment to pack up all of her belongings to take with her to Lady Noreen's house.

Late in the afternoon, they are all done packing up Marcena's apartment, plus cleaning and straightening it up. Her apartment hasn't been cleaned since the night of the big fight she had with her boyfriend, Spencer, and the police filed their report about the incident. Lady Noreen and Brook do all the work and cleaning in the house while Marcena takes a catnap. By five o'clock, Marcena is finally awake, and Lady Noreen wheels her out of her apartment in her wheelchair to the elevator to go for a quick shopping trip with her.

Meanwhile, Christopher, Joshua and Rico are setting up for the barbecue and letting the caterers deliver the other food, cake, ice cream, and beverages for the party. Marcena's friends from the hospital, the band, Orlando's dancers, Hilten's singers, Patrick, Mr. Marcuso and his wife, Claire, Joy Rhapsody and her back-up singers, Old Bessie, Nicholas, Teresa Y., and Arthur are all starting to show up for the big homecoming celebration for Marcena. Everyone is so excited about her party.

After leaving the apartment, Lady Noreen has Brook drive Marcena and her in the limo out to the mall on the Black Horse Pike so Lady Noreen can pick up a few items for Marcena. At 6: 30 p.m., it is time for all of them to return to Lady Noreen's home. The limousine is all packed up with Marcena's clothes. Marcena is now ready to officially move into Lady Noreen's house in Ventnor.

At 7 p.m. on the dot, Brook pulls up in the limousine and gets Marcena's wheelchair out of the trunk and wheels her up the ramp in front of the house with Lady Noreen. Once inside the house they push Marcena outside onto the patio, and everyone who has been invited to her party run out from behind the garden house screaming and yelling, "Surprise!"

Marcena, in shock, sees Brook hand her wheelchair over to Joshua. Then, Joshua pushes her over to see Rico, and then all of Marcena's friends from the hospital come over to visit with her. Everyone is dressed up in a mask or a costume to go with the Mardi Gras Celebration theme.

Finally, Christopher has Joshua wheel Marcena to the center of the lawn. The band plays music for her. Christopher joins in with Big Luke, the Sarge, Ogbonna, Winkie, Deuce, and Teresa Y., playing a mix of music for this happy, happy day. Brook, Patrick, Claire, Old Bessie, and Lady Noreen help serve the food. While Marc Marcuso, Arthur, and Nicholas barbecue the ribs, hamburgers, chicken, and hot dogs on the grill.

After everyone finishes eating, Orlando's group does several dances and Hilten with her back up group sing several songs for this special occasion. Then, Nicholas announces that they have a big surprise for Marcena. They are going to perform their hit song that they have been working on in the recording studio for the last several days for her.

When everyone is done performing the song for her, Marcena breaks down and cries. Joshua hands her his handkerchief and hugs her saying to her, "Are you all right?"

"Joshua, I am crying happy tears. That song is a hit. It is going to help so many kids out there who are being abused and who are just runaways on the streets."

"Well, Marcena, I think you should tell everyone that right now. Listen everyone, Marcena has something to tell all of you right now!" announces Joshua.

"I am so glad that all of you shared this day of my life with me. I now know what abuse, drugs and alcohol can do to a child. I've lived that life and I continued to live that life up to a couple of weeks ago. All of you who are a part of that song, I want you to know that your song is a big hit! I also want to thank all of you for sharing not only the song but this day with me. To my friends, Rico, Christopher, and especially Lady Noreen, all of you have made this the best day in my entire life. I will never forget this day no matter how old I live to be. Life without laughter is a slow death inside one's self. I thank all of you for giving me another chance to laugh within my life."

With that Patrick and Lady Noreen start to serve the cake and ice cream while Old Bessie and Arthur start taking beverage orders. Everyone in the backyard of Lady Noreen's house is truly having a great time.

Joshua finally goes over to Marcena and softly says to her, "I'm so glad that you are alive. You deserve so much out of your life. I've seen how you have looked out after Rico, like he is your kid brother, and how Christopher adores you like a daughter. He thinks you are the best. I really have enjoyed being with you at your party tonight. I hope we can get together again in the near future."

"Joshua, after what I've been through in my twenty-six years of life, I'd love to go out with someone who Christopher approves of me going out with. It seems like I always pick the wrong guys. I'm a caretaker, who loves abusive people in my life."

"Well, we have to end that from this day on. I'm a guy whose girlfriend left him for his best friend. I guess we have a lot in common when it comes to pain and heartbreak. I really look forward to seeing you again. Can I call on you again tomorrow, Marcena? Maybe, I can wheel you down the Boardwalk while Christopher trains with Rico for his upcoming race."

"That would be great, Joshua! I look forward to seeing you tomorrow."

Slowly the party starts to break up. Everyone starts to leave for the night from the party for they don't want it to be a long night for Marcena since she just got home from the hospital. Marcena's close friends hug and kiss her good-bye and leave early. The band and all the other members of the group say their final farewells to her, too.

Finally, Sarge comes over to Marcena and sadly says to her, "You know what you said tonight really touched my heart. I have been in rehab recovery program for the last several days and I'm starting to feel like the real me once again. But hearing you talk to all of us reminded me that I should never have walked out on my wife and two kids. I was a Vietnam hero, yet to my wife and kids, I was a deserter. Sometime the worst enemy in life isn't the enemy but one's self. Thanks for opening up my eyes for the first time at what I've done to my loved ones on my journey through this life. I wish someone like you would have represented the American people when I came home from the war. If so, I really would have been an American hero, and I would not have ended up living the rest of my life underneath this Boardwalk as a homeless man."

"Sarge, there is still time in your life to undo what you have done to your loved ones. You can always go back home and find them. You can't continue to desert your family year, after year, after year... No family should have to go through an endless maze of a loved one not returning to them forever."

"You are right, Marcena! Well, I truly enjoyed attending your Mardi Gras Celebration. It was a great party for a terrific girl. I even got to dress up as a Vietnam Veteran. Thanks for a great night!"

After the party, Christopher escorts Rico, Marcena, Lady Noreen and Tigress to their bedrooms. Lady Noreen's house is very lived in these days. Rico's bedroom is on the first floor, and Marcena's bedroom is now in the study. The dining room is now both Rico's and Marcena's therapy and workout room. Christopher and Lady Noreen's bedrooms are on the second floor. For the first time in so many years, the house that has not been occupied for years is now filled with life and laughter once again.

Chapter 13

Pass God's Blessings On...

For the next few weeks life is quite hectic around Lady Noreen's house. Every morning Christopher goes out and trains with Rico for his wheelchair event in November, while Joshua pushes Marcena down the Boardwalk. Then, they all come back home and Lady Noreen has breakfast ready and waiting for all of them to eat.

Then Rico goes to the dining room to workout with Lady Noreen, and Marcena does her exercises with Joshua. While Christopher works in the yard and walks down to the edge of the shore to feed all of his seagulls and pigeons. He looks forward to feeding his favorite seagull, Sanabrio, who eats right out of his hand.

Just lately, Christopher has been modeling for Mr. Marcuso at Marcuso's Men's Store. Also, he has been helping Nicholas Zyvosky with all of the rehearsals with the band and the group at the recording studio. Additionally, he is doing repairs on Mama Cane's house, and helping her foster children, Mariah and Jepson with their homework for school.

Lady Noreen has been busy taking care of everyone. These days, she is working with Patrick on the costumes and flowers for the song contest. She has bought a new wheelchair for Rico's upcoming wheelchair race in two months and has been busy updating Marcena's wardrobe. Marcena lost so much weight while she was in the hospital that nothing seems to fit her now.

Lady Noreen is now a picture of physical fitness from working out with Rico every day. In fact, she is so happy with herself that she has even bought a new red collar and red jacket with Tigress's name engraved on each one for her loved cat.

The band group meets with Nicholas and Christopher every day at the recording studio in preparation for the A. C. Boardwalk Talent Show. The show will be at the end of this month at the President's Plaza. Everyone in the group is really psyched about the big show, especially Nicholas.

Hilten can't believe that her dream to sing in this talent show has finally become a reality. This is because of Christopher, Nicholas, and the rest of her group. She is so happy and thankful to all of these people!

During early October, Christopher has Lady Noreen set up the trip with Nicholas for the fishing charter event. Lady Noreen is all excited about working out all of the details with Nicholas for this Cape May fishing adventure.

"Christopher, on which day of the week do you want to go on the fishing trip?" abruptly Lady Noreen asks Christopher.

"Let's book it on a Friday," responds Christopher to her.

"Who all is invited to be guests on this giant yacht?" nosily asks Lady Noreen.

"So far Rico, Nicholas, the Sarge, Joshua, Sergeant Leon Mussack and his dog, Delilah, Marc, Patrick, and myself. That gives eight passengers and one dog," patiently answers Christopher to Lady Noreen.

"What about Marcena and me?" hollers Lady Noreen at him.

"Lady Noreen, you hate to get wet and dirty, and isn't it too soon for Marcena to venture out on a fishing trip with her broken leg?"

"No! Both of us are going with you on this trip. You aren't leaving us behind! In fact, Christopher, when we are done that day, you can go with me to the Fun Money Drawing at the casino later on that night."

"But Lady Noreen…"

"There are no ifs, or buts about it, Christopher."

"Okay, Lady Noreen, you both can go on the fishing trip with me."

"Make sure you buy an extra rope, Christopher, to tie me to the yacht. I don't want to fall off of the boat and drown. I am afraid of water and I can't swim. Also, I'll make sure that everyone on the boat has a life jacket. I don't want anything to happen to Marcena or Rico either."

"Okay, okay, Lady Noreen, but I thought you wanted to die, and get your life of agony on this earth over with?"

"I do eventually want to die, but not right now! I am responsible for the two kids at the present. I have promised Rico to go to his wheelchair race in November, and Marcena won't be back to somewhat normal health until December, so that means that I am stuck living one more year on this earth."

"You better count your blessings! Every day of your life is a beginning of a new day of precious life and a miracle from the Lord to you. You know, God didn't promise any of us another day to live upon His earth, Lady Noreen."

"Okay, Christopher, stop preaching to me. I'll go and tell Marcena about the Cape May twelve hour fishing trip on the Piscean Moon Yacht," replies Lady Noreen to him.

Lady Noreen goes and tells Marcena about the Cape May fishing trip. Marcena is working out with her physical therapist in the dining room. Rico is there in the same room waiting for Lady Noreen to come and meet with him for their morning exercise. He is doing a conditioning program for his race in November with her.

Meanwhile, Christopher grabs a towel and some bread. He then races out to the beach. Once to the beach, he lays out his towel and races to jump into the chilly water of the high tide waves in the ocean. The waves are like power punches bounce off of his body. The cold sensation of the water stimulates Christopher's desire to become part of the ocean for only a moment during the last weekend of September. It gives him such a thrill.

Around him people of all sizes and races are waist high in the ocean's playful current. One boy is burying himself within the sand. The lifeguard's eyes are navigating the different sights of the water for danger. Two young boys are preparing their floats to go into the water for an adventure on the recurrent tides. A Chinese mother with her young two-year-old child is taking in the sights of the ocean and the high tide. The young mother holds her young child's hand securely to protect her from the threat of a welcoming tide becoming a danger to her young one. Two young Hispanic boys are walking the beach with their headphones on shouting the words to one of the songs they are listening to on their iPod. Umbrellas, beach chairs, and towels map out the beach like a colorful tour puzzle. These are the sights and the sounds of the ocean that Christopher treasures like a priceless seashell.

As Christopher leaves the ocean to get his towel on the beach, he feels the hot sand upon his feet. He sees the footprints of today's and yesterday's visitors upon the sand. He smells the fresh air of life deep within his nostrils. He knows that the presence of God is with him and he is just a man upon the sand within a universe that has no end.

Christopher feels energized as the seaweed blows upon his feet and the air brushes with great energy against his face. Slowly, because of the heat of the sun upon him, he stands and feeds his seagulls and pigeons. They land upon his arm, with no fear of him, or danger, as he feeds him bread from his hand. The birds know that he is not an enemy to them but a friend.

Christopher hears a young girl named, Julie Marie, call to her Grandpa, "Look how high the kite is in the air, Grandpa. You got the kite up into the air!"

Then, the grandfather's, grandson, Jeff, replies to both of them, "The yellow kite with the long blue tail is sailing in the ocean breeze, Grandpa and Julie Marie, watch as the kite is lifted higher and higher into the air."

Christopher seeing the kite, so free and high in the sky smiles at it. He knows that just like a kite, all of our lives go in different directions, too, in which we have no control. Then Christopher takes a nap upon the beach for a few hours after feeling rejuvenated from the mental stresses of the world. When he wakes up, he leaves the beach to go home to Lady Noreen's house.

On his way there, he says hello to Crazy Kay, who is a woman that after five marriages and an unhappy childhood had a nervous breakdown. After that, Crazy Kay chose to live under the Boardwalk and in the bus station for the rest of her years left upon the earth. Each day, Crazy Kay, smokes cigarette butts from the beach, eats food from the trash cans, and continuously talks to herself as she wearily walks by herself down the Boardwalk.

Crazy Kay doesn't fear Christopher; he calls her his Topaz Angel. Christopher realizes that some people are so sensitive and fragile in life that they self-destruct. He remembers, Moe, an old man, who slept in back of the Snack Store on Pacific Avenue. He was always kind to everyone, who was on his path that he ran into. Everyone in Atlantic City knew him for his kind words and sincere smile. When, he froze to death in a cold winter storm in late January of last year, everyone was in shock. One casino employee, when she saw the paramedics remove his body from the parking lot in back of the store broke out in tears. The man who had brought so many people such great laughter and true happiness was now gone from their sight. This stranger called Moe, was more of a spiritual human being to her than most of the people in her life.

Once Christopher is home, Marcena sees him and greets him in the hallway by saying to him, "Christopher, thanks for inviting Lady Noreen and me to go with everyone on the fishing trip in October. I am really excited about going with you and everyone. By the way, Christopher, I wanted to know if I wrote some lyrics for a song for the Sarge, if you could put some music to it for me. Also, maybe you could play it for him on your harmonic on the fishing trip."

"Of course I will do that for you!"

"Christopher, I have felt so bad for him ever since I talked to him at my party that Lady Noreen and you gave for me. It is so sad, Christopher, that Sarge went away an American soldier and came back a man without an American dream. He was robbed of his honor and glory! He not only lost his dreams in the war, but his wife, family, and his country. There was no patriotism for the Vietnam War heroes."

"You are so right, Marcena! The only thing worse than war, is the political system in our country. Sarge was caught up between both the war and politics of our country. Because of his love for his country, America, he served his country. Others did, too, and they died not only for their country, but for their flag, Old Glory. They never lived to come back home like Sarge did."

"Christopher, you are so right! It was all about "Old Glory". I think that is going to be the name of his song that you will accompany me on your harmonica with for the Sarge."

"Sounds great!" adds Christopher.

The days fly by so fast! Before everyone knows it, it's finally the second week in October and everyone is preparing for his or her unforgettable fishing trip on the Piscean Moon. Christopher and Marcena have been working diligently together on the Sarge's song and Lady Noreen has feared this fishing trip from the very first day that she decided to go on it. Lady Noreen swears she is going to die by drowning in the ocean on this trip.

Christopher; however, has reassured Lady Noreen over and over again, that he will tie her to the boat and put her life jacket securely around her to protect her from an untimely death. However, Lady Noreen still believes that she is going to die.

The day finally arrives for the big fishing trip. Rico, Marcena, and Lady Noreen ride with Brook in the limousine. The rest of the invited guests go with Christopher in a limousine bus. Lady Noreen rented the limo bus for the day so that everyone going on the fishing trip to Cape May would have transportation.

Sergeant Leon Mussack made sure that he brought his cherished dog, Delilah with him, so everyone, especially Christopher, could be with her. Sergeant Mussack even made Delilah a handmade foam life preserver.

After the limousine and the limousine bus arrive at Cape May's dock area at 6 a.m., they all get ready to board the yacht. They are greeted by Captain Matthew and his assistant, his wife, Marie. The Captain and Marie help everyone onto the chartered yacht. Brook, Joshua, and Christopher help Marcena and Rico onto the boat. Brook then leaves the ship, since his father is very ill today.

Captain Matthew educates all of them on the safety rules of the ship. Lady Noreen pays close attention to every word that the captain says. Then, Captain Matthew distributes the reels and all of the bait. The reels and tackle are included with the cost of the trip which Nicholas graciously hosted. Lady Noreen also provided the food and beverages for the trip, too.

Christopher, Lady Noreen and the rest of the invited guests are ready for an exciting day of deep-sea fishing. Everyone is wearing their soft-shoes, sunglasses, and sunscreen so they are prepared for the long day on the yacht.

On their way out into the ocean, they see the dolphins and their spectacular leaps into the air. Once out into the ocean, everyone teams up into three groups. Captain Matthew, the Sarge, Joshua, and Marcena are in one group, Christopher, Lady Noreen, Rico and Marc are on the second team, and Nicholas, Sergeant Leon Mussack, Patrick, and Marie are on the third team.

Throughout the day, Lady Noreen, Rico, and Marc have the time of their life by pulling in a 20" bass. Rico can't believe that he has really hooked onto a big one. With everyone's fight and determination not to let this bass go, the team brings the bass onto the ship for Rico. The rest of the day, Marie's fishing group catches blue fish and striped bass. Everyone on the yacht is so at peace within themselves.

Christopher has Lady Noreen wearing a baseball hat and sunglasses is tied to a rope secured to the cabin, plus he has her life jacket wrapped around her. Lady Noreen looks like she has gone on the trip disguised as a ghost with all of the sunscreen lotion she has smeared all over her face, arms and legs.

The sights and sounds of the ocean are like music to Christopher's ears. As he looks around at all of his friends, he sees only smiles on their faces and hears genuine laughter coming from each one of them. Christopher realizes that everyone aboard is counting his or her own blessings on this miraculous one-day expedition.

Captain Matthew and Marie help the group with fishing advice and share their skills. Halfway through the trip, Marie serves all of the passengers' hoagies and beverages. Everyone is starved and eager to eat everything in sight with their hungry appetites. As they eat, everyone talks about their day and each one shares a great fishing story. Lady Noreen does not eat due to her seasickness. All she does is look out into the water and hungers for her return back to her home. It's like she feels like a fish out of its fish tank. Lady Noreen can hardly wait to get back home to her boring, but everyday predictable pattern of life.

At this time, Marcena takes the moment to make an announcement to the group on the Piscean Moon. "It is my pleasure to present this song, and this award to Sarge for his dedication and love of America and the American people. Your song, Sarge, in which I have written the lyrics, is dedicated to you and all of our military men and women across the world. It pays respect to America, and unites her people throughout the South Jersey area. I produced this song with Christopher. It is designed to pay tribute to all of the men and women who risked their lives in the Vietnam War for us. Through this song, Sarge, we would like to honor you."

With that Sarge accepts his award with tears in his eyes from Marcena, while Christopher plays the music that he has written for the Sarge's song on his harmonica to, "Welcome Home to Old Glory". Then Marcena begins to sing the song that she has written for the Sarge-

WELCOME HOME TO OLD GLORY

FIRST VERSE

WELCOME HOME, WELCOME HOME
TO OLD GLORY
YOUR PEOPLE HAVE WON A VICTORY
IN THE WAR
AND THIS TIME WE KNOW WHAT IT
WAS FOR
THE DAYS AND NIGHTS SEEMED
SO LONG
WE WERE FOR THE RIGHT, NOT THE WRONG
THAT IS WHY IN OUR VOICES WE FELT YOUR SONG
CHORUS
SO NOW ALL THE DREAMS WE DREAM
CAN COME TRUE
THERE IS NOTHING WE THE PEOPLE
CAN'T DO
WE CAN HOUSE THE HOMELESS
FOR LIFE IN THE U.S. IS NOT HOPELESS
WE CAN FEED THE HUNGRY

WE'LL FIND THE MONEY
THE BABIES HERE
MUST NO LONGER LIVE IN FEAR
LET'S NOT ROB
AMERICANS FROM A JOB
EVEN THE POOR
DESERVE SO MUCH MORE
TIMES MAY SEEM SAD
BUT LOOK AT WHAT WE'VE HAD
IF WE CAN FIGHT A WAR
WE CAN OPEN ANY DOOR
THE SECRET IS WITHIN US ALL
IF WE ARE TO RISE NOT FALL

SECOND VERSE

WELCOME HOME, WELCOME HOME
TO OLD GLORY
YOU MUST CONTINUE TO FLY
ABOVE AMERICA SO HIGH
IT'S
THE AMERICAN DREAM
THAT MAKES US A TEAM
THAT IS WHY IN OUR VOICES WE
FEEL YOUR
SONG,
OUR SOLDIERS

REPEAT THE CHORUS TO THE SONG

THIRD VERSE

WELCOME HOME, WELCOME HOME
TO OLD GLORY
THROUGH THE GOOD AND BAD
IN AMERICA

S. L. Sharp

WE THE PEOPLE MUST CONTINUE
TO BE FREE IN THIS WORLD
AND
ALL ITS SOLDIERS AND PEOPLE
DESERVE TO LIVE OUT THE AMERICAN
DREAM
IN AMERICA

REPEAT THE CHORUS TO THE SONG

When Christopher and Marcena are finished playing Sarge's song, everyone claps for Sarge. As Sarge goes to hug Marcena and Christopher, he is very touched with deep emotions for what both of them have done for him. Today for the first time, Sarge realizes that true victory in one's life may never be seen at the very moment that one expects it to happen to them. However, it still can be experienced at a future date. Even at a later time of remembrance, a soldier can still feel his glory for serving his country as an unsung hero.

Finally, the seven-hour fishing trip is at an end and the yacht is headed back to Cape May. Everyone on the yacht is tired and sunburned, but very excited about their adventurous day. That is all except Lady Noreen. She has her rosary embedded into her hand as she continuously says her prayers out loud.

Once back at the Cape May landing, Christopher meets up with Brook. Brook comes to the ship and helps Christopher carry the coolers off of the ship, which are filled with their catches of the day.

Joshua completes shooting his video of the days happenings. Joshua has become quite close to Marcena during these past few weeks. It is like they finally have interconnected spirits.

Once everyone is off of the Piscean Moon at the dock, they gather their belongings to return to Ventnor.

Joshua on the spur of the moment decides to ride back to Atlantic City in the limo with Marcena. The limousine and limousine bus finally pull away for the trip back home. Everyone laughs about the adventure of the day. Lady Noreen sleeps and Rico keeps talking about his catch of the day – a 20" bass. He can't believe he caught one. Lady

154

Noreen has promised Rico that she will have a taxidermist preserve the bass for him and he can hang it in his room at her house. Rico is so proud of his big catch of the day. To him, it is like a treasured memory embedded in his mind forever.

Once back home at 8 p.m., Lady Noreen wakes up and goes immediately into her house to get ready to go to the casino's Fun Money Drawing. Christopher's beard has finally grown back. He goes to shower, so he can keep his promise to Lady Noreen that he will take her to her big drawing.

Joshua immediately leaves for his job at the casino.

Brook, totally exhausted from the heat of the day and taking care of his father, departs for home.

Rico goes to his bedroom to get ready to go to sleep, and Marcena goes into the living room to watch the video that Joshua has taken of the day's adventure in the ocean.

Finally, Christopher and Lady Noreen are ready for their big night at the casino. As Christopher and Lady Noreen walk up the Boardwalk to the casino, they see advertising posters going up and down the Boardwalk promoting the A. C. Boardwalk Talent Show in late October. Last year's 1st, 2nd, and 3rd place winners are on the posters.

Once at the casino, Lady Noreen hurries up the escalator to put her postcard into the large metal drum for the big drawing in the Grand Ballroom at the casino. Christopher stays on the first floor to see what machines are hitting. Christopher comes upon one happily married couple who are playing the fifty-cent slot machines. Christopher sits down next to both of them. The woman, Tynisa, introduces herself, and her husband, Raymond, to Christopher.

"Are you winning on the slot machines tonight, Tynisa?"

"Christopher, we have been truly blessed this year. I have been off work for the last 6 months due to an accident so my husband and I come down here to the casino once a month from Pleasantville. Every time we win some money on one of the slot machines, we pass the blessing on to someone else."

"I like that! Why do you have a picture of Padre Pio on the face of the machine you are playing, Tynisa?"

"It is a superstition that I have! I believe that he gives me good luck and blesses me!"

"He must! Have you won yet, today?"

"Not yet! But if I do, and I get hand paid, my husband, and I always leave what credits we have left in the machine for someone sitting near us to play on after we leave the machine. This way, we feel like we are passing God's blessing to us on to someone else."

"Oh, can I touch your picture of Padre Pio for good luck?"

"Of course, you can!"

With that Christopher touches the picture. After he does that he gets a twenty-dollar bill out of his pocket to play, but before he can, Lady Noreen finds him and asks him to come upstairs with her to the ballroom. Christopher then says good-bye to Tynisa and Raymond. As Christopher slowly stands up to walk away, he sees Tynisa's machine going off.

Tynisa yells to Christopher, "We've just won two-thousand-dollars on this machine."

Christopher is very happy for her. He congratulates Tynisa and her husband, and hurries up the escalator to Lady Noreen for the drawing. Once off the escalator, a woman with her blind husband comes up to Christopher and asks him where she should put her husband's postcard for the drawing.

Lady Noreen buts in, and directs the woman to the metal drum in the Grand Ballroom.

As a woman passes Lady Noreen and Christopher to go into the ballroom, she bumps accidently into Christopher. She immediately apologizes to him.

Christopher just smiles and replies back to her, "Don't think anything of it!"

Finally, the drawing begins. Name after name is called to come and claim their winnings. Lady Noreen is twitching in her seat because her name hasn't been called yet during the drawing.

The final winner of the night's name is finally announced. The winner is Walter Garrison. Once the name is finally called the woman which Lady Noreen and Christopher saw earlier with her blind husband stands up with her husband to go and claim their $8,000.00 check from the casino manager.

Right after the last person's name is called in the ballroom, Christopher and Lady Noreen dash out of the Ballroom to the escalator to go home. Lady Noreen is in a miserable mood because she did not win anything at the drawing. She yells at Christopher, "I can't believe I didn't win tonight, Christopher!"

"Lady Noreen, you have so much in life. A good life is not measured by how much money you have in it, but what good you do for others while you're put upon this good earth. We've had tonight another memorable day, which was created within God's own hands for us to live."

"I should have known better than to tell you my innermost personal thoughts about the drawing tonight. Christopher, you always try to put me on a guilt trip to make me feel worse. Well, I don't!" yells Lady Noreen at him.

"Come on Lady Noreen don't get so upset! Why don't you let me buy you an ice cream cone when we get outside on the Boardwalk? Then, we'll walk out to Pacific Avenue and catch a Taxi cab and go straight home. I'm tired and so are you from our big fishing trip today. You did a great job planning it. Everyone had a great time, especially, Rico."

"Okay, Christopher, that's a great idea and thanks for the compliment. I'm tired, and I've lost at the drawing. I've been deathly seasick all day, and now all I want to do is just go home."

Christopher buys both Lady Noreen and himself giant ice cream cones. Then, a Taxi cab comes and takes them both to Lady Noreen's home for the night.

Chapter 14

God Has Given Us All A Gift To Give To Others

The next two weeks in October are filled with lots of band practices for the Boardwalk Talent Show. Sarge has been committed to making his song a success ever since the song was dedicated to him on the fishing trip. Now, he really feels like an American hero.

Meanwhile, Christopher and Marcena are busy recording his song, "Welcome Home to Old Glory," at the recording studio.

Sarge listens to his song morning, noon, and night and longs to meet up with his wife and two kids since his mind is back on track. The former Vietnam War Veteran is now respected by the other members in the group as a very knowledgeable musician.

Big Luke studies every night at the library after rehearsal in preparation for his GED test and is dating one of the girls in his class. He has dreams of enrolling in the county college after he passes the GED test.

Ogbonna has become a very famous drummer at the recording studio. He is now giving a lot of people private drum lessons, and he has been asked by other performers at the studio to record with them on their upcoming production projects. His name as a highly professional drum player is well known by the recording industry in Philadelphia and New York.

Winkie hasn't drank one shot of whiskey since this project began. He says that he is off of booze forever and is now working part-time at the recording studio. The owners of the studio think he is a mental giant in the world of music. He can write, compose, and play any instrument.

In the old days, Winkie would get up and hang out on his corner in Atlantic City drinking all day. Often he would dance in the streets to amuse the people who were either walking or driving their cars nearby. At the end of his day, you would see his whiskey bottles lined up on his corner. All his bottles were paid for day after day by the people who gave him contributions for just dancing in the street. Everyone back then applauded and clapped for him. They knew he was harmless. He was just another homeless alcoholic who had no job or responsibility. Those troublesome days for Winkie have finally come to an end. Now another chapter in his life has begun for him.

Deuce still is scared to acknowledge that he lost his whole family in a house fire. He hides his emotions by playing his heart and soul out on the Boardwalk in front of the crowds for contributions. These donations are donated to the victims around Atlantic City who have experienced similar disasters out of respect for his deceased loved ones. His charity work eases his pain.

Teresa Y.'s parents wanted her to drop out of the music group in fear that the people in the band might be a bad influence on her. However, when Teresa Y. told Christopher this, he went with her to meet with her parents. Christopher then asked them if he could bring them to see Teresa Y. perform at her remaining practices and meet the people in her group.

Teresa Y.'s family, now fully support their daughter's involvement in the recording of the song and her participation in the big day of competition with the group.

Hearing this, Christopher assigns Teresa's mother and father, Mr. and Mrs. Butler, to be in charge of setting up the set and equipment for the group with Brook. Both of Teresa's Y.'s parents are so honored to be involved with Teresa Y. and her music group.

Christopher told Teresa Y. that he wasn't going to give her up. That the gold in her eyes was a mark from God for her to do good deeds and with the band, she would fulfill her prophecy in some small way.

Orlando's dancers have practiced every day with the group. Heffe, Emiliann, Jessica, and Alex are incredible stage performers. They all agree that they are ready to bring home 1ˢᵗ place for Hilten. An agency wants to hire them to perform for shows around the Jersey shore.

Hilten had to name the group. She asked Christopher what to name it. He told her to come up with an original name for it herself. At that very moment, she saw Lady Noreen walk into the recording studio with Tigress, so she decided to call the group, HiltenTigress and the Wildcats.

Lady Noreen of course was overjoyed to hear the name of Hilten's group.

Every day of the week, Lady Noreen, Patrick, and Marc work on the costumes and flowers for the group. Marc Marcuso is so very pleased with the outfits that Lady Noreen and Patrick have designed for all the girls in the show and how they complement the guy's band outfits.

Arthur these days provides sandwiches for the group since Nicholas is nice enough to include the cost of food and drinks into the recording budget.

Joy Rhapsody and her backup singers, Ngoc, P.J., and Feymale have all become great friends with Hilten. Together, they are just one big, happy family ever since Nicholas Zyvosky backed the group. Now as a group, they all have a shot at stardom together.

Rico, Marcena, Sergeant Mussack, and Joshua, long for the day to hear this big mystery surprise song once again that everyone is practicing. All three of them feel that if Christopher is behind this big musical production that it has a chance of coming in first place.

Nicholas at this point has successfully polished the group in preparation for the competition. He reflects on years of failure in the business world in spite of being wealthy; he also admits that he was a nasty mean man back in those years. He never even really had any fun doing what he was doing in his business. He just did it because his father wanted him to follow in his footsteps. Now in his later years with cancer, Nicholas is finally enjoying his life, making great friends, and his health is stable for the first time. Maybe it is because he is happy and free of stress. Who knows!

Christopher is ready for the next day to come and for the Boardwalk Talent Competition to begin. He told the group that it wasn't important whether they won the contest or not. What was, however, very important to him was all the lessons everyone had learned from creating the song. That if their song, *Shed Tears for the Teens*, ever changed anyone's life in the audience by hearing it, that is what the group's song was all about.

The next day finally came. The Boardwalk Talent Show would begin at 5 o'clock sharp. Everyone was ready to give 100% of themselves to the performance of their potential hit song, *Shed Tears for the Teens*. The group members are determined to win the contest for Christopher. They all realize that without his energy, drive, and love for his fellow mankind, this song would never have evolved to the performance level it has today.

Saturday morning arrives and everyone is sitting on pins and needles. Lady Noreen and Patrick are completing the costumes for the big event. Old Bessie is to meet the entire group at the President's Boardwalk Plaza by 4 p.m. and meet up with Christopher and Hilten earlier in the day.

Later today Patrick will show Old Bessie how to throw the flowers into the audience at the end of the performance. Both Patrick and Christopher have talked to Old Bessie on what a great job she is going to do for the group at the performance. They have finally convinced her to be part of the performance.

The rest of the group is going to be picked up by Nicholas and Brook throughout the day and dropped off with the band's equipment near the plaza.

Christopher leaves the house and gives Lady Noreen a big hug and she wishes him good luck on his big day. Christopher passes by Rico and Marcena and they tell him they will be there to support him for his big performance.

Christopher, with a smile from one ear to the other ear in a confident gait, walks down the Boardwalk to the plaza. On his way, he sees a young man and his girlfriend throwing a football back and forth on the beach. Over toward the beach huts sits an older woman next to her elderly father talking about their yesterdays together.

In the middle of the Boardwalk near Ventnor, young teens are rollerblading off to other areas of the city. Flags from the gusty wind are blowing rapidly back and forth as planes fly through the cloudy blue sky advertising casino specials and promoting area businesses.

Hilten, as soon as she is done at 2 p.m. with her shift, flies out of the casino to the Boardwalk beach. When she gets to her destination under the Boardwalk, she sees Old Bessie getting ready to greet her. Both of them plan to change their clothes in a U-Haul truck that Lady Noreen has rented for the day.

Sergeant Mussack is to drive the U-Haul truck to one of the side streets and meet the two of them with Christopher around two o'clock.

As Hilten walks closer to Old Bessie, there is a young man running toward both of them waving to them as if he knows them.

Hilten waves back at him for she thinks that maybe Sergeant Mussack or Christopher have sent him as a messenger to direct them to where they are to go.

Once the young man catches up with them, Old Bessie's eyes almost pop out of their sockets. It is Dev.

"Yo! Ladies! Can I help you?" blurts out Dev.

"No, Dev, we don't need any help from you! Thanks anyway. We're just getting ready to leave here right now," nervously replies Old Bessie to him.

"Leave, but you can't leave, Old Bessie, until I meet your beautiful friend."

"Dev, we're leaving right now! You have enough girlfriends, just let us be!" hastily replies Old Bessie in a cold sweat back to him.

Then Old Bessie swaggers through the sand and grabs Hilten by the hand. Then she goes underneath the Boardwalk to grab all of her bags.

Dev runs closer to both of them, but sees that Old Bessie and Hilten are just ignoring him.

Hilten observes Old Bessie. She sees that Old Bessie's hands are shaking and perspiration is forming on her upper lip. Sweat is all over her forehead, too.

"Old Bessie, what is happening?" in panic Hilten asks her.

"Hilten, we have to get out of here fast! We are in danger!" stutters Old Bessie to Hilten.

"In danger of what, Old Bessie?" questions Hilten.

"That boy, so let's hurry," whispers Old Bessie to Hilten.

Hilten turns around with Old Bessie to walk back to the Boardwalk, but it is too late. Dev is in front of them blocking their way to get back up the steps to the Boardwalk.

"One last time, old woman, who is your friend?" Dev screams at the top of his voice at her.

"Dev let us leave right now!" Old Bessie orders him.

With that Dev slaps Old Bessie across her face and Hilten lets out a scream.

The scream is so loud that Christopher hears it as he is walking toward their area of the Boardwalk.

Immediately, Christopher runs down the Boardwalk to the steps to the beach to find Hilten and Old Bessie.

When he does, he sees Old Bessie lying on the sand underneath the Boardwalk. Then, he sees a boy on top of Hilten kissing her passionately on the lips. Hilten is fighting him off with all of her strength.

"Let her go right now, whoever, you are!" blares Christopher at the top of his voice.

"I'm Dev to you. I thought I killed you a few months back, Dog Man," in defiance Dev answers Christopher.

"So, Dev, it's you! I meet up with you again!" replies Christopher.

"Yeah, but this time, Dog Man, you are going out of this world forever."

Christopher immediately helps Old Bessie up, and whispers into her ear to go immediately to the Boardwalk.

Old Bessie with all her strength slowly walks in the direction of the steps leading to the Boardwalk.

Next, Christopher walks closer to Hilten and Dev.

Seeing Christopher coming toward him, Dev starts to grab for something behind his back.

Christopher immediately runs right at him and knocks Dev down on the ground. Then, Christopher yells at Hilten, "Get to the Boardwalk right now!"

Dev keeps hitting Christopher, but each hit hurts Dev's hand. Then, Dev starts shooting Christopher with his gun, but the bullets just ricochet off of Christopher's chest in all different directions.

"You have a bullet proof vest on, Dog Man. What are you, an undercover policeman?" defiantly Dev screams at Christopher.

With that Christopher chases Dev to the beach.

"You're going to jail, Dev. You belong locked up. You not only hurt little animals, but humans, too. To me, you are from Hell. You don't belong here on God's earth young man," Christopher yells.

Hearing all these words coming from Christopher, Dev runs from Christopher down the beach. However, by this time the police are everywhere chasing after Dev, too.

Within seconds, Dev runs to a lifeguard boat near the beach and jumps in it. He starts rowing toward the ocean. The police move in on him. He is further out into the ocean now.

Soon a police helicopter hovers over him and Dev loses his balance in the boat and falls into the water. The police look for some sign of life from him, but he never comes back up for air from the ocean.

Sergeant Mussack runs over to Christopher.

Christopher is too busy packing up Old Bessie's bags for her. When Christopher is done doing that he walks towards the steps to the Boardwalk.

"Christopher, was he the same boy that stabbed you and almost set Delilah on fire?"

"Yes, Sergeant Mussack, but I have a feeling that this time, Dev, is out of our sight forever."

"You might be right! I just got a message from the police helicopter pilot. He can't find Dev anywhere in the ocean water. The boy fell into the ocean's waves and he never came back up."

"Well, let's get going, Sergeant Mussack. Is the truck ready for the girls to change in?

"It sure is," replies Sergeant Mussack to Christopher.

"Then, let's take Old Bessie and Hilten to it. This is Hilten's big day. She's has waited for this day for such a long, long time."

Christopher sees Old Bessie and Hilten sitting on one of the benches on the Boardwalk together. He runs over to give Old Bessie her bags, and gives both of them a hug.

Hilten grabs Christopher's shoulder saying, "Are you okay? I heard the gun shots! I thought you were dead."

"Not this time, Hilten. The boy's shots missed me each time he shot his handgun at me."

"Thank, God," Old Bessie hollers at the top of her voice. Thank, God, you are alive, Christopher."

Then, Christopher grabs both of their arms and escorts them with Sergeant Mussack to the U-Haul truck so they can change for the talent show.

Christopher, noticing that his harmonica has dropped out of his pocket, runs back to the beach to look for it underneath the Boardwalk.

Once there, he looks down into the sand and he finally finds it. As he walks back to the beach area, he sees a patrol boat coming toward a small beach area. Lots of people are gathering around that area near the "Danger Keep Away" sign in the water.

As Christopher moves closer, an ambulance drives to that beach and stops where all of the people are standing. There in front of the crowd the policeman and the paramedics are carrying Dev's body and some of his body parts they assume. Apparently, Dev was attacked in the ocean by a shark. But no one can understand how such a thing could have happened since sharks usually don't come that close to this beach area in Atlantic City.

Hearing this, Christopher takes a few steps back and sits down in the sand. He watches the waves flow in and the seagulls in almost a circular pattern standing out in the sand. Christopher spies Sanabrio as the leader of the thirty or so seagulls. Sanabrio looks so big and so patient as he watches one of the seagulls in his group that has hurt its leg standing on just one leg. Some of the other seagulls are just sitting on the sand. One small seagull lands with a big bread crumb in his mouth. The small bird just keeps flying from one direction to another direction on the beach in hopes to eat the crust of bread all by itself.

Christopher for the first time feels an inner peace of mind within himself. He feels that justice in God's world has overcome Dev's evilness. In serenity and calmness, Christopher looks out into the ocean and watches the sailboats floating into the horizon as a large number of birds huddle over the ocean in hopes of finding food.

After Christopher is reenergized from his strenuous day, he stands up and walks up the steps to the Boardwalk to meet with Hilten, Old Bessie, and Sergeant Mussack. It is getting late and it is time for them to start walking down to the President's Boardwalk Plaza to meet the rest of the group, plus Lady Noreen and Patrick.

Once Christopher is to the back of the U-Haul truck, out comes Hilten and Old Bessie. They have changed into their wardrobes and transformed themselves into stars that will go onto the stage in just a few hours. Happily they greet Christopher.

"Christopher, I want to thank you again for saving our lives. I felt that what I had wished for all this year wasn't going to become a reality," emotionally responds Hilten.

"Hilten, God knows your heart. You have a great destiny. Through your gift of singing you can help to change so many people's lives – just through your songs. So let's get you down to the Boardwalk Plaza before Lady Noreen starts to worry about what has happened to all of us."

Quickly, Hilten, Old Bessie, and Christopher make a beeline together to the Boardwalk Plaza. Sergeant Mussack follows in back of them with his precious, little dog, Delilah. Once to their destination, Orlando's group, the guys in the band, plus Teresa Y., and Joy Rhapsody with the backup singers, are there waiting for them. Lady Noreen and Patrick are putting the final touches on the costumes with Marc Marcuso's assistance.

Patrick passes out red ribbons for everyone to wear in honor of his friend who died from complications from the AIDS virus. Everyone lets Lady Noreen and Patrick pin the ribbons on them except Nicholas. When Patrick goes to pin the ribbon on him, Nicholas refuses to let him do so.

"Patrick, I can't wear that ribbon, I'm not that kind of guy," Nicholas snickers.

"What kind of guy are you?" asks Patrick.

"I'm a real man," declares Nicholas.

"Well, then Nicholas, "real men" don't wear the ribbon!" responds Patrick in an insulted tone of voice.

With that Patrick throws Nicholas's red ribbon onto the ground and walks away from him.

Lady Noreen eavesdropping on their conversation just rolls her eyes up and down as she walks away from Nicholas in disgust.

Seeing all of this happening, Christopher walks over to Nicholas.

"What's going on over here?" utters Christopher.

"Nothing, Christopher, I just didn't want to wear that little ribbon that's on the ground."

"Why don't you want to wear this ribbon, Nicholas?" Christopher asks his friend.

"Because, Christopher, I'm a real man. Aren't you?" Nicholas asks Christopher with a puzzled look on his face.

"No, Nicholas, I'm not!" Christopher utters with a serious look on his face.

"You must be kidding, Christopher? You look like a real man to me."

"You're wrong, Nicholas, I'm not a man, I'm a human being, who isn't trying to take God's place on this earth. I was not created to judge other people. I believe that I will be judged the way that I have judged others."

"I don't get it, Christopher!" responds Nicholas with a puzzled look.

"You don't have to Nicholas. Just be you! You've done everything that you wanted to do in your life, so don't wear the ribbon. It doesn't matter to any of us at all. Now, I have to go and support all of these young people, plus our friends and Lady Noreen. They are our family and we must be there for all of them."

The audience is packed with people from the casino, from the Boardwalk, parents, and lots of Christopher's friends. Everyone is so excited for the contest to begin. The judges and all of the fifteen groups that are registered to compete for the record contract are nervously waiting to participate in the contest.

Finally, the host of the show, Jeffrey Williams, begins the contest. One by one the bands and singers begin to perform at the President's Boardwalk Plaza for the big prize of a record deal and contract.

Hilten Tigress and the Wildcats are number thirteen. By the time it is their turn, Lady Noreen is a nervous wreck and Nicholas is making everyone exhausted from him continuously looking at his watch and walking back and forth as though he was expecting to be a father of a newborn baby.

Within an hour and forty-five minutes, Hilten Tigress and the Wildcats are called to go on the stage. Everyone hugs one another.

With that Christopher and the group walk out on the stage. The music begins, and everyone in the group pours their hearts and souls out to the audience through their music.

Hilten is beautiful on the stage. She comes to life. Her band complements her with the music to "Shed Tears for the Teens".

Orlando's dancers join in to excite the audience with their hip hop moves. The people in the audience join in with them by jamming.

Lady Noreen, Patrick, Brook, and Marc are in the audience. They are dancing and clapping their hands to the song. Rico, Joshua and Marcena are shouting from the audience and cheering for Hilten and her group.

When the backup singers join in everyone goes crazy. Joy Rhapsody, Ngoc, P.J., and Feymale's costume sparkle and reflect rainbow colors up on the stage. Everyone in the audience joins in with them to the chorus of the song.

Sergeant Mussack is in the audience with his kids and of course, Delilah. Sergeant Leon Mussack has Delilah held up in the air and is moving her paws to the music as he dances to the song with his children.

Next, Christopher comes out on the stage to play the bridge of the song on his harmonica. The people's faces light up and tears start coming to some of their eyes as Old Bessie throws flowers and pictures of missing children into the audience with Patrick.

The song finally ends and everyone takes their bows. Hilten comes to the center and has everyone in her group hold hands and take their final bow together. They then get up and throw kisses to Nicholas standing in the crowd near Patrick, Lady Noreen and Marc. With that Nicholas in disbelief looks at all of them with tears in his eyes and throws a big kiss back to all of them.

The audience goes crazy and cheers them all on. Loud applauses come from audience members standing in front of the stage and from the spectators standing on the Boardwalk near the President's Boardwalk Plaza.

In excitement, the group exits the stage and head to the audience to watch the remainder of the five acts.

One by one, the other acts perform on the stage until the final group performance.

Then, one of the judges announces that he will call out the judges' votes in about twenty minutes.

Immediately Hilten, Old Bessie, Sarge, Big Luke, his girlfriend, Ogbonna, Winkie, Deuce, Teresa Y., her parents, Orlando, Heffe, Emiliann, Jessica, Alex, Prentis, Joy Rhapsody, Ngoc, P.J., and Feymale gather around Christopher, Lady Noreen, Brook, Rico, Marcena, Joshua, Patrick, Arthur, Nicholas, Delilah and Sergeant Mussack with his children to hear the final results of the contest

Then, suddenly, the Boardwalk becomes very quiet. The drums start to roll and the host announces - 3rd place goes to the Latin Elites, 2nd place winners are the The Metropolitan Outskirts, and the 1st place award goes to Hilten Tigress and the Wildcats. The audience goes crazy and the Tigress and Wildcats group moves to the stage to take a bow.

Once everyone is on the stage, the microphone is handed to Hilten. She nervously takes the microphone and begins by saying, "This is the greatest day in my life, but it wouldn't have happened without all of these beautiful people on the stage with me right now. If it hadn't been for Christopher, I wouldn't be here with all of you in the audience right now. I have learned through Christopher Saint that God has given us all a gift to give to others. The greatest gift that you can give to others is yourself through your talents. All of us here have truly been blessed by knowing Christopher. We all love you so much, Christopher! Without you we wouldn't have won the contest!

Let's hear a loud applause for Christopher. We won today because of your belief in all of us!"

"Next, the group would like to give thanks to Patrick, Marc from Marcuso's Clothing Store; and a special thanks to Lady Noreen for all of our gorgeous out-of-site costumes. Also, thanks to our supporters, Sergeant Mussack, Delilah, Rico, Joshua, Marcena, and Brook. Also, a special thanks to Arthur, who wrote the music and song with Christopher. Let's hear a big cheer for Old Bessie, too," Hilten shouts out to the audience.

"The last one to be recognized, but the most important one is our manager and financial backer, Nicholas. Without his backing and business savvy, we wouldn't have ever been able to have had this great experience in our lives. This trophy is yours, Nicholas, and I'm handing the microphone right over to you now," then happily Hilten gives Nicholas a big hug and a kiss.

"Ah...Ah... I am so proud of each and every one of you. I have learned tonight that all of you are my family, and I am the lucky one. You all have made me the luckiest man in the whole world."

The host comes up to the microphone and tells the audience that the song, *Shed Tears for the Teens*, will be recorded and marketed by a major label in the months ahead. With that everyone starts screaming, cheering, and yelling in the audience. Everyone is so happy for Hilten's Tigress and the Wildcats.

Slowly, the excitement calms down and everyone starts walking down the steps of the stage and over to the U-Haul truck to change. The group is smiling and on a great high from winning the talent show.

Lady Noreen grabs Christopher and they stroll down the Boardwalk together over to the U-Haul. Once there, Patrick, Lady Noreen, and Marc help everyone change their clothes and get back into their street clothes. All except for Old Bessie, she pleads with Lady Noreen to let her keep her costume on for the rest of the night.

"Lady Noreen, this is one happy night in my life. I don't ever want to forget this moment. After all, I thought I was going to die today with Hilten and Christopher," Old Bessie shares with Lady Noreen in secrecy.

"What happened to all of you, Old Bessie?"

"Lady Noreen, that crazy boy, Dev, tried to kill Hilten and me, but Christopher defended us. It looks like that evil boy died in the water," slowly Old Bessie tells Lady Noreen.

"Old Bessie, that really happened to all of you today?" in shock Lady Noreen asks her.

"Yes, it did, Lady Noreen!" Old Bessie replies.

"Well, in that case, you wear your outfit the rest of the day, Old Bessie. I'm not going to let anything spoil this day for you," Lady Noreen promises her.

"Thanks! Lady Noreen, please take good care of Christopher. We all love him so much. To him, we are all God's people. Most people just look at us on the Boardwalk as if we are living freaks, misfits, or degenerates, but we're not to Christopher," confesses Old Bessie.

"Old Bessie, you're not a freak. I love you," with that Lady Noreen hugs Old Bessie and goes to look for Christopher.

Everyone starts leaving from the U-Haul truck to the Boardwalk for the night.

Lady Noreen sees Christopher. Everyone in the group is either hugging him, kissing him, or saying good night to him. The U-Haul is all packed up. Brook is getting ready to drive the truck back to Marc's Clothing Store, so everything in it can be stored there in his backroom.

As the U-Haul gets ready to leave, Christopher sees Nicholas on the Boardwalk behind the truck on his knees. Christopher immediately yells at Brook to not move the U-Haul yet and runs over to Nicholas.

"Nicholas, what is wrong with you?" inquires Christopher.

"Christopher, I am looking for my red ribbon, and I can't find it. I am so upset with myself. I think it fell through the slots in the boards, right here on the Boardwalk."

"Oh, Nicholas, that's okay," replies Christopher.

"No, Christopher, it isn't okay. I was wrong! I shouldn't have hurt Patrick. What I thought was right wasn't! Now, I have to undo what I did to him. Here I am dying from cancer, and I'm still judging other people, who are dying and have died from AIDS. It's so sad, Christopher. People die from so many diseases, and here I am the one who thinks he is God. I'll probably be the one that goes to Hell, and Patrick's friend is probably already in heaven with the Lord.

"Oh, come on Nicholas, get back up and let me give you my ribbon," suggests Christopher to his friend.

"You'd do that for me, Christopher? Why?" wonders Nicholas.

"Because, Nicholas, I have no right to hurt you or judge you, my friend. We are all perfect in God's eyes if we do his work. Look at all the people tonight that you helped, my friend."

"But, Christopher, will Patrick ever forgive me?" in doubt Nicholas asks Christopher.

"That question, Nicholas, can only be answered by Patrick. Now here is your ribbon. Let me pin it on you. There!"

"Thanks, Christopher, I'm going over to Sinbad's Ship at the C. T. Boardwalk Mall to celebrate. Do you want to join the group with me?"

"There's Lady Noreen, Nicholas. Let me ask her," replies Christopher.

"Lady Noreen, come over here, please," Christopher asks her politely.

"I'm coming. I'm old and I'm tired. Give me a few minutes… please, Christopher!"

"Lady Noreen, do you want to join the group for a few drinks?"

"No, I'm too busy training for Rico's wheelchair races in two weeks. I'm running in it. I need to hurry home, right now, Christopher, so I can get up early tomorrow morning and workout with the kids."

"Then, Nicholas, give everyone our best! I have to accompany my beautiful woman home," Christopher answers him with a big smile.

"See you both later. Thanks again, Christopher for helping me," Nicholas expresses his heartfelt gratitude to Christopher.

"Enjoy, Nicholas, bye for now," replies Christopher.

Nicholas in a hurry walks away from Christopher and Lady Noreen to join everyone at the restaurant.

Then Christopher immediately walks over to join up with Lady Noreen. She is silently waiting for him.

"Christopher, Old Bessie told me you almost got killed today. What happened?" sadly Lady Noreen asks him.

"Lady Noreen, the young kid who tried to kill Delilah and me, tried again today to kill me. This time, instead of him killing me, he was killed himself."

"Christopher, don't you think about leaving me by dying. I won't hear of it! I'm not going through that sad part of my life ever again. It's my turn to die not yours!"

"Lady Noreen, I'm not going to die. Everything is okay. Let me walk you home under the stars so you are in condition for your big race coming up."

"Oh, Christopher, let's go home. I'm exhausted!" moans Lady Noreen as she yawns.

Chapter 15

I Have No Right To Play God

Rico continues to train with Lady Noreen during the few weeks remaining in autumn. November rapidly approaches for the Atlantic City 5K Run/Wheelchair Race. The morning of the race, it is cool with a calm gray ocean in view.

Lady Noreen wakes up early for the event and shocks everyone as she runs around the house knocking on everyone's door to wake them up.

Christopher jumps out of bed and dresses as fast as he can. He then goes to Rico's room and helps get him ready.

"Rico, today is your day!" happily yells Christopher to him.

"Yep, it is!" eagerly replies Rico.

"You trained with Lady Noreen so hard for this big event. You will do great in it, and so will Lady Noreen in her 5K race," proudly states Christopher.

"I'm sort of scared, Christopher. What if I get tired and I just can't finish the Boardwalk wheelchair race?" softly replies Rico to Christopher.

"Rico, my son, it isn't important whether you win the race. Life isn't always about winning! It isn't important whether you win the race or lose the race. What is most important is that you continue the race today and finish it!"

"Thanks, Christopher! I just don't want to let Lady Noreen down. She has worked so hard with me every day. Even if she was tired, she got up to work out with me. If I was late getting up, she still took me down to the Boardwalk for me to practice for my race. I really owe this day to her!"

"Well, Rico let's go join her for breakfast."

In the kitchen, Lady Noreen is in her running shorts and t-shirt getting the orange juice, cereals, and water all set up for everyone to join her for breakfast. She even has little banners all around the kitchen pinned up, which say, "Good luck, Rico!"

After breakfast, all of them walk out proudly to the Boardwalk wearing their t-shirts. Lady Noreen starts to warm up, while Christopher strolls down the Boardwalk with Marcena and Rico. Slowly, they meet up with some of Rico's buddies that he has made during the last few months on the Boardwalk and Rico begins to prepare for his race with them.

As they continue down the Boardwalk, Christopher starts to collect all the people who have also prepared for the race throughout the past few months with Rico. There is Grandpa Bill, who became wheelchair bound after his stroke, Elijah, whose leg had to be amputated after a tragic motorcycle accident, and Laurel, a homeless man lost both of his legs to diabetes. Also, Christopher sees Cora and Harvey who are both from the senior citizen complex in Ventnor. Harvey has had MS for the last twenty years, and a severe car accident ten years ago, left Cora confined in a wheelchair.

As they walk and wheel down the Boardwalk to the starting line in front of the amusement park, Lady Noreen pins on her number, as they meet up with lots of other people and children in wheelchairs.

While waiting for the race to begin, Christopher spots Patrick who is with his Russ. Russ is in remission from AIDS at the present. Patrick wheels him to the starting line.

"Patrick, here we are. I'm so glad you convinced your friend to race on this beautiful November morning," happily remarks Christopher to Patrick.

"Christopher, Russ is so happy to be here. Thanks for telling us about this event. Russ used to be a runner, so when he heard about the race, he was really excited about being in it."

"Russ, this is my dear friend, Christopher," says Patrick to Russ.

"Oh, it is so nice to meet you. I've heard only nice things about you through the messages that you have sent to me through Patrick. Thanks for helping me to get back to living once again. Sometimes, we get lost in our 24/7 life. Then, someone comes along to help give us a purpose on this earth once again. You are that person to me, Christopher. At first, with my medication and diet, I didn't feel so hot. But after I mentally and physically started to condition myself for the race, I started to eat healthier, exercise, and take my medicine regularly. Now, today, you see me 20 pounds lighter and physically in better condition. Thanks, Christopher."

"Don't thank me, Russ! Thank yourself! You have been blessed by God. You still have a lot to do in your young life for the man up above us!"

"I don't know about that, Christopher!"

"Russ, no one knows what their purpose is on this earth. But I do know that you truly have a purpose. Look how you've changed your own life. Through your story, you will be able to change the lives of so many others through God's blessing upon you."

"Thanks for all your confidence in me, Christopher. However, I really don't know what my life will bring forth for me," declares Russ to Christopher.

"Take it from me, son, you'll see a change in your life from here on in," replies Christopher to him.

Then, from the crowd of runners, a lady's voice calls out in a very loud screeching tone, "Christopher, get over here right now! Stop talking! The race is getting ready to start for Rico and me. I need you here pronto with me."

"I'm coming to you right now, Lady Noreen," Christopher replies to her.

"Christopher, you promised me that you would cheer us on. Rico starts his race first at 8:00 a.m., and I start at 8:30 a.m. right after him," continuously rants Lady Noreen.

"I promise, I'll be there for both Rico and you today," Christopher pledges to Lady Noreen.

Lady Noreen spots Marcena on her crutches and yells at her, "Marcena! I'm so glad you're here with Joshua. Make sure you meet

Rico at the finish line when he gets there. It will mean so much to him. I'm so sorry Marcena that you can't race this year with us darling, but there is always another race next year, if I am still alive on this earth and well."

"I'll race with you eventually, Lady Noreen, when I am on my feet and off of these crutches. When that happens, Joshua and I plan to work out with both Rico and you, and train for next year's race," Marcena answers.

"That's great news!" Lady Noreen shouts out loud.

The announcer blurts out over the microphone, "Will all the wheelchair racers line up for the 5K Good Luck Race right now! At the shot of the gun the race will begin."

Then, the race director shoots the gun and shouts, "Go!"

The wheelchair racers take off.

Christopher follows Rico with his eyes as Rico begins the wheelchair course.

Then Christopher glances over to find Lady Noreen. He finally spots her with her headphones on in a designer jogging outfit which Patrick designed for her. Lady Noreen is lined up with all of the other runners. Christopher runs over to her.

"Christopher, please hold my towel, bag, and water bottle for me, until I'm done with the race. You know this race will probably kill me. I'll probably pass out from heat exhaustion before my feet hit the finish line," swears Lady Noreen to him.

"Lady Noreen, you won't do such a thing. You look positively beautiful! I've never seen you look so radiant. And, look at your muscles. You look great!" proudly declares Christopher to her.

"Ha! For an old 60 plus year-old, I do, I guess!" with lots of pride Lady Noreen answers him.

"You certainly do!" raves Christopher.

"Christopher, those are the nicest words that you have ever said to me. I never even thought that you ever looked at me."

"I do, Lady Noreen, and now not only do I look at you, but everyone else in this crowd is going to look at you, too. You look the best I've ever seen you look," confesses Christopher to Lady Noreen.

S. L. Sharp

"Well, thanks! I better get ready for the race before I pass out, Christopher. By the way, in case I die in this race, my will is on my desk. Please look after Rico and Marcena, I feel like they are our children," sighs Lady Noreen in deep thought to him.

"Don't worry about a thing, Lady Noreen. You're not going to die! Just enjoy your race," exclaims Christopher to her.

As soon as Lady Noreen says good-bye to Christopher, the gun is fired and the racers start off running down the Boardwalk.

Christopher then runs to the Boardwalk to catch up with Rico's race. As Christopher charges ahead, he sees Winkie Whiskey Scullen.

Winkie Whiskey Scullen sees Christopher, too, and runs over to him.

"Christopher, guess what? So far, Rico is moving as fast as he can to take the lead before the finish line. The kid's arms are like iron. He is really moving his wheelchair with great energy down the Boardwalk and around Atlantic City. The kid has moved into about 12th place," Winkie screams with great excitement.

"That's great, Winkie! Isn't it?" responds Christopher with lots of enthusiasm to Winkie.

"It sure is, man," agrees Winkie with Christopher.

Next, Christopher sees, Big Luke, running down the Boardwalk and Christopher steps toward him.

"Hi! Christopher! Rico is moving his wheels really fast. He's cruising like he's in the Indianapolis 500," hollers Big Luke out to Christopher.

"I'm so glad to hear that, Big Luke," Christopher yells back to Big Luke.

Christopher finally makes it further along the course. He is almost to the halfway mark of the course. He sees that Rico isn't far in distance from him; so he runs as fast as he can to see if he can catch up with Rico. On his run, Christopher sees Old Bessie sitting on her bench on the Boardwalk with a sign saying, "Go for the Gold, Rico and Lady Noreen." Old Bessie is all bundled up with lots of Lady Noreen's old coats and blankets, plus several pairs of Lady Noreen's heavy socks.

"Old Bessie, I'm so glad you are here cheering Rico and Lady Noreen on," replies Christopher to her.

"I'm having so much fun, Christopher. It's funny, before I used to sit and sleep on this bench and the people used to stare at me. Today, my eyes are wide open. I'm staring at all of the people in the race, and I'm having such a great time doing it," admits Old Bessie to him.

"I'm so glad, Old Bessie!" boasts Christopher.

"Have you seen Rico yet?" questions Old Bessie.

"Not yet! No wheelchair racers have come over the finish line," Christopher hollers to her.

As Christopher stands next to Old Bessie, he sees Sanabrio fly through the air in his direction. Then he sees Rico in his wheelchair moving faster than the hands of a clock down the Boardwalk.

Suddenly, Rico approaches the halfway mark. Old Bessie and Christopher cheer him on. At the turn around, he turns and begins the final stretch to the finish.

With sweat on his face, Rico smiles back at both of them. When he makes his turn, he sees Old Bessie's sign.

Christopher gives Rico a thumbs-up sign and runs off to the Boardwalk to the 5K race to find Lady Noreen. As he races down the streets to find her, he sees Brook and his father waiting patiently in the crowd looking for Lady Noreen.

"Brook, have you seen Lady Noreen yet?" asks Christopher out of breath.

"Nope, I haven't seen her yet, Christopher! But she should be here pretty soon. She is now in better shape than any of us. What have you done to the Ventnor Diva? In the old days, she never walked or ran anywhere. She just called me up to pick her up, and drive her in the limousine all over the place."

"Brook, I didn't do anything to help her get her ready for this race. Lady Noreen just decided to do it herself," smiles Christopher.

"Look, Christopher, there she is! She must be in about 80th place in the race. Lady Noreen's incredible. She looks great!" in great excitement Brooks yells out to her, "Go, Lady Noreen, go!"

Seeing her, Christopher immediately runs over to Lady Noreen and starts running alongside of her.

Without talking, for the first time in their lives, the two of them run in unison with one another. Without a sound, Lady Noreen keeps pounding her running shoes on the asphalt of the streets. Finally, when they reach Iowa Avenue to make their turn onto Pacific Avenue, Christopher waves at her. Then, he takes off to the finish line to find Rico so he can see him, and all of the other wheelchair participants that he knows when they cross the finish line.

As Christopher gets a second gust of wind for his final lap to the Boardwalk, he passes Sergeant Mussack with his precious little dog, Delilah.

"Christopher, what have you done to Lady Noreen? She is running like an Olympian. I never knew she could run so fast," blurts out Sergeant Mussack in laughter.

"Sergeant Mussack! I haven't done anything to her. She did it all by herself. She started a training program with Rico, and it got both of them fit and in condition for the race today," explains Christopher to Leon.

"They are both doing great in the race, Christopher! Rico was in about 5th place when I last saw him awhile back. Russ is holding his own, too. He is about in 19th place," reports Sergeant Leon Mussack to Christopher.

"How is Grandpa Bill doing today?" asks Christopher.

"He's about in last place, but he's having the time of his life today. I love his hat. It says, "I can't go fast, but it's great to come in last, Christopher," laughs Sergeant Mussack in good humor once again.

"He's a real character," chuckles Christopher to Sergeant Mussack.

"He sure is!" agrees Sergeant Mussack.

"Did you see anyone else go by you yet?" asks Christopher.

"I just saw the senior citizen group pass by, Christopher! They are all bunched together and having so much fun participating in this race."

"Well, listen Sergeant Mussack, I best be going. I have to meet up with Joshua, Patrick, and Marcena at the finish line so we can see Rico cross it."

Finally, Christopher gets to the finish line and sees everyone. As he goes over to it, he sees Rico coming full force down the Boardwalk up against a young athlete named Elliot for first place. Elliot, due to a gunshot wound, ended up with a spinal injury which put him in a wheelchair for life.

Right now, Rico and Elliot are racing wheel to wheel with everything they have against each other. Rico is giving all his energy to these finals moments to take the lead.

Christopher starts cheering with Marcena, Joshua and Patrick, for Rico to win the race. The cheers gets louder and louder for Rico as Christopher sees Victor, Teresa Y., her family, and Hilten all gathered at the finish line cheering him on.

Finally, Rico comes over the finish line in first place. Everyone is thrilled to death as they move down the Boardwalk to meet up with him.

Christopher, Marcena, and Joshua finally find Rico in the crowd to congratulate him on his big win. Rico is overjoyed with himself for what he has just accomplished in his race today.

"I did it, Marcena!" Rico yells out over and over again to her in shock.

This is one of the happiest days in my life, Christopher. When will Lady Noreen make it over to the finish line?" Rico asks him breathing fast and hard.

"Probably in another 15 to 20 minutes, Rico. It depends on whether she continues running at a fast pace at this point."

"I can hardly wait to see her face, when I tell her I came in first place, Christopher," Rico responds short-winded.

Next, everyone gathers together to wait for Lady Noreen to step over the finish line and place in the race.

Seeing all of the excitement taking place for her arrival, Christopher runs down the Boardwalk to meet up with Lady Noreen so she'll continue running at a fast pace over the finish line.

Christopher finally sees her, and he runs out to her to keep her running at a quick speed up to the finish line. As he appears by her side, her face lights up.

"Christopher, you saved me! Now, I can get my second wind and I can cross the finish line. I was almost afraid that I wouldn't keep my running pace up. Thanks, Christopher."

"You're welcome. Let's go!" screams Christopher to Lady Noreen. Then together they take off together, side by side. Lady Noreen gives every ounce of energy she has left to run over the finish line. As they both approach the line, Christopher runs back into the crowd so that Lady Noreen can have all of the glory of finishing the race by herself.

Once over the line, Lady Noreen starts crying from all of the excitement of the race.

At the line, she sees Rico, Marcena, Joshua, and Brook gathered there cheering for her victory.

"I did it! I don't believe I did it! I'm alive! Yeah, I made it!" Lady Noreen utters in a loud cry. Then Lady Noreen with her last ounce of energy runs over to Rico.

Rico is so excited to see Lady Noreen. He shares with her that because of her endless help and support, he was able to place first in his race today.

Lady Noreen starts yelling "yeah" from the top of her lungs with great excitement. She can't believe that he was first in his race.

Brook buts in on Lady Noreen to say, "I think you just placed first in your age group in the 5K race, Lady Noreen."

"Oh my, I can't believe it! I haven't run this well since I was 18-years-old. At that time, I was on the track team in high school. This is truly a historical day for me! Hip hooray for me!" shrieks Lady Noreen.

Seeing how happy Lady Noreen is, Christopher comes over to her and hugs her. Then, he gives her a big kiss on her cheek.

She takes Christopher by his hand and leads him, with all their friends, down the Boardwalk steps to the cabanas. There Lady Noreen has a private catering service from the casino taking orders for food and beverages from her fellow runners and friends. She also has hired Hilten's group to perform for her big victory race celebration party. Slowly, the band members, dancers, and backup singers arrive at the cabana area to set up for the big party.

Before everything begins; however, Lady Noreen rushes to her limo to change her clothes. After Lady Noreen finishes dressing, she goes back over to the Boardwalk to receive her award for her race with Julie, Christopher, Rico, Marcena, and Joshua. As she goes to receive it, everyone including Brook, his father, Sarge, Old Bessie, Victor, Sergeant Mussack, Patrick, Russ, Grandpa Bill, Cora, Elliot, the senior citizen group from Ventnor, Harvey, Eleanor, and Winkie Whiskey Scullen cheer her on. Lady Noreen places first in her age category and 67th overall in the 5K Good Luck Race.

The names are called out over the microphone for the runners who placed in the different race divisions at the President's Boardwalk Hall. Rico placed first overall in the wheelchair event. Elliot, Grandpa Bill, and Cora placed first in their respective divisions. Julie placed first in the 5K race overall.

The crowd applauds them as they receive their awards up on the Boardwalk stage.

Immediately after the award presentation is over with, the runners and friends invited to Lady Noreen's party head toward the Cabana on the beach near Ventnor. Once there, they can hear the music playing and the laughter of the festive event. They can also smell the delicious food being grilled for them on the beach. The happiness and excitement of this day is felt by everyone at the party.

As the celebration party moves on, Lady Noreen approaches the area in front of the cabanas, and Hilten hands her a microphone.

"I want to thank each of you for joining in this special celebration to celebrate today's treasured moments. I especially want to thank Christopher for making my life complete. I also want to congratulate Rico and Julie for their great accomplishments in their races today. Yeah, Rico! Yeah, Julie! You are both something else. Thank you Marcena, Joshua, Brook, Nicholas, and my business partner, Patrick, for all of your support. Special congratulations to my neighbor, Sarah, whose daughter, Julie, won the marathon race today. Julie was diagnosed with a Desmoid Tumor on her left abdominal rectus muscle last year. After her diagnosis, a surgeon removed the tumor and a two inch margin around it. The muscle and tissue were replaced with mesh. Today, she ran in this race to raise $2,500.00 to support cancer research at the Sloan Memorial Cancer Center in New York. Rico and Julie, both of you are truly great champions. Now, I would like to dedicate this tonight's celebration to both of you and the other runners with us this evening. You are all my heroes!" declares Lady Noreen to all of them.

When Lady Noreen is done recognizing all of the winners, everyone in the crowd stands up and cheers!

Then Nicholas walks over to Patrick and gives him a bear hug.

"This must be your friend; I wanted to meet him, Patrick. I am so sorry about my actions a few weeks ago. Please accept my apology," Nicholas sadly says to him.

"Uh, but, you don't owe me one," solemnly states Patrick to Nicholas.

"But, yes, I do, Patrick, I was wrong to do what I did to you. I hope you can forgive me. I had no right to play God. I must stop judging my fellow mankind. If I can ever help you in any way, please, ask me."

Patrick then introduces Nicholas to Russ who is exhausted from the wheelchair race and hopes that both of them can support each other since they both have a potentially terminal disease. He knows that sometimes people with these medical conditions can end up providing a support system for one another.

Then, as the day starts to cool off during this first week of November, everyone starts leaving in different directions on the Boardwalk to return home or back to work. Lady Noreen has her limousine waiting with Brook and his father to take Christopher, Marcena, Joshua, Rico, and herself home.

Christopher, tired from the day, walks Laurel, his homeless friend, over to see his other friend, Arthur, to see if he will give him a job. Christopher wants Laurel's life to be more stable. With a job, he might have a chance to save his money and rent a room in the area, so he wouldn't have to sleep at the bus terminal anymore in Atlantic City during the winter months.

Since Laurel ran in the race today, he wants to rejoin the human race once again. This time Laurel Mitchell knows what he wants out of life.

Chapter 16

Your Marriage Is Heaven Sent

"Christopher will you take me to the casino to play bingo tonight?" pleads Lady Noreen with him.

"Whatever you want to do, we will do, Lady Noreen," quickly Christopher answers her.

"Thanks! Marcena wants us to meet her and Joshua at Jack's Restaurant at 8:00 p.m. at the C.T. Ocean Mall. She wants us to bring Rico with us."

"Okay!"

The two of them get ready to go. Lady Noreen insists that they walk to the casino. Ever since her race, she no longer wants to ride in the limo. She is now very health conscious and exercises every day.

Rico has enrolled in a computer graphic design program. He is very involved with the Spinal Bifida Foundation now. He wants to start a newsletter for the foundation and eventually plan a race to raise money for medical research for this disease like his friend, Julie, has done for Desmoid Tumors.

Marcena, finally returns to work at the hospital. She is now volunteering to work with a Women's Abuse Group in Atlantic City. Joshua and her are now more involved than ever with each other and are dating on a weekly basis.

Today the Bingo Win Go Day Events begin at 2:00 p.m. at the casino. Christopher and Lady Noreen arrive around 1:30 p.m. at the casino after their daily walk.

Lady Noreen goes straight to the Platinum Room for the Bingo Win Go Game Event. Christopher leaves her there and goes into the main casino to gamble on the quarter slots. On his way in, he walks next to a woman who just came in on a bus trip to the casino.

"Have you won anything for the day?" Christopher asks the woman.

"No, I just got here," pleasantly replies the woman to him.

"What do you play?" inquires Christopher.

"I only play the quarter machines," responds the woman.

"Have you ever won big?" Christopher asks her.

"Yes, I won $900.00 one time. But I love playing the machines so much that I always put all of the money back into the slots before I leave the casino," confesses the woman to Christopher.

"I guess you just like playing the different slots. Don't you?"

"Oh, yes, I do! Once I start playing the slot machines I have so much fun that I can't stop! I wish the software for all of these games was loaded onto my computer. I would play these games at home all of the time," the woman tells Christopher.

"You really do enjoy the slot games!"

"It seems like when I get into the games my mind just shuts down. I don't worry about anything. I don't think about the time of day or any of my life problems. I just have fun playing the quarter slots," truthfully admits the woman to Christopher.

"Well, enjoy yourself!" Christopher eagerly tells her.

The woman sits down at a quarter machines at the end of a row and starts off her day by putting a ten dollar bill in it. Once the money registers, she relaxes, and starts her gambling ritual.

Finally, Christopher walks away from her and walks over to the dollar machines. He sits next to a man, who has already won $750.00 in credits on his machine. Christopher puts $20.00 in his machine and gets ready to play it.

"This machine has stopped winning for me. I just want another big hit before I leave it. My wife keeps bugging me to take the money out. However, I feel the slot machine is going to hit one more time," complains the man to Christopher.

Christopher starts hitting the slot button but he has no luck on his own machine.

"It won't hit! It's eating up all of my money. Oh, no, here comes my wife," the man looks very upset as he whispers this to Christopher in a low voice.

"Frederick, take the money out of the machine! Right now!" screeches his wife.

"Honey, I can feel it! It's going to hit!" joyfully the man replies to her.

"You can't take the chance of losing all of your money. You've lost a lot of money today. Take it out right now!" demands his wife.

"Just let me be by myself and play my machine!" loudly he replies back to his wife in defiance.

"Okay, I'm going to walk outside to the Boardwalk. I'll be back later and you better have won," the woman yells at him in a heated rage.

Then the woman turns away from her husband, Frederick, in disgust and rolls her eyes up into the air. She takes a deep sigh and immediately walks away from him.

"My wife always brings me bad luck. I always lose when she is behind me. It's like she is a jinx. She takes all of my positive energy away from me when I gamble," admits the man to Christopher.

"Well, good luck, sir! I'm going to go play another machine. I hope your machine hits big again for you."

Christopher then moves over to a dollar machine near the five dollar machines. He sees an older man with his elderly mother, who is in a wheelchair playing the $5.00 slots together. The man hits the button a few times and then he has his mother hit it a few times. The woman evidently has suffered a stroke and can't talk. It doesn't make any difference; however, for the two of them are having such a great time together at the slot machine.

Christopher sits and watches their machine for a while. He then realizes that it is 4:00 p.m. and it is time for him to go back to the Platinum Room and get Lady Noreen. As he gets ready to leave, he passes by the elderly woman and accidentally bumps her arm. The old woman doesn't even notice what has happened to her as she hits the button one more time. As Christopher moves away from the $5.00 slot machines the music goes off, and Bredele and another slot manager quickly run over to the woman's machine.

The woman's son is shouting, "I don't believe it! You've won, mom! You've won $5,000.00 on your machine!"

As Bredele looks away from the woman, he spots Christopher. He turns to the other slot attendant next to him, Morrie, and remarks, "Look at that man over there. He is disgusting! He has leeched onto one of the wealthiest women in Ventnor, who gambles here all of the time. On top of that, he has moved in with her. He is a con-artist. I can't stand him, I hate his guts."

"Isn't he the guy who is friends with Joshua?" remarks Morrie.

"I guess! But Joshua is stupid! In fact, he is out of his head if he chooses a man like Christopher to be his friend," Bredele snickers to himself in a malicious tone of voice.

"Ha! I thought Joshua was a pretty stable guy."

"He can't be if he hangs around with a dirt ball like Christopher," Bredele replies in a nasty abrupt manner.

Christopher seeing Bredele pointing at him just stares back at him, as Bredele and the other attendant continue talking away. He can tell that like usual Bredele is talking badly about him. Therefore, he just turns away from him and walks over to meet Lady Noreen while he mutters under his breath, "God forgive both of them!"

Finally, Christopher goes up the escalator to the second floor. There he spots Lady Noreen coming from the Platinum Room, and he walks toward her.

"Lady Noreen, I'm here!"

"Thank heavens! I didn't win anything! I am so mad. You would have thought I would have won something," Lady Noreen in an agitated voice replies to Christopher.

"It is okay, Lady Noreen. You have helped other people win. Sometimes, we give to people in different ways. You give to people with your money."

"Christopher, you always have a way of making me sadder than I already am. Just please be quiet! I want to call Brook on my new cell phone and tell him to pick up Rico at the house and meet us at Jack's Restaurant."

"Okay! When did you get your new cellular phone? You said you would never buy one," Christopher asks her with a puzzled look on his face.

"Rico begged me to get a cell phone so I would be safe, Christopher. He worries about me all the time. Plus, it is a way for me to check in on him when I need to do so."

Finally, Lady Noreen contacts Brook, and asks him to go and pick up Rico.

She then calls Rico and tells him that Brook is on his way to pick him up at the house. When she is done talking to Rico, she sends him a few kisses over the phone."

Christopher can't help but laugh to himself.

"What's so funny?" snaps Lady Noreen at him.

"When did you start sending kisses over the phone, Lady Noreen?"

"It doesn't make any difference when, I just like doing it," fires backs Lady Noreen.

"I think it is great! I hope you continue to do it. The kids need to know that you love them," sincerely responds Christopher.

Next, the two of them start down the Boardwalk to Jack's Restaurant, which is in the C.T. Ocean Mall. On the way, Christopher asks Lady Noreen if she will walk down the beach with him there instead of on the Boardwalk to the restaurant.

"Christopher, I hate getting sand on my feet, so I'll keep my sandals on as we walk on the beach. Then, I won't get my feet so dirty."

They start walking up the beach, when suddenly Christopher sees Sanabrio flying frantically in the air. As Christopher looks beyond Sanabrio, he sees two German Shepherds running down the beach free. The one Shepherd has jumped into the air and has a seagull in his mouth. The other dog tries to rip the seagull with his teeth from the mouth of the other Shepherd carrying it. Suddenly, the dogs start tugging at the seagull from both sides as if it were a toy. The owner of the two dogs calls them, but they don't come to her, so she starts to walk over to her dogs. She gets to them before Christopher can. The owner makes the two dogs drop the seagull and has them follow her.

The woman never looks back to save or help the seagull. She really doesn't care about it!

As the woman and her two dogs walk away from the crime site, no remorse is shown for the seagull that her dogs just murdered a few minutes ago.

Once Christopher reaches the site of the incident, he picks up the seagull and sees that it is dead from being ripped apart. He then walks out into the ocean and throws the remains of the dead seagull into the ocean as Sanabrio watches him from the air.

Lady Noreen is hotter than an iron on full force as she glares with rage at the woman with the two dogs. Lady Noreen can't believe what the woman has allowed her dogs to do to the defenseless seagull. She yells at the woman, "First, lady, you shouldn't have your dogs on the beach. Secondly, dogs are not permitted even on the Boardwalk without leashes. Your dogs just murdered a seagull, and you don't even care about that at all!"

The woman without responding to Lady Noreen's temper tantrum just walks away with her dogs back to the Boardwalk.

"I can't believe she didn't care about that seagull, Christopher."

"Lady Noreen, most people don't care about life. They kill nature, insects, animals, babies, children, and each other for just fun! Aren't they cruel?" Christopher asks her.

"Yes, they are! Sad to say, I never really cared about people until recently Christopher. I hated everyone and everything in my life. I just wanted to die myself."

"Well, Lady Noreen, thank God that you have changed the way you think. You now have a heart that is able to love and feel for others."

"But, Christopher, how can I change others?"

"You can't, Lady Noreen! God helps those who help themselves. You can only help yourself – that's the only person who you can change."

"We better hurry, Christopher, if we are to meet the children by 8 o'clock."

The two of them walk fast together up the beach and finally see Rico with Brook in front of the C.T. Ocean Mall.

Lady Noreen runs to get Rico as Brook is waving good-bye to everyone.

Christopher follows them into the restaurant. Once there, they see Joshua and Marcena waiting for them at a table. All of them go over to the table to join up with them.

After everyone sits down and all the orders are taken by the waitress, Joshua talks to Christopher about his promotion at the casino. While Marcena talks to Rico and Lady Noreen about her Women's Abuse Clinic Project.

Lady Noreen loves listening to everything that the kids are doing with their young lives.

Soon the food is served and everyone talks about the highlights of Rico's wheelchair race. Both Rico and Marcena are proud of Lady Noreen placing first in her age bracket and 67th in the overall race.

When all of them are done with their dinner, Christopher orders coffee for everyone except Rico and Lady Noreen. They are both still in training for their races, so he orders them water.

"Christopher, Lady Noreen, and Rico, I want to thank all of you for being in our lives. You have brought us so much happiness into our lives. That is why we want all three of you here with us tonight. I want to ask Marcena if she will marry me.

"Marcena will you marry me?" Joshua happily pops his proposal out to her.

"Oh, yes, of course, yes, I will. I don't believe you are asking me to marry you, Joshua," Marcena answers him with happy tears in her eyes.

Then, Joshua pulls out the engagement ring and places the ring on Marcena's finger.

"I love you so much, Marcena, I have finally found the right woman to share my life with, thanks to you, Christopher," replies Joshua to Christopher.

"You deserve happiness my friend, and Marcena, I love you like a daughter. I am so happy for the both of you," Christopher replies.

"Rico, I would like you to be my best man," Joshua immediately asks him.

"Of course I'll be your best man, Joshua!" replies Rico to him.

"Christopher, you have been like a father to me. Would you give me away and Lady Noreen would you be my matron of honor? My wedding would not be complete without both of you in it. I love both of you so much!" Marcena shares with them.

"Marcena, I would be so honored to be in your wedding. I want to help you plan it; we'll have so much fun doing it together," happily Lady Noreen answers her.

"Well, Lady Noreen, Joshua and I don't have a lot of money saved to have a large wedding, so we thought we'd just go to the justice of the peace and get married."

"Oh, honey, let's have it at my house. It won't cost that much money. When do you want to have your wedding?" Lady Noreen asks her.

"We'd like to be married around Christmas. That time of the year is so special to me. But it is only one month away, Lady Noreen," Marcena tells Lady Noreen.

"Well, Marcena, then, let's start planning it right now. It will be a beautiful wedding! I can see it with red and white poinsettias!" answers Lady Noreen.

"I am so proud of you, Marcena! I always knew you'd get married to each other. Your marriage is heaven sent. I can hardly wait for your big day. I look forward to being a Grandpa someday," responds Christopher so very pleased with both of them.

With that Rico starts singing to Joshua, "You're a lucky, lucky fellow, for you're a lucky, lucky fellow, and everyone right here knows it!"

Then, everyone hugs one another and starts to leave the restaurant. Lady Noreen and Joshua fight over the bill and like usual, Lady Noreen wins the fight.

Marcena and Joshua leave the restaurant arm and arm. Joshua has to walk Marcena to the hospital. She is now working the night shift.

Lady Noreen grabs Rico's wheelchair and off they go together with Christopher to the elevator at the C.T. Ocean Mall. Once down to the ground floor, they get off of the elevator and run into Nicholas. He is pushing a thin looking man in a wheelchair.

Christopher in a friendly way shouts to Nicholas, "What are you doing here?"

"Patrick had to work late tonight at the flower shop; so I brought his friend, Russ, with me here to see the water show."

"You two will have a great time here together, Nicholas, and by the way, I'd like to introduce Russ to Rico and Lady Noreen," comments Christopher.

"Hello, it is so nice to meet both of you. I have been trying to stay healthy since I raced in the wheelchair race; it is such a pleasure to participate in it even though I came in nearly last," with a lack of energy responds Russ.

"You were in the wheelchair race, too? That's right! You could work out with my adopted mom, Lady Noreen, and me, if you would like to do so, Russ. Again my name is Rico, and I know that when I was sick I only got stronger by exercising regularly each week with Lady Noreen."

"I'll keep that in mind," slowly mutters Russ.

"Well, Russ, maybe we can join them someday and work out with them if you would like to do so," Nicholas replies.

Lady Noreen is almost in tears. She can't believe Rico has called her his adopted mom. She is so happy and proud of him.

With that Nicholas and Russ go into the mall and Christopher, Lady Noreen, and Rico walk out of Jack's Restaurant to meet Brook to go home.

Once Nicholas and Russ are in the mall, they go up on the elevator to see the water show. They have so much fun watching it. Then they walk away from it to go back to the elevator to depart from the mall to get something to eat.

As they are getting off of the elevator, Nicholas runs into one of his old friends from his stock market days named Morton.

"Nicholas! Hello there, old buddy!" yells out Morton to Nicholas.

"Hi! Morton! How are you?" asks Nicholas.

"I'm here with my family, Nicholas. We are having fun with our grandchildren," proudly responds Morton to him.

"Morton, this is my friend, Russ," replies Nicholas.

"Hi!" says Russ to Morton.

Then Nicholas and Morton continue to talk as they walk together through the mall toward the exit doors.

"What's wrong with your friend, Nicholas?" asks Morton.

"Russ has the AIDS virus," answers Nicholas.

"He has AIDS! Why are you with him?" Morton shouts out in a loud voice very upset.

"He is my friend, Morton," Nicholas utters back to Morton in defiance.

"You must be kidding? The two of you have nothing in common, Nicholas!"

"Oh, no, I'm sorry, you are wrong! We are both dying. I am dying from cancer and he will eventually die from complications from the AIDS virus. You, Morton, have a mental disease that makes you feel prejudice against other people. I once had that same mental disease until a friend of mine told me that I shouldn't play God. That's my advice to you, too," states Nicholas to Morton.

"Nicholas, I have to go! You need some professional help. Your disease has distorted your train of thought, my friend. You never thought like this when we were involved with the stock market together."

"You're right, Morton! I didn't! At that time in my life, I used other people to get rich. I never cared about those innocent people. I was their pimp, they were my money prostitutes. If they made a little money or lost it all I didn't care. All that mattered to me was the greed of green money. I gambled all of those people's lives away for money and I didn't care about any of them. Like you, I wanted it all! Yes, I have lots of money, but I can't enjoy it because I'm dying from cancer. Now I'm going to help people, Morton, while I am alive. You see, for the first time in my life, I care about other people more than money and I am capable of love."

"You need a shrink, Nicholas," says Morton in a sarcastic way.

"No, I don't! I just don't need judgmental people like you, Morton, who are evil human beings in my life. You are so busy judging other people that you have appointed yourself to be a god. You will be judged the way you judge other people by the Lord, himself," comments Nicholas to him.

Nicholas then walks back to Russ and Morton walks back to his family. Nicholas can see Morton whispering to his wife about him, but Nicholas can care less.

After seeing that, Nicholas puts his hand on Russ's shoulder and says to him, "Let's go eat and buy some video games for you to take home."

"Are you sure you don't want to take me back to Patrick's apartment house so you can be with your friend, Nicholas?"

"No, Russ, I don't want you to go home. I'm having a great time with you. Morton was my friend in another life, Russ. Now, he is just another person on this earth who is breathing air and trying to hurt other people every day he is alive."

"Are you sure you feel that way, Nicholas?"

"Yes! I do Russ!" Nicholas in a serious tone replies to Russ.

"Thanks, Nicholas! Because I am having a great time with you, too! This is the first day in a long time that I feel like a happy fish in a water bowl. Before, I felt like a fish out of water ready to die. However, who knows maybe I will work out with Rico and Lady Noreen one of these days so I can improve my racing time. Maybe now, I don't want to die. Hopefully, I still have the strength left inside of myself to fight the AIDS virus, Nicholas."

"You do, Russ! You do! Let's have dinner and enjoy ourselves."

"Let's go, Nicholas!" Russ answers him with a smile on his face.

Then out of the C.T. Mall, Nicholas pushes Russ to Miletti's Italian Restaurant.

Chapter 17

Without God Or A Family One
Has Nothing To Celebrate

Throughout the month of November, Lady Noreen makes plans with Marcena for her wedding. They meet with Patrick to order the flowers. Lady Noreen loves to do calligraphy, so she starts addressing invitation envelopes to the guests, while Rico starts designing Marcena's wedding invitations on his computer.

Christopher goes to Marc Marcuso to order tuxedos for the men in the wedding party. They choose white tuxedos to add to the festivity of Christmas.

Brook has contacts with several of the limousine services for Christopher to transport several of the wedding guests to the local hotels and casinos for the day of the wedding.

Lady Noreen is having the time of her life planning Marcena's storybook wedding. As a gift to Marcena, she wants to design her dress with Patrick as one of her wedding gifts. Lady Noreen wants Marcena to wear her wedding veil that she wore when she was married. She saved the veil for her son's wife to wear one day, but since his death she just buried it in her cedar chest.

Marcena wants to have a theme for her wedding day so she goes to Christopher for some ideas.

Christopher thinks and thinks about it and then replies to her, "Let's call it, A Candlelight Evening of Love," Christopher suggests to Marcena.

"Oh, Christopher, that is the perfect name for it."

"Marcena, Lady Noreen can help you put the ideas for the theme into place for you," adds Christopher.

With that Marcena goes to the living room where Lady Noreen and Rico are starting to work on several designs for her wedding invitations and she shares Christopher's theme idea for the wedding.

"Lady Noreen, Christopher thought that you would have some great ideas for this theme. I have named my wedding day thanks to Christopher, "A Candlelight Evening of Love". What do you think of the name?" Marcena asks her.

"I love it, Marcena!" How about if we have white chairs put throughout the living room, red poinsettias lining the runway and white poinsettias in the foyers? Then, we will line the area for the ceremony with red, white, and green candles, plus two Christmas trees with white lights and red balls. Also, maybe we should spray the trees white. Do you have any other decor ideas for her wedding day, Rico?" Lady Noreen asks him.

"How about putting a Nativity set in front of the fireplace where the ceremony will be conducted? I bet Patrick can help us with that, plus he can hang angels down from the ceiling in angel hair carrying banners of scrolls saying, "A Candlelight Evening of Love". Then we can surround the fireplace with pink, red, and white poinsettias. Do you like my ideas, Marcena?" Rico asks her.

"Rico, it sounds so beautiful! But Lady Noreen it will cost you too much money to do all of this for me."

"No, Marcena, it won't, and your wedding is worth every penny that I spend on it. After all, you are only having around seventy-five guests or so in attendance of the wedding ceremony."

"Lady Noreen, what should we do about the reception?" Marcena asks.

"Marcena, let's have it in the dining room and extend the dancing to the enclosed porch. I'll have four buffet sites set up, one for Italian food, one for steak, one for Chinese, and the final one for seafood. I will move all of the furniture from the bedrooms and den on the first floor upstairs. That way, we can use the downstairs bedroom and den for serving centers since you want to have the reception at the house."

"I do want it here, Lady Noreen. All my life, I wanted a house and two parents and a brother. Now, I have it all! I am so very, very happy!" with glee Marcena answers Lady Noreen.

"What color do you want my dress to be?" responds Lady Noreen to Marcena.

"Whatever color you want it to be, Lady Noreen!" Marcena answers her.

"How about if the color of my dress is a Christmas red or a soft green, Marcena?" responds Lady Noreen.

"Whatever color you want it to be, Lady Noreen, will be fine with me! Well, I have to get ready to go to the hospital now. What are both of you going to do the rest of the day?" asks Marcena.

"I'm going to work with Patrick and Marc on all of the details of your wedding, plus call a caterer for some estimates on the prices of the food. Plus, I have my annual mammography today," replies Lady Noreen to Marcena.

"Marcena, I have to go to my graphic class and work on your wedding invitations. After that, I have to work out with Lady Noreen and prepare for our next race in February," responds Rico to Marcena.

Everyone leaves for their daily work schedules. Christopher, seeing that the house is empty, decides to leave the house, too, so he goes for a long walk down the Boardwalk. The cool air feels good upon his face as he watches the seagulls with Sanabrio flying high up in the air.

As Christopher walks further down the Boardwalk to buy a cup of coffee from Prentis's Restaurant, he sees two foreign men stopped in a rolling chair on the Boardwalk refusing to pay the attendant for pushing them down the Boardwalk to their destination. The chair pusher explains to the men his price once again, but they refuse to pay him, and they start to walk away.

The rolling chair pusher starts yelling for them to come back and pay him. Yet the men just ignore him and keep walking further and further away from the chair pusher.

Finally, Christopher approaches the two men and responds to this situation by saying to both of them, "What is going on?"

The one man sarcastically shouts at him saying, "That man is loco, we are not going to pay him fifteen dollars for his service. In fact, we are not going to pay him anything at all!"

"Sorry men, you are going to pay him the fifteen dollars that you owe him right now or else see that policeman over there?"

"Yeah," the man mutters very upset at Christopher.

"Either you pay the man his money for his services, or you will get to go to court to pay him. Then, you will have a bigger problem on your hands," suggests Christopher to both of them.

Next, Christopher motions to Sergeant Mussack and gets his attention. Then Christopher screams to him to come immediately over where they are all standing on the Boardwalk.

"What seems to be the problem, Christopher?" Sergeant Mussack asks with authority as he walks over to where Christopher and the two men who are standing on the Boardwalk.

"These men, Sergeant Mussack, will not pay the chair pusher for pushing them here."

The pusher of the rolling chair has now come over to join in the conversation with all of them.

"Is this all true, sir?" Sergeant Mussack asks the chair pusher.

"Yes, I pushed the two of them a great distance to get here, and they refuse to pay me the money that we negotiated for my services."

"Gentlemen, why don't you pay him his money, and settle this disagreement right now," remarks Christopher to the irritated men.

"Or else, you both can come with me to the police station, and we'll solve it eventually through the legal system!" Sergeant Mussack without hesitation explains to the two men.

With that the two men reluctantly scrape up the fifteen dollars that they owe the man and pay him his money.

Next, the two men say something in another language under their breath about the payment of the money to the man and depart as fast as they can from the Boardwalk.

Then the chair pusher thanks Sergeant Mussack and pushes his chair in the opposite direction of the men's direction so he can return to working on the Boardwalk.

Christopher leaves the site with Sergeant Mussack and he invites Sergeant Mussack to have a cup of coffee with him. Then the two of them walk down the Boardwalk together to see Arthur at his restaurant and buy two cups of coffee.

Once they are done buying their coffee at the restaurant, Sergeant Mussack thanks Christopher for helping him solve the problem between the three men.

Then, Christopher leaves Sergeant Mussack and walks over to the apartments on Iowa to see the Sarge. He wants him to work on the musical selections for Marcena's wedding with him.

Once at the apartment complex, Christopher pushes the apartment buzzer button to see his dear friend, the Sarge who is now working full-time for the city as a maintenance man. Lady Noreen co-signed for the Sarge, so he could rent Marcena's old apartment.

Christopher, after being buzzed into the apartment complex, takes the elevator upstairs. Once off the elevator, he walks down the hall and knocks on the Sarge's apartment door.

"Hi, Christopher, what have you been doing since I last saw you?" inquirers the Sarge in an uplifting voice.

"I have been trying to help Lady Noreen with the planning of Marcena's wedding. Did she call you, Sarge?"

"She sure did! I just love, Marcena, like a daughter. I'd do anything for her. Well, what do you want me to do for her wedding service, Christopher?"

"Why don't we have the guys in the band play some traditional holiday music, while the guests are being ushered in, Sarge. She wants everyone in the band to wear white tuxedos. Joshua's friends will usher the people to their seats. Once everyone is seated we'll play, "Pachabel's Cannon," for her to walk down the aisle to, then she wants me to play, "Ave Maria," on the harmonica, and have Hilten sing the song. That's where you come in Sarge, Marcena wants you to play, "Oh, Holy Night," with Teresa Y., on the violin with Winkie Whiskey Scullen on the keyboard. After the marriage ceremony Hilten with Joy Rhapsody, Ngoc, P.J., and Feymale will sing, "What Child is This," and finally I will play the tambourine with Big Luke, Ogbonna,

Winkie, and Deuce to "Oh, Holy Night," for the people to be escorted to their tables for the wedding reception.

"Christopher, everything sounds great! Do you have anything else to tell me?"

"For the reception we will play a mixture of music for the guests to dance to, plus a few holiday songs," adds Christopher.

"I guess we are all set! Everyone knows to go to Marcuso's Men's Clothing Store for their tuxedos. Brook has limo services hired for the day to transport people back-and- forth, and you are in charge of having all the music setup for the day. The rehearsal dinner will be at the Lost Empire Restaurant at the C. T. Royal Ocean Mall the night before the wedding. All of the invitations should be in the mail by the end of the week. Marcena, Lady Noreen, and Rico are working on all the other details for the wedding. I just have to see Old Bessie, and Daisy to remind them to pass out flowers to the guests on the day of the wedding. Mama Cane will handle the register book and Patrick will be assisted by Nicholas in setting up everything for the service. Sarge, you will be in charge of all the sound equipment and the music for the wedding service for Marcena and Joshua's wedding day."

"I would love to do that for her! It looks like we have a lot of work ahead of us to get ready for Marcena's big day, Christopher!"

"We sure do! Thanks again for all of your help, Sarge."

"Christopher, it is the other way around. I need to thank you. I wouldn't be here in this apartment, or be off of the Boardwalk and have a job; if it wasn't for Lady Noreen and you," humbly replies the Sarge to Christopher.

"You did everything all by yourself, my friend, bye for now! Enjoy!" Christopher calls out in a jovial manner to the Sarge.

"See you later, Christopher," utters the Sarge back to him in a deep voice.

Christopher goes on his way, to find Old Bessie, Daisy, and Mama Cane, so he can finalize all of Marcena's wedding plans with them.

Meanwhile, Brook is spending the day waiting for Lady Noreen to come from the local hospital. She is there for a biopsy. Her mammogram came back with some cysts in her right breast. The doctor wants to see if they are cancerous or not.

Finally, Lady Noreen comes out of the hospital. She is all upset. "I hate these tests, Brook."

"Thank God they do, Lady Noreen. These tests save so many women's lives each year. If everyone would just go yearly for their mammogram, thousands of women's lives would be saved," politely Brook tells her.

"Well, Brook, a lot of people like me never get a mammogram because we are scared to death of what the results of it will be."

"Scared of what?" Brook questions her.

"I am scared that I will have breast cancer, Brook! That's why I didn't want to get a biopsy today or ever!" shrieks Lady Noreen at the top of her voice at Brook.

"You should be smart rather than scared of getting a biopsy, Lady Noreen. Smart women protect themselves from the disease of breast cancer. Scared women often wait until it is too late for their mammogram. Then they are scared to death if their diagnosis is life threatening."

"Oh, Brook, you're so lucky you don't have to get a mammogram or a biopsy!"

"You're right, I don't, but I have to worry about prostate cancer, Lady Noreen. To men, it is like breast cancer," Brook informs her.

"I see your point! Let's go! I want to visit with Patrick. He is going to go over Marcena's flower list with me. Then he is going to help me arrange the Nativity set and design a dress for me for Marcena's wedding. We have already started making Marcena's wedding gown. It is positively beautiful, Brook!"

The weeks fly by. Plans are being made and the final details are being put into place for the wedding day. The whole house is being transformed and rearranged for the wedding.

Lady Noreen and Rico are still working out every day for their next big race on the Boardwalk in February. Lady Noreen has even changed her hairstyle for both the race and the wedding.

Before everyone knows it, it is Thanksgiving Day. For the first time since Lady Noreen lost her family, she prepares a Thanksgiving dinner for everyone she loves and cares about. She even makes a special holiday meal for Tigress to eat, too.

Everyone in the house gathers together on this Thanksgiving Day to go to church.

Then, Brook takes everyone back home for the big feast and to join all the other invited guests for today's dinner.

Once back to the house with all the other guests, Christopher and Marcena help Lady Noreen in the kitchen with Patrick. Rico and Teresa Y., who have now become best of friends, watch the Thanksgiving Parade on TV with Brook, Nicholas, Joshua, Russ, Mamma Cane and all her foster children. Sarge, Daisy, and Old Bessie help Lady Noreen with the food and the setting of the table.

The turkey and all of the other delicious dishes are placed on the table and everyone gathers around the table and throughout the house to eat the great meal. The Sarge has holiday music playing softly throughout the entire house to give it a holiday atmosphere. Lady Noreen has candles burning throughout all the rooms to give the house an aroma of enjoyment and a festive fragrance. Holiday decorations are seen everywhere in the house.

Lady Noreen is the last one to take her seat at one of the several dining room tables throughout her house. Once seated, she asks Christopher to say the prayer:

"God, we thank You for this Thanksgiving Day on which we are truly blessed to be a family with all of our loved ones around us. You have given us so many wonderful friends and great memories with them to be thankful for dear Lord. Bless all of the food that You have provided us with on this day. Always guide us into the light of Your being and prepare us for another day to serve You. This day is a day for us to give our special thanks to You for our family and extended family. Amen."

With that all the food is passed full circle around the tables for everyone participate in on the feast. Christopher grins and is truly happy for being a part of this blessed day with his new family. He realizes that without God or a family, one has nothing to celebrate or be thankful for in his or her life.

Chapter 18

I'm No Angel - I'm No Saint, I'm Just A Man!

The calendar slowly turns to the beginning of December. Tonight is the High Roller Triple Cash Night at Lady Noreen's favorite casino and Christopher is already to escort her to it.

The ballroom at the casino is filled with good food and drinks. Christopher and Lady Noreen enjoy plate after plate of rich and delicious foods at the special buffet. Lady Noreen thinks that every new plate of food is better and more delicious than the last plate of food she just ate.

Finally, the tournament begins. Lady Noreen has Christopher give her a big hug for good luck and he does.

After that, Lady Noreen goes to her machine at the 6:00 p.m. session. Then she, starts hitting the button on her machine as fast as she can, when the announcer says, "Begin now!"

The casino host announces to everyone that the winner of the tournament will win $15,000.00 at the end of the 9:00 p.m. tournament session.

This makes Lady Noreen hit the button on the machine faster than she ever thought she could hit it. Finally, she is done with her fifteen minute session in the tournament. Lady Noreen's score is 10,256. The closest to her is Mrs. Chang with 10,159 points, and Howard Davis with 10,150 points. All of them know each other since they are all in the elite high roller club at the casino. Mrs. Chang and her husband gamble at the casino for recreation every weekend. Mr. Chang is a famous international lawyer and Mrs. Chang is a physical therapist.

204

They gamble together every Friday and Saturday night at the poker tables until after midnight. Mrs. Chang stays up all night, after her husband goes to his room at the casino to go to bed, and plays the dollar slot machines in the high roller backroom. Then, promptly at 7:00 a.m., she wakes her husband up with a comp ticket in her hand to go to the breakfast buffet with him.

Howard Davis is a retired military man. His wife works as a receptionist at a doctor's office. Their one son is an electrical engineer, and their other son just got accepted into medical school. Now, their two children just want them to relax and to enjoy themselves on the weekends. So they come to the casino twice a month with their friends just to have lots of fun.

When the tournament is over at 9:00 p.m., Lady Noreen is on cloud nine. She can't believe that she has just won the tournament. She darts over to Christopher as fast as she can and hugs him yelling, "I've won! I've won! I don't believe it, I just won! I haven't had any luck for such a long time it seems!"

"Congratulations! You deserve to win! You have done so much good for others in life lately. Go get your money or check. What are you going to do with it?" Christopher asks her.

"I used to put the money back into the machines for I just love playing the machines, but this time, I am going to get a check for $14,000.00, and divide the money equally between Marcena and Rico. I want both of them to enjoy my money while I am still alive. After all, I could croak any day now, Christopher," foretells Lady Noreen to him.

"Don't be so negative about your life, Lady Noreen. Don't talk about death so much that you stop living your life to its fullest potential every day. People don't like to hear about people putting death wishes on themselves. People should talk more about living rather than about dying," lectures Christopher to her.

"I don't want to talk about death all of the time, Christopher, but my mother worried about so many things in her lifetime that she put the fear of God into me. Now like her, I worry over every little thing just to have something to worry about. This has made my life a living curse, and the only way to stop it from being that way is to die!"

"Well, Lady Noreen, you must break this evil spell put upon you and this is the time to do it!" Christopher pleads with Lady Noreen to do it right now.

With that Lady Noreen goes to the desk and gets her check for $14,000.00 and the rest in cash for $1,000.00 so she can continue to gamble the night away. After she gets her money, Lady Noreen goes with Christopher to the aisle of dollar machines in the high roller backroom, and sits down to play the "Golden Leopard Machine," her favorite slot machine. Christopher sits next to her as she plays it.

A cinnamon skinned woman in her thirties sits down right next to them and starts playing, the "Hungry Flamingo Machine." This woman keeps rubbing her religious medallion around her neck as she plays the machine she is on.

Christopher finally asks the woman, "Are you having any luck tonight?"

"Not yet! I just returned from Cancun, Mexico, and I was hoping that I can win some money for a woman who lives there."

"Why?" asks Christopher.

"The mother, Juanita, has no money to pay for her daughter's bus transportation to get to school. She works very hard at the flea market in Cancun, but it doesn't give her enough money to pay for her daughter's bus transportation to and from school."

"Do the children have to pay to ride the bus in Mexico?" questions Christopher.

"Yes," quickly the woman responds to him.

"Lady Noreen, did you hear that?" blurts out Christopher to her.

"Christopher, I'm concentrating right now. Don't bother me!" nervously yells Lady Noreen back to him.

"But Lady Noreen, a little girl needs some money for her bus transportation to attend a school in Mexico. Education isn't a privilege there like it is for our children in America," states Christopher to Lady Noreen.

"Don't bother me right now, Christopher. I've just fed this machine $300.00, and I have nothing to show for it!" mutters Lady Noreen to him in an awful mood.

In disgust, Lady Noreen, continues to play her machine. She continues to slap her slot machine and curses it at the same time.

Meanwhile, the young woman on Christopher's left keeps losing money in her machine, too. Finally, that woman's machine is down to $15.00. With great determination in her heart to win, she continues to go for broke and gamble her money away as she rubs her religious medallion. Suddenly, the medallion accidentally drops down onto the floor, and Christopher picks it back up for her off of the floor. When her machine finally reaches $6.00, the machine hits, at a 9 times 9 casino machine. She wins eighty-one times one hundred. She wins $8,100.00.

"I've won! I don't believe my own eyes! Look, I've just won enough money to help that woman and her daughter in Mexico," full of passion the woman shrieks out loud.

Christopher cheers for the woman, while Lady Noreen continues to lose her money like water in the slot machine that she is playing on. Every once in a while Lady Noreen looks up at Christopher to roll her eyes. Then she looks back down at her machine and slaps it. Lady Noreen continues to do this over and over again.

Eventually, Bredele comes over with security and asks the young woman that just won on her machine for her driver's license. She tells Bredele that she wants her money in a check.

At first, Bredele tells her that he doesn't think he can give her a check for the amount of money that she just won.

Then, Christopher intervenes into the conversation between the two of them, and says, "Bredele, you give people checks all of the time. I'm sure you can give this woman a check, too. Else I am sure she would like to talk to your manager."

Hearing that, Bredele, gives Christopher a dirty look, and goes off to get the young woman a check.

As the woman waits for Bredele to return with her check, Christopher orders drinks for both of them from Hilten, the beverage hostess.

Hilten is so happy to see her friend, Christopher.

Hilten happily says to Christopher, "How are you?"

"I'm just doing great, Hilten! When is your CD coming out?"

"Probably in six months. Nicholas is working out all of the details between the band and us with the recording studio. Nicholas is a great businessman and agent, Christopher. All of us love him so much!"

"I am so glad to hear that Hilten. You are in good hands!" replies Christopher.

"All of this happened because of you, Christopher!"

"No, Hilten, it happened because of you. You never gave up on your dream!"

"See you, Christopher! If not here at the casino, I'll see all of you at Marcena's and Joshua's wedding," shouts Hilten to Christopher.

"Bye for now, Hilten," replies Christopher.

Finally, Bredele brings the young woman, her check and says to her, "Congratulations, Juanita, here is your check. Please sign these papers for me."

Juanita signs all of the paperwork and gladly takes her check from Bredele. Then, she tips Bredele and the security guard for delivering the check to her.

Bredele walks away from Juanita and starts talking to the security guard about Christopher like he always does.

"That man next to her, Christopher Saint, is grotesque. I hate his guts. He just sits there with his rich Lady Noreen all of the time. He has even moved into her house with her. That woman must be crazy to let him live with her."

"Come on, Bredele! You gossip about everyone. In fact, you probably talk bad about me behind my back, too, so just be quiet! I'm tired of all your bad karma, racial slurs, and hateful remarks. Just shut up!" immediately replies the security guard to Bredele.

"I dare you talk to me like that! I'm above you. I'll have you fired! You're no one! Always remember that Haines," Bredele full of hate blares out these hateful words at Haines.

"I have to go elsewhere, right now, Bredele. Don't pull rank on me. You make me sick!" Haines comments back to him.

Juanita finishes her drink and stands up to leave. Before she leaves the backroom, she looks back at Christopher and happily says, "I enjoyed talking to you! I still can't believe that I just won such a big jackpot!"

"Well, you have. Now you will be truly blessed for helping those people in Cancun with the money that you just won."

"I already have been...! I'm so happy right now," the woman excitedly says to Christopher.

"By the way, whose picture is on the medal that you rub for good luck?"

"Oh, it is St. Christopher. This chain was given to me from my great-grandmother. In her time, St. Christopher was a saint until the church proved him not to be a saint. So now he's not a saint!"

"Well, it looks like he brought you lots of luck tonight."

"He did, Christopher! He'll always be my favorite saint."

"He's my favorite saint, too, for my name is Christopher. Like him, I'm no angel! I'm no saint! I'm just a man!"

"That's funny! Well, I have to go now! Good luck, Christopher."

Lady Noreen continues to lose her money at her machine. It has now eaten up the $1,000.00 that she took in cash tonight. Her machine has given her little hits, but no big hits. At the present, her machine looks dead.

In a miserable mood, she asks Christopher to take her home. He gladly obliges her.

As they walk out of the casino, he runs over to the donut shop in the restaurant to buy her two luscious glazed donuts. Then, he runs over to Lady Noreen to give her both of the donuts to eat on their walk back home.

"Lady Noreen, this will make you feel so much better," Christopher tells her.

"Sure it will! Christopher, you just want to rub it in that I lost $1,000.00 of my own dough. That's why you gave me two donuts made out of dough."

"Ha! Ha! That's funny! When you eat your donuts you'll be out of all of the dough you have in your hand once again, Lady Noreen," laughs Christopher.

"Thanks! Rub it in, Christopher. Just rub it in!" abruptly Lady Noreen replies to him.

"Stop it, Lady Noreen! You just won $15,000.00 tonight. You still have the $14,000.00 in a check left to divide between Marcena and

Rico. You don't even need the money, Lady Noreen! You are filthy rich! Don't be so greedy! You've only lost $1,000.00 of your own money tonight! You could have blown the entire $15,000.00," Christopher reminds her.

"I just hate to lose at the casino, Christopher!" Lady Noreen responds to him in anger.

"Everyone does, Lady Noreen, but life is often full of more losses than wins. If everyone won all of the time at the casino, we wouldn't need to believe there was a heaven or a hell. Would we?" Christopher asks her in a calm tone of voice.

"Christopher, stop preaching to me right now! You're not making me feel any better, so quit your sermon right now! After all, you are not an angel, nor are you a saint!" yells Lady Noreen at him.

"You're right, Lady Noreen, I'm no angel – I'm no saint, I'm just a man!" answers Christopher in agreement with her.

Chapter 19

Gift Out Of Love

The days pass from Monday to Sunday so fast. Finally, it is two weeks before Marcena and Joshua's wedding date. Christopher and Marcena have planned a big combined bachelorette and bachelor party at the casino tonight to celebrate their last single days before marriage. The ushers and bridesmaids are to meet Joshua and Marcena at the casino at 7 o'clock.

Lady Noreen is all excited about this night. She can hardly wait for the fun to begin.

Brook pulls up in the limo and picks up Lady Noreen, Christopher, Marcena, and Rico and takes them to the casino for their last big night of single fun.

Once at the casino, Marcena meets up with Joshua at the front desk, and all of Marcena's and his friends in the wedding party.

Lady Noreen gives each of their guests $100.00 to gamble and keys to their rooms. She tells the wedding party that whoever wins the most money will receive a big surprise.

Then the wedding party goes throughout the casino to gamble. Joshua can't gamble since he is employed by the casino; so he just sits with Marcena as she plays the slot machines.

Some of their friends start gambling on the high roller machines, some go to the poker tables, or to the crap tables. Others go to the penny, nickel, or quarter slots.

Someone is on Lady Noreen's dollar machine, and she is so mad at them. She doesn't want anyone on her machine to win, but herself.

Lady Noreen just stands near her favorite slot machine in hopes that the man on it, will either lose all his money, or just leave her machine. She only prays that her dollar slot machine will win just for her, if she gets the chance to get back on it.

Rico never gambles, so he just sits patiently next to Lady Noreen while she plays. He has never been in the casino before even though he lives in Atlantic City so he is enjoying his first experience there. Rico is also delighted that the casino is now handicap accessible so he can get around in his wheelchair on the casino floor.

Christopher sits next to two of Marcena's friends while they play on the 50 cent machines. One of the girls is named Taylor, and the other one is named Hannah, who is Joshua's sister. While Taylor plays her slot machine, Hannah just sits in front of her machine and plays occasionally while she talks to Christopher.

"I hear you are going to give Marcena away at the wedding next week. She really loves you, Christopher, like a father, and my brother, Joshua, has the highest respect for you. He says that without you in his life, he would never have found the right girl to marry."

"I am so lucky; Hannah, Marcena and Joshua are truly beautiful people. I love Marcena like she was my own daughter, and I think the world of Joshua. He is such a wonderful young man."

"Christopher, I gave birth to a son last year. He was a still born. It almost killed me. I am so fortunate though that my husband and family were there to support me. Even now, I feel great pain within as I talk to you about the death of our child."

"Hannah, your loss may always hurt you! You lost a perfect little angel created out of God's love. You should never forget your son. He will meet up with you in heaven one day and with those in your family who go there before you."

"That may be so, Christopher, but now I don't know if I want to have another child or not."

"Hannah, you and your husband will have to pray about it. You can either have another baby or adopt one. In fact, you can even adopt an older child if you would like to do so. Hannah, you can do anything that your heart desires you to do. I do; however, feel that you will have another child in your lifetime, for you have so much love in your heart to give to a little one."

"Well, Christopher, I guess in time we will know what is to be, won't we?"

"Yes, Hannah, not only does time heal the heart and the mind, but it also gives us rewards and surprises along our lifelong journey."

Christopher gives Hannah a hug, and then walks over to see how Lady Noreen and Rico are doing in the backroom. As he walks over to see them, he sees Lady Noreen with a very unhappy look on her face. The man sitting at her machine is being hand paid $3,000.00. Lady Noreen is ready to blow up at him, as she watches him get his money from the casino slot attendant.

Christopher seeing this immediately walks over to her.

"Christopher, do you believe that man just won on my machine? I am so mad at him! I waited all night to play my machine, and now I can't win on it, because that man just won on it!"

"Lady Noreen, why don't Rico and you come with me to the nickel machines to play?"

"Did you say, nickel machines? No way am I going with you to one of those machines! I am going to wait here until that man gets up and walks away from my machine, Christopher," Lady Noreen replies to him in a fit of anger.

"Rico, do you want to join me where the nickel machines are located over there?" Christopher asks him.

"No thanks, Christopher! I'd better stay here with Lady Noreen. She is really upset!"

"Okay, I'll see both of you at the show around 9:00 p.m. on the second floor," Christopher tells both of them.

With that Christopher walks over to the front of the casino to the nickel machines. As he nears the machines, he sees a young homeless man sitting near a woman playing on two machines.

Next, you see, Bredele in an explosive rage coming over to escort the young twenty-something homeless bum out of the casino.

"Get up, and out of this casino, right now! If you are not going to gamble on the machines here, just leave this casino," Bredele yells directly into the young homeless man's face.

With that, Christopher walks over to the homeless guy in his mid-twenties, who he knows from the Boardwalk as being named Jasper, and says to him, "Jasper, here is some money that you have been waiting for; so you can gamble on your machine."

Hearing his name, Jasper's eyes instantly light up like moonbeams.

"Oh! Christopher! Thank you so much!" Jasper replies.

Christopher gives Jasper $20.00 and Jasper starts playing the casino machine.

Bredele yells at Christopher, "Of course, you would help him. That homeless degenerate, is just like you, isn't he?"

Then, the two security guards and Bredele walk away from Jasper as Christopher sits down beside him, and begins to talk to him.

"Jasper, what is wrong with you?"

"Christopher, I've run out of cocaine, and I just want to sleep. I have no money, and my life is a big, big mess."

"Jasper, please, get some help at one of the local churches or at the mission house. They take in homeless people in. You need to get help if you are going to get back on your feet once again."

"Christopher, I can't go to those places. One, it is too late for me, and secondly, I usually have to be put on a list to get into one of their drug programs. Although those people should see that I am helpless and very much in need in of medical and psychological help."

"Then, where are you going to go, Jasper?"

"I'll just cash out the $20.00 from the machine. Then, I'll leave this casino, and go sleep on one of the benches on the Boardwalk tonight, Christopher."

"Are you sure that you don't want me to help you, Jasper?" Christopher asks him.

"Christopher, at this point in my life, I can't even help myself! So no way can you help me! Just pray for me, Christopher!"

"I'll pray for you, Jasper, but before you leave the casino, you must buy yourself some food to eat with the money that I gave to you earlier."

With that Christopher walks Jasper outside of the casino. Christopher has Jasper buy himself a large pizza and a coke with the $20.00 that he earlier gave to him. Christopher knows if Jasper has any money left in his pocket, he will just go out and spend it on some cocaine or cheap drugs."

Christopher finally gets Jasper settled down on the Boardwalk on a bench with his food. Then Christopher quickly hurries back to the casino.

Promptly at 9 p.m., all of the people who are attending the joint bachelorette and bachelor party are seated for the show on the second floor. Lady Noreen and Patrick have booked a private cabaret show to perform Marcena and Joshua's favorite songs and dance music until 10:30 p.m. tonight.

While the show is going on, waitresses are taking food and beverage orders.

Lady Noreen and Patrick are so happy that everything is turning out so perfect.

Around 10:00 p.m., Teresa Y. shows up at the party to join Rico. Rico is so happy that she is finally at the party with him.

The two of them have become a team lately. Teresa Y. had to work at her family's restaurant tonight; therefore, she wasn't able to get away from her job until late. Marcena wanted Teresa Y. especially to attend their bachelorette/bachelor party.

Finally, at 10:30 p.m., all of the dancers from the cabaret show come out onto the dance floor and escort the wedding party onto the stage to join them in dance. This sets the atmosphere for the remainder of the night as everyone dances to the band's selection of the happy couple's favorite tunes.

At 11:30 p.m., Patrick announces the name of the highest winner from the night's gambling event. It is Rusty. He won $2,500.00 on the "Lucky Horses" casino game.

Hearing his name, Rusty comes over to them, and gets his surprise. It is a complimentary room for three days nights with dinners and shows included from Lady Noreen.

Then, Lady Noreen requests Christopher and the Sarge play a song for Marcena and Joshua that they have both written. The young couple and friends assemble on the dance floor. Next, Hilten Tigress sings the lyrics with her backup singers, the Wildcats; consisting of

Joy Rhapsody, Ngoc, P.J., and Feymale. Orlando's dancers appear on the stage and together as a group they all excite the crowd like always.

Christopher then starts playing his harmonica with the rest of the band consisting of the Sarge, Big Luke, Ogbonna, Winkie, Deuce, and Teresa Y. accompanies all of them on her violin.

Lady Noreen with Patrick call both Marcena and Joshua up to the dance floor as Hilten Tigress begins singing the lyrics to this memorable song written for the two of them.

Emotionally High
Dedicated to Marcena & Joshua

I
You're all man
And you enjoy being a man
With you on my arm of love
All the beauty of life surrounds me
My living showpiece of art
I'll cherish your love forever.

Chorus
So let's get emotionally high
For the very first time
And give falling in love
A second try
Cause I'm a real live woman
Who loves holding your hand
And you're a real live man
Who loves me being by his side
So let's get emotionally high
For the very first time
And give falling in love
A second try
II

Look at me

And see within my very soul
All the secrets that I hide
And all the dreams of love I've searched for
All these lost and lonely years
That I've been deprived
From the gift of love

Chorus
So let's get emotionally high
For the very first time
And give falling in love
A second try
Cause I'm a real live woman
Who loves holding your hand
And you're a real live man
Who loves me being by his side
So let's get emotionally high
For the very first time
And give falling in love
A second try

Then, Hilten Tigress asks everyone to join in with her group and
the band for the third and final verse of Marcena's and Joshua's song.

III
Feel me near
And unite your spirit with mine
To find love's mystic secret
Eternally move
Beyond all time
To a world where hearts can love
And totally find love as one

Chorus
So let's get emotionally high
For the very first time

And give falling in love
A second try
Cause I'm a real live woman
Who loves holding your hand
And you're a real live man
Who loves me being by his side
So let's get emotionally high
For the very first time
And give falling in love
A second try

After the song is over with, Marcena rushes to the microphone and thanks everyone; especially Christopher, Lady Noreen, Rico, Patrick, the Sarge, Orlando's dancers, Hilten Tigress and the Wildcats, the entire band, and all of their loving friends for making this night, a night that neither Joshua or her would ever forget. She knows in her heart that this night was truly a gift to both Joshua and her, from Christopher and Lady Noreen.

Then, Marcena hands the microphone over to Joshua, and he says to his wedding party, "Again, Marcena and I thank all of you for coming here tonight to our joint bachelorette and bachelor party."

At the end of his speech, everyone cheers for the ending of Marcena's and Joshua's special celebration. Then their friends who are staying at the casino go to their rooms, and the rest of their local friends either walk to the parking deck to get their cars to drive home or walk home.

Christopher and Lady Noreen also depart from the casino. They leave Marcena, Joshua, Rico, and Teresa Y. behind at the casino since they are also staying all night with their friends.

Outside in the limousine Brook is waiting to pick up Lady Noreen, Christopher, Patrick and the Sarge. He plans to drop Patrick off at Nicholas's condo since Nicholas is taking care of Russ for him tonight. Then Brook will drive the Sarge to his apartment and then drop Lady Noreen and Christopher off in Ventnor.

As they drive to Lady Noreen's house after dropping off the Sarge, Lady Noreen and Christopher stand up in the limousine and look out of the open sunroof. Out of it, they can smell the ocean's misty air and see the birth of a new full moon.

Christopher and Lady Noreen's are so happy about their dream of happiness for Marcena and Joshua!

Chapter 20

You've Colored My Life

The next week is very hectic with everyone getting ready for the rehearsal dinner and the wedding. Lady Noreen's head is spinning in all different directions as she tries to make everything just perfect for Marcena's and Joshua's wedding.

Finally the Friday date for the rehearsal dinner arrives in December and everyone is getting ready for the big night and Marcena and Joshua are ready for their wedding weekend.

Most of the wedding party is local; so only a few friends of the bride and groom are put up at the casino hotel for the weekend by Lady Noreen.

Since Marcena is an only child, whose parents are deceased, there are very few relatives on her side to invite to the wedding. She has just invited her closest friends at the hospital and Rico, who is like a brother to her. Her family now consists basically of Christopher, Lady Noreen, and Rico.

Joshua's father was killed in Vietnam, when he was a child. His mother died five years ago from complications from a hip replacement. Joshua's sister, Hannah, who lives in New York with her husband, Raul, will be staying as Lady Noreen's guests at a local casino hotel. Besides Joshua's sister, most of his friends are from the casino or live locally in Atlantic City.

The rehearsal for the wedding is planned for 7 p.m. at Lady Noreen's home later tonight. Then, the wedding party at 8 p.m. will be transported to the Lost Empire Restaurant at the C.T. Royal Ocean Mall in Atlantic City for the rehearsal dinner.

Brook is prepared for the day. He has the limos scheduled for 6:30 p.m. to pick up the guests who are staying at the casino hotel. The remainder of the wedding party is to provide their own transportation to Lady Noreen's house.

Patrick and Lady Noreen have gone crazy all day looking after the final wedding details. At this very moment, they are working with the delivery people to set up the white plush folding chairs in Lady Noreen's living room.

Patrick has had the poinsettias delivered, and both Lady Noreen and he have lined the walk-way with red poinsettias, and put white poinsettias in the foyers. They lined the area for the wedding ceremony with red, white, and green candles, plus two sprayed white Christmas trees with white lights and red balls.

Lady Noreen received the delivery of the giant Nativity set earlier in the morning, which Patrick and she set up at the center of the altar area in the living room. They added pink, red, and white poinsettias to that area, where the nativity set is positioned.

Patrick covers the Nativity set and the white Christmas trees with sheets. He wants Marcena and Joshua, plus their wedding party, to be surprised tomorrow on their wedding day to see the spectacular decorations and beauty.

When everyone goes to the rehearsal dinner in the evening, Patrick plans to stay back with Brook, Old Bessie, and Daisy. With them, he is going to make the sign of angels in angel hair carrying scrolls in calligraphy saying, "A Candle Light Evening of Love," in gold and white lettering around it to put in front of the house and small miniature ones to give out as souvenirs at the marriage ceremony.

Everyone is working so hard to make this a storybook wedding for the lovely couple. Most important to Christopher is that Marcena and Joshua understand that they will be taking a sacred vow uniting the two of them tomorrow on their wedding day.

The guys in the band have been practicing the music for the big day during the past two weeks at Lady Noreen's house. The Sarge and Christopher have the music under control and are ready for Marcena's and Joshua's big wedding day ceremony.

S. L. Sharp

Patrick and Lady Noreen have the wedding and bridal gowns upstairs laid out for the girls to change in first thing tomorrow.

Lady Noreen loves the dress that Patrick has designed for Marcena. The elegant dress truly looks like it would top a Hollywood fashion list.

Marcena is at the beauty parlor right now with her bridesmaids getting her hair done for the wedding.

Lady Noreen is going to have Patrick do her hair when they are done setting everything up for the wedding.

Rico is in his bedroom working on a poem to present to Marcena and Joshua at the colored dancing water show on the first floor at the C. T. Royal Ocean Mall after the rehearsal dinner. He is going to have Teresa Y., Christopher and the Sarge, play the background music for him while he presents his poem to them.

Christopher is out on the bench feeding Sanabrio and the other seagulls. At the moment the water is so still. This calmness of the water is unusual during this summer tourist season and the air is also cool and breezy. Today the ocean and sky together are set into a picture in time as one.

"Sanabrio," Christopher says, "I am so glad that Marcena and Joshua are going to get married tomorrow. They both deserve happiness and love in their lives. Like you, my friend, they will have to overcome many challenges and tragedies on their journey throughout their lives. However, with God in their lives, they will be able to overcome these obstacles and survive life's tests."

Christopher then releases his confidant, Sanabrio. When the other seagulls see Sanabrio fly away from Christopher, they follow him and fly toward the ocean with him.

Next, Christopher walks down the Boardwalk and sees Jasper sitting on a Boardwalk bench reading a newspaper. Jasper is still living and sleeping not only on the Boardwalk, but in the library, and in the transportation these days.

"Jasper, what are you up to?" inquires Christopher.

"Christopher, not a whole lot," responds Jasper.

"Jasper, you need to get some professional help, so you can stop living on the Boardwalk," suggests Christopher to Jasper.

"Christopher, I can't! I just am part of the homeless subculture. I can't get out of it. I am a drug addict! I am too far in it. Death is my only way out of all of my problems," explains Jasper to Christopher.

"I really wish you would let me help you, Jasper!" suggests Christopher.

"You are helping me! You are being nice to me. You have to understand, I have chosen my own destiny. I can't reverse the fickle finger of fate now, Christopher," states Jasper to him.

"Well, if I can ever help you; please, ask me. Bye for now," sadly Christopher says to Jasper.

After Christopher is done with his Boardwalk walk, he returns to Ventnor to meet the Sarge, Big Luke, Ogbonna, Winkie Whiskey, and Deuce. He wants to check with them that all the instruments and music details are set in place for the wedding program. Christopher certainly doesn't want any mistakes to happen at the wedding ceremony tomorrow.

By the time Christopher has completed going over everything with the Sarge and the band, it is time for everyone to get ready for the wedding rehearsal and dinner.

Everyone throughout the house is dressing in their suits and dresses for the final rehearsal.

By 6:00 p.m., Lady Noreen has Brook on the phone making sure everyone is getting picked up on time. Then, she goes over her final list of all the details for the night with Patrick. She knows that Patrick is a perfectionist just like she is.

By the time 6:30 p.m. comes around, everyone is at the house ready for the wedding rehearsal to begin. No one can believe the beauty of the decorations throughout the house.

The priest, Father Garrison, arrives and the wedding rehearsal begins.

The priest has the band, the bridesmaids, the matron of honor, the best man, the bride, the groom, and the rest of the wedding party gathered in the living room. He then leads all of them in the practice for tomorrow's wedding ceremony.

The band plays "Pachabel's Cannon," and Lady Noreen, Hannah, Joshua's sister, and Taylor, Marcena's dear friend, walk down the aisle.

The ushers are Rico, Raul, Joshua's sister's husband, and Matthew Roberts, one of Joshua's best friends from the casino.

The priest requests Marcena and Joshua to review their wedding vows. Then he has the wedding party rehearse the service and music with him twice. Finally, the priest has them practice the closing of the service and everyone walks down the aisle to the music of the "Wedding March".

After the priest has completed the rehearsal twice, the time is around 7:45 p.m., and Brook has all of the limousines waiting to take the wedding party, the band, and the priest to the Lost Empire Restaurant.

Once at the C. T. Royal Ocean Mall, everyone takes the elevator up to the restaurant on the second floor. Lady Noreen has booked the entire restaurant for the rehearsal dinner and the restaurant crew is working only for her tonight.

The wedding party and invited guests are escorted to their seats so the waiters and waitresses can take their beverage orders. After the beverages are brought to the table, Christopher proposes a toast to the wedding couple-to-be by saying, "To tomorrow's bride and groom. Everyone here wishes you all the happiness, love, and joy possible in your lives together as husband and wife."

Then, Lady Noreen stands up and says, "This day of joy has brought me a memory of something I never dreamt of in my life. May both of you live a long life together as husband and wife. I love you both!"

Next, everyone's dinner orders are taken at the tables. The selections of food on the menu look delicious. Lady Noreen tells everyone to order anything that they wish to eat on the menu. She says to all of them, "Dine like it was your last supper!"

After the food is served, Lady Noreen has hired a show of Asian dancers and actors to perform for everyone at the rehearsal dinner.

The show goes on until 10:30 p.m., at that time the wedding party and guests are asked to take the elevator down to the first floor's dancing water show of colors for the final event of the night.

Finally everyone is there and the dancing water show in colors begins. The Sarge, Christopher, Teresa Y. and Rico go where the microphone is located in the area of the show so Rico can use it.

Once Rico finds his spot, he nervously takes the microphone and speaks into it, "I want everyone here to remember this night. Marcena has been like a sister to me since I have no family. Without her, at times, I don't know if I would have survived in this world. Tonight is one of the happiest nights in my life. I know that Marcena is marrying Joshua, and that all of her dreams will come true. Marcena and Joshua, this is the poem that I have written for the two of you. God bless both of you always in your marriage!"

YOU'VE COLORED MY LIFE
Dedicated to Marcena and Joshua

You've colored my smile,
with the color of bight passionate pink.

You've colored my eyes,
with the stars, the moon, the sun, the sky, and the earth.
In the colors of lily pearl white, dandelion lemon
yellow, scarlet rose red, heavenly light blue,
and emerald pure green.

You've colored my heart,
with the colors of flaming fire red, fragrant deep
violet, lilac-purple lavender, and brilliant reddish
fuchsia. Then you filled my heart with true
love and endless passion.

You've colored my soul,
with the colors of unblended red burgundy, satiny
lustrous yellow, radiant sunset red, royal purplish
blue, and clear greenish-blue aqua.

You've colored my life,
with all the hues, pastels, and brilliant shades
of all my deep emotional feelings and secret desires.

Like the colors of the rainbow, I feel every degree
of your love to its fullest intensity.

You as the artist, painted my whole being on the
canvas of life giving me an inner perspective
of my true inner nature.

You've colored my life,
and changed it into a living masterpiece.

After the poem, the dancing water show of colors, and the musical
selection is completed, everyone claps and says good night to one
another.

Marcena and Joshua give Rico a big hug, and thank him for his
beautiful poem.

Then everyone goes to meet Brook at the street level entrance. He
has the limos waiting there to take everyone to Lady Noreen's house
or to the casino hotel.

When Lady Noreen, Christopher, Marcena, and Rico arrive home,
Patrick has all the decorations draped off so that Marcena can't see
what Old Bessie, Daisy, Brook and he have done all evening to prepare
for tomorrow's wedding. He wants it to be a big surprise for everyone
including Lady Noreen and Christopher.

Lady Noreen wants to take the drapes off of everything to take a
peek at what he has done, but Christopher won't allow her to do so.
He wants Patrick's surprise to be for everyone tomorrow.

Lady Noreen finally gives up and says to Christopher, "God won't
let me die, Christopher. He just wants you to torture me to death."

Christopher just laughs at her and replies, "Lady Noreen, you
don't know it, but I am a blessing in disguise to you. I was put on
this earth to make your life happy and full of love. Good night, Lady
Noreen!"

Lady Noreen stomps off to her bedroom with Tigress trailing after
her saying not one word back to him.

Chapter 21

The Promise Between Two Hearts

By 11 a.m. of the next morning, Lady Noreen has almost been up half of the day having Patrick, Sarge, and Christopher carrying things to the dining room and to the extended enclosed porch. Lady Noreen and Patrick want all of the four serving buffet sites set-up before the caterers arrive in the early afternoon.

Christopher, Patrick, and the Sarge have to also carry a few pieces of furniture from the den and bedroom upstairs that weren't taken up there earlier yesterday to allow more room in the den and bedroom for the buffet serving centers.

Then, Lady Noreen and Patrick go over the to-do list for today to make sure everything is just perfect for the wedding.

Christopher calls everyone in the band to make sure they all have their white tuxedos for the wedding tonight. He then goes outside to make sure that all the white electrical lights that Lady Noreen has put around the house are turned on and all the candle decorations are lit in front of the entry steps to the house.

Lady Noreen also has a beautiful calligraphy sign written in gold and white lettering with angels around it saying, "A Candle Light Evening of Love," in front of the entry door of her house.

At noontime, Lady Noreen fixes a small brunch for everyone consisting of different types of sandwiches, a fruit salad, and chips with assorted drinks. She feeds Marcena, Rico, Christopher, Sarge, and Patrick in the kitchen to nourish them for their big day ahead of them.

Everyone in their own way starts to prepare for the day as the final touches are being made for the wedding ceremony.

The flowers start arriving, and Patrick starts getting them ready for the ushers, the bridesmaids, the band members, Old Bessie, Daisy, Mama Cane, and Christopher.

Patrick now has all of the drapes and blankets that covered the wedding decorations removed.

The food starts arriving for the reception around 3:30 p.m., and the caterers start to get everything ready for the reception. Patrick and Lady Noreen check off the list of all the foods that they have ordered for the wedding celebration.

By 4 o'clock the bridesmaids begin arriving to help Marcena get ready for her exciting day.

It is at that time when Lady Noreen and Patrick uncover Marcena's luminous white wedding dress. Everyone is in disbelief of how beautiful the bridal dress is and the length of the train. Then, Lady Noreen hands Marcena her wedding veil that she had saved for her deceased son's future bride to wear on her wedding day.

The ushers, the band members, Daisy, Old Bessie, Mama Cane and her foster children slowly begin arriving at Lady Noreen's house.

By 5 o'clock, everyone has arrived for the wedding ceremony including Father Garrison. The band, the wedding party, Old Bessie, Daisy, Mama Cane, and Patrick are ready for the wedding to start as the music begins promptly at 5:30 p.m. in the living room. The guests are being ushered to their seats, and the band starts to play, "Silent Night".

Frantically, Lady Noreen leads the bridesmaids down the stairs to get ready to walk down the aisle. Once to the bottom of the stairs the music of "Pachabel's Cannon" begins. You can see, Lady Noreen with a glamorous smile on her face as she begins to walk down the aisle. Then, Hannah, and Taylor follow her down the aisle one by one.

At the altar area arranged in the front of the living room, Joshua, Rico, and Raul are already in place. Joshua can't believe how beautiful Marcena looks in her wedding dress.

Finally, Christopher offers Marcena his arm, and he proudly escorts her down the aisle to join Joshua and the wedding party.

She can't believe her eyes as she looks around the room and sees the magical kingdom of heaven that Patrick and Lady Noreen have created for her wedding.

As they reach the altar area, Christopher lets go of her arm and whispers in her ear, "This is your blessed day, Marcena. I love you!"

Next, the priest begins the religious ceremony, and then Hilten sings the song, "Ave Maria," and is accompanied by Christopher on his harmonica. After the song, Marcena and Joshua light the two candles in front of the Nativity set. Then, Holy Communion is given to all who choose to participate, as Sarge accompanies Teresa Y. and Winkie in playing, "Oh, Holy Night".

Finally, the priest proceeds in the ceremony with the exchange of the wedding vows between Marcena and Joshua.

Rico is thrilled to death as he hands Joshua Marcena's wedding ring.

Lady Noreen is scared to death when it is her turn to hand Marcena, Joshua's ring, but she hands it to her and everything is on cue.

Lady Noreen looks at Christopher with a great sigh of relief.

Christopher winks at her to give her the confidence that everything will be all right.

After the vows have been exchanged between Marcena and Joshua the priest says in the final moment of their ceremony to the wedding audience, "The promise between two hearts can never be unlocked by temptation, by infidelity, by deceit, or wicked deeds. The promise between your two hearts can stand the test in time, in truth, in romance, and in passion. From now until death, from now thru eternity, let your own words echo in the wind of your love, in patience, in understanding, and in truth to one another. May the two of you be each other's eternal soul mates throughout all the years you live together upon this earth. May the love in your hearts that you feel today and your vows last forever. May you both love each other not only now, but in death, and throughout eternity. I now pronounce you husband and wife. It is my honor to introduce Mr. and Mrs. Joshua McBriden to all of you who are here today with us."

Everyone claps and the bands starts playing the "Wedding March," as Marcena and Joshua walk down the aisle to the music as husband and wife.

Then Hilten with Joy Rhapsody, Ngoc, P.J., and Feymale sing the song, "What Child Is This?" as the ushers escort the rest of the friends, family, and loved ones to the reception area of the house in the dining room.

The band moves all of its instruments to the outside enclosed porch so they can begin to play other wedding reception music selections.

After everyone is greeted in the wedding party and escorted into the dining room, the wedding guests are escorted to the different buffet stations by the caterers and given a selection of the following: Italian food, steak, Chinese food, or several different kinds of fish. Then, the guests can go to other stations and choose from different vegetables, potatoes or rice, different salads, and rolls. Beverages and drinks are ordered at the tables. The four serving sites for the buffet of foods turn out to be a huge success with all of the guests. The food is scrumptious and really delicious.

As the evening goes by, Rico gives a toast given to Mr. and Mrs. Joshua McBriden and says, "May this be the first day of a joyous union between the two of you. May your married lives as husband and wife be filled with lots of love and many happy moments for both of you, and remember to never take God out of your lives. Congratulations!"

Everyone toasts to the happily wed new couple. You hear cheers all around the room.

Next, Christopher makes a toast to Marcena and Joshua by saying, "Lady Noreen and I are so overjoyed for the both of you today. May God bless and keep you, and always remember Mr. and Mrs. McBriden that -

Love is Magical!
Love is mystical as a winter's day
snow covered, but reflecting –
radiant life...

> Love is a consistent shooting beam of light-
> replenished by the unknown-
> universe...
>
> Love is deviate like an unsettled brook's path-
> silent in thought, but always-
> transmitting...
>
> Love is a shooting star in a diamond studded sky-
> You can't capture love
> Because-it's magical..."

After everyone has eaten their gourmet dinner, they are escorted to the enclosed porch. There the band is playing holiday songs, and a mixture of music that Marcena and Joshua have chosen for the evening.

Finally, the wedding party is introduced, and the wedding party starts dancing.

Lady Noreen looks so happy. She is having a marvelous time on the dance floor with Christopher, Marcena, Rico, and Joshua. It is like she has turned back the clock of time in her life to when she was a young mother, married and so happy. Now, she is happily reliving a new set of memories with different people in her life.

As the night goes on into the evening hours everyone is having a great time. Everyone who has been a part of the dream since Christopher met Lady Noreen are all there having a beautiful time. Neither money nor class separates anyone of them. They are all joined together by Christopher's belief that people can live, work, and enjoy one another as equals. It is like all of them are part of Christopher's family. He loves each of them so very much, and he judges no one.

Like Mama Cane says, "It is like we are all part of his biblical tribe. Only in the Bible were there men like Christopher, who were created to carry out God's plan. Through the wisdom of those few heroic leaders, God's world was saved. Christopher is like one of those leaders who had great insight."

Finally, it is time for Brook to take the lovely couple to the airport to fly off to Bermuda. As the married couple gets ready to depart with Brook, Marcena goes to the microphone and happily says, "I want to thank everyone here for making my marriage a storybook wedding. Never did I think that I would have a day like this in my life to remember always. Since the loss of my parents, I have had no family to love in my life, but Rico. Now I have it all! I especially want to thank Joshua, Lady Noreen, Christopher, Rico, Teresa Y., Patrick, Sarge, everyone in my bridal party, Brook, Mama Cane, Old Bessie, Daisy, Hilten, everyone in the band, Mr. Marcuso, Nicholas, Russ, and all the rest of my loved ones for this magical moment. Thank you from the bottom of both Joshua's and my heart for this wedding day celebration."

Then, Marcena and Joshua have Brook help them to the limo as everyone throws bird feed at them. Their family and loved ones say their farewells, and off to the airport Mr. and Mrs. McBriden go.

Everyone then starts to gather their belongings and say their good nights to Lady Noreen and Christopher. As the wedding guests depart, they can't believe how beautiful the outside decorations are in front of Lady Noreen's house. Many of the guests are taking photographs of both the inside and outside decorations for keepsake. Everyone admits it was a cherished moment which none of them would ever forget as they hold their angel hair souvenir gift.

Christopher after all of this, takes Lady Noreen and Tigress outside for one more look at the decorations before Christopher turns the lights off in the house for the night. In the brisk air of a chilly breeze, Lady Noreen and Christopher take one last look at the mystical decorations.

Lady Noreen knows she will have happy dreams tonight for this was one dream she never thought in the world that she would experience in her lifetime. With a smile on her face, she walks arm and arm back into the house with Christopher to put the evening to sleep.

Chapter 22

I Really Don't Know

January brings so much laughter and happiness to Lady Noreen's house with Marcena's and Joshua's happy return from Bermuda as husband and wife, and with her daily workouts for the Valentine's 5K Race in Atlantic City with Rico.

Lady Noreen is overjoyed that her entire family will be with her tonight, December 31st, at the casino to bring in a new year. In fact, she can hardly wait to get there with her family!

Christopher has bought a new suit for the big New Year's Eve celebration. He is so glad to see Marcena and Joshua so happy.

Lady Noreen, like always, has made all of the plans for tonight. Everyone will eat dinner together on the sixth floor at the casino around 7 p.m. at the Sir Knight of Chivalry Restaurant. Then, they will go to the New Year's Show of 2012's Best Entertainment. At 11 p.m. the show will be over with, and everyone can go gamble on the floor. Everyone can gamble, including Joshua, since he has quit his job at the casino and is now working for Nicholas in one of his businesses as a distributor.

Rico is so excited about his relationship with Teresa Y. and his wheelchair race coming up real soon. Like Marcena, he never thought that he would ever find anyone to share his life with either.

The day goes fast with Lady Noreen making her list like always and cleaning everything if not once, twice. Lady Noreen is a true perfectionist!

Once Lady Noreen is done with her daily work, she enjoys working out with Rico for their upcoming race in February. They love preparing for their races together every so many months.

After Christopher does his daily chores for Lady Noreen, he takes his daily walk down the Boardwalk. As he gets past Ventnor, he sees Jasper. The Boardwalk police are telling him to get out of the trash can. He is eating food right out of the trash cans these days.

Jasper yells out at police, "Leave me alone, I'll eat garbage, if I want to eat garbage. I love garbage. Just leave me alone, and mind your own business!"

Before long, Sergeant Leon Mussack shows up, and tells Jasper, "Stop eating the garbage out of the can right now!"

Jasper in defiance just laughs at him and continues to sort through the trash can to look for food in it to eat.

Finally, Christopher comes to Jasper's rescue, and says to him, "Jasper, just calm yourself down! If you like garbage food that much, grab it! Then, walk down the Boardwalk steps with me and eat it!"

Sergeant Mussack asks Christopher, "Is Jasper with you?"

"Yes, Sergeant, he is with me!" Christopher answers as he nods his head.

"Okay, then Jasper is all yours, Christopher."

"Thanks, Sergeant Mussack! Bye for now," Christopher quickly replies to Sergeant Mussack.

Jasper walks over to Christopher carrying all of his garbage food and continues eating it on the Boardwalk steps in front of Christopher. Jasper seems to be there mentally less and less there these days!

"Jasper, why don't you let me help you?" pleads Christopher.

"Christopher, my days for help are gone! My life didn't play out like I planned it to and here I am. I owe no one anything! I have no bills, no wants, nothing…"

"But Jasper there is still time left in your life to live."

"Christopher, at the rate my life is going, it will be over if not today real soon."

"I don't want to hear that from you!" sharply responds Christopher to Jasper.

"You did hear that from me, Christopher!" states Jasper to him in a loud defiant voice.

"What do you want out of your life?" Christopher asks him.

"Nothing!" hollers Jasper.

"Is it the drugs that have done this to you, Jasper?"

"It is the drugs! No family! No money! No place to live! No clothes! In the old days, I would have died in a mental institution. In today's days, no one cares about me. I don't even care about myself!" philosophically remarks Jasper to Christopher.

"Why don't you let me put you in a rehab center in Atlantic City?" firmly Christopher replies to him.

"Thanks, Christopher, but most of them don't work for me. Once you are on drugs like I am, that is it!" admits Jasper.

"Did you ever want to be anything in your life, Jasper?"

"Yeah, at one time, I wanted to be a writer, Christopher."

"Well, you still can be a writer, but you will have to write about the streets. Maybe you can help someone out there since you don't want any help yourself," remarks Christopher to him.

"Christopher, I can't even spell."

"That is okay, just write something, Jasper, and I'll have a book company edit it. I want you back. I don't want to lose you!" Christopher begins to bargain with Jasper.

"You'd do that for me, Christopher?"

"Walk over to the store with me and I'll buy you some tablets and pens. If you want to be a writer, you still can be one, Jasper."

The two of them walk over to the store and Christopher buys Jasper some supplies, plus a pair of gloves, and a heavy sweatshirt.

"Christopher, maybe since I eat garbage, I can write about garbage. I won't promise you anything, but thanks for looking out after me today!"

With that Christopher leaves Jasper in front of the store with his purchases from it and continues his walk knowing in his heart that drugs are killing more of America's children and people than the war. He also knows that for Jasper, and so many others, often their fate from taking drugs is death. Even so, Christopher still won't give up on Jasper.

Christopher then goes off to find his friend, Arthur, at the Breakfast & Lunch Grill. He hasn't seen him since the wedding, and he wants to visit with him.

"Arthur, I finally get to see you. What are you up to these days?" excitedly asks Christopher.

"Things are slow today, so I am getting ready to feed the cats and kittens underneath the Boardwalk. Do you, Christopher, want to help me carry the food in the big tins for me?"

"Sure! I wish, Lady Noreen, knew you were doing this, Arthur. She would be right here with you! But she probably would leave Tigress home. She pampers that cat like it is a real baby. She even buys it clothes!"

"Well, tell Lady Noreen, that I feed the cats and their kittens once a month. I feel so sorry for them. I don't know what is worse, not caring for people or not caring about animals. Which one do you think is the worse, Christopher?"

"I think they are tied!" remarks Christopher.

The two men take several tins of cat food out and put it under the Boardwalk. The cats and kittens run real fast to eat their cat food. Christopher can't believe his eyes; there are so many stray cats and kittens underneath the Boardwalk.

"Arthur, it is so nice of you to feed them. Why do you do it?" Christopher in interest asks him.

"I decided this year instead of asking for a Christmas present from my wife and kids, I would ask for cat and kitten food because I wanted to do something to make this world a better place."

"That is great! I wish more people would do that at Christmas time. They say that people, only use 20% of what they have. Therefore, Arthur, people have too many things in their lives and not enough substance to better their world. Maybe less is more and more is less."

"By the way, Christopher, how was your Christmas?"

"It was great, Arthur!"

"Lady Noreen never celebrated Christmas since her loved ones died. This year; however, she left all the decorations up from Marcena and Joshua's wedding and bought presents for all of us including Teresa Y., and all of her neighbors. She even made breakfast for not only all of us, but her neighbors and their children, too. I thought no one would come to the breakfast, but everyone on her street in Ventnor came. The brunch was a great success and everyone who participated in it, went home after the brunch happy and in the Christmas spirit."

"What did Lady Noreen give to you and the kids, Christopher?"

"She gave me a telescope, some furniture to Marcena and Joshua for their apartment, a video camera to Rico so he could tape his races, and a new case for Teresa Y.'s a violin."

"Wow! What did you give Lady Noreen?"

"That was hard, Arthur. The kids and I thought and thought about what to give her. Finally, Marcena said that we should give her a mother's ring with all of the children's stones in it. So that is what we bought her. Lady Noreen loved the gift so much, that she cried whenever she looked at her ring on Christmas Day. Of course, she was very happy with her present and loved it so very, very much."

"I am so glad she is happy once again in her life, Christopher. She is a beautiful person. Are you going to marry her one day?" reluctantly Arthur asks Christopher.

"You never know!" jokingly Christopher answers his friend.

"Isn't it strange, Christopher, how Christmas can change your life? By either you receiving a gift or giving a gift to another person. I guess that is what the miracle of Christmas is all about."

"Yes, Arthur, just knowing that the gift of Christ was the greatest miracle upon this earth is the greatest present to all of us."

"Again, thanks, Christopher for helping me. Don't forget to tell Lady Noreen about my cat project," Arthur reminds Christopher.

"I won't! I better start finishing my walk, so I can get back in time to feed the seagulls. Then I have to get dressed up, for Lady Noreen has us all going to the casino tonight. Bye for now, Arthur."

Christopher continues his walk and walks the whole length of the Boardwalk to the end of the casinos. On his way back, he walks on the beach to Ventnor. As he gets to Ventnor, he sees a woman in her early 30's with another woman about the same age getting ready to fall down the steps from the Boardwalk to the beach. Christopher tries to get to the woman before she falls down, but he is too late. He looks at the woman's friend and says to her, "Should I call an ambulance?"

The friend looks at both Christopher, and the other woman who has fallen down and says, "NO!"

Christopher feels that the woman needs help, but he also realizes that you can't help someone who doesn't want to help themselves. So he looked at both of them and says, "God bless you both and I hope everything turns out all right for the both of you." Even though in the back of Christopher's mind, he feels that the woman needs to get off of drinking alcohol and get medical treatment for her problem.

Finally, as it gets later in the afternoon, Christopher makes it back to feed his seagulls. As always, Sanabrio sits on his shoulder to be fed.

As Christopher feeds all of the seagulls, he talks to his beloved friend, Sanabrio. "I had a vision last night that I could only choose one of my children to win at the casino tonight. If I don't, Sanabrio, I will no longer be an angel. As you know, my sainthood was taken away from me a long, long time ago. Now, I don't know if I should choose Marcena, or if I should choose Rico. This is the year that I either have to obey God, or pay the consequences for my disobedience. Oh, Sanabrio, let's hope I make the right decision."

Christopher finally leaves Sanabrio, and slowly walks into Lady Noreen's house in a solemn mood, and goes to his room to get ready for the big New Year's celebration.

Lady Noreen like usual had Patrick make her a dress for this evening's social occasion. The dress that Patrick designed for Lady Noreen is done in a gold tinted shade. Lady Noreen has bought all of her accessories to match the color of her dress.

By the time Christopher finishes getting ready for the New Year's Eve celebration, it is 6:30 p.m., and it is time for Brook to pick up Lady Noreen, Rico, Teresa Y., and himself. Brook is going to have another limo driver pick up Marcena and Joshua this evening.

Brook is soon at the house and everyone gets into the limo. Lady Noreen is all wired up for the big night. She had asked Brook and his father to join them this evening, but Brook told her that his father would rather watch the New Year's Eve celebration on TV. As for himself, he would rather pass on Lady Noreen's invitation and just pick everyone up at 2 a.m. on New Year's Day.

Everyone meets up at the casino for the big celebration. Once inside the casino, they all take the elevator to the sixth floor to the Knight of Chivalry Restaurant. Once there they are all taken to a table which Lady Noreen has reserved for them. Fine wines and beverages, are brought to their table for everyone to sample or order. All of their orders are taken and off to the salad bar everyone goes.

Christopher says a prayer before dinner. He says, "May God's will be done on earth as it is in heaven. Thank you for this day and all of our days upon the earth. May we all honor You by doing more for You in our lives blessed Father. Bless our family and all of the families of the world, and may peace one day come between America and Iraq, Iran, and Afghanistan. Amen!"

Once Christopher is done with his prayer everyone eats together and enjoys each other's company. The gourmet food and the exotic drinks are incredible. Like usual, Lady Noreen has made it a spectacular night for all of them.

After dinner everyone walks across the hall to get ready to see the New Year's Show of the 2012 Best Entertainment at the casino. At the show everyone is escorted to their front row seats. The Broadway hits are performed with professional singers, dancers, and mime performers. It is a sensational show and everyone enjoys the entertainment. The show mesmerizes the entire audience.

Once the show is over at 11:00 p.m., the whole family goes downstairs to get their New Year's Eve hats and noise makers. Lady Noreen is having the time of her life. She loves the food, the entertainment, the excitement, and most of all, her family.

By 11:30 p.m., everyone is situated at their machines. The machine in the back has the biggest jackpot in the casino. It is up to a jackpot of five million dollars. Lady Noreen wants to play in that row of machines. It is hard to get a seat at the slots there since the casino is so overcrowded tonight. However, Lady Noreen, Marcena, and Rico finally do get a seat in that area. Everyone else just cheers them on as they play to win the big casino jackpot.

As it gets closer to midnight, the excitement on all of the machines intensifies. Everyone thinks they will win a little something on the machine, but not the jackpot for five million dollars.

S. L. Sharp

So far, Rico is the highest one at four hundred and twenty dollars on the "Gold Nugget Shower," which is a one dollar game. Second, is Marcena at three hundred and fifty dollars, and Lady Noreen has one hundred and eighty dollars total on her slot machine right now. The rest of the eleven players at the same game machines are losing their money left and right and new people are taking their seats. At 11:50 p.m., Christopher goes in back of Rico and Marcena since they are sitting right next to each other. Christopher nervously goes back and forth putting his hand on Rico's shoulder, then on Marcena's shoulder. Lady Noreen looks at him like he is crazy man.

Bredele who is watching Christopher from the side of the casino is making fun of him by mimicking the same gestures that Christopher is making right now to other employees around him.

At 11:55 p.m., Bredele thinks he will walk over to Christopher and harass him.

Christopher seeing Bredele walking over to where he is standing just keeps his focus on his wristwatch and Marcena and Rico.

When Bredele approaches him, Christopher tries to ignore him. However, when Bredele doesn't let up trying to provoke him, Christopher finally reacts to him.

He looks Bredele right in the eyes, and says to him, "You are a living jackass, Bredele! Until you start saying nice things about people and doing good deeds for them, you'll just stay an idiotic jackass!" Then, Christopher looks back at Marcena and Rico, it is 11:59 p.m., and the minute hand is slowly turning. Christopher is still going back and forth with his hand motions. Perspiration is slowly pouring off his brow and upper lip.

The clock finally hits midnight and Christopher puts his hands on both Marcena's and Rico's shoulders. Immediately after that the bells go off on the two slot machines, the lights go on, and both of Marcena's and Rico's slot machines have won the five million dollar jackpot. Both of them! No one can believe it!

Everyone is singing and wishing each other a Happy New Year throughout the casino! Loved ones are kissing one another and making toasts to the new year of 2013.

Bredele runs over to both of them and says, "This can't be! There must be a malfunction or something wrong with these two slot machines!"

People are lining up in back of Marcena and Rico, congratulating them, screaming out of joy for both of them, and just looking at the lights going off on their winning machines.

Bredele comes over to Christopher and says, "What have you done? I hate your guts."

Just as Bredele says that to Christopher, he starts talking like a jackass. After everything bad he says, "Hee... haw...!"

The people surrounding Bredele start to laugh at him, and make fun of him.

Bredele doesn't know what to do. Every time he talks, the hee... haw... sound keeps blaring louder and clear out of his mouth. He can't stop talking like a jackass.

He looks directly at Christopher, and Christopher looks the opposite way from him.

Soon the security guards and slot attendants come down to the floor baffled, and get both Rico's and Marcena's identification cards. Marcena has a driver's license and Rico has an identification card since he doesn't drive a car.

No one can believe that there have been two big winners at the slots for five million dollars tonight on New Year's. Even the management is in disbelief. They can't figure out how this ever happened at midnight.

Bredele tries to get someone to listen to him. He wants to tell someone that Christopher has put a curse on him, but everyone just ignores him. No one has ever liked Bredele, and now they all think he is just plain crazy since he is talking like the jackass he really is.

Christopher and Lady Noreen are so happy for Marcena and Rico. Lady Noreen for the first time is happy for the both of them. She doesn't even gripe that she didn't win tonight.

Joshua hugs his wife and is wild in excitement saying, "Holy cow, I can't believe you've won! I just can't believe you've won the jackpot, and we are rich!"

Teresa Y. gives Rico a big kiss, and just keeps hugging him. Never did she think that Rico would win five million dollars.

Finally, the slot attendants and the security guards bring Marcena and Rico their checks. The casino staff takes their pictures. Then the beverage waitresses bring all of them drinks.

After all the excitement, Lady Noreen tips everyone and asks the security guards to escort all of them to her limo after she calls Brook to come to the casino to pick them all up.

As all of them get ready to leave the backroom, Bredele comes up to Christopher saying, "Please undo what you have done to me! I know you did this to me! Hee... Haw...!"

"Sorry, Bredele, as of midnight, I gave up my angel powers so I can't change your destiny. Now, I am still an angel, but an angel who cannot reverse his powers. I still have the power to change people's lives, but not to change the hard lessons that they must learn just for themselves! You use your mouth as a weapon to destroy other people. Now, your mouth has turned on you, and you have destroyed your own freedom of speech."

"I beg of you, Christopher. Please change me back to the way I used to be! Hee... Haw...!" Bredele speaks out in a loud rude laugh.

"Bredele, the way you were, will no longer be. I have to pass my powers on to somebody in the upcoming months. At that time, and only at that time, can you be transformed through, whomever I choose to take my place on this earth as an angel. The best thing you can do right now is not talk!"

"If I become a better person will you change me back to normal? Hee... Haw...!"

"It isn't my call, Bredele. The best thing is for you to become a nice person. One who doesn't hurt people! Then, when I choose the next person to do my job, they might change you back to the new person who you must become. However, it is only if they know your heart is pure and good. Never ask me again to change you back to who you once were ever again, Bredele. If you do, you will never be changed back into your new self."

"Okay...hee...haw!" spontaneously blurts out Bredele.

Lady Noreen and Christopher then take Marcena, Joshua, Rico, and Teresa Y. all back to Ventnor. Lady Noreen even hires some of the off duty security guards to guard her house outside for the night in fear someone might plot to rob everyone in it.

On the way home, Lady Noreen talks to Marcena and Rico.

"First, I'll get my accountant Melvin Swartz to do all of your financial planning for both of you. Marcena and Joshua, why don't you stay with us until you decide what you want to do with all of your money? I don't want you anywhere without cameras, and security system," nervously Lady Noreen whispers to both of them.

"Great ideas, Lady Noreen," Marcena says to her.

"Rico and Marcena, decide what you want to do with your money. Maybe you'll both want to start a non-profit. Marcena, you might want to establish your own abuse group or educational program, and Rico, maybe you'll want to do something for people in wheelchair racing. Those two areas are where both of your passions generate," states Lady Noreen to both Marcena and Rico.

When home, everybody goes inside the house, but Christopher. He walks out onto the beach by himself. Once out there Christopher looks to the heavens and says, "Have I done enough God? I ask you, Lord, this question each and every day of my life. I really don't know if I have. Other times, it seems like, no, I haven't done enough. For the very first time in my life, I really don't know the right answer to this question that I am asking you. All I really do know is that, I love you, God, with all of my heart, and I must commit to serve you, Heavenly Father, more each day of my life now that I am a man. So, when my earthly existence ends, I will know the real answer to my question. Now, for the first time in my life, I'm not an angel, I'm not a saint, I'm just a man. I am so sorry that I couldn't choose just one of my children to win tonight. I love them both so much, Lord, that I chose both of them, Most people would have probably chosen their son, however, I feel girls are just as important in life as sons. Therefore, God I chose both of them. I will choose my successor to be an angel on September 13th of this year. I really don't know who I am going to choose at the present. This time, I will choose just one person to be an angel not two. This won't be as complicated as tonight's decision was for me to make. Until I leave my angel position, I will continue to make people on this earth happy and lead them to a better quality of life in Your world."

As Christopher starts to walk slowly back to Lady Noreen's house, the seagulls start to swarm all around him. Sanabrio lands on his shoulder for a moment and then disappears into the heavens. It makes Christopher feel good to think that his best friend, Sanabrio, is still there for him.

When Christopher opens the door and enters the house in Ventnor, he hears laughter and talks about dreams coming true, and doing good services for others. He knows in his heart that he has done the right thing. He knows, no matter if it was the right or wrong decision, it was the right decision that he made at the casino tonight. With that Christopher joins up with his family for the rest of the evening. They have a family toast of champagne to bring in New Year's Day. Then off to bed Christopher goes, as Marcena and Rico continue to come up with ideas with Lady Noreen on how to plan their lives ahead of them with Melvin Swartz the financial planner in the next few days.

Chapter 23

The Cupid Of Love 5K/Wheelchair Race For Children

By the time the Cupid of Love 5K and Wheelchair Races get here in February before Valentine's Day, great things have begun to happen for the children. Marcena and Joshua have purchased a house two streets from Lady Noreen's residence. Marcena is continuing to support the Women's Abuse Program at the hospital and she is helping women to start career classes in interests of their choice.

Joshua is getting ready to establish his own lawn service/snow removal business. Plus from his home and on the web, establish a garden design and landscaping service. Joshua always wanted to do this, but never had the money to start his own business.

Rico, with his money has started a non-profit to help provide information to people in wheelchairs that want to be in races. Also, through his non-profit, he will provide a service to pick up participants for races with a handicap accessible van. He always dreamt that he would be able to help and encourage other men and other women to participate in these self-gratifying events.

Today the Cupid of Love 5K Race and Wheelchair Event has been sponsored by the local organizations to help Julie Riley with her team mission to support children. All of the money collected from the race today will go to a fund to help children with Desmoid tumors.

Julie personally experienced having a Desmoid tumor, comprised of abnormal cells, much like cancer cells, with the potential to grow and invade any part of the body and have a high rate of recurrence.

Doctors and scientists have limited knowledge about these types of tumors.

Lady Noreen, Rico, Christopher, Lady Noreen's neighbors, many of the doctors, nurses, and lab technicians from Marcena's hospital, Joshua, Christopher, Julie's husband, her mother, and all of Christopher's friends, Desmoid tumor survivors, and Rico's friends in wheelchairs are participating in this race. Everyone, plus people in running clubs, from the casinos, from the tri-state area, all want to help these young people overcome their obstacles through research. Atlantic City today is filled with hundreds upon hundreds of people to support this race. Lady Noreen is so honored to be a part of this 5K race with Rico. Marcena was supposed to be in the race, but she hasn't been feeling well for the last few days.

The excitement in Atlantic City is very exciting and contagious today. The race volunteers are handing out numbers and t-shirts left and right to the running/wheelchair participants in the 5K Cupid Love Race. The runners have already started to do their stretching exercises and warm-ups in preparation for their run in the running course area.

As Christopher runs aside Lady Noreen, he sees several people who he knows in the wheelchair race with Rico. He sees Grandpa Bill, Elijah, Laurel, Elliot, Harvey and Cora. As they get closer to the starting line, Teresa Y., her family, Hilten, Orlando, Brook, his father, and Nicholas are all standing at the side of the starting area to cheer everyone on.

Lady Noreen looks for Marcena to see if she is there, but doesn't see her. She is a little worried about her because Marcena is never sick even though Joshua told Lady Noreen that she wasn't seriously ill. Joshua said that Marcena just had an upset stomach.

The wheelchair racers all line up for their race on their race course. Rico is in top physical condition and is ready for his race as he lines up.

Christopher soon sees Patrick with Russ. Today Russ is ready to roll. Russ's health condition has improved since he has been eating right and exercising almost every day. His condition is still in remission.

Patrick is going to run with Lady Noreen and Christopher. As they wait for everyone to line up to get ready to begin their running course in the 5K, Big Luke, and Sarge line up next to Christopher.

Christopher sponsored Jasper to run in this race, but Old Bessie said that she hadn't seen Jasper all week. Christopher didn't know if that was good news or bad news.

Old Bessie was now living in Lady Noreen's house. She was now Lady Noreen's scheduler. Although, Old Bessie still sat out on the chairs on the Boardwalk every so often. After all these years, it was part of her life.

Soon, the mayor of Atlantic City is called to the microphone to start the race. Once the gun is fired, Julie runs in the race with her husband, Bruce. Her mother watches their children as they race together in the 5K.

The races have finally started, and thank heavens it is a cool day. The weather gives everyone an extra dose of energy.

The participants are running or participating for a good reason - to help others. Christopher felt that more charity events like this should be done across America to help the American people. He believes that charity should begin at home.

Before too long, Big Luke, takes the lead. He is now in great condition not only physically but mentally. Running next to him are Julie, Bruce, and Joshua.

Suddenly, Lady Noreen falls back in the race. Christopher stays by her side as she slows down her running pace. Lady Noreen is in excellent physical condition, but a lot of these racers are a lot younger than she. As they race throughout the city, people from all walks of life are volunteering to give the runners water.

As the miles go by, Lady Noreen and Christopher see Sergeant Leon Mussack with Delilah and his family at the halfway mark cheering them on. As they pass by him, he has Delilah wave to them.

Russ in his wheelchair is now physically conditioned to do the course of the race by himself.

Once to the final mile of the race, Winkie Whiskey Scullen passes by Christopher and Lady Noreen really, really fast. He is so excited and proud of himself that he is leaving a lot of other people behind him. He yells out at Christopher, "I am a man on the go. This I do know!"

Christopher yells at him, "Go man, go!"

Lady Noreen is still holding her own spot in the race, but she seems to be in some discomfort. She keeps holding her right breast.

Christopher asks her, "What is wrong with you, Lady Noreen?"

Lady Noreen just replies to Christopher, "Nothing is wrong with me!"

Within minutes they will soon be approaching the home stretch. Lady Noreen asks Christopher if she can stop for some water, so they do.

As they get back into the race, they can't believe their eyes, there is Father Garrison. Now, Lady Noreen has her second wind to run.

Soon they approach the final seconds of the run. Lady Noreen is giving every ounce of her determination to keep herself going as she crosses over the finish line with Christopher. Christopher, knowing this, offers her his hand so they can cross over the line together.

As they cross the line there is Old Bessie with Lady Noreen's cat, Tigress. She has Tigress in her cat carry-on case. Tigress is all dressed up with a designer collar covered with hearts.

Once over the line, Lady Noreen goes over to see Old Bessie and Tigress, while she looks for Joshua to get a report about Marcena's health. Lady Noreen is still holding her right breast for some reason. Christopher doesn't know why.

As Christopher makes his way up to congratulate Julie, Bruce, and Big Luke, who have placed first, second, and third in the race, he runs into Lady Noreen's gynecologist.

"Christopher, where is Lady Noreen?" the doctor in a worrisome tone asks.

"Hi, Dr. Vay! She is ahead of us," quickly responds Christopher.

"Christopher, my office has called her several times to schedule her to go into the hospital. Some large tumors were detected in her mammogram in her right breast. I did a biopsy on them. They came back positive for cancer. She won't come to see me because she says she is going to finally die. If we don't do something soon, Christopher, she probably will. Since she put you down as the person to contact in case of an emergency, I am contacting you right now since no one answers the phone at her house," factually speaks Dr. Vay to Christopher.

"Doc, I should have known. She hasn't been herself lately. How long has this gone on for?" questions Christopher.

"She hasn't scheduled an appointment with me since she found out the results of the biopsy in November, and now it is February," states the doctor.

"Doc, if you don't find her after the race, I will make sure that she schedules an appointment to go into the hospital as soon as possible. Thanks for filling me in on what is happening with her. I had no idea!"

As Christopher looks back, he sees Sarge cross over the line. There are still so many racers way, way back racing on the course.

As Christopher goes through the crowd, he sees Rico with Elijah. He hears that Rico has just won first place, Elijah second place, and Russ third place.

These three wheelchair finalists are so happy with their placement in the race today.

Elijah is so proud of himself winning after losing his leg in a motorcycle race accident. He never thought that he would continue to stay in great physical condition and compete in such a sport as wheelchair racing.

Christopher looks all around for Lady Noreen, but can't find her. As he slowly makes it over to the food table to get a bagel and juice, he sees Grandpa Bill.

"Grandpa Bill, what's new?" inquires Christopher.

"I'm still alive and going strong at 82! I feel so full of life once I start and finish one of these races. These races keep me from getting old, Christopher."

"You are so right! Age is a state of the mind. To me, Grandpa Bill, you are still going strong!" laughs Christopher.

Christopher soon hears his name being called. As he looks back there is Jasper. He has finally walked over the finish line.

"Christopher, I made it. I feel sick to my stomach, but I did it. I never thought that I would make it. The drugs kept me going, but being out of condition did me in. But, I made it!"

"Jasper, you did it. This race is the first thing you've ever wanted to do. Why?"

"My mother died from cancer, and she is the only person who ever loved me. Something inside of me made me do this race for her, Christopher."

"I am so proud of you! However, Jasper, if you got off of all your drugs, you would do much better in these races."

"Christopher, no I wouldn't, I would be depressed and suicidal."

"Well, Jasper, why don't you let me send you to a psychologist or psychiatrist and have you diagnosed, so you can be put on the right medication for your mental illness?"

"Either way, Christopher, I'll take drugs. All my life I have taken them either from the black market suppliers, or the white market suppliers."

"You are a hard one to help, Jasper. If you ever need my help, just find me."

"Thanks, Christopher, I know you care about me, and I thank you. I just want out of this world so I can go onto my next life."

"Jasper, I pray that something in this world will keep you here for awhile longer. You are like on a ladder of faith going nowhere. I hope you find your way, my son," solemnly replies Christopher to Jasper.

"So long, Christopher, enjoy your day! A ladder of faith! What a profound thought!" blurts out Jasper.

"Jasper, make sure that you get some real food from the tables at the finish line before you go back to the Boardwalk," pleads Christopher with him.

"Okay, Christopher, I will!"

"Bye for now, Jasper," responds Christopher before he takes off to find Lady Noreen.

Finally, Christopher starts walking toward Lady Noreen's house. Once inside of the house, he sees Lady Noreen crying on the couch.

"Lady Noreen, what is wrong with you?" whispers Christopher to her.

"Nothing, Christopher!" yells Lady Noreen back at him.

"It doesn't sound like nothing to me! Your doctor found some tumors in your one breast that are malignant as a result of your biopsy. It just won't go away, Lady Noreen. You have to see Dr. Vay and schedule surgery," Christopher urges her.

"Christopher, it is my turn to die. It's time!" sobbingly responds Lady Noreen.

"How are you talking, Lady Noreen? The kids need you! I need you!"

"Christopher, I love all of you, but I am scared to death of being operated on, having my breast removed, and going on the chemotherapy treatment every other week for six months. What if I do die while under the anesthesia?"

"You won't die, Lady Noreen, you have great things to look forward to like the birth of your grandchildren."

"Grandchildren, Christopher! Who said anything about grandchildren?"

"I did, just mark my word, they are coming, Lady Noreen! So let's get you to Dr. Vay next week."

"Do you really think I'm going to live? I have wanted to die my whole life, Christopher, and now that I am going to die, I am scared to death!"

"First, Lady Noreen, you're not going to die. Secondly, you have a lot to live for; you have me!"

"Oh, that makes me want to die, Christopher," shouts Lady Noreen in an irritable voice.

"Lady Noreen, did you eat yet?" asks Christopher.

"No, Christopher!"

"Let's go back to the race and join everyone and I'll get you a bagel and some juice. The bagels are from your favorite bakery. Al's Bakery has donated all of their pastries free to the race today. When you are done eating, let's check out what place you came in. You love knowing everyone's placement in the race."

"I don't want to eat, and I don't care what place I came in. I know that Rico came in 1st place, and that is all that matters to me right now," in a grouchy tone of voice Lady Noreen replies.

"Then let me take you over near the Breakfast & Lunch Grill, where Arthur feeds all of the stray cats underneath the Boardwalk.

You can feed the cats and we will take Tigress with us if you would like to do so."

"I don't want Tigress around stray cats, Christopher! But, you can take me to feed the cats. I'd like that!"

So, arm and arm Lady Noreen and Christopher go down the Boardwalk to feed the stray cats and kittens. On the way, Christopher has an artist on the Boardwalk paint a Valentine on Lady Noreen's face, and he buys her a heart balloon.

Lady Noreen, like a child, is scared, but willing to go back to her doctor. She now realizes it is much scarier to die than to live. Today she did run a race to save children's lives with Desmoid tumors; little did she know she might be a race in time to save her own life!

Chapter 24

The Ladder Of Faith

The very next week, Christopher calls Dr. Vay, and sets up Lady Noreen's appointment to go into the hospital to have the cancerous tumors removed from her breast and to decide whether or not to have reconstructive breast surgery is required.

Lady Noreen is scared to death. She tells Christopher not to tell Marcena, Joshua, or Rico anything about why she will be going into the hospital."

"Lady Noreen, I called Dr. Gerald Vay's office and you are to set everything up for your operation with his office tomorrow. You must be admitted to Jefferson Hospital in Philadelphia as soon as possible your doctor says."

"Christopher, but I have cancer!" screeches Lady Noreen.

"Okay, we will deal with it!" calmly says Christopher.

"Christopher, will the cancer spread to my other organs?" scared to death Lady Noreen asks him.

"I am not God. I don't know the answers to your questions but I do know that you will be okay whatever happens," optimistically Christopher responds to her.

Lady Noreen just gives Christopher a blank stare.

"Lady Noreen, what are you going to do today?" Christopher inquirers as he glances back at her.

"Joshua called me last night and asked if Marcena and he could visit us today for lunch," Lady Noreen answers.

"Is Marcena feeling any better?" wonders Christopher.

"Joshua told me that she feels a little better," states Lady Noreen.

"Good, Lady Noreen!" remarks Christopher.

Before too long, Marcena and Joshua show up at the house.

A few minutes later, Teresa Y. comes to the door and Rico greets her. Rico is at the house unexpectedly working out on his exercise equipment.

Lady Noreen looks a little baffled for she didn't know that Joshua had asked Teresa Y. and Rico to join them for lunch, too. Lady Noreen hopes she has enough food to feed everyone.

As they meet at the door, Marcena and Joshua hug and greet everyone.

While all of them are getting settled, Lady Noreen starts bringing the food in and placing it on the table. Christopher helps her.

Once they all get seated they start to eat and talk to one another.

"Lady Noreen, Joshua, and I brought you some pictures from our wedding. We framed a few of the pictures for you, too, and here is a copy of our wedding album. We can't begin to thank you so much for everything that you did for us. We love you so much!"

"Thank you, Marcena and Joshua; it was so dear of the two of you!" Lady Noreen expresses to both of them.

"Rico, here is a copy of your poem, done in calligraphy that you wrote for us. We loved it so much. Like you, it is special and means so much to Joshua and me."

"I am glad that you liked it, Marcena! It seems like it took me forever to write it for the two of you. It is truly beautifully done in calligraphy," adds Rico.

"Christopher, you are the hardest person in the world to buy a gift for because you love nature and the wildlife around us more than material things. You give to others more in life than you take from them. This gift is for you! Read what the note says inside the card out loud, Christopher," requests Marcena.

Christopher reads the card, "This year we are giving all of you at this table something that you never dreamt of getting for a gift. You will be Grandpa Christopher, Grandma Lady Noreen, and Uncle Rico in September. Your gift, Christopher, is that you get the honor of naming the baby when it is born. Good luck!"

Lady Noreen not believing what she is hearing screams out, "I'm going to be a Grandmother. I can't believe it! I have to live to be as old as I can be now! I always wanted to be a Grandmother - now I get to be one! Oh, I am so excited!" boasts Lady Noreen.

Christopher stands up with his glass of iced tea and blurts out, "This is a miracle from heaven! Life is so precious and dear. Just to think that we are going to have a beautiful baby, which will be part of both of you, is so exciting! Do you know if it is a boy or a girl?"

"Christopher, we don't want to know until the baby is born what sex it is, so you can come up with its name right on the spot," Marcena replies.

Rico and Teresa Y. are full of laughter, they are both so happy for Marcena and Joshua. Rico laughs out loud and says, "No matter if the baby is a boy or girl, I will love it so much Marcena, since both of us were only children it is so exciting to think that in a few more months, I'll be an uncle. Congratulations to both of you!"

Lady Noreen yells out, "Christopher did you know about this before today? You just told me a few days ago that I would be a Grandmother, did you already know that Marcena was pregnant?"

"Lady Noreen, I didn't know anything, I just hoped one day that we would be grandparents. Today is the day that I hoped for and I can hardly wait for the babies to come! All of us are going to have so much fun with the little ones," raves Christopher.

Joshua remarks, "Christopher there isn't going to be two babies, just one baby!"

"Joshua, that's right! I got so excited; I was giving you more children than Marcena and you are having this time. I meant when I said babies all the other little ones to come after this baby is born," Christopher clarifies himself to the both of them.

Marcena hesitates and responds, "We'll see! Let's see how this pregnancy goes first and then we'll decide if more babies will be on the way. After all I am twenty-six, and I'm not getting any younger!"

As they finish eating their lunch, Lady Noreen just continues to talk to Marcena about her nursery decoration plans, and how Patrick will help them decorate the nursery. All Lady Noreen can think about now is going shopping with Marcena for maternity clothes and decorating the nursery.

Christopher, Rico, and Teresa Y. listen to Joshua as he talks to them about his landscaping business expanding throughout the South Jersey area. Joshua has such innovative ideas on how to incorporate the growing of vegetables in house gardens. He asks Christopher what he thinks about his idea.

Christopher responds by saying, "Everyone in America should be able to maintain their own needs to grow their own fruits and vegetables. In the times that the American people live in, they must be self-sufficient in case of a terrorist attack. In the biblical times people sometimes died because of a famine. This is why people must incorporate farming in with their gardens, Joshua. It is a great idea!"

After a few hours, Marcena calls it a day, for she is getting really tired. Just looking at her, everyone can tell that she has lost a few pounds from having morning sickness.

Joshua and Marcena soon leave and Lady Noreen sends home food and bottled water with them. Then she calls Patrick and tells him the good news about the baby.

Rico and Teresa Y. continue to sit on the sofa together. Teresa Y. tries to start coming up with a violin solo to accompany Rico, while he recites his poem, "You've Colored My Life". The two young people truly enjoy working and being together.

Soon Christopher goes outside to take a walk since Lady Noreen is talking on the phone to get some ideas from Patrick on how to decorate the nursery, and Rico and Teresa Y. are creating music together, it is his time to meditate. As he walks down the steps from the Boardwalk to the beach, he sees a lost cat. He picks it up. It looks all beat up! He feels so sorry for the abandoned animal. He knows that Lady Noreen won't want this cat around Tigress, so he doesn't know what to do with it. After pondering a few minutes about what to do with the cat, he decides to walk back up to the house and put the cat inside of the enclosed porch, and give it some food. This way, Lady Noreen can determine the cat's fate. She can either throw it back into the wild, or just maybe, need another cat to love her while she is going through her breast surgery.

Once he secures the cat on the porch and gives it some food, Christopher runs away from the house as fast as he can. He doesn't want Lady Noreen to spot him, or she'll kill him right on the spot.

As Christopher starts to walk down the beach, he hears someone calling him at the top of their lungs. Christopher looks around and he sees Jasper.

"Jasper, what are you doing all the way up here on the beach? This is not part of your turf!" shouts Christopher.

"Christopher, I've waited since last night for you here. I finally wrote something down on my tablet for you to read. Do you believe it?" confides Jasper to Christopher.

"Yes, Jasper, I believe it! God doesn't make throwaway people, man does!" confesses Christopher to his young friend.

"Here is the poem that I wrote, Christopher.

THE LADDER OF FAITH

My flesh bleeds as I struggle to hold onto each new bar of the ladder to keep from falling...

I fear on my journey upward that if I fall back down to the Earth I will miss my calling...

My legs tighten in weariness as I ascend each step to another one straight in His direction...

I try not to get depressed when I fall backwards, for I am prepared for my spiritual resurrection...

Out of breath, I clasp onto each new bar above me, I am both physically and mentally drained...

Keeping my mind focused, exhausted and weak, I stumble to the heavens in agonizing pain...

I will not let go of the ladder even though rivers of sweat are streaming down my face...

I might not be the first soul saved to enter God's heaven, but who cares this isn't a race...

Each man, woman and child must climb at their own pace to find their own everlasting peace...

If I stumble, or if I fall on my way up, I must begin once again to climb, I will not cease...

For the Ladder of Faith, can be climbed by anyone on this Earth who hears God's call...

And if at times, your climb seems too endless, hold on tighter in faith so you don't fall...

I know that my Father Almighty will give me the strength needed to get to the ladder's end...

When there, I will look straight into my Father's face in true joy and triumph once again...

And then, He will have a thousand angels lift me up from His ladder into the Pearly Gates...

On that day, I will be surrounded by God's never-ending love and free of any human hate...

At the End of the Ladder of Faith...

"Well, Christopher, do you like my poem?" asks Jasper.

"Jasper, it is an incredible poem! Without faith or a belief system, a person certainly cannot survive in this world son. Your poem is a masterpiece. You must present your poem for others to hear, my friend. You recited it so eloquently. People must hear your poem," Christopher encourages him.

"Christopher, no, they don't want to hear my poem! People don't want to hear a poem from a man who eats garbage, lives under the Boardwalk, and is penniless," protests Jasper.

"Jasper, you may be right! But God wants to hear your poem! Don't you think He should?" insists Christopher.

"Well, Christopher, I don't know! I'm exhausted after this conversation with you. Here is your copy of my poem for you. I'm going to the library and read books for the rest of the day. You have truly depleted me of all of my drug energy!" Jasper sighs.

"Bye for now, Jasper!" calls out Christopher to him.

Jasper leaves as fast as he can from Christopher's presence. It seems that Jasper is more afraid of achieving success than feeling failure.

He believes that once one falls down in their life, they can never raise themselves back up ever again.

Christopher is thrilled knowing that Marcena is pregnant and that Joshua and she are expecting their first child. He hurries to find Old Bessie since she was out of the house for one of her short walks and long sits today when Marcena and Joshua told everyone they were expecting a baby. He wants to tell her the good news before she hears it from someone else.

Old Bessie is overwhelmed to hear from Christopher that Marcena is pregnant. She tells him that she is going to ask Lady Noreen if she can stay on not only as her official scheduler, but as a nanny for the baby when it is born.

Christopher encourages Old Bessie to ask Lady Noreen this immediately. He thinks Old Bessie would be a great nanny.

Old Bessie gives Christopher a hug and a kiss. Then, she slowly gets up to walk back to the house to congratulate Lady Noreen on becoming a grandmother.

As Christopher goes on his way, he runs into Sarge on the Boardwalk. He tells Sarge about the baby to be born in September. He asks him if he can write a song for the new little one coming into this world.

Sarge gets a giant smile from ear to ear hearing that Marcena is going to have a baby. He tells Christopher that he will start right away on the song, so it will be ready when the baby is born.

Finally, Christopher is so tired out from sharing the good news with everyone. He looks for Nicholas, Daisy and Sergeant Mussack, but can't find them anywhere around the Boardwalk. As he stops into Arthur's place, the Breakfast & Lunch Grill, he sees Arthur and Big Luke there. When Christopher tells them the good news, they are overwhelmed with happiness for both Marcena and Joshua.

Once Christopher leaves the grill, he hurries home to see if anyone has found the cat yet. He fears the cat's fate if Lady Noreen is in one of her moods and finds the stray cat eating food on her enclosed porch.

As Christopher enters the house he finds no one inside of it. Once he goes from the house outdoors he peeks, and sees Old Bessie combing the stray cat.

"Old Bessie, what are you doing to that cat?" inquirers Christopher.

"Lady Noreen made me its nanny. I am to clean it up before it goes with Brook to the vet to get its shots tomorrow. Brook and Lady Noreen already went shopping to buy a carrying cage, some toys, and some food dishes for this stray," Old Bessie mentions to Christopher.

"Has the cat met Tigress yet, Old Bessie?"

"No, Lady Noreen says the cat can't meet Tigress until the cat has its shots and is groomed."

"Is Lady Noreen going to keep the cat, Old Bessie?" reluctantly inquirers Christopher.

"I guess so; she calls it, Tom Cat, Christopher," laughs Old Bessie.

"You are kidding, Old Bessie! Now, she has a Tigress and Tom Cat. It looks like Marcena won't be the only one to give birth this year!" Christopher snickers to himself.

Chapter 25

Bring Flowers Everyone Just In Case

Lady Noreen puts her surgery appointment off as long as she can. Throughout the month of February she schedules her operation, and then calls back the doctor's office to cancel her operation. Dr. Vay is so sick and tired of her game playing that he finally calls Christopher to tell him that she must have the surgery as soon as possible because her life might be at stake.

Hearing that Christopher decides to have all of the people who she loves, and who are her friends meet with her at the end of February. He wants everyone to convince her to schedule her surgery for the removal of the cancerous tumors and subsequent reconstructive surgery.

On the day that everyone shows up at the house, Lady Noreen is as mad as a bull getting ready to charge. First Marcena and Joshua show up unexpectedly, then Rico and Teresa Y., next Russ and Patrick, and last, Nicholas. Finally, it is the time to convince Lady Noreen that they all want her to go to the hospital and listen to Dr. Gerald Vay.

Lady Noreen feels like this is a meeting called to fight with her. She has made up her mind that she isn't going to have the operation, and she doesn't want any interference with her decision. Once every one hears this from her, they start to respond to her.

Patrick is the first to take her on, "Lady Noreen, you can't do this to yourself; we all need you! You have started a fashion line with me; you just can't pull out on me now."

"Patrick, I'm not pulling out on you, I'm just not going to have the operation done right now. I like my body and I'm not going to do one thing to change it," in defiance Lady Noreen replies to Patrick.

Russ blurts out, "Lady Noreen, I like my body, too, but if I wasn't taking my medication for AIDS, I might be dead. Please be sensible. We are not fighting with you, Lady Noreen. This is not an intervention session, although it may seem like one. We just want you to listen to your doctor and to our advice."

"Russ, I've heard it all! No, and I mean no!

I'm not going into the hospital to be cut up and have a slow or fast death, Christopher. Why did you call this mediation session? I'm surprised you didn't call Brook's dad to be here today with us sicko people!" yells Lady Noreen at Christopher.

"I did Lady Noreen, but Brook's father passed away this morning. Brook called earlier to tell you, but you were still sleeping and I didn't want to upset you!" in a low voice Christopher responds to her.

"He died! Oh, poor Brook, what did his father die from?" wonders Lady Noreen.

"Brook's father as you know, Lady Noreen, has been suffering from prostate cancer for several years. He came down with pneumonia, and it was his time to go to heaven!" explains Christopher to her.

"Christopher, see there! He went to the hospital and just plain died. I'm not going to do that with my life. What is left of my life, I am going to live to the fullest!" angrily mutters Lady Noreen to all of them.

Marcena intervenes, "Lady Noreen, our child needs you to be a grandmother. All we have is you!"

"Marcena, I will be here for you, I just can't go into the hospital. All my life I wanted to die. Now I finally hear that I have breast cancer, I don't want to deal with it. I never wanted to take the biopsy anyway until I was ordered by Dr. Vay. This was my first mammogram. It came back positive that I had cancer. I wish they would have made a mistake, but they didn't."

Rico jumps in by saying, "Lady Noreen, I have had Spina bifida since I was born. I've had to live with the reality that I could die at any point in my life, but I haven't because I take such good care of myself, and sought medical treatment. Please, go into the hospital. You are the mom that I never had. I want to continue to run races with you."

"Rico, I love both Marcena and you. You are my children, but I can't have a mastectomy and breast reconstruction surgery. On top of those two biggies, I have to go on chemotherapy and have injections every other week. I don't want to be sick and maybe lose my hair. I just can't do that," declares Lady Noreen.

Nicholas finally interrupts Lady Noreen and says to her, "Lady Noreen, you are the most stubborn woman I have ever known. Here I am fighting for my life each day, because I want to live. You have to have this surgery to make sure that the cancer doesn't spread throughout your body. You are still young at heart, and if the cancer tissue is removed, you can live a normal healthy and happy life."

"I am sorry, Nicholas, I have made my decision, and I'm not changing it! I love all of you, but I'm not changing my decision. Now you must excuse me, but I'm going out for a walk." Lady Noreen gets up and walks toward the door.

"Lady Noreen, please don't go! We all love you, and we want you to schedule an appointment for admission to the hospital today. Dr. Vay is waiting to hear from you!" pleads Christopher to Lady Noreen in front of everyone.

"Christopher, you schedule it, and you go to the hospital for yourself. This stupid intervention session was all your idea! You go get the operation!" bellows Lady Noreen in a mean tone of voice to him.

With that Lady Noreen storms out of her house like a leopardess on the kill. She grabs Tigress out of Old Bessie's hands and out to the Boardwalk she goes to flee from everyone in her house.

Just as she leaves the house, Brook pulls up in his limo. He runs to the door to greet Christopher.

Christopher tells Brook how sorry he is about his father's death. Then, Christopher tells Brook that Lady Noreen is in a rage. She has just stormed out of the house like a powerful tropical cyclone because she is not willing to be admitted into the hospital for the surgical procedure and at this very moment, she is headed down the Boardwalk in a fit of violent wrath with Tigress.

Brook runs back to his limo, and grabs Tom Cat who is asleep in his cat cage, and runs as fast as he can to catch up with Lady Noreen and he finally catches up with her.

"Lady Noreen, stop walking so fast! I brought you Tom Cat. Here he is in his cage. He has been bathed and is very handsome. Plus, the vet says that your cat is in great health just a little bruised up from being kicked around!"

"Brook, Tom Cat is lucky, he has nine lives, and I only have one!" sarcastically Lady Noreen replies to Brook.

"I hear that you aren't going in for the surgery," adds Brook.

"You heard right, Brook! Oh, I forgot to tell you that I'm deeply sorry about your father's death. Can I help you in any way?" mentions Lady Noreen to him.

"Yes, go to the hospital and make your appointment to get your mastectomy, so you can live. I don't want to bury you because of you being so scared of what lies ahead of you," states Brook to Lady Noreen.

"No, Brook! I don't want to get this operation. I thank you for Tom Cat, and working today, but I'm not going to the hospital!" hollers out Lady Noreen in a shrieking voice at Brook.

"Fine Lady Noreen, don't go! Don't do anything you don't want to do! I don't have to be a part of your decision, so I quit your services. Get another limo driver. I can't be a part of what you are doing to the ones who love you. Yes, my father died, but he made every attempt to live for long as he could. You, on the other hand, because of your fear of death, you want all of us to be a part of your defiant decision. Well, I won't be! Goodbye, Lady Noreen. Do whatever you want to do with your life, but I won't be a part of it. I have to get ready to make my father's funeral arrangements. Have a nice life and goodbye. Here, take Tom Cat," snaps Brook at Lady Noreen.

Lady Noreen in shock grabs Tom Cat in his cage. She yells after Brook to come back, but he just keeps walking away from her as fast as he can back toward his limousine.

With that, Lady Noreen just sits lifeless on the Boardwalk next to the steps with her two cats crying. Eventually, Christopher finds her, and goes over to her. He kisses her and gives her a big hug saying, "Lady Noreen, please come back to the house. We all love you so much! Life will not be as exciting without you!" exclaims Christopher.

"Why did you kiss me? You never kiss me!" in shock Lady Noreen blurts out to Christopher.

"Lady Noreen, I just adore you! Without you, I can't take care of the children, and be a grandfather. I need you in my life!" admits Christopher to her.

"Was that the kiss of death you just gave to me?" grumbles Lady Noreen.

"Stop it, Lady Noreen, right now. Just schedule the hospital surgery today, please, if not for yourself, for Brook, and all of us. Brook is not coming back to serve as your driver unless you make your appointment today," adds Christopher.

"Okay, I'll make it! I hope all of you are happy! I want all of you to know, Christopher, it is my body, my blood, and it will be my death if I die on the operating table! Just give me another kiss, Christopher, and I'll have the courage to die!" Lady Noreen begs him.

Christopher gives Lady Noreen another kiss after he picks up Tom Cat in his cage.

Seeing that Christopher is ready to go back to her house, Lady Noreen stands up carrying Tigress in a baby pouch that she is wearing. Then Christopher and her walk hand in hand back to the house.

Once there, Lady Noreen calls Dr. Vay to make her appointment for the following week, which Christopher has already made for her, but didn't tell her. Everyone at the house hearing this good news applauds her.

Then, Lady Noreen asks Christopher to call Brook, and tell him that she needs him to pick her up next week, and that she didn't accept his resignation. Last, but not least, Lady Noreen asks Christopher to order potato salad, salad, and wraps from the new deli in Ventnor, so everyone from her intervention group and shrink session can enjoy their Last Supper with her.

Christopher does everything that he is told to do by her. He then tells everyone that they all should accompany Lady Noreen next week to the hospital for her operation.

Lady Noreen in shock just rolls her eyes up and down and says to all of them, "Bring me flowers everyone, just in case I die lying on the operating table."

Chapter 26

We Are In This Journey For Life

The big day in March for Lady Noreen's operation finally arrives. Christopher has Brook and his drivers pick up Marcena, Joshua, Rico, Teresa, Old Bessie, Patrick, Russ, Nicholas and himself at 7:30 a.m., so that they can be at the hospital on time.

Lady Noreen was admitted into the hospital last night. Everything went okay, except that the hospital wouldn't allow her to keep Tigress and Tom Cat in her room with her, so Old Bessie had to take both of the cats back home.

Although Lady Noreen struggled with both Christopher and Brook to get out of the limousine last night, they finally got her out of the limousine and Christopher carried her into the hospital. This time, Christopher decided that there would be nothing to stop her from getting the mastectomy and the breast reconstruction surgery that she so badly needs. In fact, Christopher is going to stay with her all night just to make sure she won't slip out of her room.

Christopher holds her hand all night and during the morning hours until the orderly and nurses intervene to prep Lady Noreen to get her ready for her surgical procedure.

Lady Noreen was fine with all the medical nonsense until she read the hospital legal forms that she was required to sign prior to her surgery. After reading the forms, she told Christopher that she wanted to leave the hospital immediately because she was not going to sign the forms. That she wasn't going to let the doctors legally kill her with her own written signature and blessings.

Christopher tells Lady Noreen if she leaves the hospital, he will move out of her house. Then, he walks real fast out of her room.

Immediately Lady Noreen calls for Christopher, but he doesn't return to her hospital room. Lady Noreen then looks back at the forms and signs each one of them while tears stream down her face. She then tells the nurse to request that the surgeon proceed with the surgical procedure and to administer lots of drugs either legal ones or black markets ones to her. Lady Noreen tells the nurse that drugs are all the same no matter who they are bought from so she doesn't care who gives her the drugs.

The nurse just laughs at Lady Noreen and continues to prep her for her operation.

Christopher is seen standing outside her room waiting until he finds out if she has signed the papers. When he hears she has, he goes back into her room and waits for the orderly to transfer Lady Noreen to the surgical suite. At that time, he gives Lady Noreen a big, big kiss, and goes into the waiting room with her other loved ones.

A few hours pass, and everyone in the waiting room finds out that the mastectomy was successful. Dr. Vay tells Christopher that the malignant tumor tissue has been successfully removed in Lady Noreen's breast and she will require postoperative care followed by reconstructive surgery in the months ahead. Moreover, he will inform her about successive chemotherapy treatments and reconstruction surgical options later.

Christopher runs and tells everyone in the waiting room about the results of Lady Noreen's operation.

Everyone is so happy that Lady Noreen is okay, and they all pray that she will be able to deal with her mastectomy. However, they are scared to death that Lady Noreen will blame them for losing her breast. Each of them prays that she is emotionally stable for the follow-up treatments.

Finally, Lady Noreen wakes up from the surgery, and Christopher is with her. She looks down at her breast and can tell that her one breast has been removed.

Christopher tells her, "Lady Noreen, the operation was a success. You can now live a long and productive healthy life if you just follow up on your appointments with Dr. Vay and Dr. Wigman, the plastic surgeon. I will be there every step of the way for you. Lady Noreen; please don't be scared. We have a grandbaby to look forward to being born real soon. You will have to undergo chemotherapy for the next six months, but you will get through it. All of us love you so very much!" confides Christopher to her.

Lady Noreen responds by saying, "Well, Christopher, I'll be okay, since I know that I didn't die on the operating table, I can make it through the next steps. Will you always be there for me, Christopher? Do you promise me that?" whispers Lady Noreen in his ear.

"Lady Noreen, I will always be there for you. I'm not going anywhere. The two of us have a wonderful journey to look forward to in the future together."

"Christopher, I guess I'm more afraid of dying than living. Is that normal?" Lady Noreen asks him.

"Lady Noreen, there is nothing to be scared about in life or death. This is just a short journey leading to our next life. Heaven is better than anything in this world you will one day see. Don't be afraid of death, Lady Noreen. I'm telling you the truth. Death is not the end. It is just a new beginning, but right now, we have lots of living to do in the lives that we are living together right now! Let me put my hands on the two sides of your head. See those are your two temples; in between them, your forehead, is God's gift of heaven to you. Only you can put hell into your throne of God. I hope you choose heaven."

After his philosophical talk to her, Christopher has all of her loved ones enter her room to greet her. Then, everyone leaves the hospital except Christopher. He returns to Lady Noreen's hospital room to sleep there in a chair for the night.

The next day, Christopher discusses the dates with Lady Noreen for her chemotherapy treatments to be scheduled for her in the coming six months.

Rico has researched the breast cancer health center online to make sure Lady Noreen is getting the best possible medical treatment possible.

Christopher calls the doctor's office from his cell phone to schedule her appointments. Then he has Patrick bring in several giant bouquets of flowers from her loved ones and friends to give to Lady Noreen.

Lady Noreen gives Patrick a hug and a kiss on the cheek. Then she says to Patrick, "Maybe I am dead, and I just don't know it! It is funny, but people say it is better to be given flowers while you are alive rather than when you are dead to receive truckloads of them. This is living proof of it, Patrick!"

Patrick just laughs at her and replies, "Lady Noreen, you are very much alive. The flowers celebrate your victory over death. You have a success story to tell over breast cancer."

"No, Patrick, I am a survivor over breast cancer! Thank heavens for Dr. Vay's pre-surgical instructions to me before my surgery to help me with my recovery. I am now ready to recover and seek the essential follow-up care that I need to get back on my feet. I still have a lot of living to do!" Lady Noreen yells out with great joy.

Chapter 27

Only God Knows What Will Be In Our Lives

The ocean is rolling in with rough, strong waters and strong winds. Lady Noreen's body has slowly healed and now she is experiencing mental healing. Her back is still a little tender from the tissue that her plastic surgeon removed to create a breast mound used for the breast reconstruction.

Christopher with Marcena, Joshua, and Rico are planning an Easter Day Celebration at the beach the Saturday prior to Easter Sunday. They are inviting everyone to fly their kites and donate clothing to the children at the shelter. He has provided clothing sizes for the children attending the event and contacted the casinos, hospitals, restaurants, and local casino entertainment people to participate in this event. Christopher has encouraged people to focus on charity versus the material aspects of Easter and help not only families but their children who are in need. Everyone has been requested to bring a plastic egg to the beach with a gift card inside for a child to buy a gift, food, or go to a movie, museum, or amusement park.

Rico is busy with the founding of his non-profit corporation and planning another wheelchair race for the fall. With his involvement with Teresa Y., Christopher thinks that he will be the next one to announce a wedding date.

Marcena and Joshua are so excited about the coming birth of their baby. She is now almost 3 months pregnant and getting bigger each day. Christopher has slowly been coming up with both girl and boy names for the baby. He loves his names so much that he prays that twins will be born and he can use both of the selected children's names for both of the babies.

Christopher takes Lady Noreen out for daily walks almost every day. She enjoys her life much more than before. It seems that she has come to find peace with her life, and is enjoying her life more than ever by just focusing on her family and nature.

On the Boardwalk there is quietness. The seniors living in the condos at the shore are now walking on the Boardwalk and appear to be enjoying life's energy. As they sit in the rolling chairs on the Boardwalk, they watch life pass by them. They enjoy their later years by simply talking about their families, pets, and travels with one another. It's like they hang out with their peers much like they did as kids long ago. Although at this time in their lives, they just talk mostly about their memories, dreams and disappointments.

Lady Noreen hasn't been to the casino for a while. Therefore, Christopher has invited Lady Noreen to accompany him to the casino for dinner this evening. Lately, Lady Noreen has just wanted to stay home and plan the nursery for Marcena's and Joshua's baby. She is conditioning herself slowly to begin working out with Rico again. She is also involved with her new fashion designs for women of all sizes. The woman's clothing line is constructed of colorful fabrics that have cats and wild animal designs on it.

Lady Noreen has experienced occasional sickness resulting from her chemotherapy. She is happy with the latissimus dorsi flaps. Her plastic surgeon was quite experienced and did a remarkable job to create a breast mound to match her un-operated breast. Now, she has to decide following completion of the chemotherapy treatment if she wants a tattooed nipple. Lady Noreen has talked to Christopher about whether or not, she should proceed with the elective surgery because she is scared to death to have any more surgery.

Christopher tells Lady Noreen the decision is up to her, and to wait until she feels stronger to decide what she wants to do. That elective operation can be completed weeks or months after completion of her breast reconstruction surgery.

Lady Noreen feels mentally relieved by just knowing that she doesn't have to make any quick decision right now.

After their discussion together, Christopher takes Lady Noreen on a rolling chair ride to the casino and an early dinner at the buffet there. He thinks that it is time to get her out of the house and back to living her routine life.

Once at the casino, everyone is so happy to see Lady Noreen. She is like the casino star.

Her casino hostess seats them at a table near the buffet tables. They order their beverages and gaze at all the food on the different buffet tables. The food looks so tempting to Lady Noreen, but she is afraid to overeat because of her ongoing treatment, so she just samples the healthy dishes.

Christopher, while he is ordering his steak in the grill area, notices a young Asian girl, almost in tears. An older man is yelling at her and forcing her to eat the food on her plate.

Soon, Lady Noreen and Christopher are back at their dining table busy consuming the delicious food on their plates that they have selected to eat.

As Lady Noreen gets up to go to the bathroom, Christopher again notices the young girl at the table across from them. The girl can't hold back her tears. Seeing this, Christopher walks over to the table and says to the Asian girl, "Come with me right now!"

The man with her yells at Christopher saying, "She can't; she is my child!"

Christopher yells back at him, "No, she isn't your child; she is your prostitute."

Hearing that word come out of Christopher's mouth, the man turns as red as a beet.

The girl, who the people at the table call, Odessa, hurries and gets up from her table and walks as fast as she can right over to Christopher.

"You are making a big mistake by going with that man, Odessa!" yells the hateful man at her.

"Come with me right now and let's leave him here," slowly says Christopher to the girl.

"If you take her from me right now, mister, I promise you that you will die. You'll go out feet first, sir!" the evil man says under his breath to Christopher.

"Mr., I don't know your name. This girl is nothing to you. She is just a moneymaker. Don't try and scare me or threaten me. If you or anyone else tries to take Odessa from me, or harm her in any way, you will pay with your lives," remarks Christopher to the people at this table.

"Mark my word, I'll find you, old man, and once I do, you'll be dead meat!" in a rage the man roars out in a venomous tone at Christopher.

"We will see about that! Odessa, you are coming with me right now. Let's go!" says Christopher in a strong authoritative voice.

Lady Noreen sees Christopher with a young girl at their table, when she gets back to the table. She asks Christopher, "Hi! Who is this?"

"This, Lady Noreen, is a girl who can help you in the fashion industry," exclaims Christopher to her.

"What? What are you talking about?" bewildered Lady Noreen responds to him.

"You'll see!" states Christopher.

With that the three of them leave the table, and Christopher has a rolling chair take them back to Lady Noreen's house. The young girl cries hysterically on the ride back to the house with them.

As they get further down the Boardwalk, they see a homeless man in his wheelchair going back and forth but going nowhere. It is like he is lost in time!

Once to the house, Christopher shows the girl to Marcena's old room since Marcena has moved everything out into Joshua's and her new home. Then he talks to Odessa.

While they are talking, Lady Noreen is getting as mad as a killer dog. She can't believe that Christopher has brought home another stranger with them tonight.

Soon Christopher comes into the living room with Lady Noreen.

Lady Noreen asks Christopher, "Do you know who that girl is? Do you know her?"

"No, Lady Noreen, I've never seen her before until tonight, but when I did see her I knew she was in trouble," explains Christopher to Lady Noreen.

"What kind of trouble?" inquisitively Lady Noreen inquirers.

"She was brought over to America under false pretenses, Lady Noreen. They got Odessa her citizenship, but it wasn't for her to go to college. It was for her to go straight into prostitution."

"Why didn't she run away or report it to the authorities?" shrieks Lady Noreen.

"They told her, Lady Noreen, that they would kill her if she did! On top of that, she was petrified because three of the girls living with her out of the fifteen have disappeared in the last 8 months. They told Odessa there was a serial prostitute killer in this area, and that she better stay with them or whoever the killer was would kill her, too. Odessa was scared to death of these people just like you are scared to death of dying, Lady Noreen!"

"What do you want me to do with her, Christopher?" Lady Noreen with a surprised look on her face asks Christopher.

"Lady Noreen, can she help Old Bessie and you with the chores? Also, can, Odessa assist you with the baby or babies when they are born, too?" adds Christopher.

"Christopher, she is a prostitute!" retorts Lady Noreen.

"So what if she is, Lady Noreen! Mary Magdalene was a prostitute and Christ loved her the most. Perhaps Mary Magdalene didn't judge everyone! You know, they say we will be judged the way we judge others. So if you don't want her to stay here, tell Odessa that when she comes downstairs to join us, Lady Noreen. I know she will immediately leave your house."

Odessa, after she takes a shower and gets cleaned up, comes into the living room to talk to Lady Noreen.

"Hello! I really don't know what to say to you. Probably Christopher told you my story. As you can see, I am in a mess. Although people call me a prostitute, I am really a raped woman. I got put into this mess by assuming that the organization that brought me here would help me to get my citizenship and enroll me into a university so I could get my education for free. However, the organization was an escort service that thrived on putting young orphaned Asian women into prostitution. This life has been a living nightmare for me. Death is often the only way out of prostitution. If you want me to leave your house, I will!" speaks out Odessa to Lady Noreen with lots of emotion.

Lady Noreen studies the young woman's facial expression for a moment and says to her, "No, you can't leave me, I need you! This is a busy time of the year for my fashion design industry. You can help me with it! You will be a great assistant not only to my partner, Patrick, but to me. I do hope you will stay with us. We will make sure that you are safe here. By the way, you can call me Lady Noreen."

"But what if they kill you or Christopher?" emotionally responds Odessa to Lady Noreen.

"So what if that happens, Odessa, it is okay with me! At least I won't have to go in for another operation or anymore chemotherapy treatments," laughs Lady Noreen out loud.

Odessa looks at Lady Noreen with a confused look on her face. She isn't quite sure if this woman is mentally stable or not. However, since she has no other place to go to, she decides this is as good as it is going to get for her. She also knows that Christopher has a good heart and that he will look after her. For the very first time in months, Odessa feels somewhat safe to be Lady Noreen's assistant in the fashion industry.

As the month goes by, Christopher is working on his Sky Day Easter Celebration for the children at the shelter. Lady Noreen is having Odessa take lessons from Patrick on fashion and designing, plus assisting him at the florist shop. She wants Odessa to become business savvy and to eventually get her college education like she planned to do when she came to the United States.

Marcena and Joshua are decorating their new house. Joshua has been doing the outside painting. Joshua's nursery business and vegetable gardening ideas have caught on at the shore. He never thought his concept of these gardens would be such a great success!

Rico is making lots of progress in planning races for an Oktoberfest Wheelchair/5K. He thinks that October would be such a beautiful time for a race.

As the days fly by, Lady Noreen is getting stronger, and she is excited about the celebration of Easter being here soon.

Lately, Lady Noreen is getting chemotherapy treatments every other week.

She has been a little weak lately, and recently had an upset stomach. Little does Lady Noreen know that Christopher has planned this incredible Sky Day Easter Celebration to be dedicated to her.

Some of the local charities from the Atlantic City area are donating clothes, toys and school supplies to this event. These items will be distributed to the children and their parents, who are living in the shelters. They are also donating kites to anyone who needs one to fly during the day of the celebration.

The day of the Sky Day Easter Celebration finally arrives. It is a blessed day for the wind is just right for the kite flying. The event brings people out from all walks of life to it.

Christopher can't believe how many plastic eggs with plastic gift card surprises have been donated to the people working the beach tables for him. Also, the volunteers have collected so many clothes, toys, school supplies, bikes, and computers to give as gifts to the participants in the beach kite contest.

Finally at 11:30 a.m., before all the kites are to go up in the air, Christopher runs to the house to get Lady Noreen, Tigress, Tom Cat, Old Bessie, and Odessa, to join him for the big event.

Lady Noreen doesn't know it but she is going to start the kite event off. Once Christopher takes her down from the Boardwalk to the beach, she can't believe how many people are at the Sky Day Easter Celebration.

Then, Rico calls Lady Noreen over to the microphone and instructs her to start the big Sky Day Easter Celebration kite flying celebration.

Lady Noreen is so thrilled that she can hardly speak, but with Christopher and Old Bessie pushing her forward, she finally makes it to the microphone.

Once Lady Noreen is at the microphone, Rico tells her what to say, and she says, "On your mark, get ready, and up with your kites."

People, parents, grandparents, and children are seen everywhere pulling their kites to get them up in the air. People are on the beach, on the Boardwalk, and in their own backyards trying to fly their kites. Everyone is having such a great time, and Lady Noreen is so happy!

Christopher looks out at the glimmering water and sees Sanabrio and all the other seagulls flying throughout the sky and joining a spectacular formation of kites flying high throughout the sky.

The participants are so happy and enjoying their day at the beach. The shelters are bringing people onto the beach, and the clothes and other items collected are being dispersed to these needy families. Some organizations have set up tables in the area to provide information on drug/alcohol programs and job training opportunities for the people living in the shelters. A few local area restaurants, laundry services, gas stations, groceries, and parking services are distributing employment applications to people who need to get back into the workforce. Also, churches are providing forms to be filled out for low income housing programs in the surrounding areas. Christopher has touched almost every area of human need for these people to help them to get back onto their feet.

As the day wears down, the remaining kites in the air start to come down or get lost from the wind in the sky. The people start leaving the beach. Christopher has Lady Noreen, Old Bessie, Patrick, Russ, Odessa, Rico, Teresa Y., Marcena, Joshua, Arthur, Hilten, Nicholas, Brook, Sarge, Mr. Marcuso and Sergeant Mussack handing out plastic eggs with plastic card surprises in them for the children to either buy something or do something special with for Easter.

As all of them walk home together on the Boardwalk, they feel good about knowing that the event was special for the children in Atlantic City. Everyone present at this event would always remember tomorrow on Easter Day how they put smiles on so many people's faces.

On Easter Sunday, the church bells are ringing, and the people are awakening to the smells of delicious food, Easter eggs, candy, and family dinners. Lady Noreen is all excited to wear one of the new dresses from her designer collection. She also has Marcena, Old Bessie, Odessa, and Teresa Y. wearing dresses from her designer collection to church today, too.

Once into church, the service begins. Everyone is so thankful for this day of worship and the remembrance of Christ's sacrifice. In the prayer, Father Garrison, in remembrance, remembers Brook, and his father, who has passed away.

The priest requests Jasper to present his poem, "The Ladder of Faith," on this holy day. The congregation is so astonished at what this young man has written in his poem as he presents it to them.

Christopher had to convince Jasper that he had to wear some store bought clothes for the church service today and have his hair trimmed. Jasper yelled at Christopher most of yesterday. However, he soon gave in and went shopping with Christopher to buy a shirt and a pair of pants. Lady Noreen cut Jasper's hair for him, so of course he would look not like his homeless self, but very different on this Easter Sunday morning.

After the church service, Joshua's sister, Hannah, runs after Christopher to tell him that she is pregnant again, and she will have a baby in late November. Christopher is so happy for her. He tells her, "Hannah, only God knows what will be in our lives! People can tell us what they think will be but only God knows what will be! Congratulations! Now Joshua and Marcena's baby will have a playmate. Who knows maybe you'll have twins, too."

"But Christopher, Marcena and Joshua are only expecting one baby aren't they?" responds Hannah to Christopher's prediction.

"You never know, Hannah!" jokingly Christopher laughs out.

Next, Jasper runs up to Christopher and Lady Noreen to thank them for everything they have done for him to make him human once again. Jasper tells them that it was so much easier to leave the human race and go into a subculture animal existence than to go back into the real world.

From the corner of Christopher's eye, he sees Odessa talking to Sergeant Mussack. He is sure that she is asking him if he knows anything about a prostitute serial killer. Christopher knows in his heart if there is one loose in the Atlantic City area probably no one cares. That is what is so sad about the American World.

Once everyone gets back to Lady Noreen's house from church, they get ready to enter the dining areas to enjoy their Easter dinner together. Lady Noreen, Old Bessie, Patrick, Mama Cane, and Odessa have cooked an incredible dinner. There are 10 turkeys, 5 hams, lots of stuffing, whole potatoes, mashed potatoes, yams, salad, deviled eggs, six lasagna dishes, mixed vegetables, pumpkin pie, blueberry pie, and carrot cake.

The food looks positively delicious. It appears that Lady Noreen is going to feed an army and she is. She has all of their family, Joshua's sister and family, Teresa Y.'s parents, Patrick, Russ, Brook and his girlfriend, Sarge, Nicholas, Hilten, Arthur and his family, Mr. Marcuso and his family, Sergeant Mussack and his family, Mama Cane and her foster children, Patrick, Old Bessie, Odessa, Big Luke and his girlfriend, Jasper, Tigress, Tom Cat, and Delilah.

While everyone is getting ready to be seated in the dining room and closed porch area, Christopher and Lady Noreen give Mama Cane's foster children packages of clothes, jackets, school supplies, and plastic gift cards to local department stores to purchase gifts of their choosing.

All those who attended the Easter dinner contributed a couple items to give to the children along with a little extra money to give to Mama Cane. They decided to give Mama Cane a money order for $500.00 to help her with all of her bills.

Her foster children express appreciation for what everyone has done for them. They can't believe that so many strangers care about their existence. Here they are just foster children who no one ever even heard about, but today, they are celebrated and made to feel really special.

With thanks, everyone takes their seats, and Christopher says, "First of all God, thank you for our wonderful family, Lady Noreen's health, Marcena and Joshua's baby or babies to be born soon, Hannah and Raul's baby to follow, the newest member to our family, Odessa, Jasper's beautiful poem today, and Mama Cane and her beautiful foster children from God, and all the other children of our friends here today. Also, we would like to pay respect to Brook's father who is with you in heaven, dear Lord."

"Now for the prayer, Christopher!" Lady Noreen blurts out.

"Our Heavenly Father, we are born into this life to be nurtured by You. You not only guide us through the still calm waters but protect us from both human and earthly disasters, Lord. Yes, God, You, and You alone are with us in the early dawn of our young lives throughout the darkness of the night in our older lives. In Your holy name, may You bless and watch over each and every one of us each day of our lives. Continue to bless us with your eternal love and forgiveness forever. Amen."

Then everyone passes the food around the table and digs in. They are all so thankful for all the blessings they have in their present lives. Most of them remember their prior lives. In those lives, most of them were born into a dysfunctional family and were given no love.

Chapter 28

I Am Not Prepared For This
Scary World Called Life

Throughout April and May, Lady Noreen is seen recuperating from her breast reconstruction surgery and continuing the chemotherapy treatments at the hospital. Even though she hasn't lost all of her hair, she is still wearing wigs lately. She appears to be growing stronger each day.

With the help of Patrick and Odessa, Lady Noreen is designing new fashions for their big fashion event at the end of April. The proceeds from the Safari Fashion Show will be donated to Arthur to continue his feeding and caring for the stray and abandoned cats underneath the Boardwalk in Atlantic City.

Nicholas is pleased to be the sponsor of this fashion show that Lady Noreen, Patrick, and Odessa are planning.

The models participating are Marcena, Teresa Y., Hilten, Julie, Old Bessie, Daisy, Mama Cane, Joy Rhapsody, Ngoc, P.J., Emiliann, Jessica, and Feymale. The escorts for the fashion show are Orlando, Heffe, Joshua, Rico, Christopher, Big Luke, Bruce, Nicholas, Russ, Jasper, and Sarge. All are excited about this big Gala. Lady Noreen's and Patrick's fashions are for women sizes 6 to size 22. They feel that they want women to be well-rounded in fashion.

Lady Noreen has sent Odessa with Sergeant Mussack and Christopher to deliver some of the dresses to Patrick at his florist shop. Odessa is a fast learner and has quickly caught onto the fashion business through Lady Noreen's and Patrick's guidance.

As Sergeant Mussack drops Christopher and Odessa off at the shop, he doesn't notice anything usual around him and everything seems fine. Since he is off duty today and wearing civilian clothes, he feels happy doing this as a favor for Christopher. He wants to help out in some small way with the fashion show.

Christopher and Odessa carry a few dresses at a time into the store that Lady Noreen packaged in separate garment bags. They finally carry the final load of dresses into Patrick's Floral Shop and Sergeant Mussack closes the SUV door. While he is doing that, he observes three shady looking characters following Christopher and Odessa into the florist shop.

Patrick is oblivious to everything going on around him while moving the garments to the backroom. In fact, he doesn't even see the three men enter the store as he goes to hang the dresses for the fashion show into the storage room closet.

As Christopher and Odessa wait for Patrick to come back, one of the men grabs Odessa by both arms and begins dragging her to the front door. Then he yells out, "This girl is ours, you took her from us. Now you must pay the price with your life for not listening to my boss, Christopher. My boss told you that you would go out feet first if you took Odessa from him. If I had it my way, Odessa would be buried at the bottom of my swimming pool with the other three girls, but my boss won't let me do her in!"

Christopher yells back at them, "I warned your boss for all of you to stay away from her, but I can see that none of you listened to my warning. I told him that his threat would come back to anyone who tried to get Odessa from me or harm her in anyway."

Seeing through the window what is going on, Sergeant Mussack removes his gun and enters the store. He has a gut feeling that these men are after Odessa, and they are part of the prostitution ring.

As the men see Sergeant Mussack enter the store, the one man fires his gun at him and a bullet hits the police sergeant in the shoulder.

Sergeant Mussack then fires his gun back at the man and several bullets hit that man directly in his upper torso.

When Christopher sees Sergeant Mussack shoot back at the man; he quickly pushes Odessa out of the way from any harm. He doesn't want Odessa's life endangered when the bullets start flying in the air.

Then Christopher jumps the second man. Christopher wants to make sure that that man won't fire on Sergeant Mussack.

Hearing a gun fire, Patrick grabs his gun and runs out and shoots the third man in the head before the lowlife can return fire on anyone. This man quickly drops to the floor dead holding his gun in his hand.

As Christopher struggles with the second man on the floor, the gun goes off. Patrick thinks that Christopher has been shot. As he pushes the man off of Christopher, he sees that the second man is shot in the chest, and Christopher is unharmed and very much alive.

Christopher slowly gets up and goes over with Patrick to help Sergeant Mussack on his feet. Then, Patrick calls 911 for the police and the ambulances.

When the police arrive, they find that Patrick, Christopher and Odessa safe. Sergeant Mussack; however, has a gun wound in his right shoulder.

As they go to take the three fugitives out to the ambulance, they discover that all three of the men are dead. So the crime scene is marked off, and the dead men are taken out of the florist shop in body bags.

The police question everyone and Sergeant Mussack backs up all of their stories. Patrick rides with Sergeant Mussack to the hospital in the ambulance to have Sergeant Mussack's shoulder treated.

Before Sergeant Mussack leaves to get in the ambulance with Patrick, he thanks both Christopher and Patrick for saving his life and protecting him in the shootout.

Christopher respectfully says to Sergeant Mussack, "Patrick is the one who saved us all today. If he had not shot the other man, both of us might be dead right now."

Sergeant Mussack politely whispers to Patrick, "Thanks so much, Patrick, for saving our lives!"

Patrick replies, "I had to protect both of you, or Lady Noreen would kill all of us if we don't have her fashion show ready for her by next week."

Christopher laughs out loud saying, "You are so right! I am so glad that you purchased a handgun recently and had it registered, Patrick."

"Sad to say, Christopher, the American people are no longer safe. They need to purchase guns for crime protection. Else they are sitting ducks when someone tries to rob them. These days, Christopher, they not only rob you, but they kill you. A lot of business owners around here now own guns. It will one day be a way of life that everyone will have to own a gun, I fear. The gun market is among the country's major industries. Ever since manufacturing moved overseas and people here lost their jobs, the gun and illegal drug industries have evolved to become the leading ones in America," shares Patrick with him.

Sergeant Mussack adds to this, "Yes, Christopher, he is right. There are no longer enough policemen being hired on the force to protect everyone. Crime is out of control!"

By now, Odessa, who has been in the bathroom for a few minutes, comes out with tears in her eyes saying, "I am so sorry about all the trouble that I have caused all of you. I almost got everyone killed. I can't thank each one of you enough for saving my life!"

"Odessa," Christopher, interrupts, "It is over with. No more people will come after you. Don't you worry anymore; I promise you that it is over with! Let's go back to the house, and let Sergeant Mussack and Patrick board the ambulance to the hospital."

"Okay, Christopher. Lady Noreen will be so upset when she hears what has happened to us today," emotionally states Odessa to him.

"You are so right, Odessa! We better head to Lady Noreen's house real fast," says Christopher to Odessa.

Sergeant Mussack gives Christopher his keys, so he can drive his SUV to Lady Noreen's house.

"By the way, Odessa," remarks Christopher, "when the sergeant gets back on his feet, I'll have him check the swimming pool at the one dead man's house to see if your friends are buried at the bottom of the pool there."

Then, off drives Christopher in Sergeant Mussack's SUV with Odessa to Lady Noreen's house.

Once at her house, they both see Lady Noreen waiting very impatiently for them. She can't believe it took them all day just to deliver a few dresses to Patrick's shop. You can tell that Lady Noreen is really upset with Christopher by the expression she has on her face.

After getting out of the SUV, Odessa runs to Lady Noreen, and tells her how the men from the prostitute ring tried to kidnap her at the florist shop, and that Christopher, Patrick, and Sergeant Mussack saved her life.

Lady Noreen can't believe what she is hearing from Odessa! "And these three men attempted to kill Christopher, Sergeant Mussack, and Patrick repeats Lady Noreen to herself." Lady Noreen keeps saying these words over and over to herself as her eyes get as big as cabbages. She can't believe Christopher might have been killed in the gun fight earlier today.

After Odessa is done telling Lady Noreen the details about the shootings and the deaths of the three ring members. Lady Noreen yells out at them saying, "Did those hoodlums damage any of my dresses for the show or get their blood on them, Christopher?"

"No, Lady Noreen, not a drop of blood is on any of the dresses! Your dresses are in perfect condition for the Safari Fashion Show next week."

"Thank heavens, those men are dead, Christopher, or I would have bought a machine gun myself and hunted each one of them down. Once I found them I would have killed them. They aren't going to hurt my men, my Odessa, or my dresses. They are better off dead and eliminated off our planet. Good riddance to all three of them! From now until the fashion show, Odessa and you, Christopher, are going to stay in the house with me. I'm not going to have any more soap opera dramas. I am too old for all of this! I am not prepared for this scary world called life!"

Christopher and Odessa remain in the house with Lady Noreen. Lady Noreen won't allow either one of them out of her sight. She is petrified that someone will kill the two of them. If that happens, she wants to die with Christopher. Lady Noreen never wants to live her life alone ever again.

Chapter 29

Always Remember Stay Wild At Heart!

The day for Lady Noreen and Patrick's Safari Fashion Show has finally arrived. Christopher and Odessa are so happy! Lady Noreen has provided oversight to cutting patterns, helping her sew, iron, and bag every dress up to the critical moment. She has even designed head scarves she calls "Wild Things". The scarves are designed in a multitude of colors embossed with jungle animals. She feels those beasts will assist them in fighting the deadly demon called cancer.

Odessa and Christopher have provided the craftsmanship for the cutting of the scarves and are totally exhausted from their efforts. They believe that Lady Noreen's ulterior motive in creating the new fashions was to keep them home with her. However, after tonight, Christopher and Odessa plan to regain independence and live their lives in the outside world once again.

Lady Noreen has Patrick working both day and night. Patrick can't believe the large number of garments and Wild Thing Scarves that have been produced for tonight's Safari Fashion Show.

Marcuso's Clothing Store is supplying the men's suits, tuxedos, and men's casual sportswear for the big show and Christopher promised Patrick that he would model one of his new suits during the final showing of the designer collection.

The day is hectic, like always. Brook has limos delivering both Lady Noreen's and Patrick's Designer Collection to the Mystic Black Pearl Ballroom in Longport. Limo after limo is seen transporting clothes and decorations for the big show. Everyone is on pins and needles hoping that this event will be a huge success for Lady Noreen. Her loved ones know how hard she has worked on this project, even though she is very tired and sick. Her family, her friends, and all of her supporters are determined to make this night a night for Lady Noreen to remember.

Around 3 p.m., the models and participants in the show start arriving to allow Lady Noreen and Patrick to provide the professionals to do hair styling and makeup so they can commence the show by 8 p.m. tonight.

Marc Marcuso is there, too, with the male models to make sure that their shoes and hair are all professionally styled and groomed.

Of course, Christopher now has to have his beard groomed since he has grown it back once again to make Lady Noreen happy. Lady Noreen just loves his beard! She was so disgusted with Christopher when he shaved it off.

Rico and Marcena are seen assisting Lady Noreen and Patrick in decorating the ballroom.

Odessa is making sure that every detail that Lady Noreen has requested is done to perfection. Odessa doesn't want to hear it from Lady Noreen that something went wrong at her big event.

By 7 p.m., the ballroom is fully decorated. The models are practicing their walk down the runway for the third and last time and know their cues. Everyone is ready for this evening's fashion show.

Sergeant Mussack has shown up for the purpose of providing security and making certain that there are no surprises or uninvited guests arriving at the show. His shoulder has slowly healed and he is almost as good as new. He found out a few weeks back that Odessa's friends were in fact buried underneath Thomas Hekel's swimming pool. Hekel was one of the men killed in the shootout last month. Sergeant Mussack was so pleased to confirm the information and provide Odessa with some closure so she could have a peace of mind about the fate of her three friends. After all, these young women were just like family to her since these girls had no real family. Sad to say, how these girls had suffered as victims of the prostitute ring. They were simply living out their pimp's darkest fantasy.

Jasper arrives not only to model in the show, but to help Sergeant Mussack with security at the door. Jasper has recently written a collection of poems because of Christopher's encouragement. He still is somewhat of a non-conformist, but at least he is becoming more polite and social, and staying out of the garbage containers on the Boardwalk. Jasper now sells his poetry for pocket change for food and boarding.

People from all walks of life begin arriving at the door to attend the Gala. The once in a lifetime event is sold out. Word of mouth has spread like wildfire about the introduction of the exciting line of wild fashions that bring out the beast. Fashion buyers and marketing agents from all over the world are in attendance to review Lady Noreen's and Patrick's fashions.

At 8:00 p.m. sharp, Patrick provides the models with the cue to begin the show while he conducts the narration. One by one, the models walk down the runway. People can't believe the remarkable beauty of the dresses and the gowns as one by one Marcena with Joshua, Teresa Y. with Rico, Julie with Bruce, Hilten with Sarge, Old Bessie with Big Luke, Ngoc with Heffe, P.J. with Feymale, Joy Rhapsody with Nicholas, Emiliann with Russ, Jessica with Orlando, Daisy and Mama Cane with Jasper, strut their stuff down the runway.

The audience goes wild over the array of dresses patterned with African lions, tigers, giraffes, elephants, ostriches, panthers, apes, monkeys, and other miscellaneous wild animals modeled one by one on the runway. The models are being accompanied by the band playing African dance music.

The drummers electrify the night with the beating of the drums to the upscale show.

As each model travels the aisle three to four times, lights reflect an array of colors reflecting on the models.

In the finale, Patrick changes the lighting from laser to strobe lights. He has the models pose as mannequins on the stage, and suddenly re-energize themselves into dance movements. The audience goes crazy. Patrick is overjoyed!

Lady Noreen and Marc Marcuso are exhausted from dressing the models but thrilled with the outcome. Patrick finally cues Christopher to begin modeling for the final runway performance. With that, Christopher grabs Lady Noreen against her will, and struts with her down the runway. He is so honored and proud of her. He is wearing an all gold fashion suit designed by Marc Marcuso. Lady Noreen is wearing a beautiful purple tie dye fabric dress with tigers sculptured into the fabric. Together, they happily model the final fashions for the evening.

The audience erupts with yells and shouts of joy, and gives bravos to Lady Noreen and Christopher with a standing ovation. As the drums get louder, the models return to the stage for final bows wearing their Wild Thing Scarves. The audience cheers each of the models individually. Then suddenly the models step down from the runway and begin to dispense and wrap scarves around the necks of the people in the audience.

After that, Patrick hails the audience to model, rise in their seats and show off their Wild Thing Scarves and to pay tribute not only to Lady Noreen, but to all the breast cancer victims and survivors. Patrick then hands the microphone to Lady Noreen. He gives her a big hug and kiss. He can't believe what the two of them have accomplished at this show tonight.

Lady Noreen announces the names of the models from the program and requests them to take a final bow and strut down the runway one last time. She presents each model with a trophy of a tiger for their contribution to the Safari Fashion Show. Following that, Lady Noreen calls both Patrick and Odessa to the stage to present to both of them a plaque honoring their achievements in making the Safari Fashion Show a huge success.

Next, Lady Noreen calls Marc Marcuso to the stage to present to him a plaque honoring his participation and efforts in making the fashion show a reality.

Lady Noreen then calls the Nairobi African Band to the stage to present them all with tiger trophies to honor their musical achievement for tonight's show.

After that, Lady Noreen calls Arthur to the stage to give him a check for $1,000.00 for his Atlantic City charity that feeds the abandoned and stray cats. The audience applauds approvingly about

Arthur's philanthropic efforts. Arthur receives the check and poses for photographers.

Christopher then takes the microphone from Lady Noreen and calls Rico to the stage to make an announcement. Lady Noreen looks at Christopher in bewilderment for this was not part of the fashion show's scheduled program.

Rico happily comes up to the stage and recognizes Lady Noreen's battle against breast cancer. He then declares, "I want everyone here to know that my first non-profit race will be run on the first Sunday in October of next year. This event will be dedicated to Lady Noreen. I am so proud to announce that she is a breast cancer survivor, and we plan to raise as much money as we can to donate to breast cancer research through this race. This way, we can help Lady Noreen fight this deadly disease not only for herself, but for others. We all love you, Lady Noreen!" Then, Rico gives Lady Noreen a big kiss.

At the conclusion of the show, Christopher has Marc Marcuso bring a chair on the stage for Lady Noreen and calls Jumbo Tiny Tut to the stage. Jumbo Tiny Tut Tut is modeling one of Lady Noreen's beautiful pink tie die fashions with a pattern of giraffes on it with her hair fashioned with lovely colored braids. Christopher, with great pleasure, asks her to perform the final number for the night. With that Jumbo Tiny Tut Tut begins to dance to the beating of the drums an African dance entitled, "The Wild Animals Are Wild Tonight," that the Niarobi African Band have written in honor of tonight's show for Lady Noreen.

When, Jumbo Tiny Tut Tut and the band are done performing, the audience claps and yells for them to perform the song one more time. The song is a hit with the audience as they continue to applaud, scream, and whistle for more.

Once the audience is done with their applause for Jumbo Tiny Tut Tut, she calls Lady Noreen to the microphone to award Lady Noreen a plaque for being the creator of the Safari Fashion Show. Then, Jumbo Tiny Tut Tut gives both Lady Noreen and Christopher a big hug. After Jumbo Tiny Tut Tut is done hugging both of them, Christopher hurries to present a tiger trophy award to Lady Noreen.

Only Christopher knows that Bredele used to torture Jumbo Tiny Tut Tut with awful and cruel jokes about her weight and bring her to tears. Tonight Jumbo Tiny Tut Tut proved to be among the most beautiful of musical artists. After tonight, Jumbo Tiny Tut Tut as everyone calls her, will never cry again!

Lady Noreen is now at the microphone with tears in her eyes as she says, "To all of you here tonight, I want to thank you for a night to always remember. The fashions are now available for sale at Patrick's shop or Marcuso's Men's Clothing Store. Continue to run and walk for breast cancer victims and survivors. God bless you all and always remember to stay wild at heart!"

Chapter 30

Only He Knows The Truth

In the months of June and July Atlantic City is alive with excitement. The umbrellas are viewed on the beaches. Sailboats and cruise tour ships are spotted throughout the water. The lifeguards are back on duty and people are seen sunbathing on the beach, swimming and boogie boarding in the ocean. The smell of fresh life and salt is in the air. The smell resurrects Christopher's energy and mental powers. He is now with Lady Noreen preparing for the birth of Marcena's and Joshua's baby.

Lady Noreen hears the good news that Marcena is healthy and her pregnancy is fine. She was really worried about Marcena's pregnancy at first, since she had morning sickness almost daily during the first three months followed by weight loss. Thank heavens, she is healthier now, putting on weight, and her pregnancy is going faster for her. Lady Noreen is collaborating with Patrick on the nursery design and furnishings. Marcena's delivery is expected for September. Lady Noreen is dying to know if the baby is a boy or a girl.

Marcena can't believe that Christopher wants her to have twins; so he can use both of the names that he has chosen for them. Christopher keeps saying that they will have two babies, but Marcena keeps telling Christopher that he is wrong because the doctor only hears one heartbeat. However, Marcena, sometimes thinks Christopher is psychic. That might be because once in a while she still has a dream that Christopher flew with her in the sky on the night that she was almost beaten to death, but now she thinks it was just a figment of her imagination. In fact, at that time in her life, she also thought she had died but she didn't!

Rico is now working out with Lady Noreen for his race in October. Rico thought it would be good for Lady Noreen to start and exercise with him again since she is starting to feel more like herself even though she is still undergoing the chemotherapy injection regime.

As Christopher walks down to the beach he overhears a young man by the name of Kashmir who is the head lifeguard suggesting to the lifeguards Emily and Fernando that they might consider improving their rowing skills to navigate in the high waves. This way, they might be better able to save the lives of a drowning victim.

When Kashmir walks away from both of the lifeguards, Christopher can see a lack of confidence in both of their faces so he says to Fernando and Emily, "Hi! I think both of you know me, I'm Christopher Saint. I just wanted you to know that I row my boat every Saturday morning around 7:00 a.m. in the ocean, so if either one of you needs instruction, I will be glad to help you with your boating and swimming skills. Here is my address in Ventnor." Then, Christopher hands them both a card with his name and address on it.

The two lifeguards thank him, but do not commit to meeting up with him on a Saturday morning. Instead, they both just thank him for his invitation, and walk back to their lifeguard station.

Christopher than walks back up to the Boardwalk, and sits on a bench with a bag of peanuts to feed the pigeons. At least fifteen pigeons fly right to him, and begin eating the peanuts right out of his hand.

As Christopher looks up and down the Boardwalk, he sees people playing their instruments, doing mime, dancing and rapping everywhere. He can tell that life on the Boardwalk has come back again for the months of June, July, and August.

Before too long, a young woman comes and sits beside him; she looks refreshed and full of energy. Christopher wonders where she came from; so he asks her, "Do you work at the casino?"

"No, I just came here early today to go to the casino spa to get a massage, and then to the Jacuzzi to relax. And then finally I'll go for a swim. I always feel so good after the massage. I think this routine helps me stay young. It helps to rejuvenate my blood flow and lifeline."

"Oh, I'll have to tell my lady friend about the spa, I don't think she has gone to the casino spa before. Thanks for telling me about the spa, madam. Bye for now!" enthusiastically Christopher replies to her.

Then Christopher gets up to walk back to Ventnor and determine if Lady Noreen wants to go to the spa. He believes that the spa might just be the right thing for her. Lately, she has had occasional sickness and been unable to visit the casino. Christopher wants Lady Noreen to return to doing some of her fun things again.

On his way back to Ventnor, Christopher can't believe it, but he runs right into Bredele.

Bredele runs immediately over to Christopher, and on a magic pad writes to him, "Christopher, it is so good to see you! I have lost my voice, and this is the only way that I can communicate with you. I want you to know that I am a changed man. I only see the good in people now. In fact, Jumbo Tiny Tut Tut told me she won an award at Lady Noreen's Safari Fashion Show, and I wrote to her on my magic pad telling her how proud of her I was. You were right, Christopher. Jumbo Tiny Tut Tut is truly a beautiful woman! Well, Christopher, I better get back to work now. Bye!"

As Christopher watches Bredele walk down the Boardwalk to his job at the casino; he hollers in a loud voice to him, "Keep being positive, Bredele. You are becoming a better man! Bye for now!"

As Christopher walks further down the Boardwalk, he sees Russ conditioning in preparation for his wheelchair race in the fall. He is just practicing to improve his time for it.

"Russ, keep up the good work! I can tell that you are ready for your wheelchair race in the fall. Rico has been working out daily too."

"Christopher, I am in better condition than I was in the last race. I think it is because I am eating healthier and devotedly taking my medicine."

"Russ, it pays to be in control of your life. Your body suffers when you are not controlling your weight and eating habits. Keep up your conditioning and nutrition program. It will all pay off for you in the fall.

By the way, Russ, did you tell your mother about the family secret that you shared with me and kept quiet since you were twelve years old?"

"Christopher, no, it is sometimes easier for one to live in the present than for one to go back into their past."

"Well, one day, my friend, I pray that you will be able to confront your past and be let free of it! I'll pray for you my son," sincerely Christopher replies.

"Thanks, Christopher! You mean the world to me! I have to get back to my training for the race."

"Okay, Russ! Bye for now!" Christopher says to him while waving good-bye.

As Christopher walks further down the Boardwalk he can see a number of volunteers accompanying Arthur going down the steps under the Boardwalk to feed the cats. Christopher can't believe the number of concerned people worried about the abandoned cats in Atlantic City. Christopher is proud of Arthur efforts in starting the program to feed the cats. Now, Arthur provides the cats and kittens veterinarian care with the additional money that Lady Noreen has donated from the Safari Fashion Show, for Arthur's philanthropic efforts.

Before Christopher knows it, he is finally in Ventnor at Lady Noreen's house. He sees her working in the garden. He yells at her, "Lady Noreen! Oh, Lady Noreen! Guess what? I want you to book yourself to go to your favorite casino and visit the spa and schedule a massage. While you are there you can enjoy the Jacuzzi, and even take a swim in the pool. Doesn't everything sound like lots of fun to you?"

"It does sound like fun! Now, that I am going to live, Christopher. I might as well get back to doing things again. I'll go and call my casino host right now and book the spa for the two of us. You do want to go with me don't you, Christopher?"

"Of course, Lady Noreen, we'll have a great time at the spa together. You do feel well enough to go there with me, don't you?" in a concerned voice Christopher asks Lady Noreen.

"Christopher, I must admit, I'm starting to feel like my young self again. I don't want to say old anymore, or I might just die," answers Lady Noreen in a scared to death voice.

Lady Noreen goes inside to make reservations for their day at the casino, while Christopher goes out to the beach to look for Sanabrio.

As Christopher looks out far in the sky, Christopher sees his friend's wings flying full of life. Then, Sanabrio swoops down to catch his prey. Christopher walks back to the house knowing that his friend is safe and content.

Once in the house, Christopher hears Lady Noreen humming to herself.

Christopher knows for sure that she is happy to be going back to the casino once again. She loves the excitement there.

The next day, the two of them go to the casino and have the time of their lives. Both Lady Noreen and Christopher book an hour massage, and then go into the Jacuzzi for about thirty minutes. Afterwards, they jump into the pool, and then go lie on the deck chairs to sunbathe. Lady Noreen smiles and laughs with joy the whole time. She enjoys the entire day at the spa with Christopher. She feels like her body has been purified through her activities today.

Lady Noreen, after concluding her day of relaxation, asks Christopher, "Do you want to do this again with me?"

Christopher replies, "Let's do it any day of the week that you want, Lady Noreen. This is lots of fun! We both have been rejuvenated and brought back to life! It's like we have been reincarnated back into God's world again."

Then, the two of them gather their belongings, put their towels in the bin near the pool, and walk out of the spa happily holding hands.

Lady Noreen says to Christopher, "I've had a day of healing!"

On the way down the escalator to the front of the casino there is Bredele. When Bredele sees Christopher, he runs up to him and Lady Noreen and writes on his magic tablet, "Lady Noreen, it is so good to see you! I heard about your fashion show, from Jumbo Tiny Tut Tut. Keep up the good work that you are doing!"

Lady Noreen looks at Christopher with a puzzled face, "Why is Bredele writing on a tablet for us to read?"

"Lady Noreen, poor Bredele has lost his voice. He can't talk; so he has to converse using his tablet."

"Oh, I see! But I thought he hated your guts, Christopher!" remarks Lady Noreen in a high pitched tone.

"At one time, he did, Lady Noreen, but people do change through life altering situations, and it seems like that is what has happened to Bredele," explains Christopher to Lady Noreen.

"Oh, that is what has happened to Bredele. Well, for him to have changed that much, it must have been really life-altering! The man used to use his mouth like a machete and destroy anyone in sight with his evil words. But, Christopher, if you say he has changed, I believe you," replies Lady Noreen.

As Lady Noreen and Christopher get ready to leave the casino, Christopher looks back at Bredele, and he sees Bredele waving good-bye.

Christopher responds and returns the wave back to Bredele.

For the rest of the month, Lady Noreen and Christopher go once a week to the casino, the spa for a massage, to the Jacuzzi for relaxation, and recreational swims. Lady Noreen is starting to be surrounded by wellness. She is also trying to focus more on living than on dying these days.

To Christopher's shock, Fernando and Emily join him every Sunday for rowboat and swimming lessons. When they are done with their lessons, Christopher has them workout with Lady Noreen and Rico.

Fernando, because of Rico, has bought a weight lifting set, so he can build up his muscle strength.

Emily is starting to jog with Lady Noreen, so that she can have more energy and endurance. She also wants to lose her belly fat.

Throughout the next two months, everyone is healing, conditioning, and rejuvenating in God's own world. Even for the Fourth of July, Lady Noreen just wants to stay at home for a cookout with Christopher, Marcena, Joshua, Rico, Teresa Y., her family, Brook, Odessa, Patrick, Nicholas, Hannah, Raul, Russ, Jasper, Daisy, Old Bessie, Mama Cane, and her foster children, Whitney, Mervin, Mariah, Jepson, and Gregory, who Mama Cane calls all her children, and of course, Tigress, and Tom Cat. They are all dressed up for the big July celebration.

Their summer is a summer of healing, leisure, happiness, learning, and a true appreciation of life itself. Thanks to Lady Noreen's determination and will power to return to life from her breast surgery, chemotherapy and reconstructive surgery.

Lady Noreen, at this point in her life, has realized that people have a choice in life. They can either fight to live, or give up and die, or commit suicide. Everyone has a choice! However, when the pain from a disease or life gets too great, anyone also has the right to give up and go on to the other side. There they will find peace and happiness. Heaven's doors are always open to anyone who believes in God the Father Almighty. God judges us, not other people, that is why there are so many people in Heaven not in Hell! Only God knows the truth!"

Chapter 31

Miracles Never Cease!

In August, Christopher and Rico decide that they should plan a birthday party for Lady Noreen, which is August 15th the same day as the Feast of the Assumption of the Blessed Mother, and a surprise baby shower for Marcena and Joshua.

Rico says to Christopher, "Let's plan an incredible night on the town for the two of them. Let's have a music program of exotic myriad dancers, Celtic music, and Teresa Y. can do several violin pieces for the program with you, Christopher, and the Sarge. Lady Noreen likes healing music lately. Then, Hilten with Joy Rhapsody, Emiliann, Feymale, and Jessica can sing Happy Birthday to her. Also, let's have a male go-go dancer come out of her cake and dance for her to spice up her life. This is her 64th birthday. Let's get her ready to live life to its fullest! Marcena will have no clue that her baby shower is on the same day. She will think the party is just for Lady Noreen. We will have two cakes, one for Lady Noreen's birthday, and another one for Marcena's baby shower. Everyone is really going to be surprised, Christopher!"

While Lady Noreen is exercising and working in the garden, Christopher and Rico start calling to invite all of the guests to set up Lady Noreen's big bash and Marcena and Joshua's surprise baby shower at the casino. This is going to be a birthday for Lady Noreen to remember and Marcena is going to be really surprised on August 15th.

In the morning, Marcena comes over to the house to see the clothes that Lady Noreen has bought for the baby. Lady Noreen can hardly wait until September; all she does is order baby clothes on-line for her grandchild-to-be. The baby is due on September 12th, and everyone is so excited about the baby being born. However, Lady Noreen is sick of buying just green, white, and yellow baby clothes since she doesn't know if the baby is a girl or boy. It is killing her!

Later that day when Marcena gets ready to have Brook pick her up to go home, Rico tells her about Lady Noreen's surprise birthday party and goes over the details of it with her. He tells her that he needs her to help him cut the cake and work with Patrick on the party.

Marcena is so excited about the party for Lady Noreen. As pregnant as she is and looks, Marcena hopes she doesn't deliver before August 15th.

The next few weeks are filled with secret phone calls to set up the surprise party for both Lady Noreen and Marcena. Odessa and Old Bessie have been told by Christopher and Rico to keep Lady Noreen very busy decorating the baby's nursery until the party. They have Brook taking Lady Noreen to several different children's furniture stores with him to buy the crib and accessories for the nursery.

Meanwhile, Rico continues preparation for his race and spreading the word that he has a big surprise to announce prior to the race. He has discussed with Christopher the possibility that he won't be in it this time. This would allow another wheelchair participant to win the race.

Christopher tells Rico, "Son, you don't have to win it; just be in it. Life isn't about winning or losing the race; it's about being in it, and continuing the race."

Rico is satisfied with Christopher's advice. He will be in the race, but at the last minute, he might let someone else win it. It isn't important to him anymore that he has to win the race. This is because he considers himself one of the luckiest young men in the world to have the life he has now.

Patrick is in overdrive working on the nursery for Marcena with Lady Noreen and at the same time, working on the party for Lady Noreen with Marcena. On top of working on all of their surprises, he is managing the fashion displays and orders, plus running his floral shop. Lately, he has engaged Nicholas to assist him with the florist shop and Marc Marcuso has hired employees to produce the designer dresses and fill orders for the fashions designed by Lady Noreen and Patrick, too.

Christopher is up to his neck with projects. He is working constantly on the party, working on the house, and continuation of lessons for Fernando and Emily to build up their boating and swimming skills. On top of all of this, he is sneaking away during the week to work with Sarge and Teresa Y. on the music to be played at Lady Noreen's birthday party and repairing Mama Cane's roof. He is so busy that there is no time left for him to trim his beard which has grown down to his chest.

Lady Noreen continues to work out with Rico, shop for the nursery, design new fashions with Patrick, and take Tigress and Tom Cat shopping for new toys. She also has the time to work in the garden, run with Emily, feed the abandoned cats with Arthur, and plan vegetarian food buffets for her extended family. She now feels that you are what you eat! In fact, she has created her own cabbage soup recipe with cabbage, tomatoes, carrots, jalapenos, lettuce, onion, garlic, and black olives in it. She uses the blender to prepare her new health food delights.

August 15th finally arrives. Lady Noreen is a little bit hurt for no one seems to remember that her birthday is today. Everyone just ignores her. The only one that has called her this week was her guest host at the casino to invite her to visit the casino for dinner and participate in a tournament there. Lady Noreen is very upset with everyone. She says to her host, "I'd love to come to the casino on the 15th and be in the tournament. Apparently, I have nothing else planned for that day."

Lady Noreen has no idea that it was all planned by Rico and Christopher to have the casino host call her. On top of that, Rico and Marcena have informed Lady Noreen that they have made alternative plans for that date. Lady Noreen believes that Christopher too has forgotten her birthday.

When it gets time to get ready to go to the casino, Christopher tells Lady Noreen, "I am going to wear my gold suit from the fashion show tonight."

Lady Noreen tells him, "Christopher don't dress up, you'll look stupid, just wear your casual clothes."

"Lady Noreen, please let me wear my suit. I never get to dress up anymore since we just go to the spa, the Jacuzzi, the pool, exercise, run, and eat vegetarian food. Please let me dress up like you did in the old days."

"Christopher, I was old in the old days - now I am young. Let's dress sporty!"

"Please Lady Noreen; please, wear the purple designer dress that you wore at the fashion show. It's beautiful! Please, I grew my beard back for you, if you don't wear your purple dress, I'll shave off my beard."

"Christopher, I'll wear it, but you're crazy to make me wear it! You are a crazy man! But I love your beard!"

Lady Noreen and Christopher get dressed to kill, and Brook picks them up on time. Little does Lady Noreen know that her extended family and friends are at the casino.

Meanwhile, Rico is over at Marcena's house waiting for Teresa Y. to pick them up. Marcena doesn't know it, but Teresa Y. is purposely being late in picking up Marcena and Joshua for the party.

Once Brook drops Lady Marcena and Christopher off at the casino, Christopher takes Lady Noreen to visit with her host. After the visit, the host tells Christopher and Lady Noreen to visit the Ocean Front Ballroom.

They proceed up the escalator and to the ballroom. As they open the door to the ballroom everyone yells, "Surprise! Happy Birthday, Lady Noreen!"

As Lady Noreen and Christopher are being seated at the head table, Marcena and Joshua come in the door with Rico and Teresa Y., and everybody screams out once again, "Happy Baby Shower!"

Marcena and Joshua are escorted to the main table to sit with Lady Noreen and Christopher. Christopher and Rico are proud of themselves for pulling off the surprise parties tonight with Patrick's assistance.

Patrick is standing at the microphone to begin the birthday/ shower event. First he calls those seated at the tables by number to proceed to the buffet tables to select appetizers and entrees. One by one, extended family and friends go to the different buffet tables and pile the food on their plates.

When everyone is seated, the show begins. First the exotic myriad dance company performance, then a Celtic singing group, and finally Teresa Y., Sarge, and Christopher perform.

Next, Patrick has the waiters and waitresses take the birthday and baby shower cake and ice cream to all of the tables, and have everyone sing, "Happy Birthday," to Lady Noreen. When they are done, the waiters roll out a giant paper mache cake, and out of it pops a go-go dancer that dances right in front of Lady Noreen's head table.

Lady Noreen just turns all red and laughs up a storm. The Birthday Girl is truly enjoying her 64th birthday party. She hasn't been this happy for so long.

When the go-go dancer is done, the waiters push out another giant paper mache cake and out pops a Teddy Bear that goes in front of Marcena and dances to the music of the "Chicken Dance".

The Teddy Bear then requests the guests to deliver their shower and birthday gifts to Marcena and Lady Noreen and join them in dancing to the "Chicken Dance" with the Teddy Bear.

Christopher is in shock, "He sees Bredele dancing to the "Chicken Dance," with Jumbo Tiny Tut Tut. He can't believe his eyes, and to Christopher, it looks like they are having lots of fun together.

Marcena and Joshua are laughing so hard that tears are coming down Marcena's face as she continues to dance with the Teddy Bear. This is the most exciting baby shower party Marcena has ever been to in her life.

Before Lady Noreen's, Marcena's and Joshua's family, friends, and co-workers leave the party, Marcena and Joshua thank everyone. Marcena is in complete shock at how Rico, Christopher, and Patrick surprised both she and Joshua.

When Marcena and Joshua are finished with their thanks and good-byes, Rico takes the microphone and says, "I have always heard in my life that good things happen in threes. I want to announce that Teresa Y. and I will be getting married on New Year's Eve at midnight on a cruise ship that will be docked in Atlantic City. We want to invite all of you here tonight to attend and celebrate our wedding night. I am so honored that Teresa Y. is going to marry me and that her family will be part of my family. Secondly, I am so honored to become Uncle Rico in another month, and thirdly, the Wheelchair and 5K Race-Walk in October of this year won't be called the Oktoberfest Wheelchair 5K Race, but instead it is now will be named the Lady Noreen Wheelchair and 5K Race. I want to make both women and men aware of breast cancer."

Everyone applauds and cheers!

Lady Noreen can't believe everything she just heard Rico say. First, she is going to be a grandmother, now she is going to plan another wedding for New Year's Eve, and on top of everything else, she has to take her running seriously to be in Rico's race in October since it is named after her. Lady Noreen knows this is going to be quite an exciting year for her as she celebrates her 64th birthday!

Christopher just winks his eye at Rico, and responds to him by saying, "Congratulations to both Teresa Y. and you, Rico! I was hoping that you would make that announcement tonight. Now, we are ready to celebrate your wedding on New Year's Eve!"

The waitresses and waiters put all of the gifts into bags and carry them out to the limos waiting to take the guests home. Joshua and Marcena get into one limo with their shower gifts. Lady Noreen and Christopher get into another limo with Lady Noreen's birthday gifts. Patrick, Russ, and Nicholas get into the third limo. Odessa, Sarge, Daisy, and Old Bessie get into the fourth limousine. Mama Cane with her foster children get into the fifth limo to be taken to their house. Teresa Y. and her parents get into the sixth limo to be chauffeured home. The rest of the guests either drive their own cars home or live in walking distance from the casino.

At the moment, there is a convoy of limousines traveling through Atlantic City. Tonight is truly one of the happiest memories in the lives of Lady Noreen, Marcena, Joshua, Teresa Y., and Rico.

Chapter 32

I Think God Will Cure It

Labor Day weekend comes and Lady Noreen is back to life. With her grandbaby getting ready to be born all she wants to do is celebrate. This Saturday in September, she wants Christopher to take her to the casino to get a $3,000.00 cash reward prize earned from her cash play at the casino last weekend. Lady Noreen also needs Christopher to go shopping with her since she plans to spend the money on Marcena and Rico. She is truly looking forward to the upcoming events of the birth of her grandchild and Rico's wedding on New Year's Eve.

On Saturday at noon, Brook picks Lady Noreen and Christopher up in Ventnor, and on their way to the casino they go. Once there, Lady Noreen is so excited! She goes to her casino host and to the high roller lounge to pick up her $3,000.00 rewards cash ticket to spend in the shops on the Boardwalk. Once she has the cash ticket, off to the Boardwalk Christopher and her go to shop.

At the first shop, which is Merv's Technology Store, she purchases a new TV for Rico and Teresa for their wedding present. Then, she picks up a video camera for Joshua and Marcena to take video pictures of the baby. Since Lady Noreen still has lots of money left she grabs Christopher to go into the jewelry store with her. There she makes him try on watch after watch until she decides on which one to purchase for him. Finally, after 30 minutes, she selects one for him, and purchases it. Then, she starts looking at watches for herself. After about 45 minutes, she selects one. By this time both Christopher and the sales clerk are completely worn out.

Next, she grabs Christopher, and into the Star Sport Shop they go. There she purchases two MP3 digital FM Tuners with a built-in stopwatch, built-in pedometer, and an armband for Rico and her to wear running. She is really pleased with these items. She thinks these gifts will make Rico and her jogs more relaxing and exciting.

Finally, she asks Christopher to accompany her back to the jewelry store to purchase pearl earrings for Teresa Y., and one pair of sterling silver ball earrings for Teresa Y.'s wedding shower coming up in December. Then, Lady Noreen purchases an additional two pairs of sterling silver ball earrings for Odessa and Old Bessie, and a gold chain for Patrick. Last, but not least, Lady Noreen wants to purchase a gold bracelet with a gold baby charm on it, for Marcena. Lady Noreen is so into the baby being born that she starts to cry, when the sales clerk shows her the bracelet with the charm on it.

When Lady Noreen has completed her shopping spree she says to Christopher, "Do you mind if we go back to the casino and play a little in the high roller area?"

"Of course not, Lady Noreen, that sounds great! You haven't played there ever since your operation. I'm sure that you will have fun playing at the casino for a little while."

Off to the casino they go arm and arm. Lady Noreen is feeling so much better, but Christopher is exhausted from the shopping spree. He now knows what the phrase "shop 'til you drop" means!

Once in the back room Lady Noreen sees the regulars. Her friend, Spring, is a very successful owner of an Asian Take-Out Restaurant in Sea Isle City. Like usual, Spring is on her five dollar machine. She plays it every weekend from afternoon to the wee hours of the morning and wins big jackpots up to $5,000, and loses lots of money on it at times, too, but she loves her machine. It is the only casino machine that Spring will play when she comes to the casino.

Spring is so happy to see, Lady Noreen. Yet she is more focused on the playing of her machine. Lady Noreen knowing this leaves her friend very fast and goes to one of the dollar machines in the front of the room to play.

Christopher knowing that Lady Noreen likes to mentally focus on her playing, takes a seat in back of her at a machine not being played, and watches her play the five times, ten times machine. Seeing the smile on Lady Noreen's face, she is so happy to be back at the casino, hitting the button to make the magic wheels spin once again.

While Christopher is sitting watching her, a young woman comes over to play a machine four machines down from him. Christopher watches her put a $100.00 bill into the machine. The woman plays the machine a couple of times, and then gets out of her seat, and walks down the aisle to order a drink from a cocktail waitress. Once she is down the aisle, an older man, dressed in jeans and a t-shirt, sits down at her machine and puts a $5.00 bill into her machine on top of the money that the woman left in her machine. Seeing that the people know him in the back room, no one even notices him, since he is a weekend gambler at the casino.

When the woman gets back to her machine, she notices this man in her seat playing her machine. She confronts him in front of Christopher telling him that she was playing the machine, and she had $78.00 left in the machine to play with her player's card still in the machine.

The man responds by telling her," My wife and I have been playing at this machine all night, and it is my money in the machine, not yours! I'm not leaving it. This is my machine!"

As Christopher overhears the conversation between the two of them, he confronts the man, "Are you related to this woman?"

"Heck no, I'm not! Who are you to interrupt my conversation with this woman?" in an arrogant tone of voice the man replies to Christopher.

"Sir, I am no one, but you are lying! You are a conniver, and I am going to call the casino manager over here to prove that you are lying. And, after this night at the casino, you will never win another penny, I predict this! Here is the five dollars that you put into this woman's machine, so you can't steal her $78.00."

As people in the back room gather around the conniver, he gets up disgusted from the casino machine and throws Christopher's five dollars onto the floor. Then he goes to another machine and puts $35.00 into it. He knows that he is wrong and that he is on the casino camera. The man is truly a liar. The old conniver is madder than blazes at Christopher because he called his bluff and embarrassed him in the back room in front of everyone.

"Thank you so much for helping me! My name is Marie. I always see that man back here. Most of the time, he doesn't play any of the machines in the casino. He just talks. You are right; he is a conniver! Thanks for sticking up for me. I didn't know how I would prove that I had been playing on this machine before him."

"Hi! I am Christopher. The pleasure is all mine. Feel sorry for him, he knows what he does, and doesn't care. That is what is so sad about it; he doesn't even have a conscious level of thought to reason with for his actions! If this ever happens again to you, immediately call a casino manager to help you. Don't let anyone bully you around ever again."

Marie hits the button and plays $3.00 in her machine, within a few minutes the light on her machine goes on, the music starts playing, and she has won $2,500.00. She gives Christopher a big hug and screams, "I can't believe it. Yeah! I just won!"

With that Christopher looks at the conniver. He just lost the $35.00 that he put into the machine he was playing. He sees Marie win on the machine that he just tried to steal and hustle from her. The conniver looks at both Marie and Christopher in a disgusted way and abruptly leaves the back room.

Christopher seeing that Lady Noreen is up to $900.00 on her machine asks her, "Lady Noreen, can I go outside for a few minutes? I just want to see the ocean. It will soon be fall, and I want to just take in the view of the ocean for an hour or so."

"Christopher, go right ahead! I am having so much fun! Just go to the beach and enjoy yourself. I'll call you on your cell when I am done playing here."

With that Christopher starts to walk through the casino to go to the exit to the Boardwalk. On his walk, he sees Bredele.

Bredele seeing Christopher runs over to him.

"Hi! Bredele! It is good to see you, today!" quickly responds Christopher to him.

Bredele writes on a pad back to Christopher, "Oh, Christopher, it is always so nice to see you, too. I hope you have a wonderful day."

"Thanks, Bredele. Everyone lately has been saying nice things about you, especially Jumbo Tiny Tut Tut. She told me last week that you have been so nice to her ever since you lost your voice, Bredele. You are truly changing. I am so proud of you! Bye for now!"

Christopher then goes out the front doors of the casino to the Boardwalk and walks to the steps to go down to the beach. Once there, he sits down on the sand in the 80 degree weather and studies the beach. He sees Greta the bag lady taking a bath in the ocean. She always bathes in it once a day. The people lying on the beach usually ignore her as she washes under her blouse and around her face in the ocean. By doing this, she feels that she is washing off her whole body.

Then, he sees a lady, with two children feeding the seagulls large dough pretzels. At least 15 seagulls mixed with pigeons and other birds fly to the area to join in on the feast. As Christopher watches, he can see some people walking around on the beach area watching the birds eat and fight with each other for food. He also sees some people near the area where a woman is feeding the birds upset for her feeding them in their beach area.

As Christopher looks further out into the ocean, he can see some of the local lifeguards out in the ocean in the lifeguard boat fishing, and two teens ashore having their fishing lines out in the water waiting for a catch, but at the moment no bites. The boat continues to go further and further out in anticipation to catch some fish. They even have the nets out, too.

Finally, Christopher starts to walk down the beach to Ventnor. On his walk, he sees two new homeless people lying in the sand on the beach. It looks like a mother and a daughter. As he gets closer to them, Christopher sees the mother starting to walk down the beach to ask people for a cigarette. Seeing this, Christopher looks down to the sand and shakes his head. He realizes that the numbers of homeless people are increasing not only at the shore, but all across America, and no one cares! He knows that it will only get worse with the mortgage take backs, listed homes not selling, people on fixed incomes that can't afford the accelerated cost of living, eminent domain seizure of properties from older residents with paid mortgages, repossessed homes put on the auction block, and reverse mortgages that now are the conversation pieces for retirees. More and more people are losing their homes and losing faith in the American Dream. Christopher fears for all of these people for he knows that a lot of American people if they lose their jobs are only two months away from being homeless. He fears the obliteration as he sees the spread of homeless people across the nation like a cancer that will not stop spreading around the United States of America.

Finally, he approaches Arthur's Breakfast and Lunch Grill. As he gets ready to go back up the steps to get on the Boardwalk, he sees a young man who the people under the Boardwalk named Josey. Josey is around twenty-six years old. These days, he is homeless, and he is sleeping under the Boardwalk with the cats that Arthur feeds every week. Christopher just shakes his head. He realizes that being homeless is no longer just a problem for people on drugs and alcohol, but for single or divorced women, women with children, military servicemen, performing artists, addicted gamblers, single and divorced men, men with children, runaway children, senior citizens, or any American citizen or immigrant. No longer is anyone in America free of being homeless in their lifetime. No one!

Christopher walks up the steps. He doesn't want to wake-up Josey. Josey was once a casino worker. But after the government's six day shutdown of the casinos, it put 36,000 casino employees out of work. Josey lost his job and became homeless. The casino shutdown resulted from a budget crisis preventing operation of the State Casino Commission.

Christopher tried to defend the casino workers and couldn't believe the government shutdown. Christopher at that time picketed with the casino workers in Atlantic City. He realized that the workers were just puppets. That the people in America are controlled by the politicians elected at the local, the state, and the national levels of government. That in the political arena at any time the people of America could become their peons. Here was another case of a young man without a job or any dreams. Josey, like the cats under the Boardwalk, has to now fight for his food and survival, too.

Once Christopher is back on the Boardwalk, he in a fast pace starts walking down the Boardwalk towards the amusement area.

He wants to get a little exercise before he returns to the casino to get Lady Noreen.

As he approaches the amusement area, he sees Russ in his wheelchair going down the Boardwalk. When Russ sees Christopher, he stops his wheelchair and calls Christopher over to him.

"Christopher, it is so good to see you! You look great! Your beard has certainly grown longer once again!"

"You are right, Russ! Lady Noreen likes it longer, and I don't know why! I guess maybe because it makes me look older than her, but don't tell her that Russ."

"I won't! Mmmmm... is the word, Christopher!"

"Russ, how is everything going? Do you feel ready for the race in October?"

"Yep, I'm ready! I don't know if I can beat Rico, but I am going to give him quite a race. If I lose, at least I know that I gave him the race of his life."

"It is going to be quite a race this fall. It will be here before we know it!"

"Christopher, remember way back, when you told me to tell my mother about the incident in the basement when I was twelve with my parents' best friend. Well, I finally told my mother that their high school friend, Ritz, lured me to the basement to see the construction progress on my Soap Box Derby Race Car. He abruptly pinned me up against the wall, and continually slammed my body back and forth against the wall. I was unable to neither free myself nor comprehend the actions of this man or just what was occurring in his mind. The evil man kept saying to me, "Be a man. Be a man!" I wanted to cry out for my parents, or fight him, but I lacked the strength to push him away from my body and was too scared and too young to appropriately defend myself. After that day, I always stayed away from him, when my parents would have Ritz, his wife, and his two children visit our house."

"Russ, you did the right thing. As a child, you had to keep this secret. Now you are not a child, and you have nothing to fear. I am so glad that you finally got this awful living nightmare off of your chest. Now you can live free of knowing that others know about Ritz. That you weren't crazy, and you didn't make the story up. The memory of it will probably always stay with you, but now it isn't a living nightmare but a living truth. Don't you feel better, Russ?"

"Yep, I do, Christopher, I just wish I would have told my father this story, too, before he died. I wanted to tell him, Christopher, but I feared he would think I was less of a man, or worse yet, he wouldn't believe me. Isn't that sad, Christopher?"

"Yes, Russ, it is! That is why so many children never tell their parents the truth in fear of disbelief or fear that they will confront the person who violated them and be injured. That is why there are so many young people run away from their families, commit suicide, take drugs, or alcohol. They are living with the truth stuck inside of their minds."

"Christopher, I must thank you again for the great advice. The truth does free one from their nightmares of the past."

"You are so right! Well, take care and good luck in your training for the race. You are conquering a lot of the ghosts from your past. I am proud of you son. Bye for now."

As Christopher walks a little further he sees Jasper. Jasper informs Christopher that both Marcus and Starlett have died from an overdose of bad drugs they purchased yesterday from new drug dealers in the area. Their bodies were found underneath the Boardwalk this morning. The people on the Boardwalk, the homeless people, and some of the local churches are raising money to pay for their funeral.

Jasper tells Christopher, "You know, Christopher, Marcus was raised in an orphanage and had no family, and Starlett's mother and father were both drug dealers, who were killed execution style when Starlett was seventeen years old. Therefore, all of us on the Boardwalk want to pitch in and give them a proper funeral, and by the way, Christopher, all of us were wondering if you would do the religious ceremony on the Boardwalk in tribute to Marcus and Starlett? Neither one of them ever went to church, but both of them loved and believed in you. Everyone feels that you are the one to conduct the funeral ceremony. Will you, Christopher?"

"What date will the funeral for Marcus and Starlett be held on Jasper? And where?" Christopher asks him.

"It will be this Thursday at noon in front of Arthur's Breakfast & Lunch Grill. We need you, Christopher, not only to proceed over the funeral service, but to plan it. Will you?"

"Jasper, of course I will. In fact, I would be honored to pay tribute to both of them for they were both the children of God."

Christopher is a little taken back. He was so fond of them. Marcus was always a great dancer. He had muscular arms and could dance to any dance. He had lost his ambition to be in a dance troupe because of his drug use, yet still he danced to his fame everyday on the Boardwalk with a cup in front of him for donations from his audience to make a living. Marcus had met Starlett, the woman of his dreams, a street person, too, on the Boardwalk three years ago, and they became an inseparable hot pair. Starlett gathered Marcus's crowd for him, and was always his audience. At times she danced with him, although she had no rhythm and couldn't dance. Even so, the two of them were together up until death do they part. Christopher knew in his heart that in the hereafter they would be happier there than they had been in this world. Even though they both loved performing on the Boardwalk as a team, their misery of hardly being able to survive and living under the Boardwalk was a never ending pain for both of them. That's why they finally ended life together from a drug overdose.

Christopher before leaving to go on his way responds to Jasper by saying, "Thanks for telling me about Marcus and Starlett today, I will truly miss both of them. They truly loved each other, Jasper. They were luckier than most people for Marcus and Starlett found true love before they died. But sad to say, as a couple, they couldn't survive against all of the odds that came at both of them each day. No one gets it all in this lifetime - no one! I'll see you Thursday. Bye for now!"

Christopher finally starts to walk back to the casino to get Lady Noreen. He calls her on his cell, and asks, "Lady Noreen, are you ready? I'm starting to walk back to the casino to get you, right now."

"Yes, I'm ready! I've won $1,850.00 on the machine I was playing, and another $3,500.00 on a machine way in the back of the room, Christopher. I am so happy that you let me gamble a little tonight, I feel so alive once again!"

"Lady Noreen, do you want me to call Brook to take us back to Ventnor?"

"No, Christopher, let's walk back to Ventnor. Maybe we can stop on the way back home at the Mango Tango Bar & Grill to get something to eat. Even though I'm really tired, I feel more like living than sleeping tonight. So let's celebrate the night away, and when I get home, I'll just pass out. I'm so tired, Christopher."

"Lady Noreen, it sounds great! Sometimes, we have to think more about living than dying in our life. If not, the brain feeds into our death wish."

Christopher goes and gets Lady Noreen. She has a smile from ear to ear. She is so happy that she has finally won at the casino once again. Together so happy, they walk to the front of the Boardwalk. There Christopher pays a young man to push them in a rolling chair to the Mango Tango Bar & Grill.

Lady Noreen is like a little girl with her Prince Charming as she rides in the riding chair on the Boardwalk. She is finally, for once in her life, happy to be alive. She no longer talks about dying, but fights with all of her might to live her life to the fullest.

Once to the Mango Tango Bar & Grill, the two of them eat outside at the tables in front of the restaurant, and listen to the Brazilian band and singers. The night, the air, and the music, creates an atmosphere so romantic around the two of them.

While they are eating dinner, Lady Noreen asks Christopher, "Do you love me? I've always wondered! You love the kids and all of your friends. You love almost everyone, but do you love me?"

"Lady Noreen, of course, I love you. I've loved you ever since I saw you at your machine gambling away," romantically replies Christopher.

"Well, then why don't you ever have any kind of relationship with me?" nervously Lady Noreen asks him.

"Lady Noreen, at the present we can't! But maybe in the future we can," reluctantly responds Christopher.

"Oh, do you have a medical problem, or is something wrong with you, Christopher?" questions Lady Noreen.

"Well, I guess you could say, in a way, and that in time, I think God will cure me," explains Christopher.

"How did God get into this Christopher?" wonders Lady Noreen.

"Lady Noreen, God is in everything. He made you get well, didn't He?"

"I guess so, Christopher! But what does that have to do with me and you?"

"God has a purpose for all of our lives. Next year, I feel that I'll be just a man, and I'll feel like one, too."

"Well, Christopher, what are you now?" Lady Noreen asks him with a confused look on her face.

"I'm just Christopher Saint, Lady Noreen," honestly Christopher answers her.

"Christopher, you make no sense at all to me. You talk in riddles. You've driven me crazy, and I still don't understand one word that you have told me. Maybe God saved me for you to drive me crazy!"

"No, Lady Noreen, God saved you for me! I need you in my life," blurts out Christopher.

"Christopher, you mean for our grandbaby?" changing the subject Lady Noreen asks.

"You're right like usual, Lady Noreen, for our grandbaby!"

"Okay, Christopher, enough conversation for tonight. I'm tired! Let's just get another rolling chair ride back to the house now. It is time for me to go to bed. I am exhausted, and after our conversation with you, I'm dead tired!"

Christopher gets another older man who is pushing a rolling chair to push them back to Ventnor. Once back to the house, Lady Noreen goes to her bedroom. She calls Tigress and Tom Cat to go to bed with her. She is furious at Christopher, yet Lady Noreen says nothing to him. She feels if she just goes to sleep, it will just go away like a bad dream does.

Christopher with a smile on his face goes to his bedroom and under his breath says, "Yes, tomorrow is a new day! Thank heavens for Lady Noreen!"

Chapter 33

A Day To Remember For All Of Us

Labor Day is here! This is the day that Lady Noreen has booked all of the family to go to the beach for the "Surprise Money Dig in Day," and the "Money Balloon Hot Spot Trip" winning events. Lady Noreen wakes up and without even hardly talking to Christopher since they went to the casino last night; however, she finally decides to talk to him.

"Christopher, have you called the kids to meet us at the casino? Now, that Rico is in his own condominium in the high rise, it seems so lonely here without him."

"Yes, Lady Noreen, it does, but it was time for him to become his own man, and own his own place, since he won all of that money. And yes, I've called all of the kids and they will all be at the beach for the "Surprise Money Dig in Day," by noon.

"Great! Then, Odessa, Old Bessie, plus Brook and Patrick will all join us at the beach," excitedly says Lady Noreen.

"Lady Noreen, where has Patrick been lately? Just saw him and he is back home for a while." curiously Christopher wonders.

"He has been traveling to all of the fashion shows to market our fashion designs. Later this month he will be in Italy," responds Lady Noreen in a business tone of voice.

"Look how far the two of you have taken your designer clothes. We must celebrate your success story tonight, Lady Noreen!"

317

"Christopher, you still aren't out of the dog house! I know what you are trying to do. You are trying to change the direction of my mind so that I won't dwell on last night's deep conversation with you."

"Oh, Lady Noreen, let's look forward to this beautiful day and enjoy it! Please?"

The two of them get ready, and depart for the casino beach event at 11:30 a.m., when Brook picks them up at the house. Lady Noreen is wearing a pants suit from her Safari Fashions by Patrick and her, and she looks like a model. She has Odessa and Old Bessie dressed in the designer line clothes, too. Christopher is wearing a pair of his khaki pants and a nice long sleeve shirt.

Once at the Boardwalk, Christopher and Brook escort Lady Noreen, Odessa, and Old Bessie to the Boardwalk. Marcena, Joshua, Rico, and Teresa Y. are already there waiting for them. Patrick is there, too, wearing one of the men's fashions from their line of clothing, too. He is walking toward all of them.

The only one missing for this day is Nicholas Zyvosky. Nicholas hasn't been around lately ever since he got involved in the recording business. He has been very busy flying throughout the country on business trips. On his last trip he went to New York. There, he met up with his former secretary, Tricia Ann Williams. She had always been the love of his life, but she was also married. However, six months ago, her husband died suddenly from a heart attack. Now she was single, and so was Nicholas. This being the case, he was using the contract deals for Hilten Tigress and the Wildcats as an excuse to stay in New York so he can employ Tricia to be his secretary once again.

Christopher was so happy to hear this. He knew that now Nicholas had a reason to live as long as he could because now he had someone to love and stay alive for in his life.

Finally, the attendants let Lady Noreen and the rest of her group pass.

Lady Noreen then presents their passes to the attendants in front of the Boardwalk steps. Then they let everyone go to the beach. They are all given a plastic child's shovel to dig a hole in the sand in any spot to see if they have won money. Everyone goes out onto the beach to pick out their little spot in the sand. They can win from nothing to

$10.00, $20.00, $25.00, $50.00, $75.00, $100.00, $200.00, $300.00, $400.00, $500.00, $600.00, $700.00, $800.00, $900.00, $1,000.00, $2,000.00, $3,000.00, $4,000.00, to $5,000.00 in cash. Everyone is scurrying in all different directions to find their treasures.

Teresa Y. pushes Rico down the handicap accessible ramp. Once down it, Rico has them pick a spot near the ramp. Rico and Teresa Y. dig for a few minutes. Rico finds no money in his spot. Teresa Y. yells out loudly, "I've won $1,000.00. Rico, we've won. Yippee!"

The rest of the family look back at them and cheers and yells out for them. Lady Noreen is so happy for both of them.

Joshua and Marcena find two spots to dig in. Joshua digs up $10.00, and Marcena digs up $10.00. They both just laugh at each other.

Patrick still exhausted from just getting back from Italy late last night goes over to the lifeguard stand and starts digging. He finds $100.00. He rushes over to show Lady Noreen his winnings.

Brook and Odessa go to the middle of the beach area and dig into the sand with their shovels. Odessa finds $50.00, and Brook can't believe his eyes. He has won $2,000.00. He calls Lady Noreen over to see his winnings.

Now more and more people are digging on the beach. Christopher goes with Old Bessie to find a spot. Old Bessie has Christopher dig in his spot first and he finds nothing. Then, Old Bessie digs the sand up and throws it in the air, to uncover $2,000.00. Old Bessie almost faints after she sees that she has won so much money. She gives Christopher a hug and goes off to join Brook and Odessa.

Lady Noreen frustrated and upset that she might not win any money just keeps going around and around on the beach asking everyone where she should dig. Finally, Rico tells her to dig under the trash can on the beach.

Lady Noreen thinking that it is the best advice of the day, so she digs there, and wins $5,000.00.

Everyone runs over to Lady Noreen to celebrate her winning by congratulating her, clapping for her, and giving her words of good cheer.

Christopher winks at her, but she just ignores him.

Lady Noreen has still not forgiven Christopher for avoiding to answer her question last night.

After the "Surprise Money Dig in Day Event," everyone goes into the casino to pick a balloon. Up in the ballroom inside of every balloon is either nothing or a trip for two to a hot spot in the world.

Rico decides that everyone should get their balloon and then pop it at the same time. After the last one, Patrick has gotten his balloon. Rico calls out, "One-two, three, everyone pop their balloon, right now!"

All you see in the ballroom for the "Money Balloon Hot Spot Trip," is every color of the rainbow balloon being stomped on. You see red balloons, purple balloons, orange balloons, yellow balloons, pink balloons, and blue balloons on the floor being jumped on.

Finally, people start yelling out from their excitement of winning a trip for two to a hot spot. Odessa wins a trip for two to the Virgin Islands, Brook wins a free trip to the Bahamas with all the expenses paid for two. Then, Marcena wins a trip for two to Aruba. The rest of them are losers, however they feel like winners since they can celebrate the winning of such great trips with Odessa, Brook, and Marcena.

After everyone calms down, Lady Noreen has everyone go to the casino high roller club called "The Golden Scepter Club," that has just been redecorated this last month. Then, everyone gets on the elevator to go to the second floor to go to it. Lady Noreen has the hostess put everyone at the same table together, so all of the waiters are hustling to put the tables together to make a table for nine people. They know it is Lady Noreen, and they better make everything perfect for her, or she will complain to the president of the casino about their service.

Once everyone is seated, the drinks are ordered and everyone goes over to the buffet and fills their plates. By this time everyone is so hungry, it is time to pig out.

As they eat everyone is filled with laughter, happiness and good stories. Joshua and Marcena are talking about the baby's nursery, the success of Joshua's new business and Rico and Teresa Y. are talking about their wedding plans. Odessa is telling Patrick about her classes in college. Brook is so overly excited about his trip to the Bahamas that he can't stop talking about it. Patrick is in conversation about his fashion trip to Italy with Odessa. Christopher informs Rico about how he has been fishing in the boat with Fernando and Emily and how he has caught a few fish lately. Everyone is talking about something at the table in "The Golden Scepter Club," but Lady Noreen.

Christopher seeing this yells out, "I have an announcement to make! Our Lady Noreen's and Patrick's fashion designs are going all around the world. I want all of you to applaud both of them. Then, to recognize Lady Noreen for all she did to make this a special day for all of us.

With that Lady Noreen's face lights up. She is now the center of attention and all of the conversation goes toward Lady Noreen for the rest of the night. Lady Noreen is once again the star and the living Diva of this night. She is so happy and full of laughter for the next 45 minutes. It is as though Christopher gave her some extra energy to come back to life once again. Even though in Lady Noreen's mind, she is still very mad at Christopher. At this very moment, she has forgotten about what she was mad at him about. Now Lady Noreen is just so happy to be alive and in the company of her loved ones!

Chapter 34

A Moment Frozen In Time

Thursday, finally arrives and everyone is ready. Christopher is done organizing the memorial service for Marcus Lowery and Starlett Rivera. At noon, everyone shows up for the service. The bodies have been cremated at King's Funeral Home and the hearse has delivered their cremated urns to the Boardwalk site for the service proceeding.

Christopher is with Lady Noreen. He proceeds to say, "We are gathered today at this site to pay our last respects to Marcus Lowery and Starlett Rivera. The darkness of the night has come upon both of them in which to find the dawn of a new heavenly day. We will now bow our heads as we recite the Psalm of David, Psalm 23, together, "The Lord is my shepherd; I shall not want. He maketh me to lie down in green pastures. He restoreth my soul; he leadeth me in the paths of righteousness for his name's sake. Yea, though I walk through the valley of the shadow of death, I will fear no evil; for thou art with me; thy rod and thy staff. They comfort me. Thou preparest a table before me in the presence of mine enemies; thou anointest my head with oil; my cup runneth over. Surely, goodness and mercy shall follow me all the days of my life: and I will dwell in the house of the Lord forever. Amen."

Christopher then introduces Jasper by saying, "Now Jasper will present a poem in tribute to Marcus and Starlett."

"The following poem that I have written is dedicated to Marcus Lowery and Starlett Rivera:"

PARADISE

Two Souls Sharing the Nest
Of Life,
Together As One
They Dream Of Their Future
Together...
The Pair Realize That Forever
Is Only A Moment...
A Moment Frozen In Time.
As Lovers,
Their Hearts Beat
In A Loving Rhythm
Created In A World
Called Paradise.
Together, As One,
Their Intimate Passions Exist...
In A World Conceived Of Insanity.
United And In Love,
These Two Earthly Beings
Seize Only A Moment...
A Moment Of Each And Every Living Day.
Sad To Say, They Both Know
In Their Hearts...
That If This Day,
This Endless day,
On Which They Shared A Perfect Love
For One Another
Only Lasts For A Moment...
That...
That Exact Moment
Shared In True Love And Passion,
As One,
In Paradise
Will Last A Lifetime...In Time.

"Marcus and Starlett, may you both be blessed forever in your new heavenly paradise," ends Jasper.

Next, Teresa Y. plays the traditional song, "Amazing Grace" on her violin in tribute to the two. Everyone at the ceremony feels the intensity of the music of the sound. Tears are rolling down the eyes of so many gathered to pay tribute to these two deceased souls. People from businesses, from underneath the Boardwalk, homeless people from the bus depot, drug dealers, casino workers, and Boardwalk musicians have all gathered to say their last good-bye to Marcus and Starlett.

Old Bessie, who loved Marcus and Starlett like they were her own children then reads from the Bible, I Corinthians 9:24-27, "Know ye not that they which run in a race run all, but one receiveth the prize? So run that ye may obtain. And every man that striveth for the mastery is temperate in all things. Now they do it to obtain a corruptible crown; but we are incorruptible. I therefore so run, not as uncertainly; so flight I, not as one that beatest the air. But I keep under my body, and bring it into subjection: lest that by any means, when I have preached to others, I myself should be castaway."

When Old Bessie finishes saying this biblical verse, she begins to break down and cry. Lady Noreen comes to her side to comfort her.

Next, Christopher comes forth to read the last written words that were given to him in a letter which was found next to Marcus's body by Sergeant Mussack. Sergeant Mussack, after finding the letter at the police department, drove over to Lady Noreen's house with the love of his life, Delilah, and delivered the letter to Christopher. Sergeant Mussack was sure that the last few words in poem form ever written by Marcus would have an impact on everyone at the funeral today.

Christopher, in seriousness, begins reading Marcus's words to everyone,

"These are the words we felt that Marcus would have wanted all of you to hear today."

A Candle Burns

A candle burns in all of our
hearts
flamed with passion,
lies,
and
secrets.

A candle burns in all of our
hearts
singed in old romances,
friends,
and
acquaintances.

A candle burns in all of our
hearts
smoked with the bittersweet,
sadness,
and
sorrow.

A candle burns in all of our
hearts
melted down with memories,
regrets,
and
moments.

A candle burns in all of our
hearts
burnt out in love,
laughter,
and
yesterdays.

"May Marcus Lowery and Starlett Rivera find all the happiness in their next life that they so dreamt of in this life. In life there is no death, so do not mourn today. Neither one of them would want their ending in their lives to end on that note, but rather we must celebrate their homecoming to their next life. May God bless them and keep them now and forever. Amen," concludes Christopher.

Then, Sarge on the tambourine, is accompanied by Christopher on the harmonica, Big Luke on the electric guitar, Ogbonna on the drums, Whisky Winkie Scullen on the electric keyboard, Deuce on the saxophone, and Teresa Y. on the violin. They perform a song, entitled, "Lie with Me - Die with Me," that Sarge has written in honor of the two for their memorial service. Hilten, and her backup singers, Joy Rhapsody, Ngoc, P.J., and Female accompany Sarge on the vocal part of the song. Hilten Tigress and the Wildcats have come together once again not to win the Boardwalk Talent Show, but to pay tribute to two people, who like themselves performed for a living in the city just to make a living. Sarge begins the music, and Hilton Tigress begins the song, and her backup singers join in-

LIE WITH ME DIE WITH ME

I.
Pretty Bird of Paradise
Spread Your Wings with Mine
Fly With Me
Fly With Me
Forever
You and I
Together we will find
Paradise

Chorus
Paradise
Our Own Paradise
Fly With Me
Die With Me

326

And In the Heavens
Come Fly with Me
You and I Together
With All the Love We Can Share
Will Fill This World
And Beyond This World
With All the Love
Two Hearts
Can Share
I Love You
I Love You
My Own Pretty Bird Of Paradise

II.
Lie With Me
Die With Me
And In the Heavens
Come Fly with Me
My One and Only Love
Only You
Only You
My Love

Chorus
Paradise
Our Own Paradise
Fly With Me
Die With Me
And In the Heavens
Come Fly with Me
You and I Together
With All the Love We Can Share
Will Fill This World
And Beyond This World
With All the Love
Two Hearts

Can Share
I Love You
I Love You
My Own Pretty Bird Of Paradise

III.
Only You
Only You
Have Given Me
Through Your Love Alone
All the Love
That Two Hearts Can Hold
From Your Soul
From Your Soul

Chorus
I'm Lost without You
Watching the Sun Go Down
I Think Of You
That Way
I Know
You Could
Not Stay
Pretty Bird
My Own
Pretty Bird
Some Day
Pretty Bird
We'll Find Paradise
I Love You
I Love You
My Own Pretty Bird Of Paradise

Everyone claps and applauds for Hilten Tigress and the Wildcats to do the song one more time, and they do it in memory of Marcus and Starlett.

Then, Rico in his wheelchair wheels over to the microphone and has everyone bow their heads to say the "Lord's Prayer" together, and ends the memorial service. May everyone go in peace and remember to live today, and all the rest of the days ahead of them to the fullest second in time."

Christopher reaches out to Lady Noreen, and the urns are put back into the hearse and the hearse drives down the Boardwalk with everyone following it, in remembrance of Marcus's and Starlett's last days on the Boardwalk as performers. Then, the hearse drives out to the cemetery park, and everyone follows the hearse in their cars or in a taxi. Lady Noreen has ordered limos for all the performers and people in the memorial service to take to the cemetery if they don't have any transportation to get there.

Once at the cemetery, everyone gets to see the mausoleum that Lady Noreen has purchased for the two urns to be placed in together. Then, everyone is given a candle to light.

Finally, Christopher's says these final words, "If they were here, Marcus and Starlett, would want to thank all of you for coming to their memorial service today."

Then twelve white doves are released into the air, and they fly straight up into the heavens. Everyone now is in peace knowing that Marcus and Starlett, like the doves, have gone from this earth and are free in God's world of paradise.

With that every person leaves the cemetery knowing that Marcus Lowery and Starlett Rivera did not live in vain and that they had gone onto their next life with the Lord. The funeral crowd then departs in happiness for the two souls; not in sadness. Christopher's words indeed had delivered Marcus and Starlett from this world to the next in happiness and with honor instead of sadness and shame.

Lady Noreen invites anyone who would like to come to a memorial luncheon to follow them back to her house. Only a few come to the house, for most of the visitors have to go back to work, to their business, or back to the Boardwalk. Only Rico, Teresa Y., all of the band members, Old Bessie, Hilten, Jasper, Arthur, Jumbo Tiny Tut, Daisy, Bredele, and the backup singers return to the house for the luncheon.

At the house, Marcena, whose baby is due soon, Joshua, Odessa, and Patrick are getting all the food prepared and out for the luncheon. They want the day to end in celebration for Marcus and Starlett, not a day in mourning for the dead.

Patrick has angels hanging from the ceilings throughout the rooms in the house, colored lights are shined upon Lady Noreen's house, and candles are lit throughout the rooms of different colors and aromas. Celebration balloons are given to each guest. A champagne celebration is given to Marcus Lowery and Starlett Rivera by Christopher, and everyone joins in by getting their food at the buffet stations. The dance music from the radio station that Marcus used to dance to is played throughout the house. Everyone at the memorial celebration knows that Marcus and Starlett are in a better place.

Jasper ends the celebration by presenting one of his last poems in honor of the day that he has collaborated on writing with J. Sharp-

THERE'S A BETTER PLACE

You were always in my life
I never thought you'd leave without me
There were so many more things I wanted to share
But I know we will someday, somewhere
As I feel your sweet release, I'm not afraid
I'm full of peace for
We hung on to the last light of day
And watched the sun melt away

The ocean's waves steal bits of sand from the shore
Leaving me wanting so much more
Tides go out and tides come in
Knowing not where they are or where they've been
I'm starting to let go still
Yet it's hard because I love you

But I know that I'll survive
'Cause your memories keep me alive

For there comes a time and a moment
When we must stand alone
On an edge of something we've never known, for
I know there's got to be a better place
And I feel you're in a better place
Because life's only a stepping stone behind us
Yet not too far to remind us
Of the love we shared
And in a moment in time
I'll see your face
And remember the love we shared
Of the love we will share

Then everyone with their candles in a small decorative flower pot that Patrick and Lady Noreen have made for everyone with Marcus's and Starlett's names on it, take not only it, but one of the heart shaped balloons and depart from the luncheon to go home or back to the Boardwalk. Lady Noreen makes sure that Patrick has enough limos to transport everyone.

Christopher then walks down to the ocean to see his seagull, Sanabrio, after everyone leaves the house.

Sanabrio lands on Christopher's shoulder when he sees him there. Then, Christopher feeds him and says to him, "Oh, my dear friend, it is so good to see you. Today has ended a day in a celebration of happiness, not in a day of tears and sorrow. God would be pleased to know this. Bye for now, my friend."

Sanabrio takes his food in his beak with him and flies into the two tone blue sky. Christopher follows Sanabrio's flight into the air as he is reminiscing about all of the good times he had on the Boardwalk with Marcus and Starlett. He knows in his heart, that neither one of them had lived on this earth in vain. Christopher knew that God had a plan for both of them, and they had lived out His plan for them. Now, their lives were over with, but not the memories that both of them had left in life for all the others on the Boardwalk.

Chapter 35

Children Of Dreams

On Grandparent's Day in September, Christopher makes plans for the whole family plus Teresa Y.'s family, Hannah and Raul, Joshua's family, Patrick, Odessa, Russ, Nicholas, Jasper, Fernando, and Emily to attend church at the St. Nicholas Cathedral in Longport. Christopher is so excited to become a grandfather sometime this month that he wants to begin it with a church service today.

Lady Noreen is feeling so much better and she of course is wearing one of her designer dresses that is tie dyed pink with flamingos sculptured into the dress's design. She has a pink flamingo scarf with the same pattern to match on with shoes and a handbag with the same pattern in it. Lady Noreen looks stunning. She tells Christopher, "I feel wild today!"

Earlier in the morning Lady Noreen vocalizes to Christopher, "Let's stay home and go to St. Mattress of the Springs today. I'll call everyone and cancel going to the church service!"

Christopher replies, "You will do no such thing! We have to go to church and honor and celebrate this glorious day, Lady Noreen."

Lady Noreen just gives Christopher a disgusted look and goes upstairs. She isn't going to say anymore to him, she knows she has lost the fight to stay home.

The limos pull up at 11:00 a.m. to take everyone to the church. Lady Noreen is so upset because it is pouring rain outside. On top of that, it is thundering loud and flashes of lightning are zigzagging across the sky.

Once inside of the church, everyone is so delighted to be there to pay thanks to God for all of their blessings. As everyone looks around the church, they take in the glass windows of Christ. The church looks like it was a church that was brought from Italy and placed Longport. It is the most beautiful church in the whole wide world.

The priest begins the service, and everyone follows the mass for the day. As the service progresses, you can hear giant bolts of lightning exploding right over the church. It sounds like a bolt of lightning is going to hit the church's roof as the thunder gets louder and louder.

Lady Noreen wants to leave the service. She is so scared that a thunderbolt is going to hit the church and kill all of them. She doesn't want her grandchild to be killed before the child is born.

Christopher just laughs at her and sympathetically says to her, "It is okay Lady Noreen. If we all get killed here, it is the best place to be to die. It's a church!"

Lady Noreen hushes, but every time the thunder goes off like dynamite over the church, she jumps in the pew. Everyone else tries to ignore the lightning and the thunder during the service so they can focus on the lesson for the day, but not Lady Noreen. She is quietly saying a prayer under her breath for she thinks she is going to die; however, later during the service she decides to try and tune out the lightning and thunder. This way, she can just think about the brunch that she has planned after church for everyone.

During the prayer for the day, the priest blesses Marcena and Joshua and prays that their baby to be born will be healthy as he blesses the unborn child in the daily devotion prayer. The priest then calls Jasper up to the pulpit to give a poem for Grandparent's Day.

Jasper leaves the pew with the family and goes up to the pulpit to present the poem that he has written for the day and he begins his poem by saying, "I'd like to dedicate this poem to all of the grandparents, parents, and children here today."

Children of Dreams

Children of Dreams
Are Godly Beings

Born at Birth
To Live on this Earth
To be...

Artists   Poets

Actors   Actresses   Dancers   Singers

Writers Musicians   Journalists

Lyricists Comedians

... and all that they dream
To be...

Children of Dreams
Are Godly Beings
Born on this Earth
Talented and of Worth
To be...
Children of
Dreams...

I'd like to wish everyone a Happy Grandparent's Day today. Thank you!" politely concludes Jasper.

Everyone is so proud of Jasper. He has changed so much from the person who loved to eat garbage on the Boardwalk and defy the law. He now has his hair cut, he is clean shaven, and dressed up in his suit from the fashion show. Through his love of writing, he has found a self-worth inside of his soul. As he has told Christopher so many times, he had given up on himself and his life for he had no family, no job, and no dream. Through gaining Christopher as a father figure and the rest of the family that Christopher had united him with on his journey, he found himself. Jasper always knew in his heart that taking drugs was only an outcome from not being loved, and not loving himself. Sometimes, Jasper felt that the worst crime in life was not killing someone, but not loving someone throughout their entire life. So often, he felt that children and adults only escaped to the Internet to find people to love them, and sometimes those people only love those people to kill them, so they really do love them to death. Jasper truly feels blessed to be in the pew today with all these people as his family. A functional family!

After the service, everyone comes over to Lady Noreen's house for brunch. Of course, she has both a vegetarian and a regular brunch of every kind of food you can think of to celebrate Marcena and Joshua's baby's arrival date which is coming up real soon. Lady Noreen prays that the delivery date will be on the 12th of September. She truly doesn't want the baby to be born late!

Everyone just laughs at Lady Noreen; especially Christopher. Childbirth is one of those things that Lady Noreen can't control upon this earth.

After brunch, Christopher takes Fernando and Emily out into the row boat, and they practice rowing the boat into the ocean. Both Fernando and Emily are now muscular, with great endurance, and are all ready for any emergency that faces them on the beach or in the water. Their lifeguard job has just ended for the season and they are both getting ready to go back to their local community college in the area. They have grown so much in their water and lifesaving skills, thanks to Christopher.

Christopher just loves both of these young people. He can't believe how far they both came in the training sessions he gave them this summer. He knows that they will be a blessing for someone if their life in the water or on the beach is ever endangered one day.

After Christopher is done with the ocean training session with Fernando and Emily, he goes up to the house and visits with Marcena and Joshua. He says to Marcena and Joshua, "Don't be scared about your baby or babies being born this week. God has a plan for them and they will be healthy and full of life. So please don't worry about a thing!"

Marcena looks at Christopher and replies, "Christopher, I love both Lady Noreen and you so much! I owe you everything, even my life! You have looked after both Rico and me and loved us like a father would, introduced me to my wonderful husband, Joshua, given me a storybook wedding, been with me when I won the jackpot at the casino, and most important, saved my life on the night that I thought I was going to die. I can't thank you enough Christopher. I love you so very, very much! However, even though I look enormous, Christopher, my doctor only hears one heartbeat. I am giving birth to just one baby, Christopher. Just one!"

"We'll see, Marcena! Bye for now."

Joshua gives Christopher a hug, and tells Marcena, "It's time to tell Brook to take us home. We just have a few details to complete in the nursery today to get ready for the arrival of the baby. Lady Noreen and Patrick have everything done amazingly! Patrick has storybook characters painted on one wall in a jungle scene, the room is done in an off shade of lilac. Lady Noreen had the nursery set delivered, so the crib, the dresser, and the changing table are all in place. Both Patrick and Lady Noreen have the rugs, the pictures, the lamp, the bumper pads, the sheets, the comforter and the rocking chair all set up in the room for the little one to come home, Christopher."

"Marcena and Joshua, I want to thank you so much for letting Lady Noreen and Patrick help you with everything. This project was really a lifesaver for Lady Noreen. Both of you gave her something to live for in her young life, as Lady Noreen would say," divulges Christopher to both of them.

After Marcena and Joshua take off in the limo with Brook, Christopher goes and looks for Jasper. Jasper is sitting in a reclining chair in the enclosed porch writing a poem. Jasper is now in his own little world in thought using his creative mind.

Christopher yells out to him, "Jasper, I loved your poem today! What are you writing about today?"

"Christopher, I am writing a poem in tribute to an old man named Jeremiah, who was murdered on the Boardwalk several years ago. They killed him because of their hate for people of color. The man was harmless! All he did was clean the Boardwalk everyday with his broom. He never hurt anyone in his whole life. That's why I am writing this poem in dedication to him."

"Jasper, that is so thoughtful of you! Sad to say, there is a lot of hate in America today. It is because some the American people refuse to love their own people. Our country lacks nationalism, and some people are taught just to love themselves and to self-destroy others of different colors, religions, ethnic groups and sex standards. Like a wildfire burning in California, hate in America is on a devastating course. The lack of respect for human rights by some of our fellow Americans has resulted in racial discrimination subjecting individuals to beatings, torture and even murder. No one can stop it, and God can't because he gave each man and woman free will. Just like in the Garden of Eden when Adam and Eve were tempted, well, in America the temptation is greater. The temptation is now – to kill! Today in the states, character assassination is taking place every day and it will not cease! Because, the people who care and want to change the world for the better, have no power, influence, or money to change our world. Therefore, this world will stay a world filled with hate crimes!"

"Christopher, you are so right! Jeremiah was killed just for being a person of color!"

"You are right, Jasper. Others will die across the country because they are Mexican, from Iraq or Pakistan, because they are Jewish, Asian, and others merely for their shoes, jackets, smart phones or cars. Those are the materialistic killers of our land. Others will be killed because they are gay, because they are having an affair, because they are pregnant, because their partner or family member is on drugs, from abuse, marital abuse, because they meet up with a pedophile, from being assassinated, and the list goes on and on. Jasper, the war is not only in Iraq but in America. More people die here every day than in the war, and nothing can be done to change it, for it is like a political wildfire out of control!"

"I'll bring you the poem, when it is done. It is going to be called, "Little Black Angel," Christopher.

"I want to hear your new poem, Jasper. In fact, when you get enough poems completed, if you would like, I will make arrangements for publishing a book of your poems through engagement of a self-publishing company or online publisher. You can potentially enjoy proceeds from the sale of your books. Thanks so much Christopher," excitedly replies Jasper.

Jasper then takes his poem book and says good-bye to Lady Noreen and the rest of the family. The way he holds his poem book, is like it is a treasure chest filled with millions of dollars, as he walks down the Boardwalk holding tightly on to it.

As Christopher goes back into the dining room to get some more food to eat, he runs into Hannah sitting on the couch. Hannah has had a few complications again with her second pregnancy, and has not gained too much weight. She has not shared this with anyone for she doesn't want to scare Marcena before she gives birth to her own baby. Hannah's husband, Raul, is in the workout room with Rico and Teresa Y. working out.

Hannah calls out softly to Christopher, "Please come and see me. I've missed you so much! Come sit with me."

"Hannah, it is always a pleasure to see you. How are you?" sincerely responds Christopher.

"Christopher, I don't know how to tell you this! I haven't told anyone, but I'm worried again about this pregnancy, too."

"Oh, Hannah, have you told your doctor about your concern?" Christopher asks her.

"Christopher, no I haven't because, I don't want to lose this child, too," replies Hannah with tears in her eyes.

"Hannah, you have to promise me that you will tell your doctor what you have just told me, immediately. I don't want anything life threatening to happen to you!" in a concerned tone of voice Christopher tells her.

"But, Christopher, what if I lose this baby, too? It will be my second one. I don't think I can go through the loss of my baby again," choked up Hannah answers Christopher.

"You don't have to, Hannah. You can adopt a beautiful child or children," suggests Christopher.

"But I want my own children. I want them to look like Raul and myself. I want my own blood children, Christopher," insists Hannah.

"Hannah that is what you want. God may have another plan for you. Adopted children do have your blood in them. I think all of us are related if we started out from Adam and Eve. They may not look like you, but Marcena and Joshua don't look like me either. Both of them are better looking than I am, but I love them with all of my heart. Remember, I don't want you to be scared, but I do want you to call your doctor. Also, I want you to know that I'll be there for you if you ever need me."

With that Hannah gives Christopher a big hug and she goes off to find Raul.

Hannah is starting to get tired and she wants to go home. She values what Christopher has told her and she is going to call her doctor immediately in the morning to schedule an appointment with him.

When Christopher finishes eating his food, he hears the doorbell ring. He goes to the door and to his surprise, it is Sergeant Mussack. He wants to see Odessa and Christopher. Sergeant Mussack has something very important to tell both of them.

Christopher runs around the house and finds Odessa. Odessa is helping Old Bessie to set out some healthy and also calorie galore desserts with different flavors of coffee on the enclosed porch for whomever still remains at the brunch to eat.

Christopher tells Odessa, "I'll meet you at the porch with Sergeant Mussack. He is on duty, but maybe he can have a dessert or two and coffee with us."

Sergeant Mussack follows Christopher to the enclosed porch. While waiting for Odessa to come to the porch, he shows Christopher some pictures of Delilah and his family. Sergeant Mussack just loves his little dog so much. He always tells Christopher that his little pooch saved him from not only a divorce, but from losing his family.

Odessa soon brings an assortment of desserts and coffees out to the porch to join Sergeant Mussack and Christopher. The desserts are dangerously delicious and even the fat free desserts look tempting, and of course, Sergeant Mussack has a piece of the carrot cake and a slice of the strawberry swirl cheesecake with a cup of coffee.

Sergeant Mussack then addresses Odessa, "Odessa, I am here to tell you that the head of the prostitute ring, your escort and pimp, Fritz Winetiller, was killed over the weekend in Philadelphia with a new young girl named Ming, who had just arrived on an airplane at the Philadelphia Airport. A policeman recognized Mr. Winetiller from a composite sketch of him at the Philadelphia headquarters and reported him to the authorities. Seeing that the policeman got his license plate number, the police in Philadelphia chased after him in a high chase pursuit across that area to arrest him. In the end, Mr. Winetiller lost control of his car and ran into a telephone pole killing both Mr. Winetiller, and the girl named Ming. Odessa, you don't have to be afraid of him anymore, your biggest nightmare of Fritz Winetiller returning in your life is over with for you forever."

"Oh, Sergeant Mussack, I am so happy to hear this news, although even though I didn't know the dead girl, I do feel so sorry for her. She was probably an orphan just like me, who was very naïve," sternly responds Odessa to the sergeant.

"Well now, Odessa, you can go on with your life to do what you want to do with it. Do you have any plans for yourself at the moment?" asks Sergeant Mussack.

"Yes, Sergeant Mussack, Lady Noreen and Patrick took me to the county college recently and had me enroll to take some courses. I plan to complete my college degree in the near future. I will start classes in January. I am so thrilled to be going to college. I never thought when I was a prostitute that I would ever get the opportunity to go to college in America. In fact, I really thought that my fate was to either get killed or get the deadly disease, AIDS.

The three of them finish eating their desserts and having coffee together on the porch.

You can tell by Odessa's facial expressions that she is so happy to hear that the demon, who was in her life, is finally dead. Now she can go on in her young life to live out her own dreams.

When finished with his dessert, Christopher excuses himself, and goes into the workout room to see Rico and Teresa Y., who are there exercising and lifting weights. Christopher whispers in Rico's ear, "I know you can't eat rich desserts while you are training, but here are some fat free desserts and ice cream on the porch for Teresa Y. and you."

"Thanks Christopher, but I'm pretty full at the moment, but maybe Teresa Y. would like to have something more to eat," politely replies Rico.

Teresa Y. then excuses herself and goes and joins the rest of her family on the porch to have dessert. She has to watch her weight now since she is getting ready to get married. Teresa Y. wants to look good on her wedding day.

Rico shouts to Christopher as he lifts his weights with his arms up in the air, "Christopher, I can hardly wait until I am happily married. I hope to be as happy as Lady Noreen and you are. Thanks to Lady Noreen and you, I have found a family, become a rich man from winning at the casino, found the woman of my dream through the Boardwalk Talent Show, established my own website for Wheelchair Racing on the Internet, started a non-profit, and now I'm going to be Uncle Rico. I feel like this is all a dream that came true for me, because of Lady Noreen and you."

"Thanks so much, Rico, and there are more great things to come true for you and Teresa Y. in your young lives," predicts Christopher.

"It sounds great, Christopher! By the way, I was meaning to ask you if you would be my best man. I also want Joshua and Marcena in my wedding. Plus, I want Lady Noreen to be my mother on that day, Christopher. Lady Noreen is just like a mother to me. I didn't ask Marcena, Joshua or Lady Noreen today to be in my wedding because they have enough on their minds with the baby coming so soon," admits Rico.

"Rico, I would be honored to be your best man. Although you are really the best man on the day of your wedding! Your wedding will bring in the New Year with the biggest celebration ever!"

"Oh, Christopher, I can hardly wait until midnight on New Year's Eve! This is going to be a wedding that I will remember for the rest of my life!" eagerly replies Rico.

Christopher then leaves the workout room, and on his way out, he sees Old Bessie separating Tom Cat from Tigress she knows Lady Noreen does not want Tom Cat in the same room with Tigress without her, so Christopher thinks this is very funny! He thinks Tom Cat and Tigress are a perfect match for one another. However, Lady Noreen doesn't! But, since she hasn't neutered either one of them, Christopher feels that fate will win out for both of them since cats have nine lives.

After seeing Old Bessie all upset with poor Tom Cat, he goes onto the patio to join Lady Noreen, Nicholas, Patrick, and Russ. Sarge isn't there today with all of them because Christopher helped him locate his two children in Ohio. Ever since Sarge came home from Vietnam, and got his divorce, he hasn't taken the time to ever see his children. Now they are adults with families of their own.

Knowing this, Christopher told Sarge that since he was a hero in Vietnam, he had to now be a father and a hero in America to his own children. Those words of wisdom gave Sarge the intestinal fortitude to fly back to Columbus, Ohio, to see his two adult children.

Christopher was so happy to see Nicholas living his life to the fullest. He had recently moved the love of his life, Tricia Ann Williams, to Ventnor, to work at his new office there. This way, he can help Patrick out at the florist shop. Thanks to Nicholas doing this, it gave Patrick the time to work on the new fashion line with Lady Noreen. Nicholas has been a dear friend to the family. He has spent so much of his own money to help others lately. Nicholas was never like this until he got involved in the Boardwalk Talent Show. At the next Boardwalk Talent Show in October, Nicholas is having the song, "Shed Tears for the Teens," released and sold on the Boardwalk. Everyone in the group is so excited about their winning song and CD release in the coming year. They all know that without Nicholas's monetary help they would never have won the talent show.

Patrick, like always, is doing several projects all at once with Lady Noreen. Besides working on their designer line both day and night, he is working with Lady Noreen on the nursery for the newborn to be born with both Lady Noreen and Marcena, and still working full-time at his florist shop with Nicholas's assistance. Nicholas is truly a lifesaver for Patrick at this time.

Russ is still so excited about the Wheelchair Race in October. Every day he is conditioning and working his heart out to get his body ready for the race. His mental attitude is very upbeat and determined to win the race this year.

As he looks at Lady Noreen, he can see that she has come back to life. She wants to see the babies more than anything in her life, and she wants to be a grandmother. Who would ever have thought that Lady Noreen would be fighting so hard to live and get her strength back just so she could be a grandmother?

Christopher seeing that everyone is happy and content in their lives is at peace. He says good night to all of them and walks out onto the beach to see Sanabrio. Once on the beach, Sanabrio lands upon Christopher's shoulder and Christopher feeds his pet seagull like he always does.

Christopher then talks to his friend, "Sanabrio, I had another vision last night. I am just to choose only one person to give my angel powers to. I hope there is just one baby. I don't want to get into trouble again with my assignment. Sanabrio, let's pray that I make the right decision this time and that I am obedient. I am no longer a saint, and soon I will no longer be an angel. When I am just a man, I hope that you will still be my friend. Sometimes Sanabrio, in the real world you don't know who your real friends are in your life. Sometimes, the good people are bad, and the bad people are good. This world is so very confusing to me. Thank you, Sanabrio for always being a loyal friend to me."

With that Sanabrio eats the food Christopher has given him, and flies off into the sky. As Christopher watches Sanabrio fly off, he prays to God that in the days ahead of him, he will have the strength to make the right decision. With that in mind, he heads back to Lady Noreen's house for the night, a night of more mental thought than sleep.

Chapter 36

Only God Knows!

September 10th comes and no baby. September 11th comes and still no baby. Finally, it is September 12th, and Lady Noreen is sure the baby will be born today so she has Brook bring Marcena to her house for the day, so Joshua can work with clients. Lady Noreen also has Brook bring Marcena's suitcase with her, too. She keeps telling Christopher, "This is the day; I know this is the day! We will all be ready when she goes into labor at any time today."

Christopher just laughs and goes on his merry way around the house. He knows by now that Lady Noreen thinks she is always right! In no way, is he going to tell her that he thinks she isn't right once again.

Marcena arrives to the house and Brook helps her into the house. Marcena is giant size pregnant! Everyone thinks she is going to have a 10 or 11 pound baby because she is so enormous.

Christopher gives Marcena a big hug and a kiss.

Marcena knows how proud of her he is. She loves Christopher so much!

Then Lady Noreen has her come into the house for some breakfast. She has it all prepared, and ready for Marcena to just sit down for the day, eat, and enjoy a day without stress at the shore with her.

Seeing that Lady Noreen and Marcena are all happy and content for the day, Christopher takes his daily walk down the Boardwalk. On his way, he finds Jasper on the bench waiting for him.

"Christopher, I completed my poem last night. Do you want to hear it?"

"Of, course, I do! Remember, Jasper, all these poems are going to be in your book one day."

"I hope so! Here is the poem, the "Little Black Angel," Christopher."

Little Black Angel...
Let your giant wings of darkness
Gently caress my inner soul
As magical moonbeams of harps
Dance within my childlike mind

Little Black Angel...
Let your halo cast rays of light
All around my conscious existence
To shield me with God's armor
From the wickedness of others

Little Black Angel...
Let God's voice like a thunderbolt
Of white lightning strike me
As his message of righteousness is
Transmitted throughout my total being

Little Black Angel...
Let me battle with Satan's forces
Of evil in His holy name
As I am led from the flaming
Charcoals of earthly sin

Little Black Angel...
Let your electrifying touch spiritually
Transform me both mentally and physically
As I reflect only His divine purpose
Through my human presence

Little Black Angel...

"Jasper, it is the best poem that you have written yet! I needed to hear all the words in your poem. Your poem has truly inspired me. I know that your friend, Jeremiah, Lord bless his soul, would be so honored just knowing that you thought enough of him to write this poem in dedication to him. You truly honored your friend with your poem, Jasper. Your friend, Jeremiah, did not die in vain. They say that one never dies until the last person who knew the person or knew of the person dies. That is what life after death is all about!"

"Oh, thanks so much for all of your confidence in me, Christopher. You are my biggest fan and supporter. Thanks for giving me the will to go on writing and to live. Through my writing, I am getting stronger every day, and getting the desire to become a member of the human race once again. I thank you, Christopher, for always being there for me."

"Thanks, Jasper, for the compliment, but you my friend, had the gift to write inside of yourself all of the time. Just wait until your book of poetry is published and you share all of your beautiful poems with the world."

"Well, I must thank you, Christopher, for having the confidence and belief in me that I can write poetry! Sometimes, I wonder if my book will really become a reality!" reluctantly shares Jasper with Christopher.

"Your poetry will be in a book one day, Jasper! Now I best get going for I have to meet Fernando and Emily. They want to practice their boating and swimming skills with me today. Bye for now, Jasper."

"Bye, Christopher!" happily replies Jasper.

Christopher takes off and sees Fernando and Emily down at the beach waiting for him to get into the boat to help them row it into the water. The vast ocean has a very strong current today and the water is very choppy.

It is very hard for Emily to row the boat with Fernando. Christopher helps her row the paddles of the boat into the ocean. The strength of the current against the boat is so very strong. Fernando, Emily and Christopher are using all of their muscle power to row the boat out into the giant waves.

As they start to row the boat out into the water, Christopher notices that Marcena has come down to the beach to see all of them off. He sees her waving to them as they make slow progress going out into the rough, choppy waters.

Once the boat is further out into the ocean the waves become rougher and higher in size. Today Christopher feels that Fernando, Emily and he are fighting the ocean to overcome its current to capsize them. However, with all of their strength together they are able to overcome the will of the ocean that wants to overturn their boat and drown them.

As the boat gets further out into the ocean, Christopher hears Marcena screaming, "Christopher, help! Christopher, help me! Help! Help! Help me!"

Christopher looks back, and sees Marcena running away from Spencer. Christopher can't believe his eyes, with all of his might he heads the boat back to the shore with the help of Fernando and Emily.

As Spencer approaches Marcena he yells at her in an evil, violent voice, "I bet you never thought I would reappear in your life ever again? Well, that old man out there put a curse upon me, and the only way I can end it is by killing you, I think!"

"Spencer, please don't kill me, I'm going to have a baby, please just go far, far away from me," pleads Marcena out of breath to him for her life.

"Not until you are dead," Spencer yells at her as he pulls out a switchblade from his pocket. He quickly opens up his knife as he slowly walks toward her.

"No, Spencer, I don't want to die! Just let me be and walk away!" blurts out Marcena in panic as she slowly starts running away from him toward the ocean.

"Walk away, no way! See my face? Every time I try to hurt or abuse people, I feel my pain! I feel so much pain that I either bang my head on a wall or hurt myself. I don't want to feel all the abuse that I put on others throughout my life anymore. No more, Marcena, you are going to die!" with a wicked grin on his face Spencer shouts from a distance to Marcena.

With that Marcena jumps into the ocean and starts swimming out to Christopher. She is scared to death of Spencer once more; she doesn't want her child or herself to die by his hand.

As they get closer to the shore, Emily jumps out of the boat and starts swimming toward Marcena to save her from harm. Emily with all her might is fighting the powerful current and going into the waves like an Olympian swimmer.

Marcena keeps swimming and struggling against the waves to swim further into the ocean to escape Spencer. She refuses to let him kill her without a fight. This time, Marcena is fighting for the lives of both her and her unborn child.

Christopher frantically yells out, "Sanabrio, help me! Sanabrio, my friend! Help me right now! Christopher realizes that even though Fernando and he have almost rowed the boat to the shore, they won't get there fast enough to save Marcena.

In an instant you see Sanabrio with all the seagulls flying towards Spencer.

As Spencer looks up as he enters into the ocean, Sanabrio and the other seagulls start to peck his eyes out of his head. Red blood starts to splatter everywhere out of Spencer's eyes. Spencer, feeling the pain of the seagulls attacking him and the hatred that he feels for Marcena for her not letting him continue to love and abuse her, takes this knife and sticks it right into his chest. He then falls in the ocean near the beach with all of the seagulls pecking what life is left in him to death.

Emily finally reaches Marcena and safely swims her to the shore.

Christopher and Fernando paddle the boat toward where Marcena and Emily are both located on the shore. Christopher gets out of the boat and runs to Marcena. He gently lifts her up in his arms and runs to the house with her to Lady Noreen; so Lady Noreen can get Marcena warm clothes to put on and get her wet clothes off of her. Christopher prays all of the way to the house that both Marcena and the baby will live. Christopher wants nothing to happen to Marcena or her unborn child. He begs the Lord to look over her in this life threatening time.

Meanwhile, Fernando and Emily have pulled the boat out of the ocean onto the shore. Neither one of them desire to go and see what has happened to the man who has attacked Marcena. Although since they are lifeguards, Fernando and Emily know that they must go and check on the man to see if he is dead or alive, and they both find him dead in an enormous puddle of blood on the beach. Seeing this, Fernando on his cell phone calls 911 to report to the police what has happened and where the dead man is located on the shoreline. The police ask that Emily and Fernando wait there until they arrive.

Once Christopher gets near the house he yells at the top of his lungs, "Lady Noreen, come quick, Marcena and I need you! Lady Noreen, hurry! Please, hurry!"

Lady Noreen hears Christopher and can't imagine what has happened for him to be so upset and out of breath. She runs as fast as she can to the door and opens it. There she sees Christopher with Marcena. Marcena's eyes are closed and she seems totally exhausted, plus soaking wet, like she has been swimming in the ocean. Lady Noreen can't imagine what has happened to Marcena. She knew that Marcena was going to take a short walk to watch Christopher go out in the boat today, but she wasn't going to go swimming in the ocean.

Lady Noreen hollers out to Christopher, "Oh, my heavens, what has happened to Marcena, Christopher? Is she okay? Christopher, I'll change her clothes real fast, and get her warm. We must get her immediately to the hospital."

Christopher takes Marcena as quickly as he can to her old bedroom.

Lady Noreen calls for Old Bessie to get Marcena's bag for the hospital and one of Lady Noreen's heavy robes from the closet so that Old Bessie and Lady Noreen can change Marcena's wet clothes into warm ones and put a heavy robe over her.

Lady Noreen in a high pitched voice yells at Christopher to have him call Joshua and tell him to get over to the house as fast as he can. Then, Christopher is to call Brook to come over to the house with the limo; so they can take Marcena to the hospital right away. Lady Noreen wants to make sure that the baby is okay.

Marcena is conscious but very weak. It took all of her strength to stay afloat in the ocean, and to overcome the reality that Spencer might hurt her or kill her unborn baby. Marcena slowly mumbles,

"I'm okay Lady Noreen and Christopher. I thank God thank I finally overcame that man. This time, I didn't take a beating from him. I stood up for myself, and my child to be, and ran from him. I fought for my life! I was no longer a victim! I was victorious over being an abused woman!"

Lady Noreen and Old Bessie change Marcena's wet clothes. Odessa and Christopher dry Marcena's hair with towels and a hair dryer after she is dressed in dry clothes and a heavy robe. Marcena had truly chilled in the cold water of the ocean.

Then Christopher puts a heavy blanket over Marcena.

Soon both Joshua and Brook arrive around the same time to the house.

Rico in a bit wheels into the house, he was practicing for one of his wheelchair races on the Boardwalk today. Immediately Lady Noreen tells him about Marcena's escape from being killed earlier. Rico is scared to death about Marcena's health and the condition of her unborn baby. He has in a split second changed out of his workout clothes into his clothes so he can go to the hospital with her.

As soon as Brook and Joshua get into the house, Emily and Fernando, who have just arrived at the house after finishing the police report, explains to them what has happened to Marcena and gives them some of the details.

While that is happening, Christopher carries Marcena to the limo. Once she is in it, Joshua goes immediately to her side. Then, Christopher, Rico, Lady Noreen, and Brook get into the limo, too. Then, off to the hospital they all go with Marcena as Emily and Fernando afraid for Marcena's baby wave good-bye to all of them.

Once Marcena arrives at the hospital, she is admitted. Joshua goes with her to the emergency room until the doctor comes. The rest of them have to wait in the waiting room so the doctor can examine her. Everyone is in the waiting room and they are on pins and needles.

The doctor finally examines Marcena and comes out, and says to everyone, "Everything seems okay; however, I want to admit Marcena into the hospital right now for she has started to dilate. She seems a little weak and I don't want to take any chances with the unborn baby's life."

Christopher gets a cell phone call from Fernando asking him how Marcena is. He also tells Christopher that the body of the dead man has been removed from the beach. That his eyes had been pecked out and apparently the man stabbed himself in the heart or fell on his knife.

Christopher sincerely replies to him by saying, "Fernando thanks for everything, I don't know how you were able to help me to manage getting the boat back to the shore. Also, we all thank Emily for saving Marcena's life. It would have all been different if Emily had not jumped into the water to assist in aiding Marcena and her unborn child. Please tell Emily that she is truly a heroine, and you are a hero, too, Fernando! You both saved the day for Marcena!"

Then Emily gets on the phone and asks Christopher, "Do you want us both to go to the hospital right now. Do you think the baby is in any danger?"

"Emily, I think everything will be okay! Why don't Fernando and you go home, get some rest, and change your clothes. Then, both of you can come to the hospital later on tonight and wait with us. Okay? It looks like Marcena will be at the hospital overnight under observation."

Marcena is admitted to the hospital on the day that the baby is to be born and nothing happens! Everyone just watches the clock on the wall to see if the baby will be born or not. Throughout the whole day as everyone stays into the wee midnight hours no baby is born.

Christopher is right! Only Gods knows when the baby will be born. Only God!

Chapter 37

This Is In Their Blessing And Birth Right!

Throughout the long endless evening everyone gets comfortable. Rico takes a catnap in his wheelchair. Christopher has slowly gotten comfortable after talking to Joshua and has gone into a deep sound sleep. Joshua has gone back into Marcena's room to stay with her for the night. He is truly worried about her after the events that occurred in her life today with Spencer. Lady Noreen is totally passed out and all sprawled over the hospital couch fast asleep even though she is turning back and forth to get comfortable.

Fernando and Emily who arrived earlier must both leave later that night because they have college classes in the morning. They both are so happy that they helped Christopher in some small way to help save Marcena from Spencer today. Fernando and Emily know how much Christopher loves Marcena.

Throughout the night of dreams, hope, and nightmares, the family awaits the birth of one baby. Finally, at 6:30 a.m. in the morning, Joshua comes out of Marcena's room to wake everyone up and tell them that Dr. John William-Edward has taken Marcena into the delivery room.

The next three hours seem unending to all of them. Everyone in the waiting room is excited yet worried about the baby's condition. Christopher comforts Lady Noreen and Rico by telling them that Marcena is going to be okay and so is the baby.

At around 9:30 a.m., Brook, Sergeant Mussack, Sarge, Patrick and Nicholas show up at the hospital to see how Marcena is doing, and if she has given birth to the baby yet. Everyone just adores Marcena and hopes that her delivery goes fast and that the baby is born in good health.

Lady Noreen has called Old Bessie and Odessa to bring a fresh change of clothes for her over to the hospital. She also has asked Brook to please go to the house and bring both, Old Bessie and Odessa, back with him to the hospital.

Teresa Y.'s family, drive her over to the hospital to be with Rico. Teresa Y. knows how upset Rico is about Spencer trying to kill both Marcena and the baby. She wants to be with Rico at the hospital just in case anything goes wrong with Marcena's delivery.

Finally, at 10:25 a.m., Joshua comes out to tell everyone that Christopher was right. Marcena has given birth to fraternal twins. The girl is 5 pounds 8 ounces and the boy is 5 pounds 10 ounces in weight. Joshua scratches his head and says, "The doctor can't explain it! He kept hearing just one heartbeat, while all of the time there were two babies inside of Marcena."

Lady Noreen speaks out and says, "This is great news! How is Marcena doing and are the babies in good health?"

Joshua replies, "She is so happy! The babies are both doing great! In fact, Marcena can't believe that Christopher was right once again! She said for me to tell him, he is right like usual!"

"Christopher, now you can use both of your baby's names to name the two children since one baby is a girl, and the other one is a baby boy," shouts out Rico in delight.

Everyone in the waiting room is so happy and overjoyed about the birth of the fraternal twins. No one can believe that Marcena just delivered twins! No one, but Christopher!

Christopher gives Joshua a hug, and congratulates him. Then Christopher asks everyone if he can be excused so he can go to the chapel and pray. He knows that this has been a blessed day for all of them to be so overjoyed about the birth of the twins. Christopher now wants to go and thank God, for making today's miracle such a special honor in everyone's life.

As Christopher leaves for the chapel to pray, Lady Noreen begins to plan on rearranging the nursery with Patrick, and starts to give

Old Bessie and Odessa their schedules on when to help Marcena with the twins when she comes home. Although, Lady Noreen is so happy about the two little ones that she wants to help Marcena with both of them during the day, too. Yes, there would be nothing in her life like being a grandmother.

Rico feels like a weight has been taken off of his chest. He was so worried that something might go wrong with Marcena's delivery. Now, Rico is as happy as can be in knowing that Marcena and the twins are healthy and okay. He doesn't have to worry anymore! Marcena has been the only family he has known for so long and he sure didn't want to lose her or his newly born niece or his nephew today.

As Christopher goes into the chapel no one is there, but him. He slowly gets on his knees and softly prays, "God, thank you so much for blessing Marcena and Joshua with the two beautiful babies. I can hardly wait to see both of them. I have prayed about what to name both of them for so long. I think Marcena and Joshua will like the two names that I come up with for the twins. Also, God, I know I have to choose just one of them to give a blessing to; so that only one of them can take my place as an angel upon this earth. God, this is really hard for me to do! I already feel so close to both of them. It is going to be a very hard decision for me to just choose one baby to bless. Please watch over me, God, as I make the decision to choose the right child to be blessed to become an angel for you. Please watch over me, Lord! Please!"

With that Christopher goes back to the waiting room to find Lady Noreen and Joshua, so with them he can visit Marcena in her hospital room. Christopher is excited yet very nervous about seeing the two little ones. Christopher is excited, because he always wanted to be a grandfather in his life. He is very nervous, because he has to make a major decision about which baby to choose to replace him on this earth as an angel.

Soon Joshua takes Christopher into the hospital room to see Marcena. She looks so much better today even though she has just given birth to two beautiful babies.

Once Marcena sees Christopher coming into the room she calls out, "There is my hero like always! Christopher, I want to thank you now and Emily later, for saving my life yesterday. I never thought that I would meet up with Spencer ever again in my life. Christopher, I thought you scared him off the last time you saw Spencer on the night that he almost killed me."

Christopher responds, "Marcena, no one is ever going to hurt you ever again. Spencer killed himself! You are now going to enjoy every moment of raising your twins with Joshua. Which one of the babies do you think will be the easier of the two for you to take care of, Marcena?"

"Christopher, I think they are both going to be angels! I can't choose between the two of them. The girl was born first and then the little guy snuck out of nowhere and he weighs the most!'" answers Marcena giggling.

"I know what you mean, Marcena! It is hard to choose one child out of the two to be the best. Let me see both of them. You are so right, they are both positively beautiful!" remarks Christopher.

"Christopher, are you ready to name both of them? I can hardly wait to find out what names you picked out for them," excitedly says Marcena to Christopher.

"Yes, I am ready, Marcena! Do you want me to call Joshua, Lady Noreen, Rico, Teresa Y., Brook, Patrick, Old Bessie, Sarge and Odessa into your room, so everyone can find out at one time what their names are going to be?" Christopher asks her.

"Christopher, do you think the nurses will mind if we have everyone in at once?" curiously wonders Marcena.

"Not at all, Marcena, it is fine! Lady Noreen talked to all of the hospital staff, and gave a large donation to the hospital's development fund for the pediatric ward. Then she had the nurse get gowns and masks for everyone who is coming into your room. She doesn't want the twins to get anyone's germs," explains Christopher to Marcena.

"Oh, Christopher, that is so funny! Well, call everyone into the room right now!"

With that everyone files into Marcena's private hospital room. They all are so very excited to see Joshua and her fraternal twins. Lady Noreen is the first one into the room to see her grandchildren, followed by all the other members of the clan.

Lady Noreen emotionally screeches out, "Christopher what are the baby's names? We are all dying to hear what names you have chosen for the two little beauties!"

Christopher then tries to decide which baby he is going to pick up first to give his blessing and heavenly rites to today. He looks at the little girl, and she is positively breathtaking. Her eyes are the color of the earth and the sun mixed together, and she has lots of curly light brown hair. The little guy has curly blonde hair and dark brown eyes the color only seen in the crust of the earth. Both of the twins are so little and so beautiful, but he can only choose one. Which one, Christopher thinks to himself, should I choose?

Lady Noreen yells at Christopher, "I can't take the suspense. Please pick both of the babies up at one time and name both of them. Right now, Christopher."

Christopher responds to Lady Noreen by saying, "Both of them, Lady Noreen?"

"You heard me Christopher, both of them," emphatically repeats Lady Noreen to him.

Hearing Lady Noreen's words echo in his head, Christopher reaches down with both of his arms, and Joshua helps him pick both of them up at the same time. Now, Christopher is holding them both in each one of his arms. He then says to the two, "I now give both of you a sacred blessing. You, Christianna Emily Elizabeth, with your brother, Christian Andrew Saint, will rule God's earth together and pass on the sacred blessings of God to all on your path who need to be saved, healed, or bestowed with a miracle from this day forth. You both are blessed by God."

Christopher then kisses the twins, and holds them up in the air for everyone to see and says, "Christianna Emily Elizabeth and Christian Andrew Saint, you are now both blessed with your birth names. May God bless and keep you both always in his divine grace."

Then Lady Noreen with an attitude yells out, "Why didn't you name the girl after me, Christopher?"

"Lady Noreen, I wanted both of the children to have Christ in their names, both Elizabeth and Andrew are biblical names. Andrew was an apostle to Jesus. He was a strong man and a great fisherman.

Elizabeth was the mother of John the Baptist and her name means 'God's promise'. Saint is my last name, which I wanted carried on in the bloodline, and the name Emily was chosen because Emily saved Marcena's life in the ocean yesterday. All of the names are blessed names."

"But Christopher, my name, Noreen is a blessed name, too!" snaps Lady Noreen at him.

"Yes, it is, Lady Noreen! You can call Christianna, when you want to, Christianna Emily Elizabeth Noreen, okay!" seriously Christopher tells Lady Noreen so he doesn't hurt her feelings.

"It's not okay, but I love the baby's names that you have chosen for them, Christopher. So that is that!" answers Lady Noreen very quickly to him.

Everyone in Marcena's private hospital room applauds the naming of the twins. Joshua takes videos of all the happenings in the room with Christianna and Christian so that they will always remember their birth and all the people who were with them on their miraculous day to celebrate it with them.

Marcena pulls Christopher over towards her and whispers in his ear, "Christopher, I love you so much! The names you chose for the babies are so beautiful, I will treasure Christianna and Christian and their names always like I do you, Christopher. Thanks for being in not only my life, but their lives, too, as their Grandpop."

With that Lady Noreen bellows out, "Christopher why do the babies have three names? Other children just have a first and middle name."

"Lady Noreen, these two babies are blessed! Blessings come in threes, just like there is the Father, Son, and the Holy Ghost. There is also birth, life, and death, Lady Noreen. Christianna Emily Elizabeth and Christian Andrew Saint are sacred beings in this universe, we human beings call earth. That is why I have given Christianna and Christian three names. This is their blessing and birth right," states Christopher to her.

"I get it now! Their names are beautiful! Both babies are beautiful, smart, and a blessing to both of us! You are so right like usual, Christopher!" chuckles Lady Noreen to herself.

Then Marcena whispers to Lady Noreen, "Grandma, I want you to hold your two beauties, right now!"

With that Lady Noreen lifts both of the babies from Christopher's arms with lots of help from Joshua and she cries out, "They are beautiful! Positively beautiful! I don't believe I got to live all of these years to be a grandmother. I am so blessed! Christopher, you are so right - they are blessed babies. Oh, I just love Christianna Emily Elizabeth and Christian Andrew Saint. Oh, Christopher, I am so glad that you named them both, and they both have unique names, but Marcena will you please let me name the next baby or babies you have?" pleads Lady Noreen with Marcena.

Marcena just laughs out loud and everyone takes a peek at the two infants before the nurse escorts all of them out of the room. The people in the waiting room can't believe their eyes when they see all of these people coming out of this one private hospital room with gowns and masks on. They wonder if someone has a serious disease or if the room is in quarantine.

Finally, Lady Noreen and Christopher kiss Marcena, Joshua, and the twin's good-bye. Then, Christopher helps Joshua put the babies back into Marcena's arms before he slowly leaves the room.

As Christopher looks back at the babies one more time; he says quietly under his breath says, "Dear Lord, please forgive me, I messed up once again! But, why did you give Marcena twins? The decision would have been so much easier, if there had only been just one baby! I'm so sorry, Lord. But I promise to teach them everything I know down here! I promise, my Heavenly Father."

With that Lady Noreen yells at Christopher saying, "Are you crazy or something? Why are you talking to yourself?"

"Oh, Lady Noreen, I was just trying to remember how many pounds the twins weighed and how long both of them were at birth. I just can't remember their statistics!"

"Christopher, their Grandmother Lady Noreen knows everything. Christianna Emily Elizabeth was 5 pounds and 8 ounces and 17 ½ inches long and Christian Andrew Saint was 5 pounds and 10 ounces and 19 inches long. Now you know Christopher; so stop talking to yourself or people will think you are crazy! Stop it, right now!" in an irritated tone of voice Lady Noreen yells out to Christopher.

Christopher just smiles at Lady Noreen and walks with her to the limo to join Brook. Lady Noreen is totally exhausted and wants to go home so she can go right to bed and take a catnap, before she gets ready to go shopping with Patrick to purchase more clothes for her grandchildren.

Once Brook pulls the limo in front of Lady Noreen's house; she slowly walks out of the limo to her house and opens the door. Like always, Christopher thanks Brook for taking them home, and happily starts walking to the house door that is wide open for him.

Once Christopher gets to the door he hears Lady Noreen scream.

Brook, also hears her screaming, too, so he runs from the limo to catch up with Christopher to see what Lady Noreen is screaming about.

Once Christopher and Brook get upstairs to Lady Noreen's bedroom, they see Lady Noreen sitting on the floor with Tigress and five baby kittens.

"Christopher laughs and asks, "Is that what you are screaming about, Lady Noreen?"

"Christopher, I had no idea Tigress was pregnant, I just thought she was getting fat like our Tom Cat. I never thought she would have babies on the same day that our precious twins were born," in a dumbfounded voice Lady Noreen mutters to Christopher and Brook.

"Lady Noreen, I'm so glad Tigress had kittens. Now you can name all five of baby kittens all by yourself," Christopher utters in laughter.

"You are so right! This time, as soon as I find out who is who, I will name one Lady Noreen. Now that is a beautiful name for a kitten! Isn't it?"

"You are so right about the name, Lady Noreen! You just make sure that you name the prettiest female kitten after yourself, Lady Noreen. I'm all for it!" responds Christopher.

Brook, laughingly says, "Congratulations, Lady Noreen! Now you have five new babies. You have really had a lot of excitement for one day! You must be exhausted right now?"

"You are not kidding, Brook," Lady Noreen replies back to him.

Then Brook says good-bye once again and leaves the house in his limo.

Lady Noreen is totally exhausted from all the excitement of the day. She starts getting ready to lie down to take a nap, but before she does, she yells at Christopher one more time, "Where is that Tom Cat hiding in my house? I can't believe he got my precious little Tigress pregnant!"

"Lady Noreen, I don't know where Tom Cat is right now! You just take your little nap, and I'll look for him for you later on tonight. Goodnight!" smiles Christopher.

Chapter 38

I'm Just A Man

The babies come home from the hospital in a few days. Brook has been assigned by Lady Noreen to pick up Joshua, Marcena, and the twins and drive them home. Lady Noreen doesn't trust anyone else to drive the babies safely home. In fact, Lady Noreen makes Marcena promise that on the way home from the hospital Joshua and she will stop at her house first. This way, Lady Noreen and Christopher can see the babies first, and Lady Noreen can give her all of the clothes that Patrick and she bought for Christianna Emily Elizabeth and Christian Andrew Saint.

Once they arrive at the house Lady Noreen is in seventh heaven. She is so excited about the babies coming to see her that she locks Tigress up in the bedroom so none of the kittens will get lost. Lady Noreen wants all of the baby kittens to be safe, too.

Lady Noreen named the five kittens. Their names are Tiger, Leo, Kitten, Cheetah, and Lady Noreen. Lady Noreen loves each one of her baby kittens and is only going to give the people she loves one of them. She really hasn't decided who she is going to give the kittens to yet. In fact, she is having a very hard time making the decision to give up any of her kittens right away!

Marcena and Joshua go into the house and visit with Lady Noreen and Christopher for a brief moment, while Brook carries all the bags of clothes and sleepers for the twins to wear out to the limousine. The babies are wide awake just looking around the house and at Lady Noreen.

Christopher asks Marcena if he can quickly take the twins outside just to show them the ocean before they go home. He senses that Marcena is a little tired and wants to go home right away. Christopher doesn't want her to overdo on her first day out of the hospital.

Marcena answers Christopher by saying, "Yes, you can take the twins out real fast to see the Boardwalk and the ocean and then bring them right back into the house. Joshua and I can't stay very long here, but we wanted both of you to see the twins before we go home. After all, both of you are their grandparents."

With that, Joshua helps to put the twins in Christopher's arms, and Christopher slowly walks them out onto the Boardwalk. While near the rail of the Boardwalk, Sanabrio sees Christopher and the babies and flies down and lands on Christopher's head.

"Oh, Sanabrio, I wanted to introduce you to Christianna Emily Elizabeth and Christian Andrew Saint. I wanted you to see both of them. Aren't they beautiful?" proudly Christopher tells Sanabrio.

Sanabrio just looks down upon the two tiny babies and looks from one to the other. Then, he flies out into the ocean.

Christopher, calls to Sanabrio, "Where are you going?"

With that Sanabrio returns, and lands at Christopher's feet with a starfish in his beak, then he flies out again and gets another starfish and places it next to the other one on the Boardwalk.

Christopher then proclaims, "The blessing on these two innocent children has just taken place. I thank you, Lord."

Next, Christopher carries the two babies back to Joshua and Marcena. The limo is all packed up and ready to go. Lady Noreen and Christopher kisses and hugs everyone good-bye, and Marcena, Joshua, and the twins leave with Brook to take the twins to their home.

Lady Noreen is so overjoyed by seeing her grandchildren that she starts to uncontrollably cry.

Christopher just gives her a big hug.

Then, Lady Noreen smiles at Christopher and replies, "I better go see my other five babies and Tigress. I'm going to go out with Old Bessie and Brook later today and purchase a more comfortable cat bed for Tigress. So, I'll see you later this evening, okay, Christopher?"

"Sounds like fun, Lady Noreen!" remarks Christopher.

Christopher then walks back out to the Boardwalk towards the ocean saying to the heavens, "I'm No Angel, I'm No Saint, I'm Just a Man, God. Yes, I was an angel put on this earth to help others from carrying the burdens of their lives, but eventually I couldn't choose between the children on both occasions for they always won my heart. Again at these times, it was so hard to choose, choose one over another. I just didn't have the heart to do that, Lord.

As a saint, I tried to protect those who sought my protection from physical or mental harm. Yes, I was a patron saint to so many people throughout the world at one time in my life. However, God, I was dropped and totally forgotten by so many believers in me because the church had very little proof or factual evidence to prove beyond a doubt that I was truly a real saint. I guess that is why I became a legend in religious history. Yes, I was a martyr, who refused to renounce his religion as a saint in my time! But again the church formed the conclusion to terminate my sainthood, Lord.

Now, I am just a man, God! I will promise to serve you with every breath of my life up until my death. I will cherish every living moment on this earth with you, and I will be a mentor to your chosen twins. Lord, thank you for this day, and I will bless your holy name always."

Then, Christopher rolls his pants legs up and jumps into the ocean for a swim, as Sanabrio and the rest of the seagulls fly over him. With a smile on his face, and a twinkle in his eye, he swims in the rough currents in the ocean enjoying the beauty of nature and God's world all around him. Christopher is getting ready for his next adventure in his life as an ordinary man with Christianna Emily Elizabeth and Christian Andrew Saint as the newly proclaimed angels upon this earth.

Life is just beginning once again to be lived by Christopher Saint. He must now leave all of his yesterdays behind him and go forward with all of his tomorrows following God's plans for him and His two new little angels.

THE END

About The Author

S. L. Sharp was born in Akron, Ohio. She earned a Bachelor of Science Degree in Elementary Education from Kent State University in 1969. Later she attended the University of Akron, the New York Institute of Technology, and the University of Delaware for post-graduate studies.

Her peers selected her in 1993 for the Teacher of the Year of East Camden Middle School in Camden, New Jersey. In 1993-1994 and 1997-1998, she was chosen for the Camden City's Teacher of the Year. She appeared on the Oprah Show in 1992. Awards and honors bestowed on Sally include the Kiwanis Award for Communications in 1990, the Franklin Delano Roosevelt Conservation Award in 1995, and the Outstanding Achievement Award from the Girl Scouts in 1995. She was the creator, producer and host of a weekly radio show entitled: "The Young Heroes and Heroines of Today," on WFPG AM (1450) during 1987-1994. In addition, she has written and directed several TV programs for Channel 18 and Channel 14 for CCS-TV, the Camden City School's Access Cable Television.

She has also authored the book entitled, *Baby Jules*, a book about three dynamic women who discover the power of forgiveness along with finding both love and success. It is a heart-wrenching story about two generations of women who fight for the survival of their dysfunctional family. This leads the reader through a fractured storybook marriage, the death of a beloved daughter, and a grieving mother's challenge. The bittersweet novel is about the emotional emptiness that only a parent can feel through the loss of their child.

Sally's other writings have taken many different forms throughout the years in books, plays, poetry, songwriting, and children's stories.